# The Lost Colony

## By Irina Shapiro

# Copyright

# Table of Contents

# Prologue

The morning dawned stormy and gray, the waves slamming against the shore with violent frequency. I clutched the baby to me as I stared out to sea, and if it weren't for the tiny being whose hand lay splayed like a starfish on my breast, I might have just walked in and kept on going. My limbs were lacerated and sore, my head ached as if someone had split it with an axe, and my lips and cheek were swollen and caked with dried blood where the wounds had scabbed over, but it wasn't my physical state that bothered me. My body would heal. I would even recover from what had been done to me, but I couldn't seem to find a reason to go on. Torn from the only person I trusted, not even the baby was enough to give me hope. The other women would take over and love the child. It didn't need me and would have no recollection of the damaged woman who'd cherished it for the first month of its life.

A wave crashed onto the shore, the foaming water swirling around my bare ankles. I drew in a shuddering breath but didn't move back. Instead I braced myself for the next swell and ignored the dark figure that had just stepped into my peripheral vision. I wasn't scared.

# Chapter 1

## Natalie

## October

Looking back, we can generally pinpoint the moment when our life took a pivotal and irreversible turn, but when it happens, unless it's a jarring event that changes everything overnight, the fateful day is no different from any other. There are no ominous portents, no nagging feeling of unease, no clear warning that something momentous and possibly disastrous is about to occur.

The day I took a critical turn started just like any other Sunday. I got up at my usual time, went for a run in Thompson Park, came back, and took my coffee and bagel with cream cheese and smoked salmon—my Sunday indulgence—to the couch to enjoy while I checked my email and social media. I responded to a few emails, checked my bank balance, and then logged in to Facebook to see what my friends were up to. After ten minutes, I concluded that everyone I knew lived a more exciting life, and was about to log off when a sponsored ad caught my eye.

I never pay attention to ads, and never buy anything off Facebook, but this one piqued my interest. Not only were the graphics eye-catching, the image depicting a stark, almost abstract stretch of coast in shades of muted green, blue, and gray, but the ad seemed to be speaking directly to me.

**Love history?**

**Think you could survive in the 17th century?**

**Varlet Entertainment is seeking**

**15 fearless adventurers to star in a groundbreaking reality series.**

**First prize – $1,000,000**

**Second prize – $750,000**

**Third prize – $500,000**

**All runners up will receive a cash prize of**

**$50,000 for their participation.**

Beneath the ad was a button, urging me to Learn More. I should have just ignored the siren call of that button and carried on with my day, but something inside me responded to the challenge. I had always been a history buff, particularly the colonial period, since my family could not only trace its roots back to the very inception of the Virginia Colony but was in possession of a personal account from an ancestor that detailed his experiences upon arrival in Jamestown in 1620. Captain Thomas Osborne was the romantic hero of my childhood imaginings, a dashing Tudor daredevil who had braved an Atlantic crossing three times on his ship, *Bona Nova*, before eventually settling in the New World and throwing his lot in with a mail-order bride he had not met until she'd set her dainty foot on the jetty of the fledgling colony.

Thomas and Elizabeth Osborne had had half a dozen children, but only two sons had survived into adulthood and went on to establish a branch of the family that had played a part in every significant event in American history. I had pored over Thomas's battered, calfskin-bound journal when I had studied the colonial period at school and often wondered if I would have the strength and the courage to survive the harrowing conditions that Thomas had described so matter-of-factly—or to reinvent myself the way the Osbornes had been forced to do when the political and social climate of the country changed every few generations, and viewpoints that had been acceptable only a few years before had become untenable if the family hoped not only to survive but to flourish in the newly emerged landscape.

The Osbornes had gone from struggling settlers to plantation owners to abolitionists, and then later on to wealthy industrialists who had summered in Newport and attended grand balls in the gilded mansions of New York City's entitled elite. The stock market crash of '29 and the Depression had robbed the family of its generational wealth, and the wars of the twentieth century had thinned the ranks of Osborne males, but the family had survived, and the accounts of those long-ago ancestors had lived on and made for fascinating reading for a girl who was obsessed with history and had developed something of a survival complex as a result.

So, when the ad asked if I thought I could survive in the past, my inner voice cried, *You bet!*

I should have logged off Facebook, thrown in a load of laundry, and gone to a hot yoga class before meeting my friend Jenny for lunch to discuss her latest romantic disaster and my own lack of promising prospects, but instead, I found myself filling out an application for a reality series aptly titled *Jamestown*. After all, what was the harm, and what were the chances that I would be selected? I'd probably never even hear back, much less make the cut. I completed the application, looked over the information, and clicked Submit.

And that was the day my life changed forever.

# Chapter 2

# November

"Are you absolutely mad?" my sister Diana asked as I peeled sweet potatoes for her Thanksgiving casserole. "Why would you leave everything behind for six months and subject yourself to what has to be absolute torture? And I'm not just talking about the lack of plumbing and electricity. Think of what it's like to have your every move recorded and watched by millions of people who are sitting on the couch with their bucket-size bowls of popcorn and treating you as if you somehow belong to them and they have the right to judge your every move. I mean, really think about it, Natalie."

Diana chopped a cupful of pecans so ferociously, one might think the nuts had mortally offended her. "And what are your chances of winning one of the grand prizes? None, not when you'll be competing against those bearded off-the-grid types who've perfected living off the land and rigging their own water-filtration systems and have been waiting for an opportunity to show off their survival skills and put their macho egos to the test."

Waving a very sharp knife in the air for emphasis, she continued, "Sure, you might receive the fifty K compensation prize, but after taxes and the expenses you'll still incur while you're away—because let's be honest, it's not like you'd ever sublet your condo or sell your car to offset the bills you'd still have to pay—you'll get a few thousand at most, which will hardly compensate for the loss of wages and the six months of your life you'll never get back. And you'll forfeit your right to privacy forever!" she exclaimed. "No, this, right here, is the closest anyone should come to colonial America," she said, now using the knife as a pointer to encompass the various ingredients and bowls that littered her marble island. "Thanksgiving. Consume a million calories, take a moment to be thankful for everything you have, enjoy some quality time with the people who love you but annoy the crap out of you if you see them too often, and then spend the day after Thanksgiving putting up the Christmas decorations. That, my dear sister, is the American dream."

"Are you quite finished?" I asked as I tried not to laugh at my sister's impassioned outburst. Diana's idea of roughing it was taking a bus to the mall while her car was being serviced. "Dee, you know I love history. I think this would be really fun," I argued as I measured out maple syrup to add to the casserole. "It's the closest anyone could ever come to time travel."

"And is that what you want? To time travel? Look, they make it look all romantic and inspiring in movies, because let's face it, no one wants to imagine how those people must have smelled or see their rotting teeth and lice-infested heads, but if this series hopes to get the ratings, the producers will have to get down and dirty. People want to see contestants eating bugs and peeing on each other to disinfect jellyfish stings. They've been spoiled by other survivalist shows, and at this stage, the only thing that will keep their attention is a true fight for survival."

"Don't you think you're getting just a little bit carried away?"

"You know me—I'm a realist," Diana said, and shoved the pie she had been making into the oven.

"Some would call it cynicism."

"Realism is often synonymous with cynicism," Diana replied, undaunted. "I prefer to focus on the practicalities. And say you do get selected. What about your job? The school will have to hire a new nurse to cover for you."

"I can take a sabbatical. People do it all the time."

"Not people who hope to find their job waiting for them when they return. Look, I know it's been an uphill climb these past few years, but you have nothing to prove, and running away never solves anything. Natty, you're smart and resilient, and so very beautiful. Maybe it's time you let someone in."

I didn't think I was particularly resilient, but I was grateful to Diana for her unwavering support and thankful that at a time in my life when I hadn't been sure I'd be able to make it through the day, she'd shown the compassion I had so desperately needed and didn't say *I told you so* or offer tired platitudes and clueless advice. As far as my looks went, I really didn't think I was beautiful. In my more confident moments, I thought I was passably attractive. On days when I was down on myself, I thought I was pretty average. I wasn't statuesque, nor did I have big knockers or bee-stung lips. My wavy shoulder-length hair was nearly black, and my skin was unfashionably pale. My eyes were a sea green, the unusual color accentuated by naturally dark lashes and brows, and although I had good-sized breasts, I wasn't what people would call curvy. My hips were on the narrow side, and although I ran regularly and did yoga, I wasn't as toned as I would have liked because I also liked to cook and eat, not an indulgence I was willing to give up since these days it was my only sensual pleasure. I hadn't been in a relationship in more than two years, and although I'd had offers, I wasn't looking to hook up with someone I knew I'd never see again.

"You have to give people a chance, Natalie," Diana was saying, her attention now on the string beans. "You've completely boxed yourself in since, well, you know," she added, obviously not wanting to get into that whole thing again, but her brown eyes were soft with love and concern.

"I know, and that's the whole point. I feel like if I don't take a risk, I'll wind up spending the rest of my life sitting on the couch, watching serial killer documentaries." I was only half joking, but Diana grinned, obviously believing she'd gotten her point across.

"Look, I know you were obsessed with *Colonial House* and *Frontier House* when they aired on PBS, but if you will recall, most of the people who were so gung-ho to experience history firsthand were in for a rude awakening. They thought they were going to have this great spiritual renaissance and learn life-changing lessons, but they were crying for their bras, phones, and

Starbucks lattes by the end of the first episode. It's six months, Natty. Six months of your life that you will never get back."

"What are the chances that I will even be selected?" I replied. "Practically nonexistent, so this is all a moot point. I filled out an application. I'll probably never even hear back." I was more than ready to change the subject and wished my parents would arrive and take over the conversation as they invariably did.

"Well, I hope you don't," Diana said with righteous finality. "Maybe it's selfish of me, but I want you here. And Mom and Dad will lose their minds when they find out."

"Which they won't because you're not going to tell them," I said. "At least not today."

"I would never," Diana said. "Thanksgiving is my favorite holiday, so I won't be the one to ruin it."

"Good," I said. "Now, can we please change the subject?"

"As long as you promise not to mention this reality show to Craig. Knowing him, he'll probably want to come along and prove that he's some alpha male, even though he barely knows how to change a lightbulb," Diana said, smiling affectionately.

Craig didn't need to change lightbulbs. As a highly sought fertility specialist, he could afford to hire people to change bulbs for him, but there was no need. Diana was the handy one in the family and took great pride in upstaging her mild-mannered husband.

"Craig is not going anywhere," I said, "and Mom and Dad lose their minds if I so much as drive into the city to meet a friend. They've lived in suburbia for too long. They think New York is the Wild West."

"Sometimes it is," Diana reminded me. "Haven't you seen the news? There was a shooting in a nightclub last night. Three dead, seven wounded. God knows how many traumatized for life."

"Yeah, I saw, which only proves my point. I'll be a lot safer in a seventeenth-century settlement."

"Yeah, you just keep telling yourself that," Diana said as she drained the water from the boiled potatoes and set the pot on the counter. "Get started on the mashed potatoes. Dad's car just turned into the driveway, so hopefully we'll be sitting down soon." She glanced at the clock on the oven. "Craig better be back soon. Why must people always have medical emergencies on national holidays?"

I was just about to reply when Diana's five-year-old daughter, Maddy, ran into the kitchen. "Mom, I'm hungry. How much longer?"

Diana reached for her phone and checked her husband's location. "Daddy's on his way back, so hopefully in about a half hour. If you're hungry, grab a few baby carrots."

Maddy rolled her eyes. "I don't want carrots. I want turkey, and stuffing, and PIE," she wailed.

"And you will have it all, in about half an hour. Now go open the door for Grandma and Grandpa. They're walking up the drive."

Maddy stamped her foot and walked out, and then we heard her complaining to her grandparents, who agreed that Daddy was very unfair to work on Thanksgiving.

Diana and I both put on expressions of saintly innocence as our parents erupted into the kitchen, bringing with them the smell of autumn leaves, pumpkin spice, emanating from the box our dad was carrying, and the floral perfume Mom had worn since we were little. Suddenly, the kitchen was filled with chatter and laughter, and I put the conversation with Diana, as well as the reality show, from my mind as I went to work mashing the potatoes.

# Chapter 3

# March

Thanksgiving seemed eons ago as I gripped the railing of the old-fashioned wooden ship that would carry us from a private marina in Virginia to our new home on an island somewhere in the Atlantic. The contestants hadn't been told where the settlement was located and had been informed that we would have to remain below deck for the latter half of the journey so as not to memorize any landmarks. From the moment we'd arrived at the marina, everything we did would be recorded.

We were all dressed in the clothes we'd wear throughout filming, and each contestant had been issued with a canvas sack that held our worldly possessions. Mine consisted of a hairbrush and pins, linen strips to be used during menstruation, a spare chemise, a gown of pale blue wool, and an extra pair of hose. There was also a drab hooded cloak and an apron to protect my clothes when working. All traces of vanity had been stripped away the moment I signed the contract: my make-up, clothes, and modern-day underwear taken away and replaced with items appropriate to the period.

I'd always enjoyed costume dramas, but now that I'd been wearing a chemise, thick bum roll, heavy woolen skirt and jacket in a hideous shade of mustard, wool stockings, and supremely uncomfortable shoes for a few weeks, I wasn't quite as enamored of the idea. I also had to wear a linen cap that covered most of my hair, which was pinned up in a bun. It was unseemly for a woman to prance around with her head uncovered. She might inspire unbridled lust in one of the men and have to pay with her virtue. I thought that the backers of the show were hoping for just that kind of an outcome since watching the contestants chop wood for an hour or grind corn might get a bit dull.

As the shore grew smaller in the distance and eventually disappeared from view, excitement and eager anticipation were quickly replaced by nervousness and self-doubt. Could I really do this? Had I made a horrible mistake? Why had the producers picked me over thousands of other applicants? In fact, when I hadn't heard anything by Christmas, I had dismissed the application I had so impulsively filled out from my mind until I had received the email from Varlet Entertainment, congratulating me on being selected and outlining the onboarding process. And the process had been lengthy and grueling.

It began with an interview where I was grilled by several executives, who asked endless questions and made copious notes. I was made to understand that my participation wasn't a given and I could still be cut at any time should I prove to be unsuitable. There was a physical, performed by Varlet's medical officer, and then a sheaf of papers to sign, the documents ranging from a contract to a non-disclosure agreement that stated that I was not permitted to discuss the details of *Jamestown* even after it ended, give unapproved interviews, or write a tell-all about my experience. I signed them all, never imagining I might want to tell the world what had happened on that island. At the time, I assumed the world would see for itself once the show aired.

*Jamestown* was supposed to break the mold, partly because we'd be on the island for so long, but mostly because the contestants would live and work in a settlement built according to the exact specifications of the original Jamestown colony and face similar conditions and challenges while equipped only with seventeenth-century tools and weapons. This was *Survivor* 1600s style. Of course, this meant that no modern-day items of any kind were permitted on the island, not even a tampon or an aspirin. There would be no communication with the outside world, no technology, no machinery, no electricity or running water, and no one to turn to for help, at least not on camera.

Off camera, there would be emergency stores of food and a supply of clean water. After all, Varlet wouldn't want to be held accountable for near-starvation or serious illness. Plus there would be the film crew that would consist of two cameramen who would record our every move. The cameramen would remain on the ship that was carrying us toward our destination and was outfitted with a state-of-the-art media center, as well as medical supplies that would be administered by the medical officer, who'd also remain on hand. Giving a group of twenty-first century individuals axes and muskets could end very badly, and there'd be no time to get help if someone was bleeding to death. In case of severe illness or injury, the individual would be taken to a hospital on the mainland for treatment.

All this was explained to me during a follow-up interview in which I was assured that I had a place on the show and unless I wanted to back out, I was officially a Jamestown colonist. The administrative part of the process was followed by a two-week stint on a colonial-era farmstead somewhere in Virginia. The contestants were instructed in everything from using seventeenth-century weapons and tools to planting, harvesting, cooking over an open flame, slaughtering game, and making everything we needed for survival from scratch, all while wearing bulky and impractical period clothes that were completely inappropriate to the climate. Realism at its best!

What I found most difficult, aside from having to give up my phone and all communication with the outside world, was that not only were the male and female contestants housed in separate buildings and taught different skills, but we weren't permitted to interact with one another beyond the daily lessons. It seemed the producers did not want us to get too chummy or start forming cliques. They wanted that to happen once we were in place and the cameras were rolling. I could understand the rationale, but it would have been nice to at least get to know the other women, especially when the training came as something of a surprise.

I'm not a squeamish person. I'd never have gone into nursing if I were, but reading about history or watching certain acts performed on-screen is not the same as doing it yourself. For me, the most difficult part of the training was the skinning and butchering. I have never said no to a juicy burger or a couple of slices of crispy bacon, but all my hunting until this point had happened in a supermarket, where I was safely removed from the reality of the process. When picking up a neatly packaged cut of beef or burgers, I'd never allowed myself to think where these products had come from. It's not as if I didn't know—I had simply accepted it, like most people do; otherwise, I wouldn't be able to eat meat ever again.

Looking into the trusting eyes of a rabbit you're about to kill is as far removed from shopping in Whole Foods as one can get, and then beheading and skinning the still-warm body and removing the organs before butchering the cleaned carcass is unbelievably emotional as well as disgusting, but human beings are carnivores and have been hunting and consuming their kills since time immemorial. If I hoped to succeed on the show, I had to disassociate myself from the process, just as I had to learn to shoot, even though I'd always hated guns and hoped never to have to hold one in my hands. Traditionally, though, it would be the men who'd be handling the guns since the women were relegated mostly to domestic tasks.

We were taught to shoot an authentic seventeenth-century musket, and the lesson was as sobering as it was frustrating. Putting aside the sheer size and weight of the gun, the probability of hitting a target, especially a moving one, without years of practice was about the same as winning the Powerball jackpot. I buried a number of lead balls in tree trunks and the ground, but I was never able to hit a target, even a stationary one. I wasn't the only one. All the women were way off the mark, and our instructor gave up after a few hours, proclaiming that as long as we understood the basics of firearm safety, we never had to touch the muskets again and should leave the hunting to the men. He wouldn't tell us anything about our male counterparts, no matter how many questions we asked, but he did reveal that their training had been vastly more successful.

We had seen the men from a distance but did not meet them officially until the morning we set off for the island, and although I had spent the past two weeks training with the ladies, I had yet to get to know them in any real way. There were five women, including myself, and ten men. This wasn't strictly historically accurate since the Jamestown colony had been settled by men and it was not until years later that women began to come out from England—brides whose passage was arranged by the East India Company and who were willing to marry complete strangers in exchange for the promise of a better life in a wild and uncharted place.

Would I have had the courage to undertake such a voyage and marry a man I'd never clapped eyes on, even if he was as brave and dashing as I imagined my ancestor to be? Hell no, but then the show was going to film for only six months, and then I'd be free to return to my comfortable and safe existence. I did hope that I would at least bond with the other four women. Life without friendships would be hard and uncertain, and I thought we could still support each other even if we were all competing for the same prizes.

The four ladies were Iris Maddox, Shelby Bryant, Nicky Jackson, and Theresa Zhang, and although I tried to keep an open mind, I didn't think we'd make fast friends.

Iris was a plump, motherly woman in her forties. She had artfully highlighted blond hair cut in a chin-length bob that went from fashionable curl to bird's-nest-like frizz as soon as her hair products and blow dryer were taken away and high humidity did the rest. Her skin was milky and freckled and would probably burn without daily applications of sunscreen. Iris had warm brown eyes, a friendly smile, and something of a mouth on her. She was the sort of woman who never held back and said whatever popped into her mind, a quality that could be as endearing as it was irritating. Up until a few months ago, Iris had been the owner of a trendy Brooklyn restaurant. She didn't tell us what had happened, but it was clear that for whatever reason, the restaurant had closed. She was divorced and had a teenaged son and a daughter in her early twenties who was studying abroad.

Shelby Bryant was an elementary school teacher from a small town in Louisiana. She had pin-straight silver-blond hair, lovely blue eyes, and a body that wouldn't look out of place on the cover of *Sports Illustrated*. She was in her mid-to-late twenties and the closest female contestant to my own age, and I assumed she was single, since no husband or boyfriend had been mentioned and the only people she had referred to when speaking of home were her parents and an older brother. I found Shelby to be a bit phony, but perhaps her saccharine sweetness and excessive politeness were what they referred to as Southern charm.

Nicky Jackson was a journalist from Philadelphia. She was in her early thirties, tall, golden brown, and lithe as a jungle cat. Nicky had the most startling turquoise eyes and caramel-colored hair that she wore in braids. She had a no-nonsense attitude and didn't bother to hide her competitive nature. Nicky was there to win, and she let everyone know it.

The final female contestant was Theresa Zhang. Theresa was in her early fifties and was of Chinese descent. She was a homeopath from New Hampshire and practiced tai chi every morning before breakfast. Theresa was short, lean, and compact, with small breasts, narrow hips, and very straight shoulder-length black hair that was streaked with gray. She was quiet and reserved, and I didn't think she'd be forming any lasting friendships on the island. I found it surprising that she had been selected because unlike the other ladies, she didn't seem to know or care about colonial history.

Over the past two weeks, I had wondered what the male contestants would be like. Based on the ladies, I assumed they would be a wide mix of ages, backgrounds, and worldviews. The men, when we finally saw them trooping toward the ship, were decked out in knee-length breeches, hose, wool or leather doublets, and colorful chapeaus. If not for the ship's crew, we'd truly look like a bunch of colonists setting off for the New World.

Justin Rogue, the executive producer of *Jamestown*, and his assistant Gloria Lawson were also aboard, Justin walking from contestant to contestant, making small talk, and joking with the crew. He was dressed in pleated breeches and a studded leather doublet and wore a velvet hat with a plume, the hat perched at a rakish angle, its midnight blue color complementing his chestnut hair and blue eyes. His shapely calves were clad in powder-blue hose, and he had silver-buckled shoes, unlike the rest of us, whose merited only pewter. Justin's only nod to modernity was his rimless specs, which magnified his beautiful eyes just enough to draw attention to them. He looked completely at ease and seemed in excellent spirits.

Gloria Lawson, who was a bit overweight and very buxom, looked extremely uncomfortable in her period costume and kept yanking at the bodice that did little to contain breasts that foamed over the top like dough rising over the edge of a bowl. She was probably longing for the support of a good bra and a cold drink, since she looked tired and hot as she answered endless questions and frequently consulted her clipboard.

The men all smiled and nodded, but introductions would have to wait, since Justin asked us all to gather around on deck. The cameramen were filming, and Justin flashed them a charming smile before addressing the group.

"Ladies and gentlemen, I know you're eager to get to know each other and explore your new home, but I would like to take a moment to welcome you and share a few pertinent details while I still have your undivided attention. Then you can head downstairs, enjoy a glass of champagne, your last for six months," he joked, "and meet each other properly."

Justin gazed at the cameras yet again and continued. "The competition will officially begin tomorrow morning. Tonight, you will have time to settle in and then enjoy a bountiful feast provided by Varlet Entertainment. I want to wish each and every one of you the best of luck and hope you will not only focus on winning the prizes but also have some fun and make friendships that will last a lifetime. If you have any last-minute questions, now is the time to ask, since once I leave you tonight, I won't be seeing you for the duration of the filming."

Justin gazed at the group, his expression somber. "Please remember, the viewers will be voting not only on your ability to use a seventeenth-century plow or churn butter that doesn't run, but on good sportsmanship, personal integrity, and your ability to acclimate and survive in an uncultivated and unfamiliar environment. As much as we all enjoy the occasional historical drama, the reality tends to be very different, as you will soon learn. I wish you the best of luck and hope this will be an experience you'll treasure forever. Now, if you would all bid goodbye to the modern world, I'll ask you to head downstairs. Thank you."

"Will there be a second season?" Iris asked before Justin had a chance to leave.

"That's confidential information," Justin replied with a wink. "But people are still fascinated with the Salem witch trials, so that's something we might consider as a follow-up."

Shelby shyly raised her hand, and Justin's gaze alighted on her. "Yes, Ms. Bryant?"

"Are there going to be hostile Natives?" Shelby asked.

"That is actually a very good question," Justin said. "We had initially considered including interactions with Indigenous peoples but decided against it. *Jamestown* is about the individual's physical and emotional ability to adapt to harsh and unfamiliar surroundings, so introducing the expansionist politics and racist attitudes of the time would only distract from the objectives of the show."

"Because things are just *so* different now," someone at the back said under his breath.

"Look," Justin said, adopting a conciliatory tone, "we are not here to debate the right and wrong of colonization or the version of events that was taught to us in school. That's a debate for another time and most definitely another place. We are simply reenacting an exciting moment in our country's history and giving you and the viewer a chance to understand what life was really like, and to test your ability to handle the everyday hardships faced by the brave men and women who sailed across the ocean in a ship much like this one to start a new life in a foreign land."

Justin looked around, his desire to move on obvious. "Now, if there are no more questions, let's have that drink."

Everyone stole one last look at civilization and made their way below deck, where the lighting was dim, and the space quickly became crowded. At least it didn't smell bad. Had this been a real ship sailing from England at the beginning of the seventeenth century, there would have been livestock, chamber pots and slop buckets, and spoiling foodstuffs, too precious to throw overboard with so many hungry people to feed.

Justin disappeared through a narrow door, followed by Gloria, but the cameramen, Alan and Greg, remained, filming us unobtrusively as we got our drinks and engaged in our first unstructured interaction with the other contestants. They would film us in person the entire time we were on the island, but there were also hidden cameras that would record our daily struggles without disrupting the sense of authenticity. According to Justin, the only places safe from the watchful eye of Varlet would be the not-quite-historically accurate outhouses and bathing shed, since no one would agree to be filmed while washing. And it would be washing, not bathing. If the colonists washed at all, it was in parts. Personal hygiene had not been a priority, but you could hardly tell modern-day people that they couldn't bathe for six months, so concessions were made.

I smiled bravely as Iris came to stand next to me, a glass of bubbly in her hand. "How do you feel?" she asked.

"Nervous. Excited. Scared."

"Me too. It's starting to feel awfully real now that there's no turning back."

"Do you want to turn back?" I asked, wondering if Iris was serious.

"A part of me does, the part that likes to play it safe, but to be honest, I don't have anything to go back to. My life was a steaming pile of shit when I filled out the application. I thought it'd be nice to have some time to regroup and figure out what I really want. And the money certainly won't hurt, even if I don't win one of the grand prizes."

24

I nodded in understanding. "Fifty thousand dollars will make up for lost earnings and cover the expenses we incur while on the island. I still have to pay my mortgage," I added. I could have sublet my condo, as Diana had suggested, but the idea of someone living in my home, especially when I wasn't there to keep an eye on things, made me uncomfortable. My home was my safe space, and I would rather continue to pay my mortgage than compromise my security.

"I gave up my apartment and put everything in storage," Iris said. "I don't want to go back there anyway. Too many memories." Iris raised her glass. "To a fresh start," she said, and I joined her in the toast.

Soon, we were joined by the other ladies, whose expressions ranged from terrified rabbit (Shelby) to Wonder Woman in full regalia and on the verge of kicking someone's ass (Nicky). Theresa didn't look nervous, but she had a closed look on her face that didn't invite friendly banter.

"Ready?" Nicky asked. When she said it, it sounded like a challenge, and I supposed it was. Nicky was practically bouncing with impatience.

"As ready as I'll ever be," Iris said. "What about you, girls?" She turned to Theresa and Shelby.

Shelby gave a tight-lipped smile but didn't reply. Theresa nodded, and Nicky rolled her eyes in exasperation. "Why are you two even here?" she asked, her impatience obvious.

"I just wanted to get away for a while," Shelby said softly.

"Got too hot for you in Louisiana?" Nicky teased, but her smile faded when Shelby's eyes filled with tears.

"I'd rather not talk about it, if you don't mind. Especially on camera."

"I'm sorry," Nicky said. "I didn't mean to pry."

"It's all right. It was a fair question."

"What about you, Theresa?" Iris asked. "Why did you want to come on the show?"

"My parents fled China in the 1960s to escape communism, but to be honest, I always thought the underlying concept was a good one and might work if the government doesn't abuse its power through the use of the military and deny its citizens basic human rights. Living in a settlement and sharing all our supplies is a form of communism, or socialism, if you will. I want to see if it can work when there are no soldiers to beat people into submission."

"So, this is a social experiment for you?" Nicky asked. She seemed genuinely interested.

"In a way," Theresa replied. "My parents were grateful for their freedom, but they never truly felt like they belonged in America. Everything they did and thought passed through the filter of family history and cultural mores. It made for a difficult childhood."

"I think that could be said of any immigrant family," Iris said. "My grandparents came from Poland, and my mom always complained about the same thing. You can take people away from their homeland, but you can't take the homeland away from the people. It's how they define themselves and relate to others. What about you, Nicky?" Iris asked. "What made you sign on the dotted line?"

"PR," Nicky replied without hesitation. "Not only will I get a much-needed cash infusion, but I will become a household name. It will be easier to get my foot in the door with the bigger news outlets. I want to be one of those reporters the president knows by name and calls on at a press conference."

"Which president?" Shelby asked.

"Any president," Nicky replied with a one-shouldered shrug. "I intend to grill whoever is in the White House, although I admit, I did have a soft spot for Obama. I would have loved to get to know Michelle."

It was then that we were joined by the men, who had chosen beer over champagne. We went through the introductions, but I knew it would take me a little while to remember everyone's names. The men were a mix of backgrounds, education, and professions, and although they had spent two weeks together, they seemed awkward and reserved with each other.

The oldest male contestant was Ed Barnes, an African American Methodist minister from Pittsburgh. Ed was in his early fifties and had a wife and two grown sons who wholeheartedly supported his participation on the show. Ed was rangy and had a disarming way about him that instantly made me feel at ease in his presence. I wasn't much of a churchgoer, but I thought a minister like Ed might make it easier to come to a service.

The next two contestants I met had the sort of urban polish one often saw in politicians and salesmen of very expensive cars. They were both in their forties, fit, and with full heads of dark hair threaded with gray that gave them an instant air of distinguished authority. That was where the similarity ended, though. William Abbott was a judge from Texas. He had shrewd brown eyes, a deep tan, startlingly white teeth, and the air of a man who was very comfortable with his opinions and choices, which he was happy to share whether anyone asked for them or not. William told us that he had retired the previous year, but he seemed too young and driven to play golf and lie by the pool all day. Perhaps that was why he'd come on the show. His manner clearly showed that he had something to prove.

Mark Beasley had piercing blue eyes, a smarmy smile, and a British accent that instantly made him appear more debonair than he really was. He was a single professor of European history at a private college in Massachusetts, and as he spoke, his gaze frequently strayed to Shelby. In fact, all the men were checking out Shelby since she was the youngest and most striking woman aboard. Shelby smiled coyly over the rim of her champagne glass, her earlier reticence forgotten in the face of such naked admiration,

27

and I noticed that her gaze returned most frequently to William Abbott. Nicky looked a bit peeved, but I didn't mind. I wasn't there to hook up, so I continued my study of the men.

The next batch were in their mid-to-late thirties. There was Glen Grisham, a warehouse manager from Ohio. He was sandy-haired and blue-eyed, and had the build of a boxer, with a powerful upper body and a thick neck. Although Glen didn't say or do anything that could be described as provoking, he had a barely suppressed air of belligerence that probably went hand in hand with a raging competitive streak. I found Glen intimidating and hoped I wouldn't have too many personal dealings with him.

Jesse Milford was a cattle rancher from Montana. He had the rugged look of a man who spent his life outdoors and, although not classically attractive, with his close-cropped reddish hair and brown eyes, had an air of authority and competence.

The remaining male contestants were in their late twenties and early thirties. Brendan Taft was a cuddly, bearded hipster from Brooklyn Heights. He was a carpenter who had his own line of furniture that he sold from both his workshop and an online store. While he was away, the retail end of the business would be run by his brother, who, according to Brendan, had designed some of the more imaginative pieces and posted esthetically pleasing reels on Instagram and TikTok. Brendan didn't tell us anything about his personal life, except that he was currently single.

Samuel Murphy was a potato farmer from Idaho. He was of average height, average weight, and had brown hair, brown eyes, a snub nose, and a slightly downturned mouth. His appearance was so nondescript that he could fit into any group of people and go unnoticed. He also wasn't very talkative and chugged his beer in seconds before reaching for another plastic cup.

Timothy Branham was Mohegan and came from a reservation in Connecticut, where he was an officer in the tribal police. He had also served in the military and had done a tour in Iraq, a fact he shared with obvious reluctance. His shoulder-length hair was so black, it was almost blue, and his dark eyes held a challenge. Timothy was married and had a three-year-old daughter, but judging by the tension in his jaw and his haunted gaze, I thought it was marital problems that had driven him to try his luck in Jamestown.

Gael Ramos was a communications manager from Santa Cruz. He was ridiculously attractive, a fact that wasn't lost on the ladies. Even Theresa was discreetly admiring his thickly lashed almond-shaped eyes that were the color of onyx, and the full lips that so easily stretched into a warm smile. Gael's hair fell into his eyes, and he brushed it aside without thinking, the movement so fluid and elegant, it seemed to momentarily take Iris's breath away. When he lifted his arm, the sleeve of his linen shirt slid back to reveal an Aztec sun tattoo on the inside of his right wrist. Gael was married and had a six-year-old daughter named Luna. Besides his family, his other great love was the guitar, and he played at local bars and events on weekends and had recently put out his first CD.

The last male contestant, and the one that left me wary because I caught him watching me on more than one occasion, was Declan Carey. He had tawny eyes, dark blond hair that would probably curl given the chance to grow, and heroic bone structure. Declan was tall and muscular with the wide shoulders and narrow hips of a male model. He was also a cop, on leave from the Chicago Police Department. He didn't give us the reason for his sabbatical, but I saw a shadow cross his eyes when he mentioned it, so perhaps there had been a disciplinary issue.

"We certainly have an interesting mix of people," Ed Barnes remarked, once the introductions were finally over. I noticed that he hadn't touched his beer.

"Makes perfect sense," Mark cut in, lecturing to us as if we were his students. "Most of us have professions that are in some way relevant to those of the original colonists. We have two law-enforcement officers, a minister, a carpenter, a farmer and a rancher, an herbalist, a nurse, as well as a judge. The Jamestown colony would have had soldiers, a marshal, a priest, a governor, and a magistrate, someone who was knowledgeable in the art of healing, and someone who could cook, like Iris here."

"So, why am I here?" Gael asked.

"You can be the records keeper," Mark replied. "The colonists kept detailed journals and accounts."

"Not exactly my area of expertise," Gael replied with a frown. "I'm a techie, not a scribe."

"Not much call for techies in the seventeenth century, I'm afraid," Mark replied. He was clearly an authority on the period, so everyone listened to him, eager to know more, although, by our own admission, we'd all done our own research before embarking on our adventure.

"Maybe Nicky would be a better fit," Gael said.

"I'd be the slave," Nicky said bitterly. "Ed and I would be like those poor people who were captured and brought to the colony from Africa to grow tobacco for their white masters." Nicky looked around the group, most of whom looked uncomfortable. "But as a reporter, it's my job to report what I see, so I'll accept the position of records keeper. Beats toiling in the fields."

"We'll all be toiling in the fields," Ed reminded her gently.

"I do hope you can manage to remain objective, Ms. Jackson," William Abbott cut across Ed. "Journalists have a way of twisting the truth to align with their own agenda."

I saw a spark of anger in Nicky's eyes, but she tamped it down. "I will record only the facts. Any op-ed will be done on my own time."

"Did you not sign an NDA?" William asked.

"Of course I did."

"Then any commentary on events that take place on the island will land you in court, young lady."

Mark raised a conciliatory hand. "I'm sure Nicky doesn't need to be reminded and will toe the line," he said mildly. Nicky's eyebrows lifted in outrage at the patronizing comment, but she didn't interrupt, probably because Alan's camera was pointed directly at her. "I do think it would be a good idea to assign roles to the colonists."

"Will this be a democratic process?" Timothy asked, his tone laced with derision. "Or will I automatically be expected to take on the role of the hostile Native?"

"It's amazing how you people continue to harp on things that have nothing to do with you personally," William said without heat. It was as if he was fascinated by the very notion of being outraged on behalf of one's predecessors. "One of my English ancestors was sent down to Botany Bay at the age of sixteen. His crime was petty theft. Probably stole a loaf of bread. He died of starvation a few months after arriving. Am I supposed to blame everyone in Australia for their convict colony past? Or should I hold Great Britain accountable for the unduly harsh laws of the 1800s and their policy of rampant colonialism?"

No one replied, everyone suddenly very interested in their drinks and the napkins printed with the Varlet logo, so Mark took the opportunity to regain control of the conversation. He sighed as if striving for patience and turned to Timothy. "You heard Justin, Timothy. There are to be no Natives. If you choose to be hostile, that's up to you, but I'm sure you have much more valuable skills that could be utilized for the greater good of the colony."

"I'm all about the greater good," Timothy said sarcastically.

"Well, this promises to be fun," Iris said tartly. "Six months of sniping and blaming each other for things we can't control."

"No one can blame me for anything," Sam interjected. "My ancestors fled from Ireland during the potato famine, and I grow potatoes. There's irony in that, is there not? But then the Irish were always treated like vermin everywhere they went, so don't even get me started on that."

Ed raised a tentative hand, as if asking for permission to speak. "Look, no one here is personally responsible for the moral shortcomings of our ancestors. Please, let's take pride in our own choices and accomplishments and treat one another with kindness and respect."

"It's not even Sunday yet, and already he's preaching," Glen grumbled.

"Ed is right," Declan said. "There's no need for baseless animosity. We're all coming in on equal footing. Let's keep it that way."

"Well, technically, the residents of the colony would not be on equal footing," Mark interjected. "In the original colony, the hierarchy would be established from the start, but since we have not been assigned roles by Varlet, it only makes sense that we select the candidates ourselves based on their background and obvious strengths," he said, looking around the group for approval.

"It's an odd name, Varlet," Sam said.

"Not odd at all given the context," Mark jumped in. He reminded me of a contestant on a game show who slammed that buzzer before the host had a chance to finish the question.

"What context?" Glen asked.

"It's a play on words. Varlet means scoundrel in old English, same as rogue. Justin's last name is Rogue, so the company is named after him."

"Because Rogue Productions was probably already taken," Gael remarked.

"Well spotted, Mark," William said. "I love word games."

"Me too," Theresa chimed in. "I play Scrabble every chance I get."

"I think we're getting off topic," Mark said with exaggerated patience. "We were going to assign roles to the colonists," he reminded us.

"Am I to be the marshal?" Declan asked with an amused grin.

"You're the most logical choice," Mark replied. "And perhaps Timothy can be your deputy."

Timothy gave Mark a look of barely suppressed anger. "As usual, the white man gets to be in charge."

"You can be the marshal," Declan said. "I would be honored to be your deputy."

If Timothy was surprised by the offer, he didn't show it. "All right. I accept," he said, and gave a mock bow of acceptance.

"Perhaps we should elect a governor," Mark suggested, but everyone remained silent. The governor was the most senior and respected position, and no one knew anyone well enough to nominate a candidate. Mark clearly thought it should be him, since he was well versed in the history of the period and seemed to have all the answers, but no one expressed an immediate intention to put forth his name.

"Perhaps we should wait a week or two," Ed suggested. "Get to know each other and see who's best qualified."

"That makes sense." Iris nodded in agreement. "I'm with Ed, who I assume will be our spiritual leader?"

"If you are all comfortable with that, I would be delighted," Ed Barnes said. Most people just shrugged. Ed was already a minister, so the choice was obvious.

"And William can be the magistrate," Mark said, looking to William Abbott, who gave a small nod in acknowledgement of Mark's endorsement.

"If that's acceptable to everyone," William said noncommittally. "Although I sincerely hope we won't have any crimes to try."

"I seriously doubt Jamestown will be a Utopian society," Glen said sourly. "There are always crimes."

"Glad to see you have such faith in your fellow man," Brendan quipped. "What reason would anyone have to commit a crime?"

"The same reason anyone ever has," Glen replied. "People are people. Just because you put on a pair of funny breeches and give up your cellphone doesn't automatically make you a saint."

"You think I look funny in my breeches?" Brendan asked with a mock hurt expression. "Do they make my ass look fat?" He did a little twirl, and everyone laughed.

"You look amazing," Shelby said. "In the seventeenth century, your shapely calves would be the talk of the colony."

"You think?" Brendan asked, grinning at her. "I didn't want to brag, but they are rather impressive." That broke the tension, and everyone smiled.

"You can come up now, everyone," Justin announced as he reentered the hold. "We're approaching our colony, and I'm sure you wouldn't want to miss your first sighting of land."

Everyone trooped back up on deck, and a shiver of excitement passed through the group as everyone surged forward, eager to get a look at what would be their home for the next six months.

"Welcome to Jamestown," Justin announced proudly.

The sun had been out when we set off, the ocean sparkling playfully around the wooden ship, a springy breeze caressing our faces as we watched the shore disappear amid the cries of fat seagulls that perched in the rigging and watched us with their beady eyes. Now, thick clouds blanketed the sky, and the breeze had turned chillier, the gusts tearing at my skirts and pulling the hood of my cloak off my capped head. The island rose silent and mysterious from the choppy gray waters, the tall pine trees standing like a battalion of soldiers, shoulder to shoulder to form a protective barrier that seemed to block out sunlight and cloaked the island in sullen shadow.

Jagged black boulders rose out of the water, encircling the outcropping of land except for a strip of narrow beach that led to a lone wooden jetty that stuck out into the Atlantic like an accusing finger. A gauzy mist rose off the water and floated between the tree trunks, the tips of the trees seemingly poking holes in the overcast sky. I started as a cloud of crows erupted into the sky, the birds startled by the screeching of the chain as the anchor was lowered into the churning water below, their squawking and the frantic flutter of wings surprisingly loud in an otherwise silent landscape. I followed their progress, and that was when I saw it. There, on the hill overlooking the beach, was a row of sharpened wooden spars, the wall encircling our settlement.

Welcome home, indeed, I thought as I followed the rest of the group down a narrow gangplank and onto the jetty that seemed to shift beneath the weight of so many bodies, the wood bleached and warped by relentless waves and buffeting wind. We walked in silence, following Justin up the path toward the gates set into the curtain wall, the cameramen walking backward just ahead of Justin and filming our arrival.

Despite psyching myself up for weeks for my first glimpse of the settlement, I suddenly felt terribly vulnerable and very much alone in this forbidding place. I turned to Gael, who was walking next to me, in the hope of a reassuring word or an encouraging smile, but Gael's expression was grim, his gaze fixed on the sharpened spikes as if he were walking to his own execution.

# Chapter 4

# Gael

Depression. Anxiety. Mind and mood-altering drugs. That's the prescribed way. Numb the pain. Dull the fear until you feel nothing, until no emotion is real, and you can't even remember who you once were or had hoped to become. Worship at the altar of the pharmaceutical god until he smiles down upon you and casts a spell of chemical oblivion. Is it not normal to feel depressed and anxious when all you've known is terror and loss? Is it not healthy to face your fears and emotions and actually work through them rather than medicating yourself into a stupor? Not according to my doctors, but hey, I'm not American, and I don't think like they do.

I live by different rules and apply alternative solutions to my problems. Coming on this show might have been a bit extreme. My therapist might say it was a cry for help, but maybe it wasn't a feeble cry but a bloodcurdling roar of rage. A nod to my ancestors, who had a different way of dealing with the endless shit life threw at them. I'm not about to erect a Mayan temple or offer up the still-beating heart of a human sacrifice, but I will no longer hide behind a haze of chemical indifference. Maybe, in this place, I can come to terms with the past at last and reach a moment of catharsis that will allow me to finally move on from the guilt and pain that have been my constant companions the last ten years of my life.

Unless, of course, the reason I was chosen is because someone has unearthed my secret and there will be a great reveal at the end of the show. I bet that'd bring the ratings in. But maybe I'm just being paranoid. I'm Gael Ramos, the son of Mexican immigrants from Guadalajara, the husband of Camila Ramos, proud Latina and business owner, and the father of Luna, the most beautiful child to ever grace this graceless earth. I am an upstanding citizen, a dutiful taxpayer, and a valuable asset to a company I helped to build from the bottom up. I own a house with an inground pool, and I make carnitas and homemade guacamole and chips every Sunday, just like Mama used to make when I was a kid and life was simple and happy. I am living the American dream.

Except I'm not. Because Gael Ramos is dead.

# Chapter 5

## Natalie

Once I was able to separate my expectations from the pall cast by the sullen weather, I had to admit that the settlement looked much as I had imagined it would, but it was still a shock when we passed through the gates. There were several ochre-colored wattle and daub houses with thatched roofs, earthen floors, and unglazed windows. We peeked inside one of the houses. The interior was dim and smelled of earth, musty wood, and damp straw.

The building at the far end had a cross on the roof, identifying it as the church, and contained a crude altar and several benches that were clearly visible through the wide opening in the wall. There was no door or any means of heating the space when it was cold, as it was now. The original colonists had been expected to attend two two-hour services each Sunday, but we had agreed that one service would be enough to satisfy the historical requirements. To spend four hours seated on those hard benches would have been torture.

Aside from the church and the living quarters, there were several sheds and a good-sized barn. Justin proudly introduced us to our cow, who was immediately christened Betsy and seemed completely unimpressed with our arrival. There was a horse, Wilbur, and several chickens that clucked nervously in their enclosure when they saw us. A beady-eyed rooster ignored our presence and surveyed his little kingdom with a territorial glare.

"Ooh, I love chickens," Nicky exclaimed. "We must name them."

"Knock yourself out," Sam replied. "I don't think you'll hear an argument from anyone."

Nicky cocked her head to the side and studied the hens. "Henny, Mabel, and Mathilda," she said, pointing to each one in turn.

"Well, now you have to name the rooster," Glen said.

"You name him," Nicky replied. "He looks mean."

"Roger the Rooster," Glen said. "My grandfather used to keep chickens, and Roger the Rooster ruled that roost."

"Okay, Roger it is," Justin said a trifle irritably. "Shall we continue with the tour?"

Justin led us to the storage sheds. The first was the armory. There were five muskets, a keg of powder, and several small boxes of shot. It was unclear whether the powder and shot were meant to last us until the end or only until we ran out. When asked, Justin assured us that if we needed more, both would be provided. We followed him to the grain store, where several bags of wheat and corn, and a few smaller sacks of barley and beans, were stacked against the walls. There were also several paper packets of seeds, the starter kit for our vegetable garden. We'd be growing whatever the colonists had, namely beans, cabbages, leeks, and peas. It would have been prudent to plant potatoes, but potatoes hadn't come to the New World for a long while yet, and we had to remain historically accurate.

A dozen kegs of ale stood in the corner. The supply seemed disproportionate to the rest of the provisions, but the colonists had drunk ale in lieu of water, milk, or tea, and I was sure the ale would go faster than anyone imagined, even among those of us that didn't care for the taste of beer. If anything, it would serve as a sleep aid or a much-needed source of alcohol for disinfecting scrapes and cuts. The application of alcohol to wounds had not come about until much later, probably sometime in the nineteenth century, but I wasn't about to forego the practice, not unless the medical officer stepped in and used his own limited supply to treat any injuries that occurred on the island.

In the smoking shed, two joints hung from hooks in the rafters. Several flies circled the meat, periodically settling on the dry, brownish flesh. The smell was overpowering, and I stepped outside, disgusted by the unsanitary conditions. Iris followed me out, her expression one of naked displeasure.

"Is it the flies?" I asked, keeping my voice low.

Iris shook her head. "I wouldn't worry about the flies," she said. "We'd have to cook the meat anyway, and the heat will burn away any residual bacteria. It's the lack of supplies."

"It seems like a lot," I said, wondering why Iris seemed so troubled.

"It's not," Iris replied. "It's a drop in the bucket given how much food modern-day people consume on a daily basis. People in the seventeenth century survived on starvation rations, and even our parents' generation was raised on much smaller portions. I read somewhere that a burger and fries in the 1950s were the size you now get in a Happy Meal, and the shake was the size of a sippy cup. No one was supersizing it or slurping the Big Gulp, which is probably why obesity and heart disease were not such a problem."

"So you think the stores won't last?" I asked, focusing on the part that was really concerning.

"Not if we eat the way we did back at home. We will have to institute rations from the very start if we want the supplies to last, and given that lot," she pointed to the knot of men still hanging around the armory, "that won't go over well."

"They'll understand, won't they?" Shelby, who'd clearly overheard, asked as she came to stand with us.

"Not if they think dwindling supplies will be automatically replenished," Iris said.

"But Justin did say the stores would be restocked," Shelby said.

"Yes, but he didn't say how often. Six months is a long time, and what we have in there might last two months if we're really careful."

Justin stepped outside, followed by Ed, Theresa, and Jesse, and approached us.

"All right, everyone," he called out. "Now I will show you to your living quarters. As I'm sure you know, unmarried women would not be allowed to bunk with single men, so we have all the ladies sharing one house. The men will be split among the remaining two houses. You can decide amongst yourselves who will go in with whom."

"Do we have to remain in one house for the duration of our stay?" Timothy asked.

Justin made a show of considering the question. "I suppose you can move houses if someone doesn't get along, but I hope that won't happen."

"Throw together a group of sexually frustrated men, and tensions always run high," Glen said from the back of the group.

"Who said we have to be sexually frustrated?" William asked. "There was nothing in the contract about forming relationships. In fact, I bet the producers are hoping for some drama."

"There's no rule against forming romantic relationships," Justin confirmed. "If contestants wish to couple up, they may, but they will have to consent to a fictitious marriage and remain bound to each other for the remainder of the term, since no premarital relations were permitted in the colonies. Those who broke the rules paid the price. Likewise, if two or more people choose to band together, it's their prerogative, since that would have almost certainly happened in Jamestown. There's political and social strength in numbers."

Everyone nodded again, probably considering what Justin had just said about the fictitious marriage. That condition would certainly make for some interesting developments, and it was telling that this had not been mentioned until now.

"Technically, there wouldn't be any single women in the colony," Mark cut in. "All the women who were shipped over were married to the colonists upon arrival. So the only way a woman would become single was if she were widowed."

"Well, let's hope that doesn't happen," Justin said. "But if you have your eye on some lucky lady, I suggest you move quickly, Mr. Beasley. The ratio is two to one, so the ladies won't remain unclaimed for long."

Nearly every male head turned toward Shelby, who was gazing at Mark. Mark smiled broadly, and although nothing had been said out loud, it was clear a message had been both sent and received.

"Where are the cameras?" Timothy asked before Justin had a chance to turn away. "I haven't spotted any."

"There are several cameras placed around the island. I'm not at liberty to divulge the exact locations."

"But surely we have a right to know if we're being filmed in our most private moments," Nicky said.

Justin looked uncomfortable but stood his ground. "You agreed to be filmed around the clock," he reminded us. "As previously stated, the only locations that are off limits to the cameras are the privy and the bathing shed."

"Fair enough," Nicky said, and the tension seemed to dissipate.

"Now that that's out of the way, let's start with the ladies," Justin said, and pointed toward the house closest to the church. "Gentlemen, you can sort out your own sleeping arrangements."

Inside the house, it was cold and dim despite the bright afternoon light, and smelled strongly of earth, timber, and dust. There were two small rooms, the walls and low ceilings crisscrossed by dark beams. A boxy double bed that reminded me of a Victorian hearse was overshadowed by its wooden tester and was hung with limp curtains that might have been made of beige fustian. The bed dominated the front room and was within a hand's reach of the hearth. Surely a fire hazard, especially since there didn't appear to be a fire guard. The back room, which was just through an opening in the wall, contained three narrow cots, one against each unbroken wall and made up with straw mattresses, linen bedding, and scratchy wool blankets. Given the conversation of only a few minutes before, I peered around the room, focusing on the ceiling and the corners, but I couldn't see any cameras. However many there were, they were well disguised.

"Who's supposed to share a bed?" Iris asked, clearly outraged that there weren't individual beds for everyone.

"The double beds are for the married couples, but since everyone is still technically single, it will have to be any two of you. I suggest you draw straws, unless someone prefers to be closer to the hearth," Justin replied. "This room will be warmer, and given that the nights will remain cold for several more months, that might be an added incentive."

"You have got to be joking," Shelby said. Her mutinous expression said that she'd rather sleep on the dirt floor than share a bed with one of us.

"I don't mind sharing," Theresa said. "I grew up sharing a bed with my sister."

"All right," Justin said. "We need one more volunteer or the straws come out."

"It's fine," Iris said. "I'll partner up with Theresa. Can't abide being cold."

"That's settled, then," Justin said. "The rest of you ladies each get a cot to yourself."

"Well, that's a relief," Shelby grumbled.

Nicky set her sack on the cot furthest from the window. "I get cold too," she explained.

I took the cot beneath the window, and Shelby took the remaining one. She seemed vastly relieved not to have to share a bed, and I could sympathize. Sleeping together is intimate business, even if nothing sexual takes place, and I was too used to having my own space to feel comfortable with such familiarity, especially with a woman I barely knew. I didn't relish the idea of sleeping next to an unglazed window, but given how small and stuffy the house was, I figured I'd sleep better if there was a source of fresh air.

I sat down on the cot and nearly jumped back up again. The straw mattress was thin and lumpy, and I could feel the slats of the wood digging into my legs and butt. The cot was so narrow that if I lay on my back, my elbows would hang off unless I laid my arms straight at my sides or folded them on my chest. I wasn't an exceptionally tall woman, so at least I would fit lengthwise, but Nicky's and Shelby's feet would probably stick out several inches since they were both taller than me.

"Prisons have more comfortable accommodations," Nicky said as she sat on her own cot. She didn't seem upset, though, but more amazed at how people used to live.

"They also have cable TV, internet access, and a commissary in prison," Shelby pointed out.

"And a variety of food, unpalatable though it might be. We'll be eating nothing but porridge and stew for six months," Iris chimed in. "Suddenly, I'm desperate for a salad."

"And a salad you shall have," Justin said as he motioned for us to follow him outside. "Come. Our feast awaits."

A trestle table with wooden benches had been set up in the square. It was the only space large enough to accommodate all of us. The table was set with pewter plates, wooden cups, and primitive utensils. Forks had not been around in the seventeenth century, so people ate with knives and wooden spoons. Still, the food looked appetizing, and we were all hungry, not having eaten anything since breakfast.

The boat crew had set the table with bowls of salad, platters of corn bread, ribs, vats of potato salad, and several roasted chickens. There was beer and lemonade to drink. Justin sat at the head of the table and toasted our good health while the cameramen filmed our homecoming feast. It felt odd to be filmed while eating, but after a few minutes, everyone seemed to forget Alan and Greg were there and fell into animated conversation. Once the cameramen got enough footage, they joined us at the table and loaded their plates, eating in silence. The crew and the medical officer had returned to the ship and probably had their own dinner, away from the cameras.

The feast went on for about two hours, and we even had chocolate cake with vanilla ice cream. This would be our last taste of decadence, since we'd have no refrigeration nor the ingredients to make desserts.

"Don't worry, darlings," Iris said cheerily. "I will bake you a cake, just as soon as I figure out how to use the hearth for baking and rustle up the necessary components."

"Wouldn't you need sugar?" Brendan asked, sounding unbearably sad at the thought of not having cake. "And vanilla?"

"I could manage without vanilla, but sugar and butter are a must." Iris stole a peek at Justin.

"You'll churn your own butter, but there's no sugar, I'm afraid," Justin said. "There is a small crock of molasses."

"I've never baked with molasses, but I guess I'll have to learn," Iris said.

"I have a real sweet tooth," Brendan confessed. "I'd happily forgo meat for a muffin or a tart."

"Well, if you were hoping for tarts, you should have signed up for a reality show about the French Revolution," Glen quipped. "You might have gotten one for your last meal before they asked you to lay your head on the guillotine."

"The first colonists had no sweets," Mark said authoritatively. "Which was probably a blessing since they also had no dentists. Molasses was imported from the West Indies, and the triangle of trade between England, the colonies, and the West Indies didn't evolve until later, once the colonists had tobacco, timber, and pelts to export."

"Yeah, we know, Mark," Nicky said tartly, but Mark didn't take the hint and began a long-winded lecture on the lives of the people of Jamestown.

"He's going to be the most popular guy here. I can tell," Iris whispered in my ear, the sarcasm unmistakable, and I had to stifle a giggle.

Either Mark didn't care or was oblivious to the eye rolls and butts shifting on the bench as people's patience began to run out.

"All right, colonists," Justin said, and got up from the table. "We are going to leave you now to get settled. I recommend that you have an early night, since the competition officially begins tomorrow at dawn. We will be here, ready to start filming by the time you're up, but you are not allowed to speak to us or acknowledge our presence unless it's an emergency. Good night, and good luck!" he said, and swept off his chapeau before executing an elaborate bow.

"Good night," everyone murmured before shuffling off to their respective houses. The crew would clean up the remains of the feast and then retire to their accommodation aboard the ship, which would remain moored at the jetty for the duration of the shoot. Gloria had mentioned that members of the crew doubled as sound engineers and production assistants and would review and edit the footage as it came in in order to save time later on, once our time on the island came to an end.

The sun had set and the temperature, which had been relatively mild during the day, plummeted. The interior of the house was cold and damp, and almost completely dark. Iris went to work lighting a fire by the meager light of the moon while Nicky and Shelby fitted the wooden shutters into the window in each room.

It took me a good ten minutes to light a candle using tinder and flint, and then, the light was so dim, it almost wasn't worth the effort. I took off my jacket and skirt and hung them on a nail protruding from the wall, rolled down my stockings, and removed my cap, letting my hair loose. I massaged my scalp, which felt tight after wearing my hair up all day, and got into bed. Despite the fire that cast an otherworldly red glow on the walls and our tired faces, it was still bitterly cold, and I tucked the edges of the blanket around myself to preserve every bit of warmth. I lay still, trying to ignore the slats beneath my back, thinking of all the things I would have to get used to in order to get through the next six months.

"Are you sorry yet?" Shelby asked from her cot. I wasn't sure if she was addressing me or Nicky. Probably both of us.

"Not yet, but ask me again tomorrow," I replied. My eyelids had grown heavy, and I felt myself sink deeper into the thin mattress.

"Not at all," Nicky said. "I intend to have the time of my life."

"That's a good attitude," Shelby said into the darkness.

"Life is what you make it, and I decide every single day that I'm going to make it count," Nicky said. "I have no patience for whining or regrets."

"You're going to be the best roommate ever," Shelby said nastily.

"You can count on it," Nicky said. "Goodnight, ladies. May the best woman win."

"Are you sure it will be a woman who'll take the first prize?" I asked.

"Yes, because it will be me."

"Goodnight," I said, putting an end to the discussion. I was suddenly so tired, I could barely speak.

Normally, it took me a while to fall asleep, but I was out before either Shelby or Nicky had a chance to respond, and for some odd reason, my last conscious thought was of Mark and his desire to be elected governor.

# Chapter 6

# Mark

Despite their very loud protestations to the contrary, Americans are dreadful prudes. People in Europe are much more relaxed about sex. As long as both partners are at the age of consent, no one interferes, and the age of consent is considerably lower. Not so here, and particularly not in a place of learning that's kept afloat by ridiculously high tuitions and sizeable donations the alumni are told they can claim on their tax returns. Not only do the school governors think they have the right to question a man's preference of partner, but they also reserve the right to censure, punish, and threaten with legal action.

An eighteen-year-old girl is an adult. If she wants to have an affair with her tutor, it's entirely her decision. I have never forced anyone, or even tried to emotionally manipulate them. Many young girls are drawn to older men, who are sophisticated and cultured and can offer them a gratifying sexual experience, not like some spotty youth who'll fumble for a few minutes and then embarrass himself and blame it on the girl because he doesn't have the emotional maturity to admit that he's simply not experienced enough to see to her pleasure.

What do silly college boys have to offer? All they do is get pissed on cheap beer and behave like the bellends they are. Girls that age are so much more mature, so open to new experiences and eager to learn. Besides, they're hardly virgins. You can barely find a virgin over the age of sixteen these days, and I'm being generous in my estimation. I'm certainly not their first partner, nor their last. These girls have taught me a thing or two as well, and I'm grateful. If they think I don't measure up, they'll tell their friends and then my reputation will suffer. As is, I've had quite a good run these past few years. A new *protégé* every term, and then it's "Bye, bye, darling. See you round campus. Our time together has meant so much to me." Most get it and move on.

There've been a few who mistook our trysts for true love, but I have never lied to them about my intentions. It's a casual fling between professor and willing student. Nothing more. And if the poor creature happens to develop genuine feelings for me, I see it as a life lesson she needs to learn. Unrealistic expectations inevitably lead to heartbreak.

Only once did a student involve her parents, and that was during the autumn term. The parents, who both happened to be ultra-conservative types who probably thought their little darling would still be a virgin on her wedding night, decided to escalate the situation with the school board. I could hardly defend myself by informing them that their daughter had been thoroughly fucked before. A drunken frat party that turned into an orgy had been mentioned during one of our pillow talks, but it would be beneath me to betray a confidence. Unlike those hormone-driven jocks, I took care to protect my partner from unwanted pregnancy and disease, but the parents are never grateful for the care one takes.

Well, this little sabbatical will be good for my professional reputation. By the time I return, all will be forgiven and forgotten, and I will either be $50,000 richer or I will take one of the top prizes and not need to work for a good while. I might even return home. A lovely seaside cottage in Dorset or Cornwall would be a dream come true. Fresh air, peace, and the occasional dissatisfied young wife or rebellious teen will be just the thing. I'm not looking for a life partner. I can't think of anything more tedious than being saddled with some nagging, aging broad who thinks she can control me and live off my life savings. No, I want none of that. Life can be very rewarding for an attractive, mature man with a few quid in his pocket. Very rewarding, indeed.

# Chapter 7

I woke sometime before dawn. At least I assumed it was before dawn. There were no clocks, and I couldn't see any slivers of light between the slats in the shutters. The fire had long since gone out, and the house was like a tomb, the only signs of life the even breathing of the other occupants. I would have tried to go back to sleep, but I was desperate to pee. The prospect of leaving my cocoon of warmth and going outside, where it was very cold and very dark, to squat over a hole in the ground in the narrow wooden cabin was about as appealing as joining the Polar Bear Club and going for a New Year's swim in water that was so freezing it could bring on cardiac arrest, but needs must. I couldn't wait.

I pushed my feet into shoes, felt around for my cloak and draped it over the chemise, and crept toward the door. It *was* dark outside, but sunrise wasn't far off. A narrow band of pink shimmered just above the stretch of horizon I could make out through the open gates. I took care of personal business, and since there was little point in going back to bed, I decided to stay and watch the sunrise. Unless my trip to the outhouse was being filmed, this was probably the only moment of privacy I would have today.

I walked toward the gates, pulled the cloak tighter around me, and gazed out over the beach. There was a stiff breeze coming off the water, but the air was fresh, and the sunrise was spectacular. It was going to be a beautiful spring day. It wasn't until the fiery belly of the sun skimmed the water that I realized something wasn't quite right, and it took me a moment to work out what it was as I stared at the jetty. The ship was gone. I looked up and down the shore, but there was no sign of it. Justin had said that filming would begin at sunrise, but it was time to rise, and no one seemed to be around. Perhaps the cameramen were meant to keep out of sight, but Justin had reiterated several times that the ship would remain at anchor and the crew would live aboard for the duration of the program. Perhaps I had misunderstood, and the ship would remain anchored elsewhere on the island, so as not to get into any shots.

I heard the opening of a door and watched Iris sprint toward the outhouse, her cloak billowing behind her. As if on cue, the other contestants began to emerge, looking bleary-eyed, and in the case of the men, stubbled and disheveled as they scratched their jaws and ran hands through unbrushed hair as they lined up for the bathroom.

"Natalie, are you okay?" Instead of heading toward the outhouse, Declan came to stand next to me, shivering slightly in his thin shirt. "Are you waiting to use the facilities?"

I shook my head. "The ship is gone."

Declan's head whipped to the side, his gaze fixing on the jetty. "When did you notice it wasn't there?"

"Just a few minutes ago, when I came outside."

"That's odd. Have you seen Alan and Greg?"

"No. There doesn't seem to be anyone here."

By this point, several people had joined us, with everyone staring at the beach in obvious puzzlement. "Maybe the ship took Justin and Gloria back to the mainland and will return in time to begin filming," Theresa suggested.

"Justin said a motorboat was coming to collect them," Mark said.

"Anyone hear the sound of a motor last night?" Ed asked.

"I was out like a light," said Nicky, who'd just joined the group.

A chorus of *me toos* filled the air.

"Did anyone stay up last night?" Timothy asked.

"There was nothing good on TV," Jesse joked.

This discussion might have continued for a while if a shriek hadn't torn through the settlement, forcing everyone to search for its source. It seemed to have come from the direction of the grain shed. Iris came running toward the gates, her face pale, and her eyes round with shock.

"What's wrong, Iris?" Declan exclaimed. "Are you all right?"

"The supplies," Iris panted. "Some of the supplies are gone."

"What do you mean gone?" Gael demanded as he approached.

"See for yourself."

Everyone sprinted toward the shed. There were sacks of grain, beans, and corn, but at least two sacks of wheat had vanished during the night.

"Who would do such a thing?" Theresa asked, looking from one face to another.

"Varlet people. Who else?" William declared with irritating certainty.

"But why?" Shelby whined. "And how? Surely someone would have heard something."

"Not if they added something to our drinks," Nicky said, her eyes narrowing with suspicion.

"You think they spiked our drinks?" Brendan asked. He seemed genuinely shocked by the suggestion.

"How else would you explain the fact that no one heard a thing?" Iris replied testily. "I usually have trouble sleeping, especially in a new place, but I don't remember anything after lying down."

"Me neither, and I'm a light sleeper," Declan said.

"But why would they do this?" Shelby asked again. Her alarmed gaze slid toward the jetty. "And why would they leave?"

"Maybe there was a problem with the supplies, and Justin thought it best to replace them. They'll be back," Mark said. He strove for an authoritative tone but sounded more like a kid whose mother hadn't come to pick him up from daycare on time. "Iris, why don't you start on breakfast," he suggested. "We have oats, do we not?"

"Yes, we have oats," Iris replied. "I'll get a pot of oatmeal going, but I'll need milk. Girls, it's time to do the milking," she added, her gaze going to me and Nicky. She seemed calmer now, more in control, but I saw the questions in her eyes. This wasn't what she had expected on her first morning at the settlement. None of us had.

"We may as well start on our chores," William said. "The ladies will need wood for the fire and water for cooking and washing. And then we'll need to talk about planting. Sam, you're a farmer. What do you advise?" William didn't need to try to sound authoritative. It came naturally to him, and everyone seemed pleased to have someone assume a position of leadership.

Sam preened. "The best time to plant corn is between early April and early May. We'll need to clear a field and plow it before we plant. That takes longer than you might imagine, since this land hasn't been farmed before, so we really should make a start. And we should mark out a vegetable garden and fence it off so that our produce is not eaten by animals."

"I can take care of that," Brendan said.

"The seeds could be eaten by birds," Sam said. "If that happens, there goes our crop."

"Smoldering shit buckets," Mark announced.

"I beg your pardon?" Shelby demanded, staring at Mark in horror.

"That's how the colonists protected their crops. The fumes would drive off locusts and any other threat from the air."

"That would drive off more than locusts," William said. "Perhaps we should hold off on the shit."

"Historically, shit was a valuable commodity," Mark said. "It was used as fertilizer, as fuel when mixed with straw, and as a building material. It still is in some parts of the world. It's a little-known fact how much the use of shit has shaped our world."

"It's a little-known fact that Mark is as potent as some earlier forms of ether," Nicky said under her breath. "He can put you to sleep in under ten seconds."

Shelby put a hand over her mouth to hide her grin, but it wasn't lost on Mark that he was being ridiculed.

"Laugh all you want, Nicky, but it's that sort of knowledge that can save your life," Mark replied haughtily.

"If my life depends on building a hut out of shit and then using it to cook my food, then I might as well be dead," Nicky said.

William shook his head in dismay, while Sam held up a conciliatory hand. "We can make a scarecrow," Sam suggested, shooting Mark an apologetic look. "Not as potent as shit, but it will keep the birds away."

"I can do that," Shelby offered. "I love art projects."

"Great. You're on," William said, and smiled at her approvingly. Then his gaze fell on me. "Natalie, why don't you go and get dressed," he said softly.

I had forgotten that I was still wearing nothing but my chemise, which was clearly visible through the part in my cloak. I had worn considerably less not only at the beach but in my daily life, but now I suddenly felt exposed and slightly embarrassed to be singled out in that way and wondered if the fabric was see-through.

"You're fine," Nicky said. "He was just being an ass."

"Women didn't walk around in their undergarments in Jamestown," Mark cut in.

"Shall we put her in stocks?" Nicky retorted angrily.

"No, I was just saying," Mark replied.

"Well, don't," Nicky snapped.

People began to disperse, but everyone's gaze continued to stray toward the beach, probably hoping to catch a glimpse of the returning ship. The horizon was devoid of any manmade objects, just the sea and the sky, offering the same vista they had since this stretch of shore had been created millions of years ago. I thought everyone felt better having something practical to focus on.

Having dressed and pinned up my hair, I pulled on my cap and headed toward the barn. Shelby wasn't having any success with the milking, so I offered to try. I pressed my forehead against the cow's warm flank and pulled expertly on the udders. The milk hit the bucket with a satisfying stream, and I got into a rhythm and tried not to think about the ramifications of this morning's discovery. Just then, I couldn't think past breakfast. Shelby was quiet as well as she stood behind me, lost in her own thoughts.

"I'd kill for a cup of coffee," she said once I finished milking and got up from the stool. "My head feels wooly."

"Mine too," I confessed. "But we have six months to go before we can even hope for a cup of coffee. No point moaning about it."

"I know, but still," Shelby replied, her tone defensive. "This wasn't how I expected our first morning to go."

"We have to assume it's part of the plan until we know otherwise," I replied as I carried the heavy bucket through the barn door.

"Perhaps they're testing us and filming our reaction," Shelby said. "I hope that's it because the alternative is kind of scary."

I told myself it was too soon to worry. The ship might return any minute with additional supplies and the camera crew. Perhaps someone had become ill last night or had an emergency at home. There were cameras everywhere, so Varlet would still have footage from the first day, and we had to proceed as if everything was going according to plan.

"Would be nice to have some butter," Iris said wistfully as I handed her the bucket of milk. She already had an outdoor fire going, and water was beginning to simmer in the cauldron she'd use to make oatmeal for all of us. Iris added some milk to the water, then set the bucket aside. "We'll use the rest to make butter and get started on cheese," she said.

"And after breakfast, we'll need to start grinding wheat for flour so I can bake bread. Maybe I can recruit some of the boys for that," she mused. "We can have bread with butter for lunch, and then I'll figure something out for dinner. Cooking for everyone is going to be a full-time job, especially if we become short on supplies."

"How long do you think the supplies in the shed will last?" Declan asked as he set down an armload of firewood.

"I'd say we have enough for at least six weeks," Iris said. "But we should ration the food."

"In that case, finding alternative sources of food is our first priority," Declan replied.

"Plowing a field and planting is our first priority," Mark disagreed. "If we don't plant, we'll have no crop."

"We can do both," Declan said. "It doesn't take ten men to clear a field."

Mark conceded the point and took a seat next to Shelby, who'd just set the table with the dishes we'd used last night.

"I dreamt about you," he said, his voice seductive.

"Did you?" Shelby asked coyly. "I hope it was a nice dream."

"Very nice," Mark assured her.

"Maybe you can tell me all about it later."

Their conversation was brought to an abrupt end by the arrival of the rest of the group. Everyone settled around the table and accepted the meager offering, which consisted of a ladleful of oatmeal and a cup of water. I wasn't a huge fan of oatmeal, but I was hungry, and this dollop of oats would have to last me for hours. There was nothing to supplement them with, like fruit or coffee, not even a cup of milk or ale. All at once, I felt like a real colonist: cold, hungry, and uncertain about the future.

"Is that all I get?" Mark asked as he gazed into his half-empty bowl.

"That's all anyone gets," Iris replied. "We need to ration the oats in case we don't get any more."

"Jesus," Sam exclaimed. "That's starvation rations, Iris."

"Get used to it, buddy," Timothy said, clapping him on the shoulder. "And welcome to Jamestown."

"We need to elect a governor," Mark reminded us. "Someone has to be in charge."

"And I suppose that should be you?" Glen demanded as he set his empty bowl down on the table.

"I think I'm the most obvious candidate, yes," Mark replied, puffing out his chest. "I know the most about the historical period and the laws of the colony."

"Or not," Glen said. He clearly didn't care for Mark and didn't mind who saw it.

"All right, then," Mark retorted. "Who's your choice, Glen?"

"I think it should be William. He's a judge, after all. He's made a career of making well-informed decisions."

"In all fairness, Glen, as a judge, all I do is apply the law to the decisions people have made for themselves. It's not about how I personally feel about a case or what I think is the right decision. It's like a doctor who knows that if there's an infection, they must prescribe an antibiotic, or if there's cancer, they must recommend chemotherapy."

"So, you see the people who come before you as a cancer?" Gael said with an amused smile.

"I didn't say that, Gael. My point is that certain situations come with a previously prescribed judgment. It's really not up to me. It's up to the letter of the law."

"But you interpret the law and apply it to a particular case," Iris said. "I'm sure that takes thought and consideration, much like governing."

"It does. And, of course, there are cases that get under one's skin," William admitted.

"Then you must accept the nomination," Iris said. She was clearly impressed with William Abbott and preferred him over Mark.

William smiled at her and nodded. "All right, I accept the nomination, although I think I would probably make a better magistrate. And please, call me Will."

"So, we have two candidates, Mark Beasley and Will Abbott," Jesse declared. "Anyone care to nominate someone else?" No one responded.

"Shall we vote on it?" Jesse asked.

"Jamestown wasn't a democracy," Mark grumbled.

"No, it wasn't, but since you weren't chosen to be the governor by Varlet Entertainment, everyone gets a say," Declan replied calmly. "Let's see a show of hands for Mark Beasley. And Mark, you can't vote for yourself," Declan added as Mark began to raise his hand.

Four hands went up.

"Okay, now a show of hands for Will Abbott," Declan said.

Nine hands went up. Everyone who was eligible to vote had voted.

"Will it is," Declan declared. "Congratulations, Governor Abbott."

"Thank you," Will replied modestly. "I hope I will live up to the trust you have placed in me."

"So, what's our first order of business?" Ed asked.

Will thought about it for a moment, his spoon suspended over his nearly empty bowl. "I think we should play to our strengths. Sam is a farmer, so we'll let him take charge of the planting. Glen is a warehouse manager, so he can be in charge of rationing supplies. Brendan is a carpenter, so he can put his skills to good use by building a fence for the vegetable garden and making anything else we need urgently."

Will turned to face the women. "Theresa, you're an expert on flora, so it might be a good idea for you to forage for medicinal plants. Natalie, you're a nurse, so you're in charge of keeping an eye on our general health. As they say, if you see something, say something. Nicky can keep a record of our days, and Iris is our cook. Jesse, as a rancher, I'll ask you to keep an eye on our livestock since you probably know more about horses and cows than anyone present. And the rest of you will go where you are needed unless your specific skills are called for."

Everyone nodded in agreement. It was a reasonable first decree. We got up from the table and broke up into groups. It seemed Iris had become the unofficial leader of the women.

"Okay, girls," she said. "We need to get these bowls, spoons, and pot washed. And we need someone to man, or woman, I should say, the butter churn."

"I'll make the butter, if no one objects. I have a strong arm," Nicky said with a grin, and flexed her muscle to show us.

"Great. Natalie and Shelby, you're on dish duty. It's probably more efficient to wash them in the creek, and Theresa, you can help me start on lunch." Iris smiled sweetly at Declan. "Would you mind grinding some wheat, Declan?"

"Of course," Declan replied. "I have a strong arm too. Just tell me how much."

Everyone nodded and headed off. As I washed the bowls in the icy creek, a feeling of acute anxiety spread throughout my body, a pounding headache building behind my eyes and my stomach cramping uncomfortably. I felt like a child that had been left with strangers and wasn't sure when someone would come to pick me up. I knew I was safe for the moment, but despite my earlier attempt at reasoning away my unease, the morning's events had left me feeling off-balance. If the missing supplies and the vanished ship were all part of the plan, why was Varlet playing dirty tricks on us? Were they hoping to instill panic as early as the first day? Was this how it was going to be, and we were going to be forced to react to unexpected situations for the sake of high ratings?

I was sure they were filming us and probably tutting with disappointment that we weren't running around like chickens without heads, but who knew what else they had up their sleeves and how soon they would deploy the next unexpected incident. I hated to admit it, but some part of me was already regretting my decision to sign up for the show. Six months of naked animosity, power struggles, and possible hunger didn't seem very appealing, but then again, that was what life in Jamestown had been like. What had I thought it was going to be, a walk in the park with a stop for ice cream?

Shelby and I returned to the settlement with the clean dishes and were put to work kneading dough. Nicky sat on a bench, leaning against the side of the house as she pumped the handle of the butter churn.

"I think my arm is about to drop off," she said to no one in particular.

"Would you like to change places?" I asked.

"Yeah. Thanks," Nicky said.

I took her place on the bench, and she fixed her attention on the dough. We remained thus occupied until lunch, which came later than we had expected since it took Iris some time to get the hang of baking bread in an opening in the hearth.

As we sat down to eat at last, the wind seemed to change direction, and I caught a whiff of the outhouse. We'd been at the settlement for less than a day, and already it reeked, as did the people around me. After only a few hours of chopping wood, grinding grain, churning butter, and clearing a field, everyone was sweaty, grumpy, and miserable. Only Theresa looked serene, her gaze on no one in particular as she slowly chewed her food.

# Chapter 8

## Theresa

I see the way the rest of the contestants look at me. They can't figure out why a fifty-two-year-old woman with a family would want to participate in a six-month reality show or why she would be chosen. I don't think anyone believed my explanation about the social experiment. I don't blame them. It was something I made up on the spur of the moment to forestall their questions. Few people care to discuss socialism, or worse yet, communism since the associations the term conjures up are not those of a Utopian society but of oppression, poverty, and a complete disregard for basic human rights. I have no interest in either. My parents escaped from China before I was born and still thank God for their adopted country every single day.

The truth is, I can't bear to disclose the real reason. Not because I don't like or trust the other participants, but because anything I say will air on TV. What I am doing is running away from pain, from grief. I wanted to be in a place where nothing could remind me of the life I had or the child I lost. No photographs, no Instagram posts, no Facebook page, and no concerned friends and relatives endlessly asking me how I am or pretending that everything is normal because they don't know how to deal with my pain. I know it's difficult for them. It's difficult for me too.

Christina's death broke our family into a million tiny pieces. How do you reconcile yourself to your beautiful, smart, funny twenty-one-year-old daughter hanging herself in the garage? They say time heals all wounds, but no amount of time can erase that searing final image from my mind. No amount of time can dull the ache of loneliness I feel for her or help me to understand why it had to be my Tina.

I know why she did it. She left a note, begging us to forgive her and find a way to move on, but I still don't understand. I know she was broken; she had good reason to be, but people overcome.

It takes time and work, but it's possible if one is strong enough. Tina wasn't. And neither am I. I'm still alive, but I'm no longer living, no longer seeing the beauty in anything around me. All I see is ugliness and injustice.

I know I should be at home with my grieving husband and my angry younger daughter, but perhaps I'm not so different from Christina after all. When it came to it, I couldn't deal with reality, so I created a new one, a reality in which there's nothing and no one to remind me of home. I don't care about the money or the fame this reality show might bring me. I just want to remain frozen in time, like some cryogenic experiment where the doctors can defrost me once there's a cure for my illness.

There is no cure, but there is an odd sense of peace. The best place to hide from yourself is among strangers.

# Chapter 9

## Natalie

We waited and talked and came up with various theories as to why the ship had left or why it hadn't come back, but the only explanation we invariably returned to was that this had always been the plan. It made a strange sort of sense. The ships that had brought the colonists to Jamestown hadn't remained; they had sailed back to England and returned with reinforcements and supplies. The only logical thing we could do was to go about our business and be mindful of the fact that everything we did was recorded and would be judged by an audience of millions.

Despite the knowledge that we were surrounded by cameras, we often forgot about their existence. It's not possible to be "on" all the time or to censor one's comments accordingly. Women will be women, and we gossiped about the men just like they gossiped about us. A week wasn't enough to get to know anyone well, but we had all formed opinions about the other contestants, and some of us were more vocal than others. Nicky and Iris rarely held back, and their acerbic observations were as accurate as they were cruel. Shelby had been too well brought up to criticize anyone outright but enjoyed listening to the banter, and Theresa existed in a world of her own and avoided most personal interactions.

I had formed my own opinions and shared them at times, but for the most part, I preferred to keep the harsher comments to myself, not only because I didn't want to judge anyone openly but because it would look like bad sportsmanship once the footage aired for all to see. There were several people I found unbearable, though, and did my best to keep my distance from.

The first was Mark. He grated on me in a way few people ever had, his need to be the center of attention stoking an unbridled desire to bring him down a peg or two. I couldn't understand why Shelby flirted with him, but perhaps she responded to that sort of brash, toxic masculinity. Plenty of women did, especially when the man in question was both handsome and undeniably intelligent. Besides, Mark didn't treat Shelby the same way he treated the rest of us. He seemed to genuinely admire her and never missed an opportunity to compliment her or offer her a helping hand. It was a foregone conclusion that Mark and Shelby would pair up before long, if they hadn't already, since Will, who had clearly been Shelby's first choice, didn't seem interested in pursuing a relationship with her.

The other two people I didn't care for were Glen and Sam. They reminded me of high school bullies who always traveled in packs and picked on anyone they thought didn't have enough courage or support to stand up to them. Given that they were being filmed, the two tread carefully, but it wasn't difficult to see how low they could go given the chance, and their misogynistic attitude was difficult to hide in such a small group.

Predictably, they dismissed Iris and Theresa as being too old and unworthy of their attention. They ogled Shelby shamelessly and referred to her as SB, which were her initials but actually stood for Southern Barbie in their vernacular. I had once overheard them discussing her attributes in terms so cringeworthy that I had to get away, all the while praying that I wasn't next on their list. I had seen them appraising me when they thought I wasn't looking, but I wasn't nearly as striking as Shelby, nor did I fit the blond bombshell ideal of beauty. I think the verdict was still out on Nicky, since they found her attractive but had also expressed the opinion that she was too butch for their liking.

The rest of the male contestants were much more pleasant. I liked Brendan's shy smile and Gael's megawatt one. They both had a good sense of humor and were easy to be around. Declan and Tim were a bit intense, but I supposed that was normal given their mainland occupations, and Ed was sometimes a bit holier-than-thou, which was also easily explained by his calling. He did give off a fatherly vibe and was always there if someone wanted to talk or pray together.

I still wasn't sure how I felt about Will. He was always scrupulously polite, and his suggestions were on point, but I did notice that he had to work just a little bit harder to be civil to Tim and Nicky, who obviously rubbed him the wrong way. It was hard to tell whether he disliked them as people, as professionals in fields he didn't respect, or as representatives of certain minority groups. He was always very friendly to me, and I hoped there was nothing more in his smiles than mere politeness. I wasn't looking to pair up, nor did I relish having to face someone I had rejected every day for six months, but I didn't think Will would be as vengeful as either Glen or Sam, which was a relief.

Will's presence on the island did confuse me though. He didn't seem overly interested in colonial history, nor did he relish his position as our governor. It was almost as if he had come on the show to escape from something, and maybe he had. Why else would a man who was very comfortably off—and we knew he was wealthy because he'd alluded to his status and possessions often enough—choose to spend six months on a deserted island with a bunch of strangers just to compete for a prize he clearly didn't even want?

I supposed time would tell, but for now, I thought it wise to keep my distance.

# Chapter 10

# Will

The threat couldn't have come at a worse time, but then I suppose that's what made my nemesis so brilliant. They sat on the information for nearly five years, just waiting for an opportune moment, and that moment came when I was about to announce my run for the Senate. I might have had a chance of gaining the upper hand had I known who was blackmailing me. Everyone has their price, but I was contacted anonymously, the envelope that found its way to my desk containing photographs, bank statements, and even a secret recording of a conversation that would not be admissible in court but if leaked would do irreparable damage to my reputation. My blackmailer didn't want money. They wanted me to resign, or they would make the information public, and that would lead to an avalanche of bad press, an investigation, and most likely a conviction. I had no choice but to take early retirement and watch a lifelong dream turn into a nightmare as the foundation I had been laying for years suddenly crumbled.

I'd had my life planned out since I was a freshman in college. I would graduate, go to law school, marry the right woman, make judge before forty, and then, after a few years on the bench, shift focus to my political career. President William Abbott has a nice ring to it, at least I've always thought so, but I made one mistake. One. I trusted the wrong person and took advice from an individual I thought had my best interests at heart.

If there's one thing I have learned, it is that everyone is disposable and no matter how much good you do or how many years of faithful service you put in, everything you have worked for can be undone with one bad decision. So, here I am, on this depressing island with a group of strangers who irritate me with their asinine opinions and dreams of stardom. I understand all about ratings and carefully curated drama, but nothing about this farce of a show is historically accurate or even remotely interesting.

The men who settled Jamestown might have had their faults. After all, greed, envy, ambition, and violent impulses have been around since time immemorial, but the colonists were united by common faith, a shared background, and a clear goal. The people on this island come from different walks of life, and no two contestants are on the same page, much less reading the same book. This is a carefully orchestrated charade where everyone has their own agenda and is artificially pitted against the rest of the group.

Nicky keeps trying to provoke me into saying something I'll regret. Ed's sermonizing is grating, and Tim is about two seconds away from publicly accusing me of racism. And then there are the others. Glen's shifty gaze leads me to believe that he's more nervous in my presence than an innocent man should be. Mark is a pompous windbag who's used to being a big fish in a small pond and basking in the adoration of teenage girls, and Jesse is a throwback to another time, an America where wealthy ranchers ruled the land. Well, wake up, cowboy! This is not *Yellowstone*, and you don't get to brand your minions or make your own laws.

Theresa and Iris are pleasant enough for middle-aged women who don't have one attractive feature between them. Shelby will make for a fine trophy wife for some small-town hotshot if she doesn't let herself go, and Brendan and Sam are about as fascinating as last week's supermarket circulars. I have yet to form an opinion of Natalie and Declan. Those two might be more complex than they appear at first glance.

These are going to be the longest six months of my life, but by the time I get off this island, I will be a household name, and every viewer will have witnessed both my ability to lead and my unshakable integrity. An insinuation that I had accepted a bribe to keep a prominent politician's son out of prison on charges of rape will do little to tarnish my reputation, more so if I receive an endorsement from certain members of the party whose faith in me will only serve to prove that the allegation is nothing more than an example of fake news fabricated by some internet troll.

And then, it will be the perfect time to kickstart my political career.

# Chapter 11

## Natalie

## April

The first two weeks flew by surprisingly quickly, probably because we all worked harder than we had ever worked before. Every minute of the day was filled with chores that would help us to survive our time on the island. Despite rationing, the food stores were diminishing quickly, and we spent much of our time churning butter, making cheese, looking for edible plants to supplement our daily stews, and working in the vegetable garden. The men were able to find a large meadow that they would turn over to planting corn. Even though they didn't need to fell trees in order to clear the land, the work was physically demanding and tedious. They spent days pulling up roots, clearing away rocks, and then plowing the meadow with an arcane plow dragged by our less-than-willing horse Wilbur, who quickly became known as just Flake because he was so unreliable. Most of us didn't know much about horses, but Jesse said that Flake was too long in the tooth to be working so hard.

It was decided that Declan and Tim, who'd had official firearms training, would go hunting since the meat would soon be gone, but hunting with seventeenth-century muskets proved a challenge even for them. According to our trainer at the farm, the muskets could hit a target at one hundred meters, but their cumbersome shape and weight, and the fact that they needed to be reloaded after every shot reduced the chances of hitting a moving target and wasted valuable time. Seventeenth-century soldiers had been able to reload a musket within seconds, but they'd had years of practice where we'd had two weeks. Plus, we had to conserve powder and shot if they were to last us the full six months. Tim had managed to set several traps and caught a few rabbits, but the men had yet to bag something larger that would feed the entire group.

After only two weeks, our clothes were soiled, our hair greasy, and already everyone had lost a noticeable amount of weight. But none of these things were unexpected. This was what we had signed up for, except for the unfulfilled promises made by Varlet Entertainment. The ship hadn't returned. The medical officer, who would have done a far more competent job than me of patching up Ed when he managed to miss the wood he was chopping and swung the axe at his shin instead, wasn't on hand. It was an absolute miracle that Ed hadn't severed any major arteries or crushed a bone, or that the wound did not become infected, probably thanks to the alcoholic content in ale, which I had used to clean the area several times a day. Still, Ed wasn't up to much and limped to church on Sundays to give a sermon, where he sat on a wooden stump to take the weight off his injured leg.

We hadn't seen the cameramen anywhere in the vicinity of the settlement, and if they were somewhere on the island, they were keeping well away from us. We had no way to request more supplies or get a message to shore without speaking into space and hoping someone, somewhere, heard us. We accepted this and went about our business, doing our best to get along and work as a team, but as with any group of people, tempers often flared, and people lashed out at one another out of sheer frustration and fatigue.

The group did seem in better spirits on the morning it all spectacularly went to hell. The corn had finally been planted, Tim had managed to bag a young buck, and Theresa found a patch of wild spinach in the woods. The spinach had to be thoroughly washed and cooked to avoid E. coli and salmonella, but it was a good source of nutrients, and Iris would be adding it to our stews to boost our immune systems. Sam advised us to dig up the spinach and replant it in our garden, where we could make sure it didn't get eaten or pissed on by wild animals. For the first time in days, we felt a modicum of control and congratulated ourselves on thriving rather than just surviving.

My muscles were aching, and my thoughts were fuzzy with fatigue as I dropped into my seat at the table. Despite going to sleep ridiculously early, since there really wasn't much to do after dark but tell spooky stories, I didn't sleep well since I was overtired, and my cot didn't allow for a good night's sleep. Still, I was looking forward to a breakfast of half a boiled egg, a piece of cheese, and leftover bread and butter. This was vastly preferable to oatmeal since the protein kept me full longer.

I was buttering my bread when Iris asked, "Where's Will this morning?"

Everyone looked around the table, not having realized that one of us was missing.

"He usually takes a walk on the beach when he can't sleep," Brendan said. "He should be back any minute."

Iris set aside Will's portion and sat down to enjoy her own breakfast. By the time we were finished, Will had still not returned.

"I think we should go look for Will," Tim said, stepping into his role as marshal. "Maybe he's hurt." He turned to Declan. "Why don't you take someone and go north, and I will head south. He couldn't have gone far."

"Sure," Declan replied. "Anyone want to come with?"

"I'll go," Brendan said.

"Me too," Glen volunteered.

"Okay, since we don't have any way to check in with each other, let's meet back here in about an hour." We had all learned how to tell time by the sun, at least approximately.

"Will do," Declan said, already getting up from his seat on the bench.

The two search parties set off, and we all started on our chores, although with even more reluctance than usual.

"What do you think happened to Will?" I asked Nicky as we washed the breakfast dishes in the creek.

"Maybe he just needed some head space. It does get claustrophobic in those houses."

"It does, but I feel oddly comforted to know that the rest of you are there," I said.

"I do too," Nicky admitted. "I've lived on my own since I started college, but here, it's so different. There's nothing to do on your own anyway. It's not like I can read, or write, or watch a movie. Or play on my phone," she added wistfully. "If you're not working, you're sleeping. God, I miss my phone," Nicky said with feeling. "The not knowing what's going on out there in the world or being able to check my social media or send a text is driving me mad. It's like I lost a limb."

"I used to call my mom first thing every morning," I said. "And then I'd text my sister to see what sort of day she had ahead of her. We were in touch all day long. And I never even realized until I had to give up my phone just how much time I spent looking stuff up, sending my friends funny memes, checking Facebook, and catching up on the news. I'd give anything to speak to my mom," I said, and heard the quaver in my voice.

"I haven't seen my mother in years, and I'm not really close with my brothers these days, but I miss them too." Nicky laughed. "I hope there's no camera here, so they don't hear me say that on air."

"Are you sure they're filming?" I asked, finally voicing my concerns. There was something solid and reassuring about Nicky, if a little intimidating since she always spoke her mind, but I needed to hear her answer.

"Of course they are. Otherwise, what would be the point?" Nicky replied with a shrug.

"You think they're just setting us up?"

"You bet. They're just trying to stir the shit."

"I hope so," I said. "I feel very anxious sometimes."

"I think we're meant to."

"But they didn't send anyone when Ed hurt himself," I reminded her.

"They were probably waiting to see if it was necessary."

"The wound could have become septic."

"But it didn't. The colonists didn't have antibiotics. They worked with what they had."

"And dropped like flies," I reminded her. "That was a big chance to take with a contestant's well-being."

"Think about it, Natalie. Varlet Entertainment has invested all this money into training us and setting up this colony. What would be the point of abandoning us here? When in doubt, follow the money," Nicky said confidently. "And the money flows back to Varlet."

We finished with the dishes and headed back toward the settlement. We reached the gates just as Tim and Glen approached from the other direction.

"Any sign of him?" Iris called out from within.

"No. We walked a couple of miles but saw no footprints or any sign that anyone had been there."

"Didn't the tide come in this morning?" Jesse asked. "Might have washed away Will's footprints."

"It could have," Tim agreed. "Let's hope Declan had better luck."

Declan burst through the gates a few minutes later. Alone. He scanned the group and settled on me. "Natalie, I need you to come with me."

"Do I need to bring anything?" I asked, already hurrying toward Declan.

He shook his head. "No. Just come."

A few others made a move to follow, but Declan held up his hand. "Everyone must remain here, except for Tim."

Tim's face creased with concern, but he silently followed us through the gates. "What did you find?" he asked as soon as we were out of earshot of the others.

"Will's body," Declan replied.

I felt like someone had punched me in the stomach. I had expected an injury, maybe even a panic attack or a near-drowning, but I hadn't realized that the reason I hadn't needed to bring anything was because it was already too late.

"How did Will die?" Tim asked, and I turned to Declan, needing to hear his answer in order to make some sense of this tragedy that had come like a bolt out of the blue. Will was a capable, intelligent man. He would never do anything foolish, so what had happened to him?

"I'd like Natalie to examine the body before I commit to an answer," Declan replied cryptically.

"I'm not a doctor, Declan," I said.

"I know, but you're a medical professional, and although I have on-the-job experience, I would like to hear what you have to say."

My stomach twisted so viciously, I thought I was going to be sick. As a nurse, I was accustomed to dealing with the living. I could offer basic first aid, but I had no knowledge of pathology, and no matter how many times you'd seen a corpse, it was always a shock, a brutal reminder of how quickly a person went from being an individual to being a thing, a shell of their former self, a carcass that began to decompose the minute the heart stopped pumping and the blood stopped flowing.

"How long has he been dead?" I choked out.

"Not long," Declan said. He smiled at me apologetically. "Don't worry. He doesn't look too bad."

"Did you move him?" Tim asked.

Declan shook his head. "I left him just as he was."

Tim's dark eyes widened as he took this in. "You think there was foul play," he said, watching Declan for a reaction.

"I wanted to be sure the cameras pick up all the details. The police will want to examine the footage."

"Jesus Christ," Tim exclaimed under his breath.

Declan was walking so fast, I had to jog to keep up with him, but I didn't care. I wanted to get this over with, whatever this was. And although I was frightened, I was thankful for Declan's businesslike attitude.

Brendan was standing vigil over Will but came toward us as soon as he saw us coming, clearly relieved to have discharged his duty.

"Natalie, I want you to take your time," Declan said. "And talk us through it. Throw out your every impression, no matter how insignificant. It's important."

I nodded and forced myself to look at the body as I approached slowly, taking in all the details. Will was lying on his front, his face turned away from me, his head mere inches from the waterline. I didn't have to be a forensic expert to notice the wound on his head or the dry and crusted blood gluing the matted hair to his scalp.

The men stood back as I squatted next to the body. I took hold of Will's wrist, but there was no pulse, and the hand, which was cold and damp, was growing stiff with rigor mortis. The head wound was about two inches in diameter, and there were specks of sand and grit trapped in the blood and the hair. On closer inspection, I could see exposed brain matter and had to take several deep breaths to calm myself before continuing my examination.

Will's clothes were damp and sandy, but the fabric was intact, and there were no obvious wounds to any other part of his body. Will's skin was tanned and unblemished, his body toned and well cared for. He must have tanned regularly before coming on the show. I pulled down Will's breeches and took a cursory look at the genital and rectal areas, but there were no signs of sexual violence or anything that aroused my suspicion.

"Well? What do you think?" Tim asked as I straightened up and turned to face the waiting men.

"I think that Will was hit from behind with something like a rock. The blow was forceful enough to fracture his skull. I can't say for certain, I'm not a qualified pathologist, but my guess is that the cause of death is blunt force trauma. I would also hazard to guess that Will never saw the attack coming since his hands are clean and there's no obvious bruising or signs of struggle. He did not fight back."

Tim clapped slowly, the corner of his mouth quirking in a smile. "Wow, you're good."

"You can learn a lot from watching TV," I replied, embarrassed by the praise since I had learned most of what I had just deduced from watching crime shows.

"Wherever you learned it, it's spot on," Declan said. "The position of the body is interesting," he added, turning to Tim.

Tim nodded. "He's facing toward the water, which means someone came up behind him while he was looking out to sea."

"There were no footprints," Brendan pointed out. "If the person walked below the tideline, Will would have seen them coming."

"And maybe he did," Declan said, "but had no reason to be afraid. At some point, the person stepped behind Will and struck. He fell where he stood, since there are no drag marks either."

Feeling faint, I walked a few paces away from the body, sank onto the sand, and rested my head on my knees. I was trembling and thought I might be sick if I made any sudden moves. I shut my eyes and took deep, measured breaths, but the calming technique didn't make me feel any better. Seeing Will's lifeless body was bad enough, but the realization that someone had murdered him was almost paralyzing. As far as we knew, there was no one else on the island, which meant that one of the contestants had followed Will down to the beach early this morning and struck him over the head when he wasn't looking.

The fact that Will did not appear to have struggled with his assailant meant that he had trusted the person and had known of no reason they would want to kill him. And they had wanted to kill him. That blow had been vicious and well aimed. Intent was obvious.

"Natalie, are you all right?" Declan asked as he came to stand before me. "Are you going to faint?"

I shook my head, unable to look at him.

"Brendan, would you mind taking Natalie back?" Declan asked. "Tim and I will be along shortly."

"Sure," Brendan said. "I'm more than ready to get out of here."

Brendan offered me his hand, and I took it gratefully, holding on to it until I suddenly realized that Brendan could be Will's killer. I let go of his hand, and we walked together in silence, me staring at my feet as I tried to regain control of my emotions. I knew of no reason Brendan would want to hurt Will, and I had never noticed any animosity between them, but then again, I knew of no reason anyone would attack Will. He was a bit full of himself, and I suspected from several veiled comments he'd made that he might be a bit racist, but as far as I knew, no one had it in for him. We had all managed to offend someone in the group at one time or another, but no one seemed to dislike anyone to the point of wishing them dead.

"Are you sure it wasn't an accident?" Brendan asked at last, probably unable to bear the silence any longer.

"Unless something dropped from the sky and hit Will on the head, someone did that intentionally."

"But what if something did fall?" Brendan asked. "Is that completely impossible?"

"I saw nothing that might have been the instrument of Will's death. There were no rocks, tree branches, or manmade objects near his body. If something fell on his head, it would be there, and it would be covered in blood."

"Yeah, you're right," Brendan said. "It's just unimaginable to think that someone did that on purpose. I guess this will be the end of the show. Varlet will notify the police, they'll come and take our statements, review the tapes, and then shut down production." Brendan suddenly perked up. "Or maybe they'll just arrest the person responsible and allow us to continue."

"I don't know about that," I said. "To air a real murder on TV would be pretty controversial."

"I don't want to go home," Brendan said miserably.

"Because of the money?"

"No, because I don't really have anything to go home to. My boyfriend broke up with me shortly before I filled out the application. I felt lonely and depressed, and my brother kept giving me pep talks and telling me to get back on the horse. Like it's so easy to find someone who's going to love you and want to commit to you. It took me years to find a partner I could love," Brendan added wistfully. "And we were happy. And then, suddenly, Jon decided that he didn't want this anymore. Didn't want us. Just like that. And I had no say in it."

Brendan looked like he was about to cry, and I reached out and squeezed his hand. "It seems a number of us were in that situation. Perhaps they were betting on lonely people hooking up and making trouble."

I had suspected Brendan might be gay, but he had never said so outright, and I'd never asked. I wondered if anyone else in the group might be either gay or sexually fluid.

"Well, someone really went above and beyond in that department," Brendan said. "I still can't wrap my head around it."

"Neither can I."

Everyone was waiting for news when we returned to the settlement, and Brendan and I had no choice but to tell them what had happened. A chorus of questions and comments erupted all around us, but I couldn't bring myself to speak to anyone. I retreated to the house and lay down on my cot, praying that no one would follow me inside and force me to discuss Will's death.

# Chapter 12

## Brendan

This was a mistake of epic proportions! What was I thinking when I applied to be on this hideous show? So I was a little depressed, worried that Sean would press charges, but he never did. He knew it was never anything more than a drunken pass. I thought he was gorgeous, and I went too far. I apologized, and he accepted, but you never know these days. Someone can come after you years after something happened. And what did happen? It's not as if I had assaulted the man. I simply pulled down his pants and sucked him off. He was a little drunk, some might say unconscious, but all I did was give him pleasure. There was plenty of evidence that he'd enjoyed it, but I swallowed the proof.

Had Jon not walked in when he did, no one would be the wiser. Sean would have gone back to sleep and thought he'd had a lovely dream, and Jon and I would still be together, cozy in our little apartment, brewing gourmet coffee and baking croissants on Sunday mornings. Instead, I'm here, keeping watch over a corpse and allowing Varlet to check the box for their sexual diversity quota.

Okay, it was all my fault. I'm man enough to own that. I apologized and tried to make amends, but neither Sean nor Jon was interested. They were too busy cozying up to each other, giddy on the high of a new romance. I never meant to bring them together. I never meant to hurt anyone, least of all myself. I know it was wrong, and I'd do anything to turn back the clock and resist the urge to act on my impulses. After all, if I were straight and I pulled down the underwear of a woman passed out on my couch and went down on her, I'd probably be charged with sexual assault. There'd be no excuse for my behavior. Jon made me see that just because a man is not viewed as being as vulnerable as a woman doesn't mean I can perform a sexual act on him without his consent.

I have learned my lesson, and when I get back, I'm going to be a changed man. Maybe Sean and I can still be friends, even if Jon doesn't want to see me. And there's always the possibility of a new relationship. As soon as I get off this fucking island, I will begin a new chapter.

# Chapter 13

## Declan

After Natalie and Brendan left, Tim and I settled in to wait. We could hardly leave the body unattended, and the police would want to examine the crime scene. I'd seen plenty of bodies and had been first on the scene in cases involving a fatality, but seeing Will's body lying on the beach just didn't square with my past experience. If not for the head wound, he'd look like a sailor or merchant that had washed up on shore after a shipwreck. Like something out of *Twelfth Night*.

My mind teemed with questions and observations, but Tim didn't seem inclined to talk. He'd left his hair loose this morning, and it cascaded around his face as he crossed his legs and looked downward, rolling his head from side to side as he tried to expel the tension from his body. He raised his arms and did a few more yoga-like stretches before twisting his hair into a bun and turning to face me.

"So, what do you think?" he asked.

"Aside from the obvious?"

"Do you think it's possible that Will was murdered by someone other than a fellow contestant?"

"Anything is possible, but is it probable?"

Tim and I had walked the length and breadth of the island while out hunting. The island was just what it had appeared to be when we had first seen it from the deck of the ship, a thickly wooded expanse of land dotted by several lush meadows, crisscrossed by freshwater creeks, and surrounded on three sides by jagged outcroppings of rock. The only manmade structure we had encountered was a decrepit one-room cabin that must have been abandoned decades ago, probably longer. Either that or the last person standing had died and there had been no one left to bury them. Tim and I had found three graves within walking distance of the cabin. The mounds had long since been covered by crabgrass and a layer of fallen leaves and twigs, but the crosses, although weathered and leaning to the side, were still standing, the names on the crossbars still visible, having been carved deep into the wood.

*Mary Ellen Barnett*

*Elizabeth Dove Barnett*

*Thomas Arthur Barnett*

The dates of death ranged from November 1891 to January 1892, but no dates of birth were marked so it was impossible to know how old the Barnetts had been at the time of their passing. What was evident was that they had died within months of each other, so perhaps it had been an illness or maybe even starvation. If they had lived on the island for years and had continuously hunted, they might have depleted the wildlife population and not been able to travel to the mainland for supplies. After so many years, there were few clues, and Tim and I had decided not to explore the interior of the cabin. At best we'd find nothing. At worst, we'd make a grisly discovery.

Tim had speculated that the Barnetts had been trappers, since we had seen a pile of moldering skins piled up inside the cabin when we peered through the window, and several fox skeletons hung nailed to what might have been the chicken coup. There may have been a vegetable garden, but it had since been reclaimed by encroaching nature. The cabin was a creepy place, so we hadn't hung around.

"Let's say that someone did come to the island last night," I said. "Did they come with the express purpose of killing Will? Did they somehow know that Will would be there at precisely that time?"

"I was considering the practicalities," Tim said. "Did they land on the beach, in full view of the cameras? It would be extremely dangerous to attempt to come ashore anywhere else on the island, and even if they did manage to avoid the rocks, they'd have to walk a good distance to get to this spot. Also, unless whoever it was came in a rowboat, we'd have heard a motor. I didn't hear a thing. Did you?"

"No, I didn't," I admitted.

After years of living in Chicago, I found the silence of the island almost painful, the pervasive hush ominous, especially at night. My life had been filled with manmade sounds, everything from traffic to the constant chatter on my police radio. To be surrounded by such dense silence was unnerving, and my ears strained to identify every sound and every unfamiliar noise. I would have heard a motor. I was sure of it.

Tim squinted at the sun. "It's about eight o'clock. If someone gets into the office by nine and reviews the footage from last night and this morning, they'll call the police. It took us several hours to get here under full sail. The police should get here in a fraction of the time since they have motorboats. They should be here before noon. They might even know who's responsible, if they've seen the footage. So, our only job is to secure the crime scene and keep an eye on the body until the coroner arrives. I hope someone brings us something to eat," he added.

"That's four hours. Why don't you go back, have some breakfast, grab our cloaks, and bring me back something to eat," I suggested. A cold wind was blowing off the Atlantic, and I was shivering in my linen shirt and doublet. I was also really hungry.

"I'm not leaving you here alone." Tim suddenly smiled, the grin lighting his grim face. "Our angel of mercy will be back soon with both food and cloaks."

"I hope you're not referring to Iris," I muttered.

"I was talking about Natalie. Given her earlier assessment of the situation, I'd say she's someone who pays attention to detail. She'll realize we're cold and hungry. Just watch."

"I hope you're right."

86

"I am," Tim replied, and went back to doing stretches.

The morning dragged on, but only one of Tim's predictions came true. Natalie did return. She brought sandwiches made with butter and smoked meat from the shed and a jug of milk. Our cloaks were draped over her arm, and she handed them to us as soon as we took the food from her, smiling gratefully.

Natalie avoided looking at the body, but her gaze went to the horizon, most likely searching for any sign of the police that had yet to show up. Her forehead creased with anxiety, but she didn't say anything. Instead, she took the empty plate and pitcher when we finished and walked away, leaving us to continue our vigil. As we sat there, I grew restless and angry, but Tim seemed as calm as a clear lake on a windless day. I couldn't help but wonder about him. Tim never talked about himself and avoided personal questions by either changing the subject or giving such an innocuous answer as to make it pointless to continue the conversation. My granny would have said that Tim is a hard egg to crack, and she'd be right.

# Chapter 14

## Tim

I still see him in my dreams. He doesn't deserve my pity, and I have none to spare, but I think of his mother. I remember her face, tear-stained and bewildered, begging for information on her boy as she sat next to the chief of police at the press conference. She's the one I feel bad for. Does a mother know her child is capable of great evil, or does she only see the sweet boy who kissed her goodnight when he was a toddler, or the awkward teenager whose body grew faster than his understanding of the world?

Only two people in this world know where the body is buried, me and my brother Talon. It's not a pretty place. He didn't deserve that. It's a rocky, barren patch of soil that will bleach his bones until they look like nothing more than the stones that litter the ground. He will never graduate from high school or go to college and make his mother proud. He will never marry and have children of his own. That's the price you pay for destroying a man's family and desecrating his eight-year-old child.

He did not die by my hand—that was Talon's due as a father—but I helped to bury him, and I made sure there was no evidence to link Talon to the disappearance or to link this monster to the little boy whose life will never be the same and who will never again trust another man for fear of being hurt.

Yes, I still see his face in my dreams. And I smile.

# Chapter 15

## Declan

The hours crept by at a snail's pace, the wind picking up and the sky going from an aquamarine blue to a menacing gray with undertones of yellow. My partner used to call it a Mackerel Sky. We could no longer see the sun, but it had to be around two in the afternoon.

"I think we should move the body and mark the spot where Will was found," I said.

Tim pushed to his feet. "I think you're right. Leaving him here to get soaked will destroy any forensic evidence the killer left behind."

"Tim, I don't think anyone is coming," I said.

"If they saw the footage, they're dutybound to inform the police."

"But what if they haven't? Who's to say they review the footage every day? They might do it once a week, for all we know."

"So you're telling me that they left us here with no way to contact the mainland and they don't even check the footage to make sure we're all right?" Tim demanded.

"They didn't send anyone when Ed got hurt."

"Natalie patched him up," Tim replied.

"Yes, but the wound could have become infected. Worst case scenario, Ed could have lost his leg." Or his life. But I didn't say that. "It was Varlet's responsibility to make certain he received proper medical care."

"What are you saying, Declan?"

"I'm saying that we appear to be on our own."

"Today or in general?"

"I don't know, but I think we should proceed as if no one is coming," I replied.

"All right, then tell me this before we return to the settlement. What's your theory on what happened? I don't think we should discuss this in front of the others."

"I think it's possible that someone came ashore and killed Will, but my gut feeling tells me that's not what happened."

"Talk me through it," Tim said. He was watching me intently, as if he wanted to see inside my brain.

"If someone from the mainland wanted to kill Will, why would they wait until he was on an island outfitted with multiple cameras? Likewise, why would they chance him not being here when they arrived or resort to using a rock when they could have come armed with a weapon?" I paused, needing to organize my thoughts. "If this was planned, they could have forced him into the boat and then dumped his body, making sure no forensic evidence survived and no footage of the murder itself existed. Whatever happened here does not strike me as a premeditated crime."

Tim nodded but didn't interrupt.

"My theory is that someone saw or heard Will leaving his house before sunrise and followed him to the beach. Maybe they argued. Maybe the other person had already decided they were going to kill Will. Whatever took place, I believe the murder was committed by one of the contestants."

"Man or woman?" Tim asked.

"Impossible to tell, but I think we can safely rule out Natalie, Iris, and Theresa."

"Why?"

"Because they're not tall enough to bring down a rock on Will's head with enough force to crack his skull. Everyone else is a suspect."

"Have you noticed any unusual tension between Will and anyone else?" Tim asked. He didn't seem overly upset about being named a suspect.

"Will clearly didn't like Nicky, and I think both Mark and Glen got on his nerves, but that's hardly a reason to kill him."

"Perhaps he had an altercation with someone."

"If he did, I know nothing about it. I think we should interview everyone at the settlement. No one will admit to killing Will, but maybe someone has seen or heard something that might offer us a clue."

"What about me and you? Technically, we could have killed Will."

"I had not left the settlement since dinner last night until we went out to look for Will. If anyone was awake in the early hours, they will be able to vouch for me."

"I was awake," Tim replied. "I know you didn't leave."

"Can anyone vouch for you?"

Tim shrugged. "I didn't kill him, Declan. I didn't like him much, but I didn't kill him. First of all, I'm not a murderer. Second, I had no motive."

"Do you think any of the contestants knew each other before coming on the show?" I asked.

"I haven't noticed a spark of recognition between anyone, but we can't rule out the possibility that there was some sort of previous relationship. I doubt anyone will admit to knowing Will before, though. That would give them a clear motive, especially since they never admitted to knowing each other."

"We have to tread carefully, since we have no idea what we're dealing with."

"I agree. In the meantime, let's get Will back to the settlement and leave his body in the corncrib, since it's still empty. Then we should interview all the contestants."

"Should we split them up?" I asked. "It'll be faster if we conduct the interviews simultaneously. Less time for them to talk to each other and compare notes."

Tim shook his head. "No. I think you and I should interview them together, in case one of us misses something."

"All right. I wish we had a board to lay him on, but I suppose we'll just have to carry him."

"Nothing like lugging a dead weight for a mile," Tim said with a sigh of resignation.

We found a few pebbles and laid them out to mark the spot, then lifted Will and began the long trek back to the settlement.

# Chapter 16

# Natalie

The rest of the day passed in near silence with occasional bursts of speculation that fizzled out quickly and came to nothing. I think we were all listening for a motor or the whirring of helicopter rotors, but the island was eerily quiet, the only sounds the wind moving through the trees, the waves crashing against the rocks, and the stakes in the palisade creaking ominously.

We were all dealing not only with the shock and horror of Will's death but trying to wrap our minds around the fact that he may have been murdered by one of us and the fact that no one had come. That could mean only one of two things. Either no one was manning the cameras, or someone had seen what had happened and made a conscious choice not to alert the police.

Both possibilities were equally disturbing, just as it was impossible to conceive of one of the people at the settlement picking up a rock and bashing Will's brains in. But someone had, and it wasn't very likely that it had been an outsider. There was nothing to suggest that anyone had visited the island at precisely the time Will had decided to go for his early morning walk. Had he done so every day, it might have been more likely, but Will only went out so early occasionally and not on any particular days.

After Declan and Tim laid Will's body on a board in the corncrib and covered it with a blanket, they set up in the church, where they proceeded to speak to each contestant privately. The interviews didn't last long, since no one had seen or heard anything, or, if they had, weren't willing to admit to it. Mark made a big production of claiming the position of governor and insisted on interviewing both Tim and Declan in the presence of Jesse and Ed, declaring it was only fair that they had to answer for themselves as well. Neither Declan nor Tim protested, and they gave an account of their evening, night, and morning willingly. By the time Mark was finished with his interrogation, we were none the wiser.

Once we sat down to dinner, everyone was even more subdued, the events of the day having sunk in and settled in their consciousness. Will was dead. Someone had killed him. That someone was most likely still on the island and sitting at the same table with the rest of us. The thought was as mindboggling as it was terrifying. Few people have never watched a crime show or read a murder mystery, but to suddenly find oneself a part of a real one, and to also become a suspect, was not what anyone had expected when agreeing to do the show.

Where were the people from Varlet? Why had the police not come? Was it really possible that no one was aware of Will's death, and we would be forced to carry on as if nothing had happened?

Unable to keep still, I pushed away my plate and stood, needing to walk. Declan was beside me in seconds, his cloak billowing behind him in the stiffening wind.

"You can't go alone."

"Then come with me. I can't bear to sit there another minute, knowing that one of those people might have killed Will," I whispered, so that only he could hear me.

"Natalie," he began, but I cut across him.

"Did you find anything out from your interviews?" I asked.

Declan shook his head. "Nothing we didn't already know. Sam and Glen said that Will occasionally went for an early morning walk. They also said they were both asleep when Will left and didn't hear anything."

"What about Gael?"

"Both Glen and Sam said that Gael was still asleep when they woke."

"So they all alibied each other?"

"Pretty much."

"What about the people in your house?" I asked.

"Tim said he woke early but he didn't hear anything. He also confirmed that everyone was asleep. Besides, I didn't hear the door opening or closing. I'm a light sleeper."

"So that leaves the women."

"Only Shelby and Nicky are tall enough to have hit Will from behind. No one saw them leave or come back, and neither seems to have a motive."

"Someone murdered him, Declan. Are we supposed to pretend that it was a terrible accident and just get on with our lives?"

"We don't have much of a choice. Unless we can figure out who did it and why, we have no basis to accuse anyone, especially since there's no physical evidence. The tide washed away the footprints, and the murder weapon is probably lying at the bottom of the sea, now clean of blood and DNA."

"How long will you wait for the police before you bury him?" I asked.

"A few days. If they come afterward, they'll just have to exhume the body. To be honest, my biggest worry is that no one will come."

"But why?" I cried. "Why would they not?"

"That's the million-dollar question, Natalie. Why would Varlet leave us here and not even bother to watch the footage?"

I looked up because I needed to see Declan's expression when I asked him my next question. "Have you noticed that not a single plane has flown overhead the whole time we've been here? And I haven't seen any boats on the horizon."

Declan nodded. "I have."

"And how do you explain that?"

"We are not that far from Virginia," Declan said. "We only traveled a few hours in a non-motorized boat. For all we know, it was going in circles while we were all down below to make us believe we were further away than we really are. I don't know why there are no boats or planes. It doesn't make sense. The island might not be near a shipping lane or lie beneath a busy flight path, but we'd still see private craft in the water and planes passing overheard."

"That's what I thought," I replied as a shiver of apprehension ran down my already stiff spine. "I'm really scared, Declan. And to be honest, I don't want to be here anymore."

"Neither do I," Declan said. "I've made some impulsive decisions in my life, but I think this one takes the cake."

*Why did you come here?* I wanted to ask but didn't. If Declan opened up to me, that'd give him license to ask me questions as well, and I had no desire to explain my motivations.

The conversation died away, and we walked the rest of the way in silence, then turned back for the settlement and headed toward our respective houses. It was growing dark, and all I wanted was to climb into bed and pull the blanket over my head. And for the first time since arriving on the island, I wished there was a deadbolt on the door.

# Chapter 17

## Declan

I lay down on my cot but couldn't get to sleep. The rain that had managed to hold off until nightfall drummed against the wooden shutters, and the smell of mud and wet thatch was pervasive inside the stuffy confines of the house. It was cold and damp, and the wind howled outside as if a gale were heading for the island. I could hear Tim's even breathing and Ed's soft snores from the other room. Brendan wasn't asleep, and neither was Jesse, but no one spoke. More than enough had been said for one day.

Images of Will's body floated before my closed eyes, so I opened them and stared at the ceiling instead. I had come on the show to escape reality for a while, and to work through problems that had plagued me back in Chicago, but despite a voluntary leave from the police force, I was once again in the midst of a murder investigation. At least this time, I didn't feel responsible for a person's death. Small mercies.

The bodycam footage had exonerated my partner in the death of Noah Peters, a thirteen-year-old inner-city boy who'd pointed a gun at us and threatened to shoot when we found him squatting in a condemned building in Englewood. My partner had done what he was trained to do, had followed protocol, but how could he have known that Noah's gun wasn't loaded, or that the poor kid was terrified and depressed after the death of his best friend, who had gotten caught in the crossfire between two rival drug gangs while walking home late one night? I wasn't the one who'd pulled the trigger, but Noah's death haunted me as if I had.

I still saw Noah's face every day and prayed for forgiveness. I could have saved that kid. I could have made a difference to his life. Instead I stood by while my partner pulled the trigger, believing it was either him or Noah, and now Noah was rotting in the ground, my partner had been suspended pending further investigation, and I was trapped in this weird alternate reality.

My sergeant had managed to keep my name out of the press, since I wasn't directly responsible, but I have to live with my part in Noah's death for the rest of my life, and I have yet to forgive myself. I told the Varlet selection committee that I had a girlfriend back in Chicago, but the truth is that I gave up my apartment, put all my stuff into storage, broke things off with my girl, and said goodbye to my friends. I hid out at a friend's lake house for several months, glad the weather was too cold to have to deal with vacationing neighbors. When chosen for the show, I had hoped that six months away on an island with nothing to do but plant, hunt, fish, and chop wood would heal my soul and allow me to make peace with myself. I had still believed that until today.

As I lay there in the dark, I considered every person on the island once again, trying to determine if they might have had a reason to hate Will Abbott. Will was an arrogant son of a bitch, the sort of person who unapologetically flaunted his privilege and talked down to anyone he thought intellectually or socially inferior to him, but I couldn't think of a compelling reason for murder. In fact, the only incident that sprang to mind was a conversation that had happened a few days ago as we sat outside after dinner. The ladies had gone in, and Will, Gael, Tim, and I remained. The rest of the guys had wanted to get a head start on their beauty sleep.

Gael had asked Tim about his most memorable case, and Tim told us that several women had been raped by a guy who'd come to play at the casino on the reservation and then followed the servers he found attractive home when their shift ended and assaulted them. Tim was still outraged by the man's actions against these defenseless women, but Will could barely hide his impatience.

"Women get raped everywhere, Tim. I wish you people would stop playing the victim."

For a moment, I'd thought Tim would charge him and beat the crap out of him, but Tim had simply stood and walked away. As far as I knew, Will had never apologized. Having attended seminars on race relations, I found the "you people" more offensive than the implication that the Native Americans were somehow playing the victim in what was clearly a criminal case with specific victims and a suspect who had been proven guilty by a court of law and was now serving time.

Did I honestly suspect Tim of killing Will? My gut feeling told me that this wasn't the first time someone had made an offensive comment to the man. Tim had gotten angry, as anyone would in his place, but I thought he had learned to control his impulses years ago. Nothing he said would change someone like Will, who'd clearly been born with a silver spoon in his mouth and could only respect individuals who came from a similar background and had a sizable enough bank account and connections to validate their worth.

Will had also made a comment to Nicky, something about the #MeToo movement using its momentum to victimize innocent men. The gist of his point was that boys would be boys. Nicky had ignored him, her only reaction a slight lift of the eyebrow, as if she were assessing the shit on her shoe. In her profession, she was probably used to dealing with pricks, and her not taking the bait had taken the wind out of Will's sails. He'd probably realized that what he'd said wouldn't sound too good on TV, except to the people who shared his views and would vote for him at the end of the show, and had immediately backtracked, conceding that in some cases, the men accused had it coming.

I sighed heavily, hoping to turn my frustration into a cleansing breath. The one person I really felt sorry for was Natalie. She'd clearly never seen a murder victim, and she was terrified. It was written on her face. She looked as lost and frightened as a child who'd witnessed something incomprehensible, and I felt awful for asking her to confirm our suspicions. I thought she had hoped I would put her fears to rest when we went for a walk, but I'd stoked them even more, since I didn't think it'd be fair to lie to her. Maybe I should have. I was sure she was lying awake in the women's house, asking the same questions I was.

Inevitably, my thoughts turned to Varlet. What the hell were they playing at? We'd had no contact with the production company since the day we were dropped off. Was this even legal?

We hadn't agreed to this when we'd signed on to do the show. There had always been the understanding that several Varlet employees, as well as a medical officer, would remain on the island, and we would have the means to ask for help should we need it and to leave if things became unmanageable. We had walked in willingly, knowing there was always going to be a back door. The door had not only been shut but bricked over.

I angrily turned onto my side and felt the slats of my cot digging into my ribs. Was there some clause I had missed when reviewing the contract? I didn't think so, which was what made me even more upset. I could understand them leaving us alone and taking some of the supplies in order to create tension and drama sooner rather than later, but a man had been murdered. It was their duty to notify the police. Why had no one come?

# Chapter 18

## Natalie

I barely slept that night, tossing and turning as I wondered what had happened to Will. Shelby's quiet weeping didn't help, and sometime in the middle of the night, Iris came into our room and tried to comfort her.

"I just want to go home," Shelby said over and over again.

"Why did you even come here, Shelby?" Nicky asked irritably. "You were miserable before this happened, and now you're carrying on as if Will was the love of your life. Or do you think you're next?"

I couldn't see Shelby's expression in the dark, but I could hear a quavering intake of breath.

"I came because I messed up," Shelby said softly, ignoring the jibe about Will.

"Messed up how?" Nicky asked.

Some part of me wanted to tell Shelby to be quiet and keep her secrets to herself. It was easy to forget while lying in the dark that there were cameras inside the house and whatever Shelby confessed would be broadcast to the world. But Shelby clearly needed to unburden herself.

"I had an affair with one of my students' dads," she said, keeping her voice low.

"That's not illegal," Nicky replied.

"No, it's not, but things are not always legal or illegal, are they?"

"What happened, Shelby?" Iris asked kindly.

"My boyfriend was married and didn't want to be seen coming to my house, so we found other places to meet. One time, we had sex in my classroom. It was after hours and no one was around, but the next day a video was posted on the school's Facebook page. A janitor was still in the building and filmed us."

Shelby sighed heavily. "Of course, it spread like wildfire. Everyone shared it, and in a town the size of a postage stamp, it was mere moments before everyone had seen it, including my parents, my brother, and my boyfriend's wife. I lost my job, got kicked out of the teachers' union, and was banned from church. Even the cashier at the grocery store wouldn't ring me up. I was blacklisted, and my parents and brother had to take sides in order not to be treated like pariahs."

"Isn't that a bit extreme?" Iris asked, clearly outraged. "I mean you shouldn't have used your classroom as your personal boudoir, but it's not as if you had conducted an affair with a minor. Your boyfriend is at the age of consent and should have borne some blame."

"This is not New York City, Iris. This is a town whose morals haven't evolved much since the 1950s," Shelby said. "People said that my boyfriend had 'his head turned,' a quaintly vicious expression that painted me as the Jezebel and the man who was screwing me as an innocent victim. I was the irredeemable homewrecker, while he was a naughty boy who only had to act contrite and promise he wouldn't do it again."

"Did he do anything to support you?" Nicky asked.

"He is the sheriff," Shelby said bitterly. "He got the video taken down within the hour, and the janitor was arrested and charged with the distribution of pornography. His defense was that one of his underage children found the video on his phone and was the one to upload it."

"What happened to him?" Theresa asked.

"The janitor was eventually cleared of all charges since his ten-year-old son admitted to posting the video, but he lost his job and the family left town. Everyone was glad to see them go because they were—" Shelby suddenly went quiet.

"What? Black?" Nicky asked.

"Hispanic," Shelby admitted. "There are very few minorities, or immigrants. The townspeople don't make them welcome."

"I bet not," Nicky muttered under her breath.

"Let me guess," Iris said angrily. "No one dared to call your boyfriend out, even though he was the one to commit adultery, not you, and had used his position to intimidate and run this family out of town."

"He was treated as the town hero," Shelby replied, her tone now resigned. "That was when I applied for the show. I guess it was an excuse not to make a decision that would change my life forever. Some part of me still hoped that it would all blow over and everyone would forgive me in time."

"Did they?" Iris asked.

"By the time I left, I was able to shop at the grocery store and attend Sunday services, but everyone still treated me like the Whore of Babylon, even my parents. They were embarrassed in front of their friends."

"And your boyfriend?" I asked.

"He made a show of playing the devoted husband and father. Last I heard, he and his wife were expecting another baby."

"I'm sorry, Shelby. That must have been horrible for you," I said.

"It was. I just needed a refuge for a few months, until I could figure out what to do. I never expected this," Shelby wailed.

"None of us did," Iris said. "From now on, we must stick together. No one should go off by themselves. We'll institute the buddy system."

"And how do you know one of us didn't kill Will?" Nicky asked.

I could almost hear Iris smiling in the darkness. "I can vouch for every one of you. I was wide awake for hours before sunrise. None of you left the house, not even for a few minutes to pee."

"But can we vouch for you?" Theresa asked from the confines of the bed.

"And what reason would I have to kill Will?" Iris cried defensively.

"Who knows?" Theresa said. "I have a feeling the producers of the show picked us for a reason. Perhaps we are not all complete strangers to each other."

"Did you know any of the contestants before coming on the show?" Iris demanded.

"No, but that doesn't mean that there isn't some obscure connection that might come out in the wash."

"Have you ever considered becoming a crime reporter, Theresa?" Nicky quipped.

Theresa chuckled. "Much more fun to observe quietly from the sidelines."

"Are you having *fun*?" Shelby asked incredulously.

"It's like being inside an Agatha Christie novel," Theresa said. "I always did like Agatha."

I hoped she was joking, but at this point, I couldn't be certain of anything. Theresa was the proverbial closed book, so who knew what really went on in her mind.

# Chapter 19

The days following Will's death were indescribably difficult. Not only were we reeling from the fact that someone, possibly one of us, had murdered Will, but with every hour that passed, it became clearer that no one was coming. That knowledge was even more disturbing. We kept speculating as to why no one had shown up, but at the end of the day, there were only a few possibilities that made sense.

A. No one was reviewing the footage.
B. Someone was reviewing the footage but had made the decision not to inform the police.
C. The cameras weren't working.
D. No one realized the cameras weren't working because no one was reviewing the footage.

All the options were equally difficult to rationalize. Varlet Productions must have spent a tremendous amount of money to get this operation up and running. Why would they suddenly drop the ball? It didn't make any sense. What was even more frightening was that our families believed we would return in September, which meant that no one would start to ask questions for five more months.

It was impossible to imagine that no one would make contact for five months, but the possibility was becoming more likely with each day that passed. It was now three days since Will's death, and it was becoming painfully obvious that it was time to bury him. The smell that emanated from the corncrib was growing stronger and creating unsanitary—or more accurately, more unsanitary—conditions in the settlement.

Tim and Declan chose a pretty spot, not too close to the settlement, where Will would be buried that afternoon. I had never expected to have to attend a funeral during my time on the island, and the prospect made me want to weep, not only for Will but for myself. I was more scared today than I had been on the day we'd discovered Will's body, and unless I found some way to cope with this new reality, my time on the island would be spent living in terror. I spent more time with Iris and Nicky, since Theresa kept to herself, as usual, and Shelby seemed to find comfort in Mark's arms. Personally, I couldn't see the attraction, but I supposed Shelby responded to Mark's authoritative presence and his matter-of-fact way of dealing with the situation. If she felt safer with Mark, then more power to her, I thought.

Desperate for something to do, I filled a pitcher with cold water and headed toward our newly created cemetery, where Declan and Tim were hard at work. I told myself they'd be thirsty, but really I just felt safer when I was near them. I thought I might just find a place to sit and wait for them to finish. Watching two men digging a grave was a morbid occupation, but it was still better than returning to the settlement, where I didn't have a single real friend.

# Chapter 20

## Declan

I welcomed the physical exertion after days of fruitless speculation. I had never dug a grave before and never realized what it took to move six feet of packed soil that's crisscrossed with stubborn roots and interspersed with pebbles and rocks. Tim was across from me, his hair tied back, his hands gripping the shovel, and his face a mask of intense concentration. I was grateful for his reassuring presence and glad to have a partner I could rely on, since despite first impressions, I really liked the man.

Tim and I had spent the last few days trying to make inroads into the murder inquiry, but although we had discussed it to death, we still didn't know any more now than we had right after it happened, and everyone seemed to be sticking to their story. I hated the idea of having to abandon the investigation and pretend nothing had happened, but that was what we'd have to do if we were to move forward and not live in constant fear.

Tim drove his shovel into the earth next to the hole. "I think that should do it. What do you think?"

"I guess. I've never done this before."

"I have. Once."

"Should I even ask?"

"It was when my grandfather died. He wanted to be buried in a specific spot on the reservation, so my brother and I dug his grave. It was a sobering experience."

"I bet. I feel sobered enough for the rest of my life," I replied.

Tim nodded. "I'm worried, Declan. Really worried."

"Yeah, me too. I really think we're on our own here."

Tim nodded again, his dark eyes narrowing against the afternoon sun. "Something is very, very wrong, and now everyone realizes it."

"What are you suggesting?" I asked, fingers of apprehension dancing up my spine.

"If someone has an axe to grind, now is the time to do it."

"You don't think this was an isolated incident?" I asked carefully.

"The only thing I know for sure is that I don't know what to think, but it would be foolish in the extreme to let our guard down."

"I agree. Which is why we should pretend to close our investigation. Let whoever did this feel like they got away with it, but keep an eye on everyone."

"You think the murderer will slip up and make a mistake?"

"They always do on TV." The joke fell flat, possibly because Tim's gaze fixed on something just behind me.

I turned to find Natalie walking towards us, a pitcher of what I hoped was water or cold milk in her hands. I smiled despite the grim fact that I was waist deep inside a grave, and Natalie smiled back, and for a moment the task didn't seem as awful. But then I remembered that in a few hours Will would occupy this hole in the ground and the smile slid off my face.

# Chapter 21

## Natalie

"Goodness, have we really been here only a month?" Iris asked as she adjusted her cap. "Feels more like a year."

"It does," I agreed. "I can't recall ever being this tired. Who needs the gym when you can pull weeds and lug water all day long?"

"I plan to be gorgeous and svelte by the time I leave here," Iris said, running her hands along the length of her plump form. "I'll be the hottest I've ever been and find me a new man."

Since Will's funeral, we had all been striving to regain some sense of normality, and everyone was joking more than ever to lighten the atmosphere, but the tension and mistrust were there, plain to see. As was the fear.

"You're plenty hot now," I replied. "Especially after standing by the cooking fire for two hours."

Iris laughed and tied an apron around her waist. "You are right there. I think we need to do the laundry again. We all stink."

"But we'll have to wash the men's clothes too, and I'm not looking forward to that. Maybe we should wait a few days."

"Yeah, you're right. Too much work."

"Maybe we should volunteer Mark to wash the men's clothes. Not like he's busy," I said, my gaze following Mark as he approached Shelby, who was watering the vegetable garden. Mark leaned in and gave Shelby a lingering kiss, which she seemed to welcome.

"That man is lording it over everyone as if he were the king of England," Iris muttered under her breath.

Mark was constantly making speeches and urging us to come together in this time of uncertainty. Meanwhile, he did less and less actual work and spent his days finding ways to distinguish himself as the new governor. He was also trying to secure a commitment from Shelby by asking her to agree to be his "settlement wife." Shelby seemed to be considering his offer.

"Why doesn't she just tell him to screw off?" Iris asked after Mark shut the garden gate when he noticed us watching.

"Perhaps she's attracted to authority figures," I replied. "Her boyfriend was the sheriff."

"Mark has the cocksure attitude of a man who's never been rejected," Iris said. "I do hope Shelby turns him down. She's safer with us, in the women's house."

"Do you really think so?" I asked as I began to set the table for breakfast.

Iris shrugged her meaty shoulders. "Who knows? We're all telling ourselves we'll be all right, but it's impossible to predict what someone will do, or what will set them off."

I gave Iris a sidelong glance. I knew her husband had left her, and her restaurant had gone under, but like everyone else, she spoke little of her life before the island, probably because she didn't want her hurts and disappointments broadcast to the world. At this point, I wasn't even sure if anything we said or did was being recorded, but we had already fallen into the pattern of keeping things to ourselves.

# Chapter 22

## Iris

I've always loved food. Food is my drug, my crutch, my solace. It's not just that I like to eat. Cooking is a form of art. There's great satisfaction in creating something wonderful that brings people pleasure. Cooking is also a form of therapy and a way to show people that I care and want to make them happy, if only for a short time. But I don't enjoy cooking for the contestants, and not because of anything they've done or the lack of ingredients. My heart is simply not in it. I thought coming on the show would help me to make peace with the shambles my life had become, but you can't run away from yourself or from the people who've let you down, no matter how far you go and how drastically you cut yourself off.

I met my husband when I was fourteen. In chemistry class. He helped me with my Bunsen burner and explained what I had to do. I hated chemistry, even though cooking is a form of science and a way of combining elements to form a substance. Brad became everything to me: my boyfriend, my best friend, my study partner, and my unfailing support. We were married at nineteen and had a very small wedding because we didn't want a big party. It was us, our immediate families, and a few close friends, and that was all we needed.

As I got older, I looked at those sad, lonely thirty- and forty-somethings going on internet dates and hanging out at bars in the hope of finding their soulmate, and I congratulated myself on being so lucky, so blessed. Whatever else happened, Brad and I had each other, and together we would overcome any obstacle, even the failure of the restaurant that had been my dream since I'd attended culinary school. It seemed so easy on paper to run a successful business. Not so easy in real life. No business plan can predict that a trendy gastropub owned by a minor celebrity will open across the street, or that some troll will write a nasty review that will go viral. Or that a dozen people will get food poisoning from a bad batch of oysters.

But I could have coped with all those things. I could always get a job as a chef and make enough money to live comfortably, even if Brad had decided to retire at forty-five because his accounting job was sucking the life out of him. What I couldn't live with was the loss of my husband. Like most devoted wives, I had ignored the signs, explained them away as fatigue, depression, midlife crisis, a passing phase. Brad would get over the slump. He had before, just as I had gotten over my own frustrations and disappointments. After all, we had a charmed life. A solid marriage, a beautiful daughter and a loving son, a nice house in Brooklyn Heights. Everything else would fall into place.

Well, when it fell, it really fell. I never saw it coming. Never saw Brad as one of those middle-aged men who'd get involved with a woman half his age and get her pregnant. When he finally found the courage to tell me, at first I thought it was a bad joke. My Brad, with his thinning hair, flabby paunch, and crow's feet around the eyes who I had loved since I was fourteen, engaged to a woman who was twenty-seven and expecting his child. Who was this woman, and why did she want my husband, who'd already been married for twenty-six years and had children who were only a few years younger than her? Would Brad want to make a life with her if she weren't pregnant? Did he really want to start that part of his life all over again? As I recall, he wasn't all that excited about night feedings, changing diapers, and spending endless hours at the park while the kids ran around like little lunatics, trying to throw themselves head-first off every monkey bar and slide.

In the end, I had no choice but to accept it, but I'm not the sort of woman that goes down without a fight. I decided to be gracious, mature. I even invited Brad and Sandy over to the house to discuss the divorce. After all, Sandy should see the house she was trying to take from me. I made a fruit plate, herbal tea, and caramel cheesecake. Sandy's favorite. I'm such a masochist, I made it from scratch instead of just buying it from a local bakery. I suppose I wanted to impress her.

No one suspected me when Sandy lost her baby. Why would they? I was just the discarded wife, the older model who had become obsolete. How could this dumpy, middle-aged woman be responsible for Sandy and Brad's heartbreak? No pubescent NYC emergency room doctor would suspect that I had slipped a crushed abortion pill I'd taken from my daughter's bathroom cabinet into Sandy's tea. And neither did Sandy. The sweetness of the cheesecake had masked the bitterness of the tea.

Miscarriages happen. Better luck next time, Sandy. But there will be no next time because Sandy and Brad split up and he came begging me to take him back. A sad, tired, middle-aged man who'd dodged a bullet and gotten the chance to turn back the clock and undo the biggest mistake of his life.

Maybe I'll take him back, eventually, but for now, I need time to figure out what I really want and to decide if that sad sack of shit is deserving of a second chance after the agony he put me through. Maybe it's over with Sandy, but no breakup or miscarriage will erase the pain and shock of Brad's betrayal or fix the life that he so carelessly broke.

Sometimes, in the dead of night when I can't sleep, I offer up a prayer for that baby. It was the true victim of this situation, but in the clear light of day, I have no regrets. Tough luck, kid!

# Chapter 23

## Natalie

# May

After Will's funeral, everyone worked hard to pretend that Will's death had never happened, both because we couldn't live with the possibility of another murder and because we had other problems. By the beginning of May, our supplies were running dangerously low, and despite careful rationing, we all realized that no bag of wheat or oats was bottomless. With no new supplies coming in, we had to think long and hard about how we were going to survive for several more months.

Without a calendar, it was easy to lose track of the days, but I thought it was the first week of the month when Mark decided to officially address the situation.

"Your attention, please, everyone," Mark said as breakfast drew to an end. It didn't take long since there wasn't much food. "I know everyone is doing their best to contribute to our food stores, but I think we need to double our efforts. Iris informs me that we're nearly out of wheat flour, we have enough oats to last a few more days, a week at most, and the chickens are not laying enough eggs to provide us with an inexhaustible supply of protein."

"What are you proposing, Mark?" Glen asked.

Mark actually winced at the use of his first name. He expected everyone to refer to him as Governor, something we all had yet to do since it seemed rather ridiculous.

"I think that until it's time to start harvesting our vegetables and corn crop, we must hunt, fish, and forage."

"Theresa is out foraging every day," Iris said defensively.

"Theresa is one person. I think we need to allocate more people to looking for natural resources. Hunting is our best bet," Mark said.

"If I may," Jesse interjected. "Hunting has always been a way to feed hungry people, but we must be very careful in how we approach the hunt."

"What on earth do you mean, Jesse?" Mark demanded irritably.

Jesse looked around the table. "We are on an island, so the wildlife population is not unlimited. If we hunt too aggressively, the deer might become extinct within a few months. Likewise, our own resources are scarce. We have five muskets and a finite supply of bullets and powder. We are not about to get more. I think that we need to be judicious in how much we hunt and who we send out into the forest."

"What do you propose?" Mark asked. He clearly saw the wisdom in Jesse's argument.

"I propose that we send out only the people who have an actual shot at hitting the target. And we should hunt only as needed."

"And what do you suggest we eat between hunting trips?"

"We should make better use of the sea," Jesse replied. "There isn't enough fish in the streams to feed us for long, but if we fish off the rocks, we'll have a better chance of a steady catch."

"That's a good idea," Tim said. "We should start fishing and catching shellfish. Brendan, do you think you could make traps and maybe carve some hooks to use for fishing poles?"

Brendan nodded. "For sure, but we don't have any fishing wire."

"We have linen," Tim said. "Maybe we can cut Will's sheet into thin strips and then tie the pieces to form strings. It's primitive, but it should work."

"Anyone enjoy diving?" Theresa asked.

"Diving? Why?" Jesse asked. It was obvious he didn't enjoy that particular sport.

"Seaweed is a good source of iodine and fiber," Theresa said.

"It's disgusting," Sam said.

"It's no more disgusting than organ meats or tripe," Jesse pointed out. "It's all about what you're used to."

"I love seaweed salad," Brendan chimed in. "And sushi. Maybe once we catch something, we can make sashimi, since we don't have rice. I really miss sushi."

"I miss my mama's enchiladas," Gael said dreamily.

Suddenly, everyone was talking about what food they missed, and I found myself salivating, my stomach twisting with hunger. Physically, I suppose we got enough to keep us going, but there was little satisfaction to be had from the food we ate. Our diet was monotonous at best, unhealthy at worst. We had no vegetables, no fruits, and no supplements to take should we start to develop vitamin deficiencies. And we would, if we didn't find a way to make our diet more varied.

"Perhaps we should say a prayer," Ed suggested, stepping into his role as minister.

"Why? It's not Sunday," Glen protested.

"We're all feeling worried and homesick. It might help to make us feel less alone."

"Count me out." Glen rose from the table. "I don't believe in prayer. I believe in myself and my ability to make things happen."

"Me too," Tim agreed.

Most people left the table, but a few remained. They bowed their heads as Ed intoned a quick prayer, then everyone went to work. It was my turn to weed and water the vegetable garden. I hated weeding, but there was something comforting about being close to the earth and watching things grow, and after two months of mostly cold weather, it was a pleasure to feel the sun on my shoulders as I set to work. Soon, we'd start seeing the fruits, or more accurately, the vegetables of our labors. I really missed greens and hoped we'd have a good harvest. I would have sold my soul for a tomato or a potato just then. And Gael mentioning enchiladas made me crave avocados. I could have murdered a bowl of guacamole served with tortilla chips.

I missed certain foods, but what I missed more was the knowledge that I could get anything I wanted anytime I wanted it. Living on nothing but oatmeal, bread, and the occasional egg and slice of venison after a lifetime of taking all my food choices for granted was a rude awakening, and I realized what a huge part eating played in all our lives. Not only were people angrier when they were hungry, but they craved the sensual pleasure food offered, and without family, friends, and partners, this was just another comfort that had been ripped away from us. It was hard not to think of the men who'd settled Jamestown and lived on starvation rations for years before even seeing women again. Except for Mark and Shelby, no one appeared to be pursuing a relationship, and the absence of physical touch and the knowledge that someone had your back was in some ways even more difficult than the lack of food. We were all in this together, but we were very much alone, and that to me was the hardest part of all.

As I yanked on the weeds, I considered the men from a romantic perspective just for fun. Gael was, hands down, the most attractive man on the island. He smoldered even when his face was damp with perspiration or when his hands were covered in fish

117

guts, but I wasn't attracted to him, nor did I trust him. Besides, even though Gael never really talked about his wife, he was very much married. As was Tim, who was also very good-looking and just as tight-lipped as Gael about his homelife. If I were honest with myself, the only person I was drawn to was Declan. Declan did not smolder. He didn't have the coloring for it, but he had the sort of open face and friendly smile that I had always found attractive.

Declan also had expressive eyes—another one of my musts in a man. Tim and Gael had such dark eyes that it was impossible to make out their pupils. Declan's eyes were that pale brown that became darker when he was upset or angry but seemed more amber when he smiled or when he became emotional. My gut instinct told me to trust Declan, even though I had no real reason to trust anyone. And that went to the root of my sense of isolation. I trusted some people more than others, but when it came down to it, I'd be foolish in the extreme to trust anyone completely, more so since Will's death.

I was startled out of my reverie when Shelby joined me in the enclosure and shut the gate firmly behind her.

"Want some help?" she asked.

"Sure. You'll never hear me refusing help with weeding."

Shelby bent down and pulled up a few weeds, but I could see her mind wasn't really on gardening. She looked sad and tired, and her face was gaunt after weeks of stress and eating a poor diet. I caught Shelby sneaking glances at me, as if she were unsure whether she wanted to speak, but I was certain she hadn't come into the garden just to offer her assistance.

"Shelby, are you all right?" I asked at last. I had straightened and used the moment of rest to massage my lower back, but my gaze was fixed on Shelby, who looked like she was about to cry.

"No," she whispered.

"What is it? How can I help?"

Silent tears slid down Shelby's sun-reddened cheeks. "I'm pregnant, Natalie."

I stared at her. Even if she had slept with Mark on the first day we were at the settlement, which I was pretty sure she hadn't, she'd only be a week or two late, and with no pregnancy test, it was impossible to know for sure. There were many reasons a woman's cycle might shift, especially when she was suddenly sharing a house with four other women. It wasn't uncommon for women's cycles to become synchronized over time—nature's way of making certain that the women who lived in such near proximity became pregnant around the same time and delivered around the same time as well, so that if a woman died in childbirth or had no milk, the other women in the tribe or village would be able to feed her newborn. We'd only been on the island for two months, but Shelby, being the youngest, might be the most susceptible to the hormonal changes.

Shelby wiped her nose with her apron and said quietly, "It's not what you think."

"What do I think?" I asked carefully.

"You think it's Mark's. It's not." Shelby sighed heavily. "The baby is Matt's. My boyfriend back home."

"The one who left you without a backward glance and had you blackballed?"

Shelby nodded. "Yes."

I opened my mouth to protest, then closed it again. This didn't make any sense. I had applied to be on the show just before Thanksgiving and had had a physical at the beginning of January. By her own admission, Shelby had applied after the breakup with Matt, so she had to be well into her second trimester.

"Shelby, how far along are you?" I asked.

"About five months."

"What?" I cried, despite having already worked out the timing in my mind.

Shelby nodded again, tears dripping onto her bodice. "The last time I had sex with Matt was about two weeks before Christmas, after I had already applied. He came over, supposedly to talk, and one thing led to another."

"But we all had a physical. They wouldn't have let you come on the show if you were pregnant."

"They never did a pregnancy test," Shelby said.

"But—" I began, then stopped. Shelby was right. The doctor had asked me if there was a chance I might be pregnant, and I'd said no. They had taken blood and urine, but maybe they had never tested for pregnancy. Even so, most women would suspect they were pregnant by the second trimester, which was how far along Shelby would have been by the time we left for the island.

"Did you never suspect?" I asked.

"My periods were never regular, and there were several times when I was a teenager that my period stopped altogether when I was really anxious. I just thought this was one of those times. I didn't realize I was pregnant until I started sleeping with Mark."

I stared, willing her to elaborate.

"I noticed that my breasts were fuller and more sensitive, and everything felt different," Shelby added as she lowered her eyes in obvious embarrassment.

"Shelby, does Mark know?"

Shelby shook her head. "Mark is too desperate to fuck me to pay much attention to my belly. He probably thinks I need to start doing sit-ups. Besides, we usually have sex in the woods, and I never took my clothes off, in case there are cameras, so Mark has never seen me fully naked. The bum roll and skirts hide my belly, and it's really not that big yet," she explained.

I couldn't help but stare at Shelby's middle, but she was right. It was impossible to tell, especially since she was wearing an apron.

A sudden and terrifying thought came into my head. Shelby might have her baby on the island. Putting aside the birth, Shelby needed prenatal care. She wasn't getting enough nutrients, and she'd never seen an obstetrician. What if there were serious complications? And what would happen when her time came? I had never delivered a baby. Maybe Declan and Tim had some experience, being police officers, but we didn't have anything we might require for a child. What if Shelby needed a Cesarean, or a blood transfusion? I took a deep breath and told myself to calm down. Perhaps Shelby was wrong, and this was a result of extreme anxiety. That was the more likely scenario.

"Shelby, would you allow me to examine you?" I asked.

Shelby sighed and nodded. "I hoped you would. I just want to be sure."

"Well, I don't know if I can tell you with one hundred percent certainty, but I can at least try to figure out what's going on."

"Can you do it now?"

"Let's go to the creek, where no one will see us. Besides, I need to wash my hands, and so do you."

We left the enclosure and headed toward the woods. It was sunny and cool by the creek, the water flowing rapidly and sparkling in the morning light. I washed my hands thoroughly and asked Shelby to do the same. I was not qualified to perform any sort of internal exam, but I still wanted to avoid any sort of contamination.

"Lie on the ground, please."

Shelby lay down on a patch of grass that was shadowed by a leafy maple, and I knelt next to her and slid my hands beneath her skirts to feel her belly. It was strange to touch another woman this way when she wasn't wearing anything beneath the chemise, but my discomfort evaporated as soon as I laid my hands on her stomach, and I let out a strangled breath. No internal examination was necessary. Shelby's belly was taught and round, the child within moving gently. It was too small for its kicks to be hard, but I could feel the ripples as it shifted inside.

"Have you experienced any morning sickness?" I asked.

"I felt queasy before leaving for the training farm, but I thought it was just nerves. And I have to pee a lot, but I've been going in the woods so no one would question the frequent trips to the bathroom. I'm scared, Natalie," Shelby whispered.

*And I'm scared for you*, I wanted to say, but that wouldn't be helpful.

Shelby's desperate gaze met mine. "Look, I know you all probably think I have daddy issues and need to use better judgment when it comes to men, but I'm not the sort of woman who does well on her own. I know that's terribly unfashionable these days and I should be spouting all these women's lib slogans, but I like older men who feel grateful to be with me because they know I'm out of their league. It boosts their ego to have a younger woman on their arm, and it makes me feel special."

*Until they drop you and stand well back as the whole town gets in line to stone you*, I thought, but kept my mouth shut.

"Besides, I thought Mark might step up when the time came," Shelby was saying.

"Step up how?"

Shelby looked embarrassed, but too much had been revealed to hold back now. "With extra food rations and less work. He's the sort of man that would protect his girlfriend, if only to show that he has the power to do so."

I saw no logic in her argument, since Mark didn't really have any power at all, but I could see how she might turn to a father figure, or in this case a sugar daddy, for comfort. But in this instance, if anyone could offer Shelby more food, it was Iris. Then another thought occurred to me.

"How do you feel about this baby, Shelby?"

Shelby sat up and shrugged. "I don't know. A part of me really wants it, and a part of me wishes it'd never happened."

"What would you have done if you were back home?"

Shelby looked like a deer trapped in the headlights, and I realized that she still loved Matt and probably hoped that he would come to the rescue once he found out about his baby. Matt sounded like a total dick to me, but now wasn't the time to point that out, not when she was already frightened and uncertain about the well-being of her baby.

"Whatever Matt wanted me to do," Shelby confessed. "If he said he'd look after us, I'd have kept it. If he said he didn't want it, I'd get an abortion. I never wanted to be a single mom." Shelby let out a shuddering breath. "Please, don't tell anyone, Natalie. I can't bear for everyone to know. Not yet."

"I think we need to tell Iris and Theresa," I said. "Iris can make sure you get enough food, and maybe Theresa can help you to get the nutrients you need."

"I'm not going to take some weird concoctions while I'm pregnant. Women had babies long before prenatal care and vitamins. As long as I get enough to eat and don't have to do any heavy lifting, I should be fine. Please, let's not tell anyone for a few more weeks. I can hide a belly beneath these pleats and apron for another month, at least."

"Don't you think you should at least tell Mark?" I asked carefully.

Shelby shook her head vehemently. "No. I'm not ready for him to know. Promise me you won't tell him."

"All right," I said, but I felt uneasy about making such a promise.

# Chapter 24

## Shelby

I wasn't completely honest, and I'm sorry for that, but how could I tell these understanding, supportive women that I'm the one to blame for everything that happened? I was a fool. I overplayed my hand and lost everything I held dear. I put about the story that the janitor had filmed me with Matt, but Matt, and even my parents, quickly realized there was more to the narrative. The janitor had filmed us, but I'd paid him to do it and asked him to post the video on Facebook, where I knew Bella would see it. The end game was to torpedo Matt's marriage and sink that already leaking ship.

Bella knew Matt was cheating on her, but she wasn't ready to admit defeat. She dragged him to endless marriage counseling sessions and threatened to fight for sole custody of their children if he forced her hand and she filed for divorce. Still, she held on. I figured that if everyone saw us together, she'd have no choice but to do something, if only to save face in a town where her family has lived for generations. A quaint, all-American town with white picket fences and colorful flowerbeds can quickly become the seventh circle of hell when people you've known your whole life snigger behind your back and feel sorry for you because you couldn't hold on to your man. Makes it nearly impossible to hold your head high and walk with dignity, not when your rival is the Homecoming Queen and beauty pageant winner two years running.

I'm not a bad person. Really, I'm not, but I had been in love with Matt since I was a little girl. He was the captain of the high school football team, and I only went to the games with my older brother to watch him on the field. But Matt never had eyes for anyone except his Bella. She was a stunner when she was sixteen, but at nearly forty-five, she is bitter and middle-aged, and no longer a fitting partner for such a handsome, ambitious man.

I really thought my plan would work and Bella would throw Matt out and file for divorce at long last. And then we'd build our own little family, with charming holiday traditions and glossy family portraits. How wrong I was. Matt was furious, and I was the one who was consigned to hell and nearly run out of town. Not to mention the janitor and his kid, who was forced to take the blame in order not to make the whole sorry episode appear premeditated.

And now I'm pregnant, and I don't even know who the father of this baby is. I went on a bit of a bender in New Orleans and was too drunk to ask the two guys I fucked in an alley behind a bar in the French Quarter to use protection. Still, I feel a sense of obligation toward this baby, and maybe even a little bit of love. And if everyone thinks the baby is Matt's, then I might reclaim something of the support I once enjoyed in the community. And if Bella thinks I have had her husband's baby, well, that will just make my day, every day.

# Chapter 25

## Natalie

"Would you like to take a walk?" Declan asked me after dinner that night.

It was Nicky and Shelby's turn to wash the dishes, so I had some free time, and I longed to get away from the settlement for a little while. Leaving with Declan seemed like the safest option, and I hoped that the walk would help me sleep better. I hadn't been sleeping well since Will's death, and Shelby's revelations of that morning had left me shaken. I didn't want to betray her confidence, but there were things I felt Declan and I needed to talk about.

It was a gorgeous evening, and the sun painted the clouds pink and gold as it started its journey toward the horizon. The ocean was calm, the waves washing over my bare feet. I had left my shoes and hose on the sand and tied up my skirt to keep it from getting wet. Just as we were about to walk away, I pulled off my cap and released my hair, enjoying the gentle breeze as it ruffled the strands.

"You were very quiet at dinner," Declan said as we walked a little way from the settlement.

"Was I?"

"You looked worried." Declan stopped walking and turned to face me. "Natalie, anything you share with me will be kept in the strictest confidence. You have my word."

I considered his offer and knew I would accept. I needed to unburden myself, and I trusted him more than most. Declan hadn't moved, his warm gaze inviting me to confide in him, so I took a deep breath and told him.

"Everyone is trying to act normal and pretend that Will died of natural causes. It's easier that way; I get it, especially since after all this time, when we still don't know what happened or who was responsible. No one wants to believe that we are living alongside a murderer or that we have been abandoned by Varlet, so they have rationalized it in their minds and decided to downplay their fears. They're choosing to believe that if we just carry on as normal, this will all be over in four months. But what if it's not, Declan? What if no one comes to get us?"

Declan nodded. "I haven't rationalized it, and neither has Tim. We've been over it a thousand times, Natalie, but when it comes to Will's death, we have nothing to go on, which leads me to believe that the crime we thought to be unpremeditated was actually meticulously planned. Whoever killed Will had thought everything through and made sure there was nothing to connect them to the murder." Declan took a deep breath. "And as for Varlet, I honestly don't know what to think. I can't think of an explanation that fits, but I think you are right, and we need to prepare for the worst, which is why it's even more imperative that we lay in supplies and ration the powder and shot. We'll be fine for the next few months, but if we're still here come winter..."

Declan's voice trailed off, the implication obvious. Not only would we go hungry if we weren't able to hunt, but without electricity and hot water, we'd be fighting against bitter cold as well, since the island would be buffeted by winter winds off the Atlantic. The only protection we had against frostbite was our thin cloaks and firewood that would only keep us warm if we remained within a foot of the flames.

"And what if there are unexpected developments?" I asked.

"You mean besides a murder?"

I inwardly asked Shelby for forgiveness, but I couldn't keep my promise. I felt responsible for Shelby's well-being and that of her baby and needed to take steps to prepare even if she wasn't ready to deal with the reality of her situation. "Did you ever deliver a baby?"

Declan stared at me. "No. Why would you ask me that?"

128

"No reason." There was no point in telling him the truth, since he clearly wasn't equipped to help.

"Aw, come on, Natalie. No one asks a question like that for no reason. Are you pregnant?" Declan looked momentarily stricken but instantly rearranged his features into an expression of quiet competence. "Look, I won't judge. I only want to help."

"I'm not pregnant," I said.

"It's Shelby," Declan said, coming to the obvious conclusion since Shelby was the only one in a relationship. "I should have known."

"Why would you say that?"

Declan looked away, embarrassed. "I overheard Glen and Sam talking a few days ago. They said her breasts got bigger even though she'd lost weight. They were speculating that Mark got her pregnant."

"That's disgusting," I snapped, even though Declan had probably amended some of the terminology. Glen and Sam would have been considerably more crude when discussing Shelby's attributes.

"I'm only telling you what I heard. Is it Mark's?" he asked carefully.

"No. Shelby was already pregnant when she came on the show. She's about five months along."

Declan's mouth fell open. "Five months? Are you sure?"

"I examined her this morning. I felt the baby move."

"That means that Shelby might have her baby on the island," Declan concluded.

"She needs prenatal care. And what if something goes wrong? What if there are complications? I'm a school nurse, Declan. I'm not equipped to handle this."

"We'll do our best to deal with whatever problems arise. For now, all we can do is hope that we're off this island by the time Shelby goes into labor." He sighed wearily. "Does Mark know?"

"No. She hasn't told him."

"I don't see that going over well."

"You think he'll break up with her?"

Declan gave me a look that said, *You don't really understand men, do you?*

"Mark is a raging narcissist," he said. "He not only needs to be the smartest person in the room, but he has to believe that he's envied by all the little people he looks down upon. The only reason he wants Shelby is because he thinks she's the best-looking woman on the island, and to possess her adds to his cachet since he believes all the other men are hot for her."

"Aren't they?" I interjected.

"Not all of us dream of Shelby," Declan replied, a ghost of a smile tugging at his lips.

"So, what do you think Mark will do when he finds out?"

"If Shelby tells him in private, he will probably walk away from her and make sure everyone knows it was his decision. If he finds out publicly, his reaction will reflect his humiliation."

"You don't think he will hurt her, do you?" I asked.

"No, but he will try to punish her for embarrassing him. He's just that sort of man."

"Declan, is it possible that Mark is the one who killed Will? He's the only person who gained anything by Will's death. Not only did he eliminate the competition for Shelby's affections, but he also became governor, which is what he wanted all along."

"To be the governor of a pretend colony is not exactly worth killing for, but I suppose people have killed for less," Declan agreed. "However, there's nothing to tie Mark to the murder. He never left the house that night."

"Surely you must have some idea," I prodded. I simply couldn't accept that two law-enforcement officers had utterly failed to come up with even a plausible theory.

Declan shifted his gaze toward the setting sun and remained silent for a while. To all the world, he looked like a man watching a glorious sunset, but his jaw was tight, and his neck and shoulders too tense for someone who had nothing to hide.

"Declan, please tell me," I pleaded.

Declan turned to face me. With the sun directly behind him, I couldn't make out his expression, and his eyes looked nearly black as his gaze met mine.

"I believe that whatever led to Will's murder has roots in the past."

"How can you be sure of that?" I asked.

"It's the only theory that makes sense."

"You don't think any of us have been selected at random, do you?"

"No, I don't, but unless people admit to a historic connection, there's no way for me to connect the dots." Declan took me by the arm and gently turned me around. "Come on, we'd better head back. It's going to get dark soon, and I don't think we should be out here alone."

It shocked me to hear him say that. He didn't think we were safe, and that was a frightening thought.

# Chapter 26

## Natalie

Shelby was carrying very small, until one day, about a week after she had told me she was pregnant, she popped. I had seen this happen with my sister. One day she'd looked like she might be a little bloated, and the next day she'd had a full-on baby bump. Even with the voluminous skirts and the apron, it was noticeable that Shelby suddenly had a belly, just as it was noticeable that Mark was furiously angry. I didn't ask Shelby if she had told him or if he had finally figured it out for himself, but it was clear they weren't speaking to each other, and Mark did everything possible to avoid her at mealtimes. Everyone noticed that something had changed, but since they weren't aware of the situation, they simply assumed it was just a lovers' tiff.

The day Mark lost it, tensions were already running high. We woke to find that our chickens had been killed. Someone must have left the door to the coop unlatched and a fox had gotten in through a narrow opening in the curtain wall and slipped into the chicken coop. Everyone knew it was Shelby, since she'd been the last one in the coop, but no one wanted to point the finger at a woman who was already so emotionally fragile. The chickens were strewn across the enclosure, their throats ripped out, their feathers covered in blood, and their eyes glazed in death.

Nicky, who'd gone to collect the eggs for our breakfast, came running out, screaming bloody murder as she vowed to disembowel the predator that had destroyed her "girls," as she called them. I had no idea Nicky had grown so attached to the chickens, and it nearly brought me to tears to see her weep. Perhaps it wasn't the chickens she was crying for but the loss of control and the knowledge that there'd be no more eggs, but it was a personal loss for us all, and we were understandably upset.

"We should boil the chickens," Mark said. "To bury them will be a dreadful waste of food."

"It's not safe to eat them," Sam said. "You don't know what disease the animal that attacked them might have been carrying. We need to dispose of them."

"Do you know what this means?" Mark cried. "No more eggs. We're already low on supplies, and it doesn't seem that more will be coming."

Like the rest of us, Mark had lost weight, and there were lines of strain around his eyes, but this appeared to be the final straw. His normally calm demeanor had finally cracked, and he looked like a madman, capable of anything.

"Sam is a farmer, Mark. He knows about these things," Shelby said softly.

She may as well have pulled out the pin of an unexploded grenade. Mark turned on her, his face growing a mottled red with fury, his eyes blazing. "Shut up, you filthy slag! How dare you question me? Or are you cozying up to Sam now that I no longer want your bloated carcass?"

Everyone stared at Mark, their faces showing varying degrees of shock. Seeing their stunned reaction, Mark roared, "Oh, they don't know? Well, why don't you tell them?"

He glared around the silent group. "The bitch is pregnant. And no, it's not mine. She was stringing me along all this time, thinking I was so pussy-whipped I'd be willing to be a father to her brat. Well, I'm not interested in playing happy families, especially not with you," he bellowed, pointing a finger at Shelby's chest. "You're too thick to realize that the only thing you have going for you are those big tits and your tight—" Mark seemed to realize that he'd gone too far and went quiet, but the damage was done.

"Don't you dare speak about me that way!" Shelby shrieked. "You were the one who pursued me."

"Yeah, I did, because you're the only decent piece of arse on this island, but that doesn't mean I don't have my pride. I'm not interested in whores. Lord, do you even know who the father is, or will you fuck any guy that buys you a drink and tells you you're pretty?"

"You bastard!" Shelby screamed, and went for him.

It happened so fast, no one had time to react. Shelby slapped Mark across the face, leaving a livid red mark on his cheek. She was crying hard, her sobs shaking her whole body and making her look like a heartbroken little girl. Had Mark managed to retain even an ounce of self-control, he would have taken a step back and accepted his punishment. God knew he'd earned it, but Mark had crossed a line he could never uncross. He slugged Shelby in the face, sending her flying onto her back in the chicken-shit-strewn mud of the coop. She cried out as she landed with a thud, her hand going to her belly. I didn't think the baby was hurt, but Shelby's nose was bleeding, and she had a split lip. Her teeth were crimson with blood that was dripping down her chin. Shelby wailed even louder as she tried to get up but slipped and fell right back into the mud. To make matters worse, she wiped a hand across her face to keep the blood from running into her mouth and left a fat smear of slimy, shitty mud across the lower half of her face, making her look like a brawling fishwife from a historical drama.

Everyone sprang into action. Declan and Tim tackled Mark and pinned his arms behind his back, while Iris and I went to help Shelby, who seemed unable to find the strength to stand up on her own. Nicky untied her apron, wet it, and used it to gently clean Shelby's battered face. Shelby was weeping quietly. Her shoulders were hunched, and her arms were wrapped around her middle protectively. Iris slipped her arm around Shelby's waist and maneuvered her toward the gate of the enclosure. Nicky followed them toward the women's house, but I remained behind. I had to know how the guys planned to deal with Mark. I was so furious, I would have liked a go at him myself, but I wasn't careless enough to get in his way. He'd probably hurt me too if he managed to break free.

"Let me go, you cretins," Mark hollered as Declan and Tim dragged him away from the scene. "She's a filthy whore, and you two couldn't organize a piss-up in a brewery much less maintain order in this godforsaken settlement. A man was murdered on your watch, but you know fuck all. Not a fucking clue between the two of you.

Declan and Tim frogmarched Mark toward the settlement gates, then pushed him through. They could hardly arrest him for domestic battery or lock him up, but something had to be done.

"Don't come back until you're ready to apologize to Shelby and to the rest of us," Tim said.

"And if I don't apologize?" Mark challenged him. "What are you going to do about it?"

"Then you will be cast out of the settlement. This sort of behavior will not be tolerated."

"Oh, really? Who died and left you in charge, you filthy mongrel?" Mark demanded, his lips curling into an ugly half-grin.

Tim didn't take the bait but turned and walked away. In fact, everyone turned their back on Mark, even Ed, who normally tried to defuse any tense situation. Mark was left standing alone just outside the gates. When I turned to look back a few moments later, he was panting, his face scarlet with fury, but it was obvious he was beginning to realize just how badly he'd erred, and what it would cost him.

Jutting out his chin defiantly, Mark walked away toward the beach, and I turned toward the women's house. As I passed Declan, our eyes met, and I silently acknowledged that he'd been right in his prediction. But even Declan had not anticipated the violence of Mark's anger or the repercussions his outburst would have on the rest of us.

# Chapter 27

"Come now, sweetheart," Iris cooed. Shelby stood on the threshold, her busted lip quivering, and her eyes huge with horror as she watched Mark walk away. We had all known Mark was a bit of a jerk, but the things he'd said and done had showed a side of him none of us had suspected was there. Least of all Shelby.

"Let's get you inside," Iris tried again. "You need to get out of those filthy clothes and lie down for a little while. I'll bring you a nice, cold cup of ale." Iris's expression changed as she realized that Shelby shouldn't be having alcohol in her condition. "A cup of milk," she amended.

"Thank you," Shelby muttered.

I followed Shelby inside and helped her out of her soiled clothes. Once in her chemise, she washed her face and hands in the basin and watched in horror as the water turned murky with blood and mud. Shelby gingerly touched her nose. I didn't think it was broken but couldn't be sure without an X-ray. Shelby would be swollen and in pain for several days, but the best I could offer was a damp cloth. We didn't even have ice to bring down the swelling.

I sat with Shelby for a while but left her to rest when she drifted off to sleep. It was time for lunch, and I was hungry since I'd never gotten my breakfast. I would bring Shelby a plate when I came back to check on her, since I didn't think she would be leaving the house that day. She was terribly shaken by what had happened but also embarrassed to have been treated so badly by the man she had trusted.

Appalled as I was by Mark's behavior, some small part of me acknowledged the fact that he must have reached the end of his tether to lash out like that. Whether it was Will's death, the demise of our chickens, Shelby's perceived betrayal, or just the reality of our situation finally sinking in, this day had tipped the scale and Mark had gone from cool civility to jaw-dropping ugliness and violence. I didn't think I could ever fully forgive him for the way he'd treated Shelby or the way he'd spoken to Tim.

When I came outside and took my place at the table, I was relieved to see that Mark hadn't come back. Still, everyone looked angry and tense as they took their seats and accepted bowls of watery stew. Iris set aside a portion for Shelby, then joined us at the table.

"So, what do we do about Mark?" she asked as she looked around the table, her spoon suspended in midair.

"The things Mark said were awful, but we can't censor what someone says. However, resorting to violence, especially against a defenseless pregnant woman, cannot be tolerated," Jesse said. "There must be consequences."

"What sort of consequences?" Theresa asked. She looked tired and upset, and just a little bit older than she had that morning.

"We can banish him," Tim said, reiterating his earlier threat.

"We can't do that," Gael argued. "He'll never survive on his own, and I won't sentence a man to death, even if he's a complete dick."

"Casting him out would not be the Christian thing to do," Ed said, using his ministerial voice.

"And hurling abuse at a pregnant woman and knocking her to the ground is?" Declan demanded.

"No, but two wrongs don't make a right," Ed replied calmly. "We're all worried and upset. We've just lost our chickens, and no one knows what's going on with the show. Everyone is on edge. If we handle this incorrectly, we'll only escalate the situation."

"Are you suggesting that we pretend nothing has happened?" Nicky asked. She looked at Ed angrily. Normally, the two of them got on well, but now she looked ready to smack the man across the face.

"I'm suggesting no such thing. Why don't you let me talk to Mark?" Ed said. "I'm sure I can make him see sense."

"What would constitute seeing sense in this scenario?" Jesse asked sharply.

"He must apologize to Shelby and do some sort of penance," Ed replied.

"This is not a Catholic convent, Ed. We don't do penance, and I seriously doubt that Shelby will give two fucks for his apology," Tim retorted. "What he said was bad enough, but he assaulted her. Viciously."

"I agree," Declan said. His voice was level, but it was obvious he was angry and frustrated with Ed.

"So what do you suggest?" Ed demanded, his voice rising in anger. "That we string him up from a tree? Banish him into the wilderness? Brand him?" Ed's thin chest was heaving with outrage. "Is this what we have been reduced to? Colonial justice?"

"We are not going to string people from trees or brand them," Tim replied hotly, "but we can't let them get away with shit either. Every action has a reaction, and every crime should have a punishment."

"He's right," Iris chimed in. "What Mark did was a crime against Shelby."

"She did go for him first," Glen said with a smirk. "Mark was defending himself."

"Shelby slapped him," I cried, unable to remain silent any longer. "And he had earned that slap, and much more. Mark punched her in the face with a closed fist. He might have broken her nose, and he could have hurt her baby."

Iris shook her head. "God, I'm still processing that bit of news. I can't believe I hadn't noticed."

"Shelby was doing her best to hide the pregnancy," I said, "but she's pretty far along. There's a very real chance that she will have the baby while on the island."

"A woman's first pregnancy is so emotional," Theresa said quietly. "It's not only the physical changes but the realization that nothing will ever be the same again and life as you knew it is over forever. You can no longer put your own needs first or make decisions based on your own desires. You now have a tiny person whose very existence depends on you, and you must put their well-being above all else. To have to go through that alone and with no doctor to turn to must be absolutely terrifying. We must do everything in our power to support Shelby."

Everyone stared at Theresa in surprise, probably because this was the longest speech she'd made since coming to the island, and the most impassioned. She was right. Punishing Mark was secondary. We had to focus on Shelby's well-being and help her in whatever way we could.

"We must give Shelby extra rations," Declan said. "And the lightest chores."

"We're barely getting enough to eat as it is," Glen complained.

"She doesn't need much," Iris interjected. "And extra cup of milk, and an extra serving of vegetables once we bring in our harvest, will make all the difference. I will see to it that Shelby gets what she needs."

"That's all well and good, but we still need to decide how to deal with Mark," Tim said.

I had never seen him so angry, and I wondered if the slur Mark had used had gotten under his skin more than he was willing to admit. I wouldn't blame him if it had. Everyone had their breaking point.

"I think we should ask Mark how he intends to make up for his behavior," Ed said. He seemed calmer now, more reasonable. "Give him a chance to atone."

Tim threw up his hands in disgust and walked away, but the rest of us remained seated.

"We should cut his rations for a week," Iris said. "Nothing is as punishing as hunger."

"That's actually a good idea," Jesse said, smiling at Iris with obvious approval. "Boy, I'd hate to get on the wrong side of you, Iris."

"Then don't do anything stupid," Iris replied, and began to gather the dirty dishes. "Time to get to work, guys. Another few hours and it will be dinnertime. I have things to do. Sam and Glen, I need more wood. Nicky, it's your turn with the butter churn. Natalie, dishes. Gael, perhaps you can help Natalie, since Shelby is not feeling well. Declan, you really should have a word with Tim. He seems really upset. Ed, help me grind some wheat."

Everyone nodded, glad to have something to focus on. Iris handed me the stack of dirty plates, and Gael followed me to the creek with a basin full of cups held against his torso with one hand and the pot Iris had used for the stew in the other. We stood side by side, washing the dishes in silence, the greasy water flowing away from us toward the ocean.

"I'm tired," Gael said quietly.

"Take a break."

"Not of doing dishes. Just tired of being here. Everyone is so pissed off. This is not going to be an isolated incident, not when everyone is angry and frustrated. And what about Shelby?" Gael went on. "My wife became severely anemic when she was pregnant. She needed a blood transfusion. What if Shelby gets sick, or needs a C-section?"

He was clearly thinking about the birth of his own child, and I wondered why he'd chosen to leave his family to come on the show.

"Coming here was a mistake," Gael said, as if I had spoken out loud. "My wife and I were having some problems, and I thought time apart would help. When I was a kid and my brother and I fought, my mother always used to send us to separate corners to cool down." Gael smiled wistfully. "My wife and I were angry with each other so often, I thought a few months in separate corners might help us to remember what we love about each other, but what works for brothers doesn't always work in a marriage."

"You clearly miss her, so maybe it has worked," I said.

"I'm not so sure she feels the same. She was against me coming on the show, and we had a huge fight the night before I left. She wouldn't even say goodbye to me." Gael looked heartbroken, and I wished I could say something that would comfort him, but I thought it was probably helping him just to talk. He wasn't the sort of person who opened up easily, so perhaps this was cathartic for him. "I see now that I should have been a better husband, a more devoted father, but I never had a role model growing up. My dad was murdered when I was eight." His voice was barely audible, and for a moment I wasn't sure I'd heard him correctly.

"Murdered?" I echoed.

Gael nodded. "Tortured for hours, then executed. His body was tossed out of a car onto the steps of the police station."

"Why? Who by?" I cried, horrified.

"By the cartel. He didn't want to work for them, so they showed him what it meant to refuse."

"Was this in Santa Cruz?"

Gael shook his head. "No. In Mexico. Sorry, I still can't talk about this without breaking down." His voice sounded thick, and his beautiful eyes were swimming with tears. "I'm sorry to burden you with this, Natalie."

Gael grabbed the washed items and walked off through the trees, leaving me alone with the horror of the images he'd planted.

# Chapter 28

Mark didn't show up for dinner. Neither did Shelby. She lay on her cot, staring at the ceiling as her face swelled and her bruises turned a deeper shade of purple. She didn't cry or speak to anyone, just remained stoically quiet. I had a feeling that if Shelby got hysterical, she wouldn't be able to stop screaming. The rest of us sat around, staring into our plates, and left the table as soon as we finished. No one was in the mood for conversation, and there was still a lot of anger and resentment over the morning's events. No one mentioned Mark.

It normally took me a while to get to sleep, but I was so tired, both emotionally and physically, that I felt myself drifting off as soon as my head hit the pillow. I woke at dawn, my thoughts scattered, my back aching from those damn slats, and a headache building behind my eyes. With great sadness, I recalled that there would be no more wake-up calls from Roger the Rooster or fresh eggs from Henny, Mabel, and Mathilda. I would have liked to take a walk on the beach and watch the sunrise, but some part of me didn't think that would be a good idea. I couldn't take my safety for granted.

I was surprised to find Declan standing outside his house when I finally got up and headed to the outhouse to beat the morning rush. He was staring through the gates, his brows knitted with tension, his stubbled cheeks and gently curling hair gilded by the golden rays of the rising sun. His hair had grown, and with a two-day beard, faded velvet doublet, less-than-clean hose, and scuffed shoes, he could pass for a real colonist.

"What's wrong?" I asked as I came to stand next to him.

"Mark never came back last night."

"He's probably ashamed of the way he acted. Imagine how this will look if it's aired. This would be the one thing people would always remember about him."

Neither of us remarked on the fact that no one might ever see this footage since at this point we had serious doubts about whether the cameras were even working.

"Mark is a pompous ass, but he's not stupid," Declan said. "Sleeping out in the woods is not safe, especially if he doesn't have a fire to keep the animals away. And if he wanted to save face, the best thing he could do would be to come back, grovel shamelessly, and blame his behavior on an emotional breakdown. People would still judge him, but they would be able to sympathize with him a little more. To stalk off and not return shows a lack of remorse."

"He may have made a fire," I said, ignoring the bit about the groveling. Mark wasn't the begging for forgiveness type. He'd probably never apologized to anyone in his life, and the prospect of swallowing his pride publicly would seem way worse than any danger he might face when sleeping rough.

Declan shook his head. "He didn't. There was a southerly wind last night. We would have smelled the smoke from his fire since he went south."

"What are you thinking?" I asked.

"I think we should look for him."

"I don't think the others will agree."

"Maybe not, but we still need to do the right thing, even if we're angry with him."

I nodded. "I'll come with you if you need me. But I'd like to have breakfast first."

Declan smiled, and the grin brightened his worried face. "Better than washing dishes, ha?"

"I'm sick of washing dishes, milking the cow, and shoveling horseshit."

"I bet. I'm pretty sick of chopping wood and killing innocent animals. I hate hunting," he said miserably. "But I'm also sick of being hungry. I would literally sell my soul for a burger and fries. And I wouldn't have any regrets," he added, still smiling.

"I know how you feel. We took so much for granted, all those little things we never gave a second thought to, like a hot shower. God, I'd give anything for a shower. And conditioner." My hair alternated between feeling greasy when it hadn't been washed and brittle after using the horrible lye soap and rinsing it in nearly cold water.

"A shower would be nice, but the water is getting warmer. We'll be able to go swimming soon."

"We don't have bathing suits."

Declan gave me a lopsided grin. "At this point, I honestly don't care who sees me in the buff. Better to go skinny dipping and dry off in the open air than to spend hours walking around in soggy woolen breeches."

We were talking of trivialities when Shelby lay battered on her cot and Mark was missing, but imagining Declan rising out of the sea, his skin shimmering with sunlit droplets of water, did make me feel a little bit lighter. We all needed tools for dealing with stress, and mine had always been fantasy. I would have traded that bottle of conditioner, if I had one, for a stack of novels. I'd read anything as long as it took me away from this claustrophobic island and the people on it.

I turned at the sound of an opening door. Iris stepped blinking into the light and gave us a brief wave before hurrying to the privy.

"Since you're up, Declan, I need some firewood," she called out once she emerged. "Time to make the donuts," she moaned theatrically.

Declan and I were too young to get a cultural reference from the 1980s, but my dad used to say that all the time before

145

heading off to work, and the memory nearly made me cry with longing for my parents, as well as with a visceral desire for a cup of Dunkin' Donuts coffee and a double chocolate donut.

"I'd kill for a donut," Declan said under his breath, and headed toward the chopping block.

As expected, Declan's suggestion that we look for Mark was met with opposition, but eventually, a few people agreed to participate in the search, most likely because they hoped that if it were them who went missing, we'd come looking for them, not because they felt any sympathy for Mark. Also, it was a way to get out of doing their chores, and who could blame them? Iris, Theresa, and Shelby remained behind. Likewise, Tim and Jesse decided to attend to their morning chores.

The rest of us split into several groups and went off. I went with Declan because I really didn't care to be alone in the woods with Sam and Glen, and Gael seemed to be avoiding meeting my gaze since his confession by the creek. I was also ashamed to admit that I didn't want to be stuck with Ed. I wasn't in the mood for his preachy comments and glad that he had paired up with Nicky. We agreed to meet back at the settlement in about an hour, whether we found Mark or not.

"You really don't trust Glen and Sam, do you?" Declan asked as we set off.

I shrugged. I didn't want to admit to actively mistrusting other contestants, especially if our conversation was being recorded, but Declan was right. I always made sure to give those two a wide berth.

"They give me a bad vibe as well," Declan said. "I can't help but wonder what they're running from."

"What makes you think they're running from anything?"

"I think everyone here was running from something. They just never realized that what they were running toward would be considerably worse."

The words hung between us as we entered the shadow of the woods and lost sight of Glen and Sam.

# Chapter 29

## Glen

I hate this fucking island and everyone on it. Still, the show couldn't have come at a better time. Things were getting a little too hot at home, and difficult questions were being asked. I thought I'd been really careful and had covered my tracks, but even though my boss was fucking clueless, even he eventually realized that something was up. Took the moron nearly two years, though, because I had created an eBay account with a name and IP address that couldn't be traced back to me and transferred the money into an offshore savings account as soon as the payments came through.

I really don't think they can trace the stolen goods back to me unless they follow the money, but for that they'd need a warrant. I figured that disappearing for six months would turn the spotlight onto the other employees, who are running their own scams and are probably nowhere near as careful. I've always been good at creative accounting, and I never got greedy. A box here, a crate there. Inventory that never quite made it into the system or was written off as damaged or returned even though it had never left the warehouse.

Over the years, I'd built up a nice little nest egg. The plan is to retire to the Cayman Islands. God, I love it there. It's not like the other Caribbean islands, where all the cruise ships stop and the beaches are overrun with overfed, sunburned tourists who act like they own the place. The Caymans are classy, and expensive. A little house on the beach, a boat, an occasional fling with a pretty lady, and I'll be happy as a clam.

And speaking of flings, maybe I can even manage to have a little fun here. If Theresa and Iris were the last women on Earth, I'd probably get calluses on my hands from jerking off, but Shelby, Nicky, and Natalie are prime cuts of beef in this sorry little meat market. Nicky especially. Shelby is too whiny and probably wants to be loved, and now that she's knocked up, I'm completely turned off, even if she gets an itch she'd be willing to let me scratch.

Natalie looks like the sort of woman who thinks she should only have sex with a guy if they're in a serious relationship. She's cute, but too prudish for my taste. I bet she creams herself at the thought of Gael. It should be illegal to be so pretty. Even Brendan has the hots for him but tries to hide it. The poor bastard really got the short end of the stick when he came on the island, since there's no one for him to cuddle with. If I got horny enough, I'd let him blow me. I bet he really knows what he's doing, given how long he's been practicing.

Nicky would be my first choice, though. She's a fine piece of ass, and I bet she likes to be in charge. I don't mind. She can do whatever she wants as long as I get to fuck her in the end or watch her suck me off with those gorgeous bee-stung lips. I get hard just thinking about it. I wonder if she ever takes it up the ass. That'd be one way to get my rocks off without worrying about getting her pregnant. Last thing I need is a kid.

I don't think Nicky likes me, though. I see the way she looks at Tim. I guess she prefers his brand of brooding masculinity. Tim is married, but when did that ever stop anyone? Still, I always did enjoy the chase, no matter how long it took, and in this miserable place, we have nothing but time.

# Chapter 30

## Natalie

Declan and I hadn't gone very far into the woods when we found Mark. He must have been sitting with his back to a tree trunk, but by the time we got to him, he had slid sideways, and his nose was almost touching the ground. Mark's limbs were stiff, his unseeing gaze fixed on the ground.

"Jesus!" Declan exclaimed. He didn't immediately approach the body but stood well back and surveyed the scene.

"How long do you think he's been dead?" I asked, glad of an excuse not to get too close.

"A while."

"I don't see any wounds or bruises," I observed.

"No, but there's something on his mouth and chin." Declan moved a few steps closer and peered at the ground beneath Mark's face. "I think he might have vomited. And there's something…"

I stayed back while Declan approached the body and sat on his haunches, staring at the ground.

"What is it?" I asked.

"He scratched something out next to his body. Looks like H-E-L. I think he was trying to write HELP. His index finger is covered in dirt."

I sighed heavily. If Mark had died before he could finish spelling the word, chances were he had known help wouldn't arrive in time.

"I don't think he really expected anyone to help him," Declan said. "I think this message has another purpose."

I thought I knew what Declan meant but needed to clarify. "What do you think his intention was?"

"He wanted to let us know that this wasn't suicide."

"Is it possible that it was, and he changed his mind at the last minute?" I asked.

Declan shook his head. "I really don't think so. I'm not an expert on poisons, and I have no idea how long or how much it would take to kill a grown man, but I would think that if you were trying to kill yourself, you'd take a lot, just to be sure. Given that Mark hadn't eaten since dinner the night before he stormed off, his stomach would have been empty, and the poison would have acted quicker than it would if there was food and liquid to dilute the toxins. Mark would most likely have died very near where he had ingested the poison."

I looked around. Mark was at the base of a tall pine, one of many in that part of the forest. The ground was littered with pine needles, dry pinecones, and twigs, but there were no leafy plants. Mark's hands, except the index finger, were also fairly clean. There were no traces of crushed leaves or berries. I inched a little closer and peered at the substance on Mark's lips and chin. It looked like he might have vomited, then frothed at the mouth as death approached.

Declan followed my gaze, but he was looking for something else. "I don't see any evidence of a struggle or of the body being dragged. Nothing looks disturbed. There are no broken branches or tracks in the underbrush, and there are no traces of blood. Had the ground been wet, we might have been able to make out footprints, but it hasn't rained in days, so there's no way to tell if anyone else was here. Does anything look suspicious to you?"

"No," I replied with one hundred percent certainty. Everything looked precisely as it should in a forest.

"Do you know anything about poisons?" Declan asked.

"I can identify signs of poisoning in a patient, but it's impossible to tell what Mark ingested since I wasn't here to see the reaction. Also, I'm more familiar with the effects of household poisons since that's what people are more likely to ingest, either by accident or by design. These days people rarely use little-known plants to knock someone off."

"Little known to you and me, but someone like Theresa would know a poisonous plant if she saw one."

"Yes, she probably would, but what reason would Theresa have to kill Mark?"

Declan nodded. "Theresa and Mark had virtually no dealings with each other. I never even saw them speaking to each other."

I looked away for a moment, wondering if I should tell Declan what was on my mind.

"What is it?" Declan asked, noting my consternation.

"There are others who would know about poisons."

"Who do you mean?"

"Tim, for one. Also Sam."

"Okay, I can understand Sam. A farmer would probably be able to identify poisonous plants, but why Tim? Do you think because Tim is Native American he would automatically have that knowledge?"

"I think certain knowledge is passed from generation to generation. People who have a history of living off the land would certainly know which plants and mushrooms were dangerous and which were safe to touch and eat. I'm not pointing the finger at Tim, I'm simply saying that he might know more than we do."

Declan nodded. "Mark called Tim a filthy mongrel. At that moment, even I wanted to kill him."

"The person who had the most obvious reason to want Mark dead is Shelby, but Shelby never left the house yesterday, or today."

"Who was unaccounted for yesterday?" Declan asked.

"Nearly everyone, except Iris. She hardly leaves. I think she feels safer within the confines of the settlement."

"So aside from Shelby and Iris, anyone could have found an opportunity to poison Mark."

I nodded. "Yes, they could have."

Declan ran a hand through his hair in frustration. "Without a discernable motive, it's impossible to say who might have wanted him dead."

Declan looked at me as if he expected me to offer him a motive for Mark's murder, but I had no idea. Mark's conceit was irritating, but until his nasty outburst the day before, he'd gotten along with everyone, and no one seemed to dislike him enough to top the list of suspects.

"Natalie, would you mind getting Tim? I don't want to touch the body until he's had a chance to see it."

"Of course."

I was glad to get away. As much as I had hated Mark yesterday, seeing him like this had absolutely gutted me. I felt sick to my stomach and braced my hand against a tree as I vomited my breakfast. I think what had disturbed me the most was the insects I had seen crawling over Mark's face and into his nose. There was something profoundly terrifying about seeing a person who had been alive only yesterday as nothing more than a decaying carcass. I was sick again, then wiped my mouth with the back of my hand and set off in search of Tim.

Tim was walking on the beach with Brendan. They were heading back to the settlement from the opposite direction. I explained what Declan and I had discovered but didn't share any of our observations. Declan would not want Tim to be predisposed when he examined the body and the scene, and Brendan was something of a gossip. The suppositions would come thick and fast once he told everyone what I had said.

Tim asked Brendan and me to return to the settlement, which we were happy to do. I didn't want to see Mark's body again, although I was sure I'd have to. At this stage, no one really expected an intervention from Varlet, so we would have to deal with the preparation of the body for burial. I don't think any of us could have imagined when we arrived on the island that we'd be leaving behind a cemetery.

News of Mark's death spread within moments, and we all settled around the table since it was comforting to share our shock and disbelief rather than process it on our own. Even Shelby came out and sat at the end of the bench, her face resembling a boxer's after a losing match. She didn't comment, and we didn't ask how she felt. We were more worried about the manner of his death and its impact on our little community.

Declan hadn't asked me to involve myself in the investigation, but I couldn't help but dissect everyone's reactions to the news, looking for anything that seemed off or staged. To my great disappointment, I didn't notice any sentiments that rang untrue. Everyone seemed stunned and genuinely upset, if not for Mark then for once again finding themselves in this situation. They were frightened, and had every right to be, since no one believed Mark could have killed himself.

"Are you sure you didn't see a wound?" Iris asked again.

"We didn't turn the body over," I replied woodenly. "But from what we could see, there were no signs of an attack or any blood."

"He could have been killed elsewhere on the island and left beneath that tree," Ed said.

"I don't think so," I said. "He tried to leave a message where we found him, so he was still alive. And there was no evidence of him being dragged."

"It had to be an animal or some insect," Brendan said. "Maybe he was bitten."

"Or maybe it was suicide," Jesse said quietly.

"You need something to kill yourself with," Nicky pointed out. "He didn't hang or shoot himself. He didn't drown. So how would he have done it?"

"Maybe he consumed something poisonous," Shelby said, speaking up for the first time.

"Theresa, have you seen any poisonous plants on your foraging trips?" Sam asked.

"There are poisonous plants everywhere. You don't have to go far to find something that can kill you," Theresa replied.

"But have you seen any specific plants here?"

"Yes, I have. And mushrooms as well," Theresa said. "Amanita muscaria, for one. They're highly poisonous."

"I don't even know what they look like," Nicky said.

"They're the ones with the spotted red caps. I always found it bizarre that children's books frequently depict poisonous mushrooms in their illustrations. They're meant to look colorful and quaint, but in reality, they're killers. So is mistletoe," Theresa added. "Another quaint tradition that can kill."

"Perhaps you should examine the scene," Ed suggested. "See if there are any poisonous plants or fungus nearby."

"I'll gladly help," Theresa said. "But we should probably wait for Declan and Tim to return."

The two officers returned to the settlement about an hour later, groaning under the weight of Mark's lifeless body. They took him to the corncrib, as they had Will's remains, and then asked me to take another look since now I could examine him properly. I dreaded the task but nodded and followed Declan to the shed. Declan helped me to undress Mark, but I didn't see anything that aroused my suspicion. I still believed Mark had been poisoned.

"Can we speak privately?" Tim asked as he entered the shed behind us. "Too many people can hear us if we confer in here."

The three of us walked down to the beach, where we could see anyone approaching. It was such a peaceful scene, and so at odds with the almost crippling anxiety that was gnawing at my insides. I looked out toward the horizon, hoping against hope to see a vessel headed for the island, but there was nothing, just an uninterrupted expanse of sea and sky.

"I think Mark might have been poisoned with jimsonweed," Tim said once he was sure we couldn't be overheard.

"What's that?" Declan asked.

"It's a toxic plant that was sometimes used in tribal rituals. It causes hallucinations in small amounts, but if ingested can be fatal."

"Would Mark have been familiar with the plant?" I asked.

"He may have been," Tim replied. "Mark was knowledgeable on a variety of subjects."

"Are you suggesting he took it himself?"

"Without a forensic team, a postmortem, or a toxicology work-up, we don't have enough physical evidence to know anything for certain," Tim replied. "But he could have."

"I'm only a nurse, but I worked in a psychiatric practice before taking a job at a school. Nothing about Mark suggested that he was suicidal. He lost it with Shelby because he felt duped and she had humiliated him in front of other people on a day when he was already upset about the chickens, but someone as narcissistic as Mark would reason it away and decide it wasn't his fault. He'd say that he was provoked. He had reacted irrationally. His emotions got the best of him."

I took a deep breath and continued, needing to make Tim and Declan understand that I did not agree with the possibility that Mark had killed himself. Not for a moment.

"Look, I'm sure he regretted his outburst, and especially the physical violence, since it showed a side of him he would rather have kept hidden from the world, but I can't imagine that he'd just go off and kill himself by chewing on some plant he'd probably never seen in real life."

Tim nodded. "I tend to agree with you, Natalie. Mark was lapping this all up, until Shelby made him look like a fool. Angry, upset, maybe even ashamed, but suicidal? I don't see it," he said forcefully. "Mark was in the woods for hours, and plenty of people left the settlement during the course of the day. Someone might have fed him the poison."

"Would he not have realized he was being poisoned?" Declan asked.

"The thing about jimsonweed is that it doesn't taste bad. You wouldn't immediately suspect foul play," Tim said.

"But why would anyone want to kill him?" I asked. "The one person he hurt directly was Shelby, and she remained in the house all day. Who else would have a motive?"

"I don't know, but I don't think it was the same person that killed Will. Totally different MO," Tim replied. "Perhaps this is an opportunistic killer who uses whatever he or she can find. A rock with Will. A poison with Mark."

"That would imply that there's a serial killer among us," Declan said.

Tim smiled wryly. "So, what's better, one psychotic killer or two separate killers in a group of fourteen?"

"Either possibility is terrifying," I said.

"It is," Declan agreed. "Where do we go from here?"

"I'm going to nominate you to be the next governor at dinner tonight," Tim said.

"Why me?" Declan asked, clearly surprised.

"Because you're a cop. People accept your authority."

"You're a cop too."

Tim rolled his eyes. "First of all, they don't see me as a real cop. And second, they don't want their governor to be some dude off the reservation." He lifted a hand to stop Declan from replying. "Look, we can debate this all day, but deep down, you know I'm right. People have their prejudices and always will. They accepted Will because he was a middle-aged white judge. They voted for Mark because he was a middle-aged white guy with a respected degree. People like me don't really fit into their vision of America."

"Look, Tim, I will grant you that we all come from different realities, but the reality I've seen is even more violent and dangerous than that of your people, at least in this century," Declan argued. "I don't want to be the governor. I would much rather observe from the outside and try to figure out where the danger lies than paint a big red target on my back."

"Are you saying Will and Mark were murdered because they were governors?" I asked.

"I'm not saying that, but we had two governors, and they're both dead. I don't want to be the third," Declan replied.

"We need a leader, Declan, or we will descend into complete anarchy," Tim pointed out. "Hunger, fear, and loss of hope can lead the sanest person down the path of violence. The people back there need to believe that someone has a plan and knows what they're doing."

"What about Jesse?" I stepped in. "Jesse owns a big ranch in Montana. He employs many people and deals with the everyday issues that arise when managing a business. He has leadership skills and an air of authority. I also think he's a much nicer person than either Will or Mark were. He treats everyone equally and with respect."

"That's a great idea, Natalie," Declan said. "I think we should nominate Jesse and see how the rest react."

"We need an alternative choice," Tim said.

Declan shrugged. "No one stands out. Ed is too mild-mannered. Brendan and Gael will never get the votes. And Glen and Sam are not even an option as far as I'm concerned."

"What about Iris?" I interjected. "Iris is capable and sympathetic. People would get behind her."

"That would be historically inaccurate," Tim pointed out. "Jamestown never had a female governor."

"Look, at this stage, we don't even know if there's still a show," Declan said. "We've had no communication from Varlet since the day we were left here. I think being historically inaccurate is the least of our worries."

"I second that," I said. "Let's offer the job to Jesse and Iris and see which one of them wins."

"Sounds like a plan," Tim agreed.

"And what do we tell everyone about Mark?" I asked. "They're already in a panic."

"I think we should tell them we believe Mark died by suicide," Tim said. "It may or may not be true, but at least it will keep the rest of the group from completely losing their shit. To have two murders in less than two months is enough to terrify anyone."

"Agreed," Declan said.

Tim strode toward the settlement, but Declan and I hung back, neither ready to return to the unsavory reality.

# Chapter 31

"Declan, I think we need to start thinking ahead," I said as we strolled along the sand, leaving two sets of footprints that were very clearly male and female. "And I don't mean to our next leader or Mark's burial."

"Go on."

"We have no way to contact anyone on the mainland, and no way to get off this island."

"Yeah, I've noticed that," Declan replied sourly.

"We have an IT specialist and a carpenter. Perhaps we should turn our attention to them if we hope to get out of here."

Declan looked out over the calm water, his facial muscles tense and his shoulders squared against the tide of tragedy. "I've been thinking the same thing, but I'm really not sure that there's anything Gael can do without electricity or an internet connection. And Brendan is a hipster from Brooklyn. What does he know about building a boat?"

"You won't know until you ask," I said.

Declan turned to face me and smiled ruefully. "I have asked. The best Brendan can do is build a raft. Would you feel safe getting onto a raft and trusting your welfare to the vagaries of the ocean? We don't even know exactly where we are."

"We're in the Atlantic, correct?"

"Yes."

"So, we know that's east," I said, pointing toward the sun that had risen a few hours before. "That's west." I gestured toward the woods behind me.

"And?" Declan asked.

"We can figure out which way is the mainland."

"Can we? Or we can make a mistake and sail further out into the ocean."

"Surely, between all of us, we can figure something out. We all have such diverse professional backgrounds. We must know something useful."

"What do a cattle rancher from Montana and a preacher from Pittsburgh know of building rafts?" Declan asked. "And what do a homeopath and a chef know of geography? Our skill set is useless," he declared darkly.

"Are you saying we're completely helpless?"

"I'm saying we shouldn't do anything rash."

"We might get rescued if someone spots us," I tried again.

"Natalie, how many passing ships have you seen since we've been here?" Declan asked.

"None," I admitted, recalling our conversation from a few weeks ago.

"Exactly. This island must be too far offshore for some random fisherman to drift past. Given the flora and fauna and the temperatures for this time of year, all we can safely deduce is that we're aligned with one of the middle states. Virginia, North Carolina, maybe."

"Well, if that's east and we sail west, we should reach the shore," I said stubbornly. "Because sailing east would take us further out into the Atlantic."

"Are you willing to risk your life to prove that? I'm a cop from Chicago. I'm no mariner. I know nothing of navigation. And it'd have to be a pretty big raft to hold more than a dozen people."

"It doesn't have to. It can hold two," I said. "Someone could go for help."

"Who?"

"You," I blurted out before even considering Declan's question.

"I'm not leaving you here on your own with a killer, or possibly two, on the loose."

"Tim can go, and one other person."

"And if something happens and they drown, we'll never get rescued, and two more people will be dead."

"Well, when you put it that way," I grumbled.

"I don't want to be responsible for anyone's death, Natalie. If they say they want to build a raft and go, it's on them. If I propose it and then send someone other than myself, then I'm to blame."

"You are not. You'll be asking for volunteers."

"And who among us is qualified to sail a raft?" Declan demanded. "This is not a movie with Tom Hanks. This is real life. And in real life, there are very few happy endings."

"I need hope, Declan," I said. "Without any hope of getting out of here, I feel I might…" I wasn't sure exactly what I wanted to say, but Declan stopped walking and stared down at me. He looked stricken by my confession.

"Natalie, please don't give up. We will get out of here, but we need to be smart, and careful. I don't believe Mark killed himself. I think someone saw an opportunity to knock him off, but I couldn't tell you who. Unless we pen everyone in and keep a watch on everyone's activities, anyone can do anything. We have an unlocked armory. If someone decides to arm themselves, we'll have no way to stop them, yet I can hardly declare that I will supervise access to the muskets. I don't have that authority."

"Saying we must be careful is hardly a solution," I replied.

"You're right. It's woefully inadequate, but until we figure out what's going on, it's the only thing we can really do. Don't go anywhere by yourself. Stick with people you trust. Who do you trust?" he asked, watching me intently.

I considered the question. "I have no reason to actively distrust anyone, but the only person I truly trust is you," I said simply.

"What about Tim?"

I shook my head. "Tim is angry and frustrated and feels defined by his heritage. And we can't be certain that he didn't poison Mark. He didn't deny having knowledge of poisonous plants. In fact, he admitted to it."

Declan nodded. "What about the others?"

"I don't know enough about any of them to trust them. All we have is their word, and since we have no way to verify anything, the only thing we have to rely on is our gut instinct."

"What does your gut instinct tell you?" Declan asked. I hadn't realized he'd moved closer to me, and his head now blocked the sun.

"My instinct is telling me to seek support because it's too scary to be on my own," I said softly.

Declan placed his hands on my arms and looked deep into my eyes. "You will have my support, no matter what happens. You are the only person on this island I am willing to put my faith in."

I raised my face to look at him, and he lowered his head and kissed me. It wasn't a hungry kiss, but a tender admission of affection. A question Declan needed me to answer. He understood that I was horrified by what had happened, deeply worried about our immediate future, and emotionally vulnerable, and he was asking for my unequivocal consent to go further. Had we been back home, I might have clung to him and imagined a future in which we could be a couple, but given the circumstances, I wasn't

164

in a place where I could contemplate a romantic relationship. I didn't trust myself to make the right decision, and perhaps I didn't entirely trust Declan's motives.

I had no doubt that he meant what he'd said and that he had feelings for me, but he was on an island with a grand total of five women, two of them much older than him. Just as I longed for support, so did he, but Declan had a life back home, possibly a partner he hadn't told me about, and what would happen once we were back in the real world? Would Declan simply return to Chicago and pick up where he'd left off? Would he expect me to follow him or just walk away, our relationship having served its purpose? Now wasn't the time to address these questions or to embark on an emotional roller coaster that would cloud my judgment at a time when I needed my wits about me.

I gently pushed Declan away. "I need time," I said, and lowered my gaze so I wouldn't have to see the disappointment in his eyes.

"I understand. I'm sorry if I overstepped. I didn't mean to make you uncomfortable."

"You didn't. Can we go back now, please?"

"Of course. I'm sorry," Declan said again.

"Me too." And I was. For all of it.

# Chapter 32

After returning to the settlement, I went directly to the vegetable garden. It was the only place I could be alone while remaining surrounded by people. I didn't even pretend to weed but sat with my back to the wooden fence and buried my face in my folded arms. Like most people who are forced to deal with trauma, I had buried the fears that had stemmed from Will's death in order to carry on, but now they all came rushing back and I was even more afraid.

Whoever killed Will had probably used a rock, a weapon they might have picked up moments before the attack, so the murder had most likely been a crime of passion. Mark's death was different. Someone had followed him into the woods, but that someone had not simply ripped off a few leaves from a poisonous plant and told Mark to chew on them. I'd made sure of that. I had looked in Mark's mouth and studied his gums, tongue, and teeth. There were no bits of greenery or any indication that he had eaten a mushroom or berries. I had not seen any undigested particles in his vomit or smelled anything that would appear out of place.

I was certain that whoever had given Mark the poison had done so stealthily and without arousing suspicion, because they had come prepared. One of the contestants—for I was certain that no one had come ashore simply to kill Mark—had probably offered Mark a drink and he had accepted, grateful for their kindness. And as soon as he ingested the poison, it would have been too late. The deed done. The killer had simply removed the contaminated receptacle and gone on their way, leaving Mark to scratch out his final message before he died.

This killing had been premeditated, so chances were that it hadn't been spurred on entirely by Mark's outburst. What, then? Who'd want Mark dead? Until yesterday morning, I hadn't noticed any obvious tensions within the group aside from the basic differences one would expect in any pool of people who were stuck together and came from different walks of life.

And who among us besides Theresa would be knowledgeable about poisons? The answer was that it could be anyone. Just because their choice of occupation didn't revolve around botany didn't mean they weren't aware of which plants were poisonous. Anyone who read murder mysteries would know which poisons could be used to kill one's enemy. Likewise, anyone who enjoyed hiking, fishing, or camping would also know which plants to avoid. Didn't Boy Scouts teach their members about such things?

And the obvious answer was that if someone was planning to commit murder, they could have researched plants native to North America at any time before coming on the show. It would be impossible to make headway into the investigation without isolating the motive, but as far as I knew, no one had one, and they weren't about to reveal their motive now, not when they had committed the perfect crime. And they had committed a perfect crime because I was sure the cameras weren't recording and there would be nothing to connect the killer to Mark's murder.

I didn't realize I was crying until the patch of apron beneath my cheeks became damp. I angrily wiped my eyes and glared at the sky, hoping I'd see a plane that would reassure me that we were still in the twenty-first century and hadn't somehow been transported to the past. God, what I wouldn't give for that magical little rectangle that would allow me to call for help or at the very least contact my family. But even if I had a phone, it wouldn't work, I reminded myself. For one, there was nowhere to charge it, and for another, there was probably no cell tower within miles of the island, so there'd be no service. We were completely, utterly cut off from the outside world, and now there'd been another murder. Which of us would become the next body to be buried in the cemetery?

# Chapter 33

Tim called for attention after everyone finished their meal, yet another stew made of meat I couldn't readily identify, a bit of barley, and beans. It had been neither tasty nor filling, but we had to eat, so everyone had dutifully scarfed it down with the minimum of complaining.

Tim stood and held up his hand, asking for silence. "As you all know, Mark's body was found in the woods today," he began.

"Was he murdered?" Sam demanded.

It was inevitable that everyone would begin to speculate despite Tim's veiled suggestion that Mark's death had been a suicide. No one really believed Mark had been suicidal, even after yesterday's meltdown, and even fewer thought that Mark would have resorted to using some unknown poison. We had plenty of rope, knives, muskets, and an ocean. If Mark had wanted to kill himself, he'd had his pick of available methods.

"At this time, Declan and I can't confirm or deny that Mark was murdered. We simply don't have enough evidence."

"You two are like Dumb and Dumber," Glen snarled. "What can you confirm or deny?"

"I can confirm that you're a total dick," Tim replied calmly. "Does that help?"

Glen made to rise, but Jesse clapped a hand on his shoulder and pushed him back down. "You started it, Glen. Don't dish it out if you can't take it."

Glen had the decency to look chastised. "I'm sorry, guys," he muttered. "We're just all scared and frustrated."

"Don't bring us into it," Nicky said. "If you're going to belittle someone, at least have the courage to own it."

Glen nodded but didn't say anything else.

"As I was saying," Tim continued, "without forensics or toxicology, we can only guess at the cause of death, and as you already know, we believe he died by ingesting poison. Since it's getting warmer, I think it's best we bury him as soon as possible. In the meantime, we think it's important we vote on a new governor."

"It seems to be a life-threatening position," Nicky said bitterly.

"We don't think that either Will or Mark died because they were the governor," Tim said.

"Then why did they die?" Shelby asked. Her voice quavered. Despite Mark's treatment of her, she was deeply upset by his death.

"We don't know, and unless someone has something to share or confess, we're not likely to find out," Declan said. Everyone remained silent.

"Tim and I thought that Jesse or Iris would make an effective leader. What do you guys think?"

Iris raised her hands as if to ward off the very suggestion. "Thank you for the vote of confidence, Declan, but I have enough to do. Preparing meals three times a day is enough of a responsibility, especially when there are only about three ingredients to work with and even those are in short supply."

Jesse looked around the table. "If you think I can help, then I will step up. I have some ideas, if you're interested in hearing them."

"Please," Nicky said. "I would love to hear your ideas, Jesse."

There wasn't a hint of sarcasm in Nicky's voice, and I sensed that beneath the acerbic exterior, she was actually pretty rattled.

Jesse stood and addressed the group. "I know we all have our theories about what's happened and why no one has come even after two contestants have died. Whatever the reason, we need to focus on our own survival. Assuming someone will actually come for us at the end of this ordeal, we still have four months on this island, and unless we replenish our supplies, we'll be playing Hunger Games of our own. I think we should channel all our energies into finding and storing food."

"Jesse is right," Iris said. "By next week, we'll have no more barley, and we're already out of wheat and oatmeal. We still have some dried corn, but it will go quickly, and our own corn has yet to ripen. The vegetable garden is not likely to produce enough to support fourteen—sorry, thirteen people. We need not only food, but we also need nutrients." Iris turned to me. "Natalie, do you know anything about preventing scurvy?"

"Scurvy is prevented with vitamin C," I said.

"Theresa, is there anything on this island that contains vitamin C?"

"Vitamin C can be found in citrus fruits, tomatoes, dark green vegetables, and kiwis. None of which we have," Theresa said. "I will continue to look for spinach. If someone will come with me, maybe I can go further afield and look for wild strawberries. Blueberries and raspberries ripen during the summer months, so maybe we'll find a few bushes, if we're lucky."

"Have you seen any blueberry or raspberry bushes?" Shelby asked. Theresa shook her head.

"What else do you suggest, Jesse?" Tim asked.

"I suggest that every day, the men go fishing and hunting. Anything we bring back will keep hunger at bay a while longer. Theresa and a companion should go foraging, and the other three ladies should remain in the settlement to see to the daily domestic chores." Jesse smiled ruefully. "Sorry, ladies, I know that sounds awfully sexist, but we still need to eat and have clothes to wear."

Our clothes were becoming threadbare from constant use, and whenever we had free time, we darned hose and sewed up rips in our chemises and skirts, and the men's shirts and breeches.

"Theresa, is there anything we can use as a mosquito repellent?" Shelby asked. "The little suckers are eating me alive."

Theresa just shrugged, but Tim stepped in. "There are many natural mosquito repellents, but we don't have any of them. Lemon and eucalyptus oil, tea tree oil, even garlic will work."

"Cedar and pinon wood repel mosquitoes," Gael said. "I don't think there's any pinon here, but maybe I can find cedar. The smoke will drive the bugs away."

Tim looked thoughtful. "We could crush pine needles into animal fat and make a cream. That might help."

"I'll slather myself with whatever you give me," Shelby said.

"You have to be careful, Shelby," I said quietly. "The cream will get absorbed into your skin and might harm the baby."

Shelby's face fell. "I didn't think of that," she said.

"I'm not pregnant, but that sounds absolutely disgusting," Nicky said.

"Most things we use are disgusting when you realize what goes into them," Tim said. "Did you know that they use beaver ass juice to simulate raspberry flavor in ice teas and other products? They call it 'natural flavors.'"

"No way!" Nicky cried. "That's gross."

"Personally, I'd like to know who discovered that ass juice tastes like raspberries," Glen mused. "Dude must have been one sick motherfu—" His voice trailed off when he caught sight of Ed's thunderous face. Ed despised profanity and made sure everyone knew it. "Person," Glen finished.

"Woodsmoke keeps mosquitoes away," Jesse said. "If you remain at the settlement and stay close to the fire, you'll be fine. You shouldn't go into the woods anyway. There are ticks and woodlice. Being pregnant, you're vulnerable."

"Thank you," Shelby said. "I'll stay here."

"Brendan, how are those lobster traps coming along?" Jesse asked.

"Two are ready."

"Anyone want to keep an eye on the traps?" Jesse inquired.

"I can do it," Gael said. "It's preferable to hunting or fishing."

"Are you kidding?" Sam exclaimed. "You don't like to fish?"

Gael shook his head. "I'll leave the fishing to you and Glen. I don't have the patience to sit there for hours, hoping something will bite."

"I'll happily fish from morning till night," Sam said. "Beats having to do chores."

"Well, we know who's going hunting," Nicky said as she smiled at Tim and Declan. "If not for you two, we'd be eating grass by now."

"Please don't kill the fawns," Jesse said. "If you do, you will wipe out the deer population on the island."

"Are you implying that we might still be here when that happens?" Ed asked, his face drooping like melting wax.

"I'm not implying anything, Ed, but if we do find ourselves still on the island come winter, we'll starve without venison."

"Oh, God," Shelby moaned, her hands going to her belly. "I need to get home. I want my mom."

"I think at this point, we all want our moms," Brendan said miserably.

"I know I'm not your mom, Shelby, but I'm here for you. Whatever you need," Iris said.

Shelby nodded and sniffled. "Thank you. I don't know what I would do without you all."

Theresa reached out and patted Shelby's hand in what she probably thought was a comforting manner. Then the conversation moved on to more practical topics once again.

We hadn't taken a vote, but it seemed that Jesse was our new leader. I liked him and thought him knowledgeable and hoped that he would be able to defuse some of the panic that was growing among us like a cancer with his no-nonsense suggestions.

Once we returned to our house, it was unanimously decided that we would leave the windows unshuttered that night. The house was stiflingly hot, and the lack of even a sliver of light made us all feel like we were trapped in a coffin. Given that tomorrow Mark would be buried, the fear was uncomfortably real.

Theresa brought a few small pine branches and spread them around the room to keep the mosquitoes away. I had no idea if they would help, but the fresh, piney smell was a vast improvement on our body odor, so no one complained.

# Chapter 34

## Jesse

I grew up on stories of survival and always hero-worshipped my ancestors, who staked out a few acres of land and went from running a small farm to owning half the county. I welcome the challenge of helping this disparate group of people through the ordeal we find ourselves in the midst of. As long as we have food, water, and shelter, there's no reason to panic. We'll be just fine. And if Varlet is still watching and hoped to record our helplessness and desperation and show it to the bored, desensitized viewers who want to watch someone's breakdown on TV, I will not give them the satisfaction of being the one who falls apart. I've withstood greater storms, and I will not only remain calm and practical, I will win the grand prize and use it to pay the money I owe to the IRS.

I do think it was wise to keep my distance until I knew more about the other contestants and had an opportunity to assess their strengths and weaknesses. I pride myself on being a good judge of character, but this group didn't fill me with confidence when we first arrived and inspires even less trust now. The contestants range from shifty and secretive to arrogant and somewhat lost, and now that we've had two fatalities, it's becoming more difficult to imagine that the deaths might have been tragic accidents. Declan and Tim certainly don't think so, but I am not about to take their word as gospel. They have little to go on, and both suffer from something of a hero complex.

I refuse to give in to panic. I've seen plenty of death in my time on the ranch, but I don't intend to become the next victim, nor do I want to see those I'm partial to get hurt. Declan, Tim, and Brendan are useful members of the group, as are Iris and Theresa. And Natalie is not only lovely but has that air of quiet competence and serious intelligence that I find so alluring. Nicky is a hard worker and isn't afraid to speak her mind, even if her opinion differs from the rest of the group, which I respect.

The rest of them get my hackles up, but I hope to see them safely through the rest of this failed experiment and intend to put their skills to good use. Ed doesn't contribute much, but people like to have a man of the cloth close at hand. It makes them think God is watching. Glen and Sam love to fish, and Gael doesn't mind walking miles to check the traps. Any supplies they bring back will be most welcome. Shelby was purely ornamental, but now we must all work extra hard to keep her safe and well fed.

Given the number of ranch hands I've gone through over the years, I've definitely worked with worse. All these people need is a guiding hand and a competent leader.

# Chapter 35

# Declan

I woke up with a start and knew I wouldn't be able to get back to sleep. The house was hot, and although by this point we all slept naked beneath the rough linen sheets, I was still sweating. I reached for my shirt, which was long enough to cover all the pertinent parts, and stepped outside into the moonlit night. Although I would have loved to walk down to the beach and take a midnight swim, I didn't think wandering around by myself was the wisest thing I could do, so I settled for sitting on the bench, my back against the wall of the house, my face raised to the heavens.

Ever since I was a child, I had found solace in looking at the sky, but tonight, the cold, distant stars did little to calm me. We were entering *Lord of the Flies* territory, and it was just a matter of time until the next body showed up. We had no concrete evidence, but I wholeheartedly agreed with Natalie. Mark wasn't the sort to kill himself. He was too vain, too arrogant to ever take such a step. The only way a man like Mark would kill himself was if he felt he had absolutely no other recourse and suicide was the lesser of two evils. I didn't think Mark had been anywhere near such desperation. He had been angry, frustrated, humiliated, but not hopeless or scared out of his wits. In a few days, if he'd apologized profusely enough, the incident would have been, if not forgotten, at least not as fresh in everyone's minds, and with time, he might have found a way to redeem himself.

No, Mark had been murdered. Just as Will had. Someone on this island was picking us off one by one, and it was time to get off this lethal carnival ride. And it would be up to me to figure out how to do that, since no one seemed to be putting forth any practical ideas. Everyone was angry and scared, but on some level, most of them probably still believed that we would be picked up by Varlet come September and this was somehow all part of the plan. I might have bought into that idea if I hadn't found and examined the corpses myself. I know a dead body when I see one, and I'm pretty sure no one who was playacting would permit us to bury them.

If Varlet had planned to take out the contestants one by one to boost the suspense, I didn't think this was what we were dealing with here. It would be both easier and safer to have the contestants vote on who got booted off the island if they failed to pull their weight. In fact, that would make it easier to determine the winner. But I didn't think we were playing the game anymore. This was way too real, and all too terrifying, since we had no idea what we were dealing with.

As I looked at the stars, I recalled that I had been dreaming before I woke, and I now remembered the dream was about Jake McDowell. Jake was one of the IT guys at my station in Chicago, and a more irritating person would be hard to find. He was always either complaining or lecturing, and we all avoided him like the proverbial plague. But in my dream, Jake had been telling me something. Urging me to remember. What was it?

It took some time for small bits of the dream to finally return to me, but then I finally pieced together Jake's message—or more accurately, the wake-up call from my subconscious that had arrived in the form of Jake. I sat up straighter, grateful for the sudden moment of clarity. Like most people of my generation, I was always attached to some device, but I rarely gave much thought to how they worked or where the information went. The cloud, cyberspace, ether. Who really knew? In my dream, Jake had been urging me to focus on the practical. I think I actually groaned out loud at my own stupidity.

In the two months we'd been on the island, I had never actually seen a camera, not in our house, not in the trees, and not in any of the communal spaces within the settlement. But if there were cameras on the island, they had to be connected to a power source. If they ran on batteries, they'd all be dead within a few days of our arrival. That was a possibility, since there was no evidence that anything was being recorded or transmitted, but that theory didn't make any sense. If this whole thing was some elaborate hoax, then what was the point? And who would benefit

177

by spending all this money to recreate a seventeenth-century colony and bringing us all here if there was no guaranteed return on investment?

Whatever was happening here had been orchestrated and funded by someone, and in order to keep an eye on their investment, they had to know what was going on. Tim and I had walked the length and breadth of the island numerous times but had never seen anything that might house a generator or any sort of power station. There were no electricity poles or cables of any sort, which meant that the only way the cameras could be powered was by a source that was underground. What Jake had been telling me in my dream was that I should question Gael.

Now that I thought of it, it made perfect sense. Gael was a techie, a younger, hipper, more personable version of Jake. He would know this. Why had he not said anything or tried to discover how the cameras operated on his own? Was it because he still believed we were participating in a reality show, or could it be because it suited his purpose to keep us in the dark? Was it possible that Gael was actually a Varlet employee sent here to maintain the equipment? If he was, surely he had a way to call for help, especially in view of the fact that two people were now dead. And if he wasn't connected to Varlet, then what was he up to?

In the past, I'd tended to go in guns blazing, but I thought I should think this through and then discuss it with Tim before confronting Gael. Perhaps there was a reasonable explanation and cornering the man would only create more unnecessary tension. I had time, so I would keep an eye on him for a few days.

Tired at last, I went back in the house and tried to sleep. As I started to drift off, my mind turned to Sam, who, like Glen, gave off some very unsavory vibes.

# Chapter 36

## Sam

Sometimes I wonder if it was really even a crime. I mean, the soil in the United States is layered with the relics of its history. Dig anywhere, and you'll find lead balls, buttons from Civil War era uniforms, and unmarked graves of people who were either once revered or dumped into an out-of-the-way hole. People were interred that way for many reasons, especially during the influenza epidemic of 1918. It was a way to avoid contagion, to stop the spread of the killer disease. Both my great-grandparents died just that way. They were twenty and twenty-one, and they left behind a six-month-old baby, my grandfather. I don't see anyone making a big deal about their hasty burial because they were farmers, people history wasn't overly interested in unless there was a famine, in which case they either became heroes or scapegoats.

I love being a farmer. Working the land, watching things grow. These are the things that bring me satisfaction. But if I had reported that Native American burial ground I'd come across, I'd never get a moment's peace. There'd be swarms of reporters, representatives from the local tribe, archeologists, and government officials. The land would be cordoned off and maybe even requisitioned if it was of historical significance. That land is mine. It has been in my family for generations, since before the Civil War, which would probably raise the question of how those people had died and why they were buried on Murphy land. For all I know, they'd had a dispute with one of my ancestors. Or maybe they had carried some illness or died of hunger and my ancestor had allowed them to bury their dead on his property. An act of kindness that would haunt future generations.

Truth is, I don't want to know. I dug up their remains, excavated their weapons and jewelry, and threw it all on the fire. I don't care what happened to them then, and I don't care what happens to them now. But it's concerning that a Native American law enforcement officer is one of the contestants. Was this intentional or simply a weird coincidence? A nod to inclusivity or a way to flush me out and get me to admit to what I did? Good thing I didn't try to sell any of the artifacts, or I would really be in the shit.

This way, they can't connect anything to me unless they go digging in the municipal dump for the blackened pieces of metal and bits of bone that I threw out with the ashes. The fire burned away any traces of DNA, and I wore rubber gloves while cleaning out the furnace. No proof, no foul.

# Chapter 37

# Declan

# June

Despite my best intentions, I wasn't able to keep a lid on my suspicions for long, especially since Tim and I were going hunting and would be alone in the woods for hours. Plenty of time to talk when you're traipsing through the woods.

Tim heard me out, then shrugged. "I have considered a power source, but the cameras must be battery operated. If they were still recording, someone would have come."

"But what sense does that make?" I argued. "They leave us on an island, take a portion of the supplies, then let the camera batteries run out? What's the point of this exercise?"

"I have no idea, but I have a feeling none of this was planned," Tim replied.

"What do you mean?" I demanded. I had been operating under the assumption that this was all part of some mad scheme.

"I mean that there must have been some sort of plan in place, but something happened to derail it."

"Like what?"

"I don't know. Companies go under all the time."

"And you think that if the company went under, they would just leave us here?"

Tim shook his head. "Look, Declan, I've been thinking about this around the clock, like you, but nothing I come up with makes any sense."

"So now what? What do we do?"

"I think we should speak to Gael. You are right about one thing, it's odd that he never mentioned any of this. For someone with his background, it would be second nature to question the tech side of this operation." Tim froze at the sound of an animal moving somewhere in the distance. "Let's park this for now and concentrate on dinner."

We didn't get back to the settlement until the late afternoon. It had to be around four, and we were exhausted from walking all day and then carrying back the deer we'd bagged, but we still had the carcass to butcher before we could call it a day. I was starving, not having eaten anything since breakfast, but there was nothing I could grab and I would have to wait for dinner, which would thankfully be plentiful for a change since we had to use the meat while it was fresh.

The men were sitting around the trestle table, nursing cups of ale, but they came to join us outside the gates as we strung up our kill from a sturdy tree and went to work. We'd have to exsanguinate the carcass and remove the organ sack before getting on with the butchering, and we preferred to do that outside the settlement for obvious reasons.

"Hey, where's Gael?" Tim asked as he glanced around the knot of men who were watching us hungrily.

Glen looked surprised. "We thought he might be with you."

"Why would he be with us?" Tim asked. "Wasn't he going to check the lobster traps? That was hours ago."

Sam turned to Brendan. "I saw you talking to Gael on the beach. Did he say anything about where he was going?"

"There was nothing in the lobster traps," Brendan said. "Gael said he was going to check the traps we'd set in the woods. He was hoping to bring back a rabbit for lunch. I offered to go with him, but he said he preferred to go alone."

"And he never came back?" I asked, wondering why no one had gone to look for him.

"We figured he ran into you two," Ed said. He looked anxiously in the direction we had come from. "You didn't see him?"

"No," Tim said.

"Oh, God," Ed groaned. "I do hope he's all right."

"Should we go look for him?" I asked Tim.

"Give him a little time to come back on his own. There's no reason to think he's in trouble."

"There was no reason to think the other two were either," I pointed out.

Tim sighed heavily. "We've been on our feet since daybreak, and then we carried a dead weight for miles. I don't know about you, but I'm tired and hungry. Gael will have to wait."

I opened my mouth to argue but couldn't bring myself to disagree. We needed to rest and eat.

"The deer is not going to butcher itself, is it?" Iris demanded as she came striding through the gates. "Come on, boys. Let's get this done if you want to eat today."

"Let me help," Jesse offered. "You two look dead on your feet. Go wash up. I'll see to the deer."

"Thank you," Tim said.

"I'll help too," Sam said, and came forward.

I handed him my knife, and Tim and I walked down to the beach, where we stripped off and ran into the waves, the water around us turning a hazy pink as the blood was washed off our hands. The water was still bitterly cold, but it felt good to be clean, and the chill gave me a jolt of energy. By the time we walked through the gates, Iris was already cooking the meat. It would last longer if she added it to stew, but everyone was hungry and unwilling to wait hours for the stew to be ready. Instead, Iris speared chunks of meat onto sticks and invited everyone to roast their portion over the open flames.

My stomach growled with hunger. I'd forgotten what it was like to have enough to eat. At this point, it wasn't even about missing certain foods or craving something sweet. It was that primal hunger that will make you eat anything to get your fill. We didn't have any bread or sides to go with the venison. Just a handful of beans since we were out of everything else. If not for the cow, we wouldn't have any milk products either, but we weren't allowed to drink the milk since there wouldn't be enough left over to make butter and cheese. Cheese made me think of cheeseburgers and pizza and cheese omelets, and I felt even hungrier. I had to stop thinking about food.

As a reward for bringing back the deer, Tim and I got double portions of meat, and I ate mine slowly, savoring every bite. I inwardly apologized to the deer for taking its life and thanked it for keeping us fed. Perhaps I was being fanciful, but since coming to the island, I'd felt more connected to nature and the creatures we shared this space with. Or maybe I was just slowly losing my mind. It was easy enough to do when trapped in a tiny settlement with people you didn't trust.

By the time we finished eating, there were a few hours of daylight left, so the men broke up into groups and set off to look for Gael, leaving the women on their own. I didn't want to alarm Natalie, but I was beginning to worry about leaving them alone. There was no reason to suspect that there was someone on the island with us or that one of the men meant them any harm, but the way things were going, I was worried for their safety and instructed them to shut the gates and lock them behind us. For once, no one argued.

# Chapter 38

## Natalie

After the men left, Iris and Theresa headed to the shed to see to the remaining meat, since if left uncovered it'd be crawling with insects by tomorrow morning, while Nicky, Shelby, and I set to work. Declan had said we shouldn't leave the settlement, so we got some water from the well and set it to boil. Nicky and Shelby would wash the greasy dishes, while I was tasked with cleaning out the deer's intestines. Iris would use the last of the barley and bits of meat and fat mixed with the deer's blood to make sausage. I had never been a fan of sausage at home, and I liked it even less now that I knew how it was made, but I could hardly afford to turn down food. I tried to distract myself from the disgusting task by talking to the other women.

"What do you think happened to Gael?" I asked. I couldn't bring myself to ask if they thought Gael was dead.

"I think he just wandered off," Nicky said. "I can't see anyone targeting Gael. He's always nice to everyone. Maybe he just needed some time on his own."

"And you think someone targeted Will and Mark?" I asked.

"Will's and Mark's comments could be incendiary," Nicky said.

Shelby stared down at the bowl in her hands. She seemed upset, but it was only normal, since she'd had a personal relationship with Mark.

"I think Gael is dead," Shelby said suddenly.

"Why?" Nicky demanded. "What do you know?"

"I don't know anything. I just think someone wants to kill us all. It's like that Agatha Christie book, *And Then There Were None*. We all have sins, and now we're being punished."

"And you think someone will kill you because you had an affair?" Nicky asked.

"I had an affair with a married man. That's a sin," Shelby said stubbornly.

"And I had an affair with a woman," Nicky said. "That's a sin too, in some people's eyes. But there are people out there who shoot up elementary schools and torture animals. Why aren't they here?"

"Maybe they are," Shelby said. "What do we really know about each other?" She fixed me with a baleful look. "What about you, Natalie? What's your sin?"

"I stole a candy bar when I was six," I confessed.

"I doubt that's why you're here," Shelby snapped. "Why were you chosen, Natalie?"

"I honestly don't know. I was surprised when I got the email."

"So, what, you're perfect?"

The conversation was making me uncomfortable, but I could understand her fear and desire to know more about the people around her. "I'm not perfect. I don't have a lot of friends. I have commitment issues, and I'm jealous of my sister. I always have been. I feel like a fuck-up around her."

"Wow, call Dr. Phil!" Nicky exclaimed. "This is sure to boost our ratings."

Shelby gave me a pitying look. "Show me a woman who's not jealous of her sister. I don't have sisters, but I have three female cousins and they're total bitches sometimes, but I love them, and I do envy them their lives from time to time. They're married to nice guys and have adorable children and pretty houses."

"I don't believe in marriage," Nicky said.

"Really? Why not?" Shelby asked, clearly shocked by Nicky's admission.

"Probably because I don't know a single happily married couple. The very idea that you can be happy with one person for the rest of your life is a fantasy. Even if you're happy at the start, what are the chances that you will grow and change in the same direction? It's an impossibility. The person you are at twenty-five is never the person you are at fifty."

"So, what do you suggest?" I asked.

"I think people should simply cohabitate for as long as the relationship works and then separate amicably and move on. No costly divorce. No custody battles. Just two people who agree that it's time to move on for the sake of their personal growth."

"What about the kids?" Shelby asked.

"The kids would probably be a lot happier if their parents remained civil to each other rather than watch them duke it out in court."

"And what if one person wants out and the other doesn't?" I asked. "People don't always feel the same way at the same time, as you have rightly pointed out."

"I think the people who don't want out are coming from a place of fear," Nicky said. "If their partner wants out, then the relationship is clearly not working anymore. They're just afraid to admit it. We are conditioned to want a home and a family. These expectations run deep and have been perpetuated by society for centuries, especially when it comes to women. No matter how successful you are in your own right, you're nothing if you don't have a man and a baby."

"I want a baby and a man," Shelby said miserably. "I just went about getting them in the wrong way and in the reverse order. And now I'm alone, with a baby on the way, and no way of getting off this awful island. My baby and I will probably die here."

"Come on, Shelby," Nicky said, her expression softening. She reached out and put a hand over Shelby's wrist. "We're not going to let you die. We're in this together, and we will be okay."

"How can you be so sure? Gael probably thought he was going to be okay too when he set off this morning. And where is he now?" Shelby cried.

She dropped the bowl she was washing, hiked up her skirts, and ran into the house. I looked at Nicky, not sure if I should follow.

"Let her go," Nicky said. "She's understandably scared and upset. I would be too in her position, but no one can help her make peace with the situation. It's all on her."

"I'm scared too, Nicky," I said, my voice barely above a whisper.

"So am I. I feel like we're in a horror movie and there are audiences out there, sitting on the couch with their popcorn and taking bets on who'll be the next idiot to get themselves killed."

"I don't want to die," I whimpered.

"Neither do I, and I don't plan to. I'm getting out of here alive, come hell or high water."

Personally, I thought hell and high water weren't too far off.

"I wish Ed was a better minister," Nicky said wistfully.

"What do you mean?"

She sighed. "A gifted minister who can gauge the mood of his flock can really make a difference to his parishioners' emotional well-being. He's like a father figure, only he's the sort of father you can trust and admire. Ed means well, but his sermons are uninspired at best, painfully boring at worst. We need to band together if we hope to get home."

"Do you honestly think that a more eloquent sermon would make any difference?"

"I don't know." Nicky sighed. "I guess I'm just grasping at straws, but I do wonder why Ed is here. He never did seem very interested in colonial history."

"Must be for the money," I said.

"Must be, but why did he get picked? Why him?"

"I would hazard to guess that not too many ministers applied. Perhaps it was his occupation that tipped the scale."

Nicky wrinkled her nose and shook her head. "Somehow, I doubt it."

# Chapter 39

## Nicky

I never met my dad. Maybe I would have found him once I got older, but my mother didn't even know who he was. He was one of the countless guys she'd met while working bachelor parties and boys' nights out. My mom wasn't picky. If someone was willing to pay the price, she was willing to roll the dice. And she did roll that die since protection was apparently optional. I have two half-brothers who came into the world in much the same way, by accident. They got out as soon as they could. Barry joined the navy when he was eighteen, and Cory got a full scholarship to the University of West Virginia and never came home after graduation. Why would he? What was there to come home to?

I wish I could say we were close and had bonded as children because we were so neglected and unloved, but we didn't. The boys did their own thing, and I was always expected to babysit since Mom had better things to do. I don't know why she'd even bothered to keep us. She would have been better off on her own, going wherever the promise of a good tip took her.

My counselors and teachers always said I had an attitude. Damn right I did. Hard to be a sweet, trusting girl when no one has ever spared you the time of day, or night. The only time people were nice to me was when they wanted something from me. Our next-door neighbor wanted me to feed her cat while she was away and thought that a thank you was payment enough. The men my mother brought home were sometimes friendly because they thought they had to make nice with the kids if they hoped to impress the woman, but they quickly learned that wasn't the way to my mother's heart. And as I got older, they were nice to me for a different reason. I never fell for any of it. I asked the superintendent of our apartment building to put a lock on my door and locked it whenever anyone came over. That was the only way I felt safe, but I saw that doorknob rattle as they tried to come in.

There was only one man who ever saw the inside of my room—Barry's friend Keith. I still love Keith and wonder if I made a mistake by letting him go, but I wasn't ready to get married at nineteen. I wanted a life for myself, a future that was built on something I was good at. And I am good at what I do because I have nothing holding me back. I have no partner, no children, and no fear of failure. The only thing I fear is the truth coming out. Not only did I lie on my college applications, but I plagiarized an essay I found online. It was that essay that got me in, the perfect combination of emotional and factual, heartbreaking and uplifting. The girl's story wasn't so different from my own, except she had laid it all out so much better. It actually made me cry. Of course, I had to change a few things, in case someone clued in, but I don't think anyone ever questioned my story. I was a shoo-in.

I have discovered my own voice since then, and I'm proud of the work I've done, but if that teenage misdemeanor comes to light, everything I've accomplished will be torn down and Nicky Jackson will get canceled, just like all those other fools who thought they were invincible, and no one would ever come for their privileged ass.

# Chapter 40

## Ed

My calling is to preach the word of God, but what right do I have to speak for Him when I'm an unrepentant sinner? Oh, I confess to any wrongdoing and ask for forgiveness, but then I sin again. I've been doing it for years and nothing has changed. This was my last-ditch attempt to cure myself of the cancer. Here, on this remote island, I'm cut off from the world, and from the temptation that has possessed me for decades. It started with my daddy when I was only thirteen years old. He allowed me to come into the room and bring beer and snacks when he and his buddies were playing poker. We had a secret language, me and him, and I would steal a peek at the other players' cards and signal Daddy. Sometimes he'd act on my intel, other times he wouldn't, so no one would suspect that he was cheating.

It was then that a love of gambling took root in my soul. The thrill of winning and the despair of losing are like nothing else I've ever known, since no joy or sorrow takes one to such dizzying heights or such bottomless lows. Daddy had a talent for the cards, not because he occasionally cheated but because he could read body language the way others can read the Sunday paper. He knew every expression, every tell, and he always kept his head above water. That was how he made his living, not on the fishing boat that brought in just enough catch to keep us in beer and basic groceries. He always took care of my momma too. Whenever he won big, he didn't keep his winnings to himself. He always bought her a little something: a new hat for church, an electric mixer, a pretty new dress to wear to the neighbor's barbecue on the Fourth. Daddy was generous, and it made him happy to spoil his family. He took care of me too. A new basketball, enough quarters to play for an hour at the arcade after school, a weekly allowance with enough left over from my daily expenses to take my girlfriend Latisha out for a burger and a shake on Friday nights.

Soon enough I grew into a man. My daddy died, drowned when a storm came in and he didn't have enough time to make it back to shore. I married Latisha, had me a family, and became the minister of our church. But I never lost my love of gambling. Except I didn't have the knack for cards Daddy did, nor did I want to involve my sons. Instead, I took up a collection at church every Sunday. Dry rot, leaky roof, fund for victims of Hurricane Katrina, help for survivors of the tsunami in Thailand. You name it, I used it. Except the money never went anywhere but in my own pocket. And I lost it all, time and time again.

The donors never found out. I was never called out or shamed, at least not publicly, but my boys figured it out, and they called me to account and gave me a choice. I either pay back every cent I took from those hardworking people who put their faith in me, or they will stand up in church and tell everyone what their daddy did. And it won't end there. I will be disgraced and run out of town, and every local newspaper and social media account will carry the details of my misdeeds.

I never wanted to be on this island. I don't belong here and stand no chance of winning one of the bigger prizes, but fifty thousand dollars would cover my debts and make things right with my boys. And then I will get help for my gambling addiction. See if I don't.

# Chapter 41

## Natalie

It was a clear night, the sky strewn with stars, the gibbous moon as bright as a light bulb. We sat around the fire, both because we drew comfort from its light and the smoke kept the mosquitoes at bay. I was sweltering in my woolens, but it seemed wrong to wear nothing but my chemise, especially since there was nothing underneath. The men began to trickle in about an hour after the sun set. Brendan and Glen came first, followed by Ed, Sam, and Jesse. Declan and Tim came back last. They didn't need to say anything. Their tired, grim faces said it all. They hadn't found Gael. Once everyone was back, they settled next to us and stared into the fire, as if they could divine some message in the leaping flames.

"It's like he vanished," Brendan said at last.

Tim sighed deeply. "Either Gael was murdered and his body hidden, or he has left the island. We found no evidence of either."

"What now?" Nicky asked.

"Tomorrow, we'll resume our search. Until then, we lock the gates and remain together," Declan said.

"What if Gael comes back?" Shelby asked.

"He'll knock on the gates, and we'll let him in," Tim replied patiently.

"He's not coming back," Jesse said. "Either he made sure we couldn't find him or someone else did."

"But who?" Shelby wailed. "Who would do that?"

Declan looked around the firelit faces. His own face was set in stern lines, his gaze speculative and direct. "I'm going to ask you a question, and I would appreciate an honest answer. Did any of you know any of the contestants before coming on the show?"

Everyone shook their heads.

"Are you sure?" Declan asked. "Maybe you had never met in real life but had heard of the person or knew someone who's had dealings with them."

"We're from different parts of the country, Declan. How could we have known each other?" Ed asked.

"With the internet and social media, the world is a lot smaller than it once was."

"What are you suggesting, Declan?" Jesse asked.

"I think that someone really did their homework. They researched each and every one of us and selected people who would clash, either in front of an audience or in private. Whoever killed Will and Mark had a motive, a motive they brought with them to the island."

"If all our secrets were online, then everyone would know what that motive was as soon as they Googled us," Iris said. "It'd be pretty difficult to get away with anything."

"The connection might not be obvious to someone who doesn't know what they're looking for," Declan said.

"I had never met or heard of any of you before meeting you through the show," Jesse said.

"Same here," Brendan said. "Although I might have eaten at Iris's restaurant once."

"Did you?" Iris asked, obviously pleased. "What did you think?"

"It was fantastic, but I never saw you there."

"I would have been in the kitchen."

Clearly not interested in Brendan's restaurant review, Declan turned to the others. "Sam?"

"I've never met any of these people before the show," Sam said. "To be honest, I don't even have a Facebook account. A friend of mine saw the ad and told me about it. He helped me fill out the forms."

"Ed?" Declan asked.

Ed shook his head. "No."

"You know, it is possible that only some people's paths had crossed in real life," Nicky said. "And those people are now gone."

"But how could anyone predict that they would snap?" Iris asked.

"Maybe the producers didn't think they would," Nicky replied. "They might have just been hoping for tension and drama to boost the ratings."

"Perhaps there were certain emotional triggers that were planted," I suggested. "We might not have noticed, but the person who was meant to react did just that."

"You're giving these people way too much credit," Glen said. "They'd have to be diabolical to plan something like that. And even if they had, it'd be of no use to them unless they could profit from it. If all this is being filmed, then they're taking a huge risk since they could be held liable."

"How so?" Ed asked.

"Surely they're breaking the law," Glen said, turning to look from Declan to Tim. "What say you, boys?"

"If it can be proven that the execs at Varlet pitted people against each other deliberately and their actions resulted in death, then they can be charged with being an accessory to murder," Tim said. "And if they made a conscious decision not to alert the authorities, then there are additional charges that can be filed. Failure to report a serious crime. Withholding evidence. Even unlawful imprisonment, since we have no way to call for help and ask to be returned to the mainland. Their show would never air, which is why I strongly believe that no one is watching the footage."

"But if they are not watching the footage, where the hell are they?" Glen demanded angrily.

"That's not something we can figure out without connecting with someone from Varlet," Jesse said. "Whatever happened had to be major, though. I can't imagine the production company would be willing to lose their considerable investment over some minor snafu."

"Two deaths and one missing person are hardly a snafu," Tim retorted.

"I didn't mean to imply that they are, but if Varlet stopped watching, it must have happened before Will's death."

"I agree with you there," Tim said. "I think something happened shortly after our arrival on the island."

"Well, it's been months," Iris cut in. "Surely they've had time to figure things out."

"Maybe they're limiting their liability," Brendan said. "If they claim they haven't seen the footage, then they can't be held accountable for not informing the police."

"Or maybe they have seen the footage and wiped it as soon as Will was murdered. And then they all bailed," Nicky said. "Losing the money is better than losing your freedom."

"And you think they just left us here?" Iris asked, clearly shocked by Nicky's suggestion.

"They could be on a beach in Bora Bora by now or living under a new identity in another country," Sam said bitterly.

"The people at Varlet know that no one will start to ask questions until we fail to reappear in September. That's months from now. Without physical evidence of a crime or those recordings, no one will be able to prove anything. It will be like the mystery of Roanoke Island. People will just say that the colonists mysteriously disappeared or died of starvation," Nicky said.

"There will be plenty of evidence," Declan replied. "There will be a paper as well as a money trail to follow. There will be graves and postmortems carried out. They will be able to figure out exactly what happened."

"But it might be too late for us by then," Shelby whispered. "We could all be dead."

"The only way to remain safe is to stick together," Tim said.

"We can't all watch each other all the time. If we do that, we'll starve," Jesse said.

"As was suggested before," Declan reiterated, "we need a buddy system. We go out in pairs, and no one goes off by themselves. Gael went off unexpectedly and on his own."

Iris suddenly turned to Ed. "Wait a minute. Weren't you with Gael on the beach? I thought I saw you two going off together."

Everyone turned to stare at Ed, who looked like he was going to be sick.

"I'm a strong swimmer, so I went with Gael in case he had any issues in the water, but I didn't go in. I watched him from the beach. After Gael checked the traps, he came out and said he wanted to stay on the beach, so I left," Ed said.

"So, why are we just hearing about this now?" Jesse asked.

"Because there was nothing to tell," Ed snapped. "I never denied going to the beach with Gael."

"You never mentioned it either," Iris retorted. "You hoped I forgot."

"No, I didn't. I simply didn't think it was important. Gael was alive and well when I saw him last," Ed cried. "I had no reason to hurt Gael. I've never met the man, and as you all know, we got along just fine."

"Maybe it was all an act," Iris said.

Ed looked around the group, his gaze panicked. "You were there. You said you saw him going into the woods to check the other traps," he said to Brendan.

"I did," Brendan replied.

"What time was that?" Declan asked.

"Around ten, maybe."

"Where was everyone between ten o'clock and lunch?"

"The women were all accounted for," Iris said. "We were at the settlement."

Declan turned to the men. "Tim and I were hunting. Where were the rest of you?"

"Glen and I were fishing," Sam said.

"I was collecting firewood," Ed said.

"Alone?" Tim asked.

"Yes."

"I was mucking out the barn," Jesse said. "Ask the cow."

"Brendan?" Declan asked.

"I had to find some thin branches to fix the hole in the garden fence. Shelby saw me."

Declan turned to Shelby, who nodded. "I saw Brendan coming back with the sticks."

"So everyone is accounted for," Tim said, shaking his head.

"It would seem so," Jesse replied. "We might not have been paired up, but everyone saw everyone at some point around that time."

Tim let out a deep sigh of frustration. "Well, I guess that means we're back to square one. Again."

"I'm going to bed," Shelby said.

"Me too," Theresa added, and stood.

Once they'd left, everyone slowly dispersed. I got the impression that Declan wanted to speak to me, but I honestly couldn't bear the thought of rehashing this any further, so I wished everyone a good night, if such a thing were even possible, and followed Theresa and Shelby into the house, Iris trudging behind me.

# Chapter 42

## Declan

As the weeks passed, I found it harder and harder to sleep and often sat outside at night, listening to the sounds of the ocean and the forest. On clear evenings, the sky was full of stars, but I never saw any planes overhead, nor did I ever spot the lights of a passing boat. Once, I thought I'd heard a motor, but it was probably just my imagination since it had to be after midnight and the sound faded away within moments. If I had been surprised and disturbed by the deaths of Will and Mark, I was terrified by Gael's disappearance and tried to think back on his movements in the weeks leading up to it.

He'd sometimes gone off by himself but always came back with a rabbit or a basketful of mushrooms. I had no reason to suspect Gael of any wrongdoing and had not noticed any tension between him and another member of the group. Gael was friendly and helpful and had a good sense of humor. He wasn't the sort of person to make anyone the butt of a joke or use their vulnerability for sport.

Natalie told me that Gael's father was murdered by the cartel, but I saw no connection between something that had happened in Mexico when Gael was a child, tragic though it might be, with what had happened on the island. And I strongly doubted that if Gael had any ties to organized crime, whoever he had pissed off would send someone on a six-month reality show to dispose of their target. That was just ludicrous. If Gael had gotten on the wrong side of someone, he'd likely get a bullet between the eyes or a knife in the back. Quicker, easier, and much more difficult to investigate in a city of millions than a colony of a dozen.

We were working on the assumption that Gael had been in the woods when he'd vanished, but he might have returned to the beach. The only answer that made sense was that Gael had drowned. Perhaps he'd gone for a swim and gotten caught up in a rip current, or maybe he'd thought he'd spotted a boat and struck out without thinking but never made it. If Gael had drowned, then his body could have washed up anywhere. Or it could have been carried further out to sea and picked over by fish until there was nothing left but his bones, which would even now be resting on the ocean floor. In a way, the not knowing was even worse than having two fresh graves to remind us of how fragile life on the island was.

I was still determined to find the power source for the cameras, if there was one, but I could hardly look for it in the dark, and we spent all our daylight hours hunting for food. We had completely run out of the stores Varlet had provided and relied entirely on whatever we killed and grew. The vegetable garden was providing some produce but not nearly enough, and the animals we managed to kill fed us for only a few days at a time. The mood was grim, and what I found most disturbing was the lack of communication. Whereas in the beginning we'd often sat around the table after dinner and talked of life back home and the tasks we had to undertake the next day, now most people just said goodnight and walked away, too depleted after the day's efforts to keep up a conversation. The women looked drawn and tired, and the men were hungry and irritable.

Even Iris, who had always been good-natured, had become quiet and short-tempered, sniping at anyone who asked for more food or made any comment regarding the cooking and distribution. Everyone's patience was stretched thin, and I feared that some minor altercation might lead to a full-blown fight.

As in any stressful situation, alliances had formed, and the members of the group made no secret of disliking someone. Glen and Sam, in particular, were unpopular. They both had an abrasive manner that didn't endear them to the rest of the group. The women had closed ranks around Shelby, and Ed had stopped taking Sunday services after suffering weeks of heckling by Sam and Glen and rapidly declining attendance. No one was in the mood to listen to a sermon when they were angry, frightened, and hungry.

But certain bonds did blossom. I noticed Tim and Nicky sneaking off together a few times, and although Tim didn't comment on their relationship or make excuses about cheating on his wife, I could tell that something in him softened when Nicky was around. He probably noticed the same thing when I was around Natalie. Aside from Tim, she was the only person I trusted, and some caveman instinct to protect my woman reared its head whenever anyone so much as looked at her the wrong way. Except that she wasn't my woman, and she was probably better off. To give in to a desire for companionship would put Natalie at risk of getting pregnant, and the last thing I wanted was to endanger her in any way. We had grown closer, though, and I looked forward to our talks. I wished I could talk to Natalie when I couldn't sleep, but I could hardly wake her and expect her to sit with me. She was tired and needed her rest, and I needed to find a way to calm my racing mind before the anxiety attacks I'd suffered from after Noah's death came back and made me feel even more vulnerable in an already volatile situation.

I wasn't a religious man, but even I was beginning to pray that something would give.

# Chapter 43

## Natalie

## July

Our grim mood lifted for a few days in July when Sam declared it was time to harvest the corn. We went into the field with our baskets, thrilled that we'd have something to eat besides venison, fish, and rabbit. We were lucky to get a decent first crop, but although we'd be enjoying corn on the cob with butter today, we couldn't afford to consume too much for fear of working through our reserves too quickly.

We had decided as a group that we didn't have enough resources to manage three meals a day, so we were down to two: breakfast and a late lunch around three o'clock. It was a long time between meals, especially since breakfast was hardly more than a piece of cheese and a thin slice of the meat Iris had been smoking in the shed.

"Corn takes four to eight weeks to dry," Iris informed us. "We need to set enough corn aside to make cornmeal. Hopefully, it will supplement our diet for a few months."

No one asked if Iris thought we'd be getting off the island in September. We had no way of knowing, and we had to make our harvest last as long as possible. That first night, we had a feast. Roasted venison, corn, and creamed spinach. That spinach was the only thing that kept us from getting scurvy, and we rationed it out a spoonful per person since there was only the one patch that Theresa had found.

"I have a surprise for you," Theresa said once everyone had finished eating and sat back, smiling happily now that they felt full.

"Really? What is it?" Shelby asked.

She sounded as hopeful as a child, and my heart went out to her. I couldn't begin to understand what she was going through or how terrified she must be, for both herself and her unborn baby. Shelby's belly swelled beneath her apron very noticeably now, especially since her limbs were as thin as a scarecrow's. Her blond hair had grown out at the roots, and she had about two inches of dark brown hair closer to her scalp. She was terribly pale despite the hot sun that had been baking the island for weeks now, and she was often too tired to get through the day and needed to lie down for a few hours in the afternoon. By my estimation, Shelby's pregnancy was coming up on seven months, and I worried about her incessantly, praying that help would come before she went into labor.

Theresa smiled widely and then raised a finger, instructing us all to wait. She headed toward one of the lesser-used sheds and returned with a wooden bowl covered with a linen towel. She set the bowl on the table with great pomp and whisked off the towel like a magician revealing a white dove he'd conjured out of thin air. The smell of fresh raspberries wafted from the bowl, making my mouth water.

"Oh my God," Shelby cried. "Where did you get those?"

"I found some raspberry bushes and have been waiting for the perfect moment to pick the berries. Wait too long, and the birds will eat them," Theresa explained. "There'll be more berries over the next week or two. I'll pick those bushes clean," she promised.

We all got a handful of berries and savored them as if they were the most decadent dessert we'd ever had.

"If this place has taught me anything, it's to appreciate every tiny miracle God performs," Ed said.

"Oh, shut up, Ed," Sam said irritably. "God didn't put these raspberries here for you. These bushes have probably been here for decades. If your God is so accommodating, why don't you ask him to send a boat?"

"And He will," Ed replied calmly. "When the time is right."

"You mean when we're all too weak with hunger to move?" Glen piped in.

"It's not for us to question the ways of the Lord."

"You really are an ass, you know that?"

"Your words have no power to hurt me, Glen. Sticks and stones," Ed said, referring to the refrain from his childhood.

"Actually, words can hurt far worse than bruises," Iris said. "But please, let's not ruin this lovely meal."

"I'm sorry," Glen said contritely.

"It's not me you should be apologizing to," Iris replied.

"I'm not apologizing to him. I'm sick and tired of being lectured on the glory of God when my stomach is empty most of the time and I can barely sleep through the night for fear of dying on this fucking island."

"Yeah, keep it to yourself, Ed," Sam said. "Not everyone shares your faith."

Tired of their bickering, I got up and started to collect the dirty dishes. Nicky collected a pile as well and followed me to the creek.

"I hate those two," Nicky said as we scrubbed the plates.

"They're angry and scared, and they're taking out their feelings on anyone who won't fight back," I said.

"Yeah, I know. Glen called Brendan a fairy yesterday."

"Did Brendan respond?"

"No. Brendan doesn't go in for confrontations."

"Well, thank God for that. We have enough people here who are on their last nerve as it is."

Nicky smiled serenely. "I was very angry, but I feel better since I've been with Tim. It's nice to have someone who cares about you."

I bit my tongue just before I said something about Tim's wife. I didn't need to remind Nicky. She knew and chose to ignore it.

"Why don't you give Declan a chance? He's pining for you like a sad puppy."

"I don't trust myself, Nicky."

"What does that mean?"

"Declan is a great guy, and I really like him, but if I give in to my feelings for him, I will become a burden to him because I will cling to him for dear life."

"I think he'd actually like that. He has a superhero complex. He wants to feel needed and admired. He'd welcome your adoration."

"It's not adoration. It's fear. It's like a drowning person dragging their rescuer down with them."

"You're not drowning, Natalie. You're strong and capable."

"I don't feel strong. I'm terrified."

"Of anything in particular or just the prospect of never being rescued and dying on this godforsaken rock?" Nicky asked conversationally.

I was petrified of not getting rescued and living out what was left to me on this island, but my fear was more immediate.

"Shelby will turn to me when she goes into labor. I'm the only one here that has any medical knowledge. What am I going to do? I have nothing. I'm powerless to help her."

"Women have given birth on their own since the dawn of humanity. It will be messy and painful, but as long as there are no dire complications, everything will be okay."

"And if it's not?"

"If it's not, you will do everything in your power to help Shelby. I know you will."

"And the baby? How will we care for it?" I asked.

"The same way women have cared for their babies through the centuries. Shelby will breastfeed it for as long as it takes for us to get off the island."

"Did you see how thin she got?"

Nicky nodded. "Shelby is getting enough to eat. Iris gives her a cup of milk twice a day on top of the rations, and she gets a double portion of the spinach and dried seaweed. It's not prenatal vitamins, but it's something."

"I hope it's enough," I said.

"Natalie, there are still people out there who were born in concentration camps to terrified, emaciated mothers. They survived, and so will Shelby's baby. Do you think it's a girl?" Nicky asked.

"I don't know."

"I'm getting a girl vibe," Nicky said. "Girls are resilient. *We* are resilient," Nicky reminded me. "Come on, cheer up, and go screw that pretty boy from Chicago. I bet he'll make you forget your troubles for a little while."

I shook my head. "I'm too afraid to get pregnant. Aren't you?"

"Nope. I got that contraceptive implant. It's good for five years, and I have three more to go."

I nodded. Suddenly, I envied Nicky her decision. Declan wasn't the only one pining. I was pining too and would give anything to walk straight into his arms and stay there until I no longer felt so scared and alone.

When I returned to the settlement, I saw Declan coming out of the armory. He turned, his shy smile silently asking if I was ready to take our daily walk now that I was finished with the dishes. Everyone had to be in before dark so we could shut the gates, even though we were probably shutting the killer in with us.

Declan looked worried as we walked along the beach, his jaw tight with tension, his hands balled into fists.

"What is it?" I asked gently.

"We don't have a lot of powder and shot left. We won't survive long if we can't hunt. We need to get off this island, and soon."

"How long have we got?"

"If we're very careful, we can make it for another two months or so, but after that…" Declan's voice trailed off.

No one was allowed to help themselves to powder and shot except Declan and Tim, since they were the most proficient hunters and didn't waste our resources on shots that went wide, but even they couldn't hunt without bullets or the powder that propelled them.

"Some naïve part of me still hopes that they will come for us as they promised," I said.

"Some naïve part of me hopes so too, but the realistic part says that no one is coming and we're heading for disaster. The corn won't last forever, and without meat, we'll starve."

We walked in silence for a while, each lost in our own thoughts.

"Nicky and Tim are hooking up," Declan said. The change of subject seemed abrupt, but I thought that Declan probably needed to think about something less catastrophic than dying of starvation or he'd snap.

"I know. I can't say I blame them. They're trying to snatch whatever happiness they can from this place," I said.

"You don't disapprove?"

"It's not my place to judge. I don't know anything about Tim's life off this island."

"We could snatch some happiness," Declan said, his gaze pleading with me to let him in, even a little.

"Funny, that's what Nicky just said."

Declan looked momentarily surprised, then decided to press his advantage. "Natalie, I promise that I will respect whatever boundaries you set. I just really want to be with you."

I felt the prickle of tears and looked down at my feet to avoid Declan's intense gaze. Every cell in my body wanted to say yes, and to give in to my desire to be with Declan, but I hadn't been exaggerating when I'd told Nicky that the constant fear and uncertainty were taking up all my emotional reserves and I was afraid that if I let go, I'd go to pieces. I was barely holding it together, and it wasn't fair to dump my emotional baggage on Declan, who was struggling himself.

He had told me about what had happened with Noah, and although I had reassured him that it wasn't his fault and he had done what any other police officer would have done in his place, I knew that my platitudes meant nothing. Declan had to make his own peace, and now we also had to carry the deaths of two people and the disappearance of a third. Declan blamed himself for not being able to prevent the tragedies that had struck our little community, and the rest of the group seemed to blame him as well. For some reason, they did not have the same expectations of Tim, maybe because they didn't see tribal police in the same way they saw Chicago PD, or maybe because Tim refused to accept the blame. He didn't seem as emotionally vulnerable, or maybe that was just my perception because I knew Declan better than I knew Tim.

I wondered if Tim talked to Nicky when they were together or it was just a physical thing between them, an outlet they both needed and weren't afraid to explore. I'd be lying if I said I didn't crave physical intimacy, and at this point, even the touch of a hand or a hug were so much more meaningful than they had been back at home.

A wave of loneliness washed over me, and despite my reservations, I walked into Declan's arms. He held me tight, his heart beating against mine in a way I found extremely romantic. We were both sweaty, our hair unwashed and our clothes soiled and worn, but I didn't notice any of that. All I knew was that we were stronger together, and Declan would have my back no matter what happened.

I raised my face to his, and he kissed me. Just for a moment, my fears receded, and it was just the two of us on a beautiful beach, enjoying a moment of intimacy.

Suddenly, Declan tensed, his head cocking like a dog's. And then I heard it—someone was calling for Declan. It was Tim.

# Chapter 44

## Declan

Tim's holler couldn't have come at a worse time, but Tim wasn't the kind of guy to raise the alarm for nothing, so I reluctantly let go of Natalie and pulled her along toward the gates, unwilling to leave her alone on the beach. Tim was standing between the gateposts, hands on hips, looking absolutely murderous.

"What happened?" I asked as soon as we were within earshot.

Tim held something up between two fingers, and I peered at the tiny object. It was a camera. We had been searching for the cameras for the past few weeks, going over every inch of the settlement when we had time off from hunting and the never-ending chores, but had found nothing. If there were no cameras inside the houses, then where were they? In the trees? Affixed to the roof? If the cameras were that high up, the only thing they'd get a clear shot of was the tops of our heads, so it didn't really make sense from a practical point of view. They had to be low enough to capture our facial expressions and words, but the task of locating them had proved about as easy as looking for the proverbial needle in a haystack, and without any modern tools, like a tall ladder, we were at a disadvantage. We could hardly climb every tree within the vicinity of the settlement.

I held out my hand, and Tim dropped the tiny camera into my palm. "Where did you find it?"

"Come, I'll show you. The camera is not all I found," Tim said. He looked grim.

The three of us walked in silence toward our house. He approached the window and pointed to a spot in the corner of the window frame. It was no bigger than a dime and was positioned in such a way that the light would not reflect off the lens. The camera had been worked into a whorl in the wood, and unless someone looked very closely, it would appear to be just a natural knot that happened to be at the perfect height to see us all clearly, whether we were standing or lying down.

I peered into tiny hole where the camera had been and noticed that there was an opening that led out through the wall and now allowed in a chink of light.

"What happened to the wire?" I asked.

"Come and see."

We headed back outside and stood before the window, which faced the back of the house. I could clearly see the opening now that I knew what I was looking for and could trace the thin wire that ran along the length of the post. And then I saw what Tim was so angry about. At the very bottom, where the post met the ground, the wire had been severed, so the camera had definitely not been recording.

"Let's see if we can find the camera in the women's house," Tim said. "Maybe it's in the same spot."

We crossed the square and examined the window frames carefully. "Here it is," Tim cried triumphantly as he used the tip of his knife to pop the camera out of its hiding place. We trooped outside and found the post that hid the wire. This one had been cut as well, the damage buried beneath a tiny mound of earth. I was actually relieved that no one could see us congregating behind the house because what we had discovered would set off a panic. To speculate was one thing, to know for certain was quite another.

"Someone has intentionally disabled the cameras," Tim said, keeping his voice low. "I bet all the other cameras have been tampered with as well, so Varlet has no idea what's been happening here."

"Why wouldn't they send someone to check on us and fix the cameras?" Natalie asked, her face pale with alarm.

"Because I don't think anyone was watching the footage," Tim replied angrily. "If they had been, they'd know what's been happening here."

"But it doesn't make any sense," Natalie protested.

"No, it doesn't, which is why it's so worrying," I said. "We need to see where the wires lead. If there are wires, there's a power source."

"It's buried in the ground. How do you propose to excavate it?" Tim asked.

"Very carefully," I replied, determined to get to the bottom of this. "We will follow this wire to wherever it takes us." I held up the length of wire I had pulled away from the post.

"I'll get the shovel," Tim said.

As soon as Tim brought the shovel, he began to dig around the stub that disappeared into the earth to see how far down it went. To our surprise, the wire was buried only about a foot deep, and we were able to gently pull it out of the ground and follow the trail. The wire ran toward the wooden palisade and disappeared underneath, but we were able to pick it up on the other side.

"How far do you think it goes?" Natalie asked as she trailed behind us.

"Possibly all the way to the other side of the island," Tim said. "Whoever laid the wires made sure to seed the ground so that there'd be no trace of a recent excavation."

"But we've walked every inch of the island," Natalie said. "There was nothing that could house a power source."

"That's because they buried it," I said.

Tim nodded. "The power source is well disguised since no one ever found it."

"They didn't need to find it," I said. "Someone sabotaged the cameras to make sure there's no evidence of the murders. And Gael is still missing. Either he's a victim or the perpetrator."

"Gael is an IT guy," Tim said with disgust. "I highly doubt he's the victim. He's probably the one who sabotaged the cameras."

"Let's reserve judgment until we know more," I said, although my gut feeling agreed that Tim was onto something.

We were at the approximate center of the island when the wire stopped, and no amount of yanking would pull it out of the ground.

"The power source must be beneath our feet," I said. "There has to be an access point. Whoever laid down these wires would have made sure of that, in case maintenance was required."

Tim gave me a look of astonishment. "Maintenance? You see anyone here?"

I couldn't begin to explain why no one had bothered to come, but we were too close to give up now.

"Let's spread out from this spot and search for anything that might lead below ground, like a manhole of some sort. It will be well hidden, so take tiny steps and shuffle your feet," Tim said.

We spread out, our eyes glued to the ground, our shoes making no sound since the ground was covered with a layer of pine needles, leaves, fallen branches, and patches of moss.

"There's nothing here," Tim said with disgust.

"There must be," I replied stubbornly.

"It's going to get dark soon, and we don't have a torch," Natalie said.

She sounded nervous, and I couldn't blame her. Darkness was pooling in the hollows, and the shadows lengthened as the sun began to set. The light was fading quickly, and we had no more than a half hour to get back to the settlement.

Tim nodded. "We now know where to start looking. Let's pick this up again tomorrow. Honestly, I'm beat."

I was reluctant to leave, suddenly fearful that the telltale wire would disappear, but Tim tied it to a low-hanging branch to mark the spot. "We'll start again first thing tomorrow, Declan. I don't think anyone is coming tonight to undermine our efforts."

"At this point, I can't be sure of anything," I said. I sounded pessimistic, but the whole situation was becoming more bizarre by the day. "Let's keep this to ourselves for now."

"Agreed," Tim said, and looked at Natalie.

She nodded. Our kiss on the beach seemed like it had happened a year ago.

# Chapter 45

Tim and I returned to the forest immediately after breakfast the next day. I had convinced Natalie to remain behind and attend to her usual chores. If she went with us, the rest of the group would become suspicious. This way, they assumed we were off to check the traps. Once back on site, Tim and I split up and searched the forest floor. Whatever that wire was attached to had to be right beneath our feet.

In the bright morning light, I was able to make out the minute differences in the texture beneath my feet. There was a pattern to it, an order created by nature, but then I spotted a patch in deep shade that was somehow different, the leaves and pine needles too staged to have been placed that way naturally. I walked over and tried to brush away the debris with my foot, but only the top layer came away. The moss and pine needles underneath were fake.

"Tim," I called.

Tim was by my side in moments, staring down at the camouflaged trapdoor I had uncovered. He smiled happily and patted me on the shoulder. "Well, done, brother. Let's see what's down there."

The trapdoor came equipped with a leather pull and was easy to open, which was something of a surprise since I expected it to be either locked or booby trapped. Maybe it had been before someone else had found it first. The opening was square and only wide enough for one average-size person to get through. A metal staircase descended into darkness. I set my foot on the top rung before Tim had a chance to preempt me. I couldn't wait to get down there and see what we were dealing with.

The bottom of the shaft was in darkness, but there was enough daylight to allow me to see a switch at the bottom. I flipped it and squeezed my eyes shut as a bright fluorescent light seared my retinae. Amazing how quickly our bodies had forgotten the things we had been so used to only a few months before. I opened my eyes slowly, allowing them to adjust to the brightness, then looked around. The ladder led to a square cinderblock room equipped with a computer desk with a hard drive, several dark monitors and a keyboard, an ergonomic chair, a refrigerator, and a narrow cot that looked like it had been slept on.

"Tim, come down here," I called.

Tim was down in a flash, his eyes widening when he saw the setup. "Looks like someone's been down here," he said. "Let's see what we can find."

I turned to the computer, but Tim went straight for the fridge and yanked open the door. The inside of the fridge was dark, and a foul smell filled the small room almost immediately.

"Oh, that's gross," Tim said, and slammed the door shut. But instead of walking away, he opened the fridge again and pulled out a six-pack of Coors. "Beer doesn't spoil," he explained, and set the beer aside for later. Tim walked around the fridge and peered behind the unit. "Someone's cut the cord."

"Same here. The power cord has been cut in two."

"Bastards," Tim hissed, then turned and walked back to the fridge. He opened the door and stared in as if he could find the answers to all his questions in a chunk of petrified cheese, while I checked out the small bathroom that contained a toilet, a sink, and a tiny shower cubicle. I flushed and watched as the water swirled inside the toilet. After using the reeking privy for months, running water was a minor miracle. Some part of me wanted to strip off and take a shower, but now wasn't the time to think about my creature comforts.

When I came out of the bathroom, Tim was rummaging through a small cabinet in the corner. There were a few cans of tuna and baked beans, and a bag of chips, which Tim grabbed as if it might vanish. There was also a jar of instant coffee and nondairy creamer, and a full box of oatmeal packets. The top shelf contained two mugs, two bowls, a small pan, and utensils. Tim collected everything that was edible and put it in a duffle bag he found at the bottom of the cabinet.

"Come," he said at last. "Let's get out of here."

Tim grabbed the beer, and we climbed out and shut the trapdoor behind us. There was a shallow stream nearby, and Tim submerged the cans in the cold water and left them to cool as we settled on the bank, each lost in our own thoughts as we stared at the rushing water and tried to find a logical explanation for what we'd found.

The beer tasted amazing when Tim finally thought it was ready to drink, and it reminded me all too painfully of the real world. I'd experienced bouts of homesickness before, but nothing like this. It was a visceral pain that took my breath away and threatened to leave me paralyzed with grief. Tim didn't say anything, but the faraway look in his eyes was enough. We each finished a can of beer and savored a few chips before we were ready to talk about what we had found.

"The food in that fridge spoiled a very long time ago," Tim said as he handed me a second beer and took one for himself. "Most of it has liquefied. Whoever cut the cord must have done it weeks ago, if not months."

"But who cut it and why?" I asked.

"It had to be Gael," Tim said. "You thought you heard a motor a few nights after Gael vanished. Gael must have overheard us talking about finding a power source and realized that his days were numbered, so he hid down there, waited until we called off the search, then called for help. Once he was sure he was getting off the island, he disabled the computer and the fridge."

"But why?" I exclaimed, throwing up my hands in frustration. "And how did he even know the bunker was down there?"

"You said it yourself, Declan; Gael was in IT. Perhaps he was able to hack into Varlet's servers and download a map of the area as well as the location of all the cameras. He'd know there'd have to be an electricity source somewhere on the island if the cameras were to record for six months. The outlet in that bunker is probably connected to fiberoptic cables that run along the ocean floor. Those cables would also provide an internet connection."

"If Gael armed himself with all this information before coming on the show, then he must have had a plan," I said.

"Maybe he had hoped to use the information to help him win the top prize," Tim said.

"If Gael was able to hack into Varlet's servers, then he would have had access to all the personal information we provided."

"Exactly," Tim said. "He could use that to disqualify the others."

I shook my head, unable to get on board with this theory. "Gael disappeared three months after we arrived on the island. In that time, I have not seen or heard anything that would make me suspect him of trying to undermine the other contestants. He got along with everyone. And why would he disable the cameras? How would he benefit if the plan was to win?"

Tim exhaled loudly. "That's what I'm trying to figure out."

I swallowed hard and took a sip of my beer, almost unwilling to say out loud what I was thinking. "There might be another reason," I said at last.

"Which is?"

"Maybe Gael's agenda wasn't monetary in nature."

"What are you driving at?"

"Perhaps Gael disabled the cameras because he planned to commit murder."

Tim raised his eyebrows and moved his head from side to side as he considered this suggestion. "Okay, let's go with that. So presumably, his plan wasn't to kill random people. He could have done that in Santa Cruz. Your theory suggests that he had targeted particular contestants. Yet neither Will nor Mark showed any signs of recognition when they met Gael. We were all there that first day when the introductions were made."

"Maybe they didn't remember him," I said.

"They might not have noticed him in a crowd, but when he was there, every day, how could they not recall meeting him?" Tim asked. "Especially if they had done something to wrong him."

"It's possible that they never met in person. Perhaps there was a connection they knew nothing about."

"Will was a judge from Texas, Mark a teacher from Massachusetts. What connection could there be?"

"I don't know, but it doesn't mean there wasn't one," I replied stubbornly. I was growing attached to this theory, but there was nothing I could do to back it up. Without internet access, there was no way to verify whether Gael, Will, and Mark had somehow connected online.

"Okay, say there was a previous relationship of some sort. Why kill Will a few weeks into the show and then wait a month to kill Mark? If Gael knew the cameras weren't working and he could get off the island anytime he wanted, he could have killed them both right away and hightailed it. But he didn't disappear until you and I started discussing the existence of a power source. And why cut the electrical cords?" Tim added, almost as an afterthought.

"Cutting the power cord to the computer would not prevent the police from downloading the information stored on the hard drive. So, he must have cut it to prevent us from using it to contact the mainland. And the fridge—that was just pure spite."

"Yeah, that was petty," Tim agreed. "We could have used the fridge to store the leftover meat and milk."

Tim popped a chip in his mouth, chewed it thoughtfully, then continued. "Let's say, for argument's sake, that Gael never meant to kill either man. Perhaps his only intention was to sabotage their efforts. Maybe he confronted Will over some past injustice, things got out of hand, and he picked up a rock and bashed him over the head. Instead of making a run for it, Gael disabled the cameras and decided to stick around to see what would happen. No one came, so he thought it was safe to remain. Then Mark had that public showdown with Shelby, and a few hours later he was dead."

Tim sucked in a deep breath, a faraway look in his eyes as he hashed out his theory. "Again, Gael waited to see if anyone would point the finger at him. They didn't, so he hung around, perhaps still hoping to win the prize if Varlet finally got around to fixing the cameras. But then something happened to spook him. He must have known the bunker was there, so he hid for a few days, during which time he made inroads into the supplies, then called someone for help, and they came to get him. He knew that as soon as he disappeared, he would become the prime suspect for the murders, so he disabled the computer to prevent us from contacting the police and cut the cord on the fridge. By the time we get off this island, there will be no physical evidence to link Gael to either crime, and no footage to implicate him."

"That theory is the only one that loosely fits the facts, but there are some things that still bother me," I said. "The two methods of murder were completely different, and as far as we know, Gael was accounted for at the time of Mark's death."

"Gael is our only plausible suspect since he's the only one missing. Out of curiosity, what did you make of him when you first met?" Tim asked.

"Observant, intelligent, personable."

"Most psychopaths are," Tim said stoically.

"Gael didn't strike me as a psychopath."

"I think the producers were hoping for a confrontation and chose the people most likely to lose their shit."

"I can understand bringing together people who would irritate each other. I can even understand them leaving us here to figure things out as we go along, but what I can't figure out is why no one has come. Will was murdered shortly after we arrived on the island. If we are to assume that the cameras were disabled then, it would stand to reason that Varlet Entertainment has been aware of a problem since early April. It's the middle of July, and we've had another murder, an unexpected pregnancy, and we're completely out of supplies. Forget the financial liability of what they have done, but what about a moral obligation? Would Varlet really leave fifteen people on a deserted island with no way to call for help and not tell anyone?"

"It's almost like they're all dead," Tim said.

"That's impossible."

"Is it? If someone came to pick up Gael, then obviously he had an accomplice. What if that accomplice took care of things on the mainland?"

I nearly choked on the chip I was chewing. "Are you seriously suggesting that the accomplice has murdered every Varlet employee?"

"Or only those in charge."

"I don't know about that, Tim. I think something has happened at Varlet, but I can't think of any scenario in which they would willingly leave us stranded."

"What if it wasn't Gael who sabotaged the cameras? What if the cameras were disabled before we even got here, or on the night we arrived? One of the crew might have done that," Tim said, pointing toward the bunker.

"Yes, they could have, but Justin Rogue would know by the following day that the cameras weren't operational. Why would he not send someone to fix them?"

"We could probably answer that question if we knew why he told us that the cameramen and doctor would remain here for the duration of the show and then left as soon as we went to sleep," Tim replied.

"Which brings us back to the theory that something has happened at Varlet," I reiterated.

"God dammit!" Tim exclaimed, and struck the ground with his fist. "We keep going around in circles, and nothing adds up. Are we really lousy cops, or is this some intentional mindfuck meant to drive us insane? Maybe the real show is something entirely different, and there's an alternate set of cameras we know nothing about."

"You mean they want to see what will happen to fifteen random people when they think they've been abandoned on a deserted island?" I asked sarcastically. "Well, we've lost two so far, and one is unaccounted for."

"So, what do we tell the others?" Tim asked. He suddenly looked really worn out.

"I think we should tell them the truth of what we found. For one, someone might remember something. For another, maybe we can figure out how to fix the power cord. We know the power is still on since the light is working. And we have to share the supplies we found. It might not be much, but it's still communal property," I said.

"But not the beer," Tim replied, and I watched his Adam's apple bob as he drained the can. "We deserve the beer for finding the bunker." He let out a small burp and wiped his mouth with the back of his hand.

"All right," I said. "Let's finish the beer and bury the cans, or we'll have a lot of explaining to do."

We finished the chips as well. We were too hungry and frustrated not to give in to some small measure of selfishness. We buried the garbage and returned to the settlement, neither of us looking forward to delivering this sobering new truth.

Despite the gifts of coffee, canned food, and oatmeal, the group was nearly silent, everyone stunned by the news that not only was there electricity on the island but that someone had intentionally sabotaged our chances of calling for help. Everyone wanted to blame Gael, and there was little sense in telling them different since the theories Tim and I had discussed would only lead to more questions and increased panic. Everyone was scared enough as it was, and it would be irresponsible to add fuel to the fire.

"Our only chance of getting off this island lies in fixing the power cord and hoping the computer is still operational. Does anyone know how to reconnect the wires?" Tim asked as he looked at the tense faces around the table.

"I can try," Brendan said.

"Why don't you start with the fridge and see if you can get it to work," I suggested. "We have one chance to get this right, so a little practice might be a good idea."

Brendan nodded. "Yeah. Sure. I'll start working on it tomorrow. Did you happen to notice if there are any tools or electrical tape in that bunker?"

"Didn't see anything," Tim said. "Does anyone else know anything about electrics?" Everyone shook their heads.

"Brendan, you're our only hope, so you had better not screw up," Iris said. It was probably meant to be a joke, but it sounded more like a threat.

Brendan looked distinctly uncomfortable, and who could blame him? At this point, everyone's patience was so frayed that any perceived failure could lead to misplaced blame and even repercussions.

"So no pressure, then," Brendan said, and stood. "Goodnight, all."

# Chapter 46

## Natalie

I woke early the next morning, having spent a restless night. The discovery of the bunker and the fact that the island had been wired for electricity was both frightening and exciting. Varlet had clearly intended to use the base on the island for monitoring the cameras and maybe keeping some additional supplies that required refrigeration. Was it possible that someone had been there from the start but had been taken off the island for some reason, or had the bunker been empty the whole time and Gael had made use of it when he decided it was time to save himself? Neither possibility was reassuring, especially since whoever had been there had felt the need to disable both the fridge and the computer. That took a special kind of callousness when we were all scared and struggling to find enough food.

Feeling angry and hot, I quickly pulled on my clothes and went out into the vegetable garden. One thing I could count on was that there would always be more weeding and watering to do. I found the work both soothing and gratifying since I could actually see the result of my efforts. I hadn't been at it long when I heard Iris's voice calling a greeting from the other side of the fence. I thought she was speaking to me and was just about to reply when I realized she hadn't seen me and was addressing someone else. Her voice became low and urgent.

"Jesse, I need to speak to you."

Jesse was an early riser and sometimes went for a walk around the settlement before the rest of us were up. He'd never struck me as someone who exercised for the sake of it, but we were all searching for ways to relieve stress and get along with people who were becoming angrier and more short-tempered by the day.

"Of course. How can I help?" Jesse asked politely. They were just on the other side of the fence, and I wasn't sure if I should make my presence known or go about my business.

"Someone's been stealing supplies," Iris said quietly.

"Are you sure?" Jesse asked.

"I'm sure. They're taking a little bit at a time, but it's been consistently happening over the past two weeks."

"What are they taking?"

"Corn, butter, slices of sausage and cheese." Iris sighed irritably. "I wish there was a lock on the storage shed, but as it is, anyone can walk in. I can't be expected to stand guard over the food."

"Do you have any idea who it might be?" Jesse asked.

I heard Iris's sharp intake of breath. "I don't want to point fingers at anyone without proof, but I think it might be Ed."

"Ed?" Jesse echoed, clearly as surprised as I was.

"I saw him near the shed twice in the past week. He had no business being there. And there were yellow flecks in his beard when he sat down to dinner. It looked like bits of corn."

"That's hardly proof."

"I know. That's why I haven't said anything until now."

"Until now?" Jesse asked carefully.

"I think we need to make some changes. We don't have a harvest to look forward to, so whatever we have now is pretty much it, except for the fresh meat and fish the others bring in, and with powder and shot running out, we might not even have the meat. I think we need to figure out how to lock the shed and cut the rations."

"The others won't like that," Jesse replied thoughtfully.

"No, they won't, but we have no idea if or when anyone is coming for us. We need to think ahead."

"I'll have a quiet word with Ed, and then, tonight at dinner, we can talk about the rations."

"Thank you."

"No need to thank me. I'm the governor," Jesse said, his voice dripping with sarcasm. "If only I had any actual power to go with the title."

"None of us have any power here. The only way we can survive on this island is through goodwill and trust."

"That's a tall order, Iris."

"I know, but what else have we got?"

"I could hardly sleep all night," Jesse said. "I kept thinking about that bunker and praying that Brendan can fix the cords. I'd give anything to leave this cursed place and go home. I swore to God I'd never complain about anything ever again and will spend the rest of my life helping others."

"Yeah, I was thinking that as well," Iris said. "I don't want to get my hopes up, though. Brendan is a handy guy, but there are limits even to his talents."

The opening of a door put an end to the conversation, and I returned to the weeds, angrily yanking them out of the ground. I really wasn't all that surprised that someone was helping themselves to the food, but I would never have expected it to be Ed. Maybe Iris was wrong, and it was someone else. I did not find the prospect calming. Whoever it was, they were taking food away from the rest of us, and with the proposed decrease in rations, desperation would only escalate as hunger prevailed.

# Chapter 47

## Declan

I've been in plenty of dangerous situations, but I was as nervous as a rookie cop on his first patrol when I pulled open the door to the bunker and watched as Brendan descended the ladder. It was only as I watched him disappear into the gloom that I realized how much weight he'd lost. Had Brendan still been the same size as he was at the start, he'd have had trouble getting down the narrow opening. I supposed in this situation, this was a blessing in disguise since we could hardly lift the fridge out if Brendan couldn't fit into the shaft. I waited until he reached the bottom, then followed him down.

This time I was prepared for the brightness of the light and the claustrophobic interior of the cinderblock space. The inside was cooler than the outside, but it was stuffy, the smell of rotting food hanging in the air. Brendan stood at the center of the room and looked around, taking in the blank computer monitors and the narrow cot. He peeked inside the bathroom.

"Is there running water?" he asked.

"There is."

"So there's plumbing as well as electricity."

I nodded. "There must be a filter that desalinizes the sea water."

"Nice," Brendan said.

Having completed his tour, Brendan approached the refrigerator, pushed it away from the wall, and unplugged the remaining length of cord. He then rotated the fridge so that the back faced the center of the room in order to take advantage of the light and sat on the floor to get a better look at the severed halves.

"What do you think?" I asked, my heart hammering against my ribs. If Brendan said this was a lost cause, we'd be right back where we had started.

Brendan sighed. "Look, it's not that difficult to fix a broken cord if you have the right tools, but all I have is my knife and my fingers."

"What would you need?"

"A soldering iron, for one." Brendan pushed to his feet and looked around the room. "We need to search this space from top to bottom."

"What are we looking for?"

"Anything that can be useful. A razor, duct tape, pliers. But what I really need is a lighter."

"What for?" I asked.

"To use in place of a soldering iron. Come on," Brendan said. "Maybe there are some built-in lockers or something."

We spent the next half hour searching but didn't find any tools or duct tape. There were two clean bath towels in the bathroom, a metal trashcan, and a plastic shower curtain that Brendan took down.

"What's that for?" I asked.

"I don't have any heat shrink," he said. "This is the closest thing to rubber, so maybe I can use it to insulate the repair."

I nodded. I didn't know anything about electricity, but I knew enough about leaving live wires exposed.

"I'll need a flame. Can you build a small fire in the trashcan and then give me a light when I tell you to?"

"Sure," I said, eager to help. "Brendan, do you think you can do it?"

"I can't promise anything. In theory, I think I can get this to work. In reality, I'm not so sure."

I watched as Brendan took out his knife and very carefully cut through the insulation to expose about an inch of wire, then I climbed the ladder and stepped outside into the stifling morning. I was sweating profusely after the long walk to the bunker, my shirt clinging to my back as I searched for dry grass and kindling. I had honestly never thought I'd miss Chicago winters, but right now, I wouldn't have minded a blast of cold air and some snowflakes on my tongue. It was so hot, and so humid. The forest was alive with insects and small creatures that darted through the undergrowth as they went about the business of living through another day. Thankfully, it hadn't rained, so at least the twigs weren't damp, and I quickly collected an armful.

I filled a leather bottle with water from the creek, had a drink, then took my kindling and climbed back down into the hole. I was more proficient at using tinder and flint than I had been two months ago, but it would still take time to get a good fire going, and I was sure Brendan was ready for me.

As soon as I was able to hand him a burning taper, he held the flame to the copper wires he'd reconnected and allowed the heat to do its work. Brendan tried to keep the white, black, and green wires separate as he applied the flame. He sat hunched over the cord, his shoulders tense, his forehead beaded with perspiration as he tried to keep the three wires from fusing together.

At last, he let out a loud breath and set aside the smoking stick. The flame had gone out, but it seemed that Brendan was finished with it. He cut a small strip of plastic off the shower curtain and wrapped it around the repair, then held the still-smoldering stick to the plastic and allowed it to melt around the cord.

He set the mended cord on the floor and stood, taking a deep breath. "I need some water."

I offered him the bottle, but he shook his head. "Let's go outside for a minute."

Brendan climbed out, walked over to the creek, and squatted on the bank. He washed his face and poured some cold water over his neck before drinking his fill. I could tell he was really nervous and almost afraid to find out if the repair had worked. I splashed some cold water on my face and followed Brendan back down.

We moved the fridge back in place and plugged the cord into the outlet. Nothing happened. There was no humming noise as the fridge came back to life or any indication that anything had changed. Brendan's gaze momentarily slid toward me, probably to gauge if I blamed him, then he opened the fridge door. The stink of decay hit us, but we didn't care. The light was on, which meant that the electricity was flowing.

I'm not a touchy-feely kind of guy by nature, but I grabbed Brendan and gave him a huge hug, patting him on the back as if he were a crying five-year-old.

"You did it," I panted. "You did it, Brendan."

"I can't believe it worked," Brendan said as I let him go. "Don't tell the others."

"Why not?"

"A fridge is nice, but it won't get us off the island. Why don't we see if we can fix the computer cord tomorrow before getting their hopes up?"

"Okay," I agreed. "But I will tell Tim. He needs to know."

"All right," Brendan said, and moved toward the ladder. "Let's get out of here. This place gives me the creeps."

# Chapter 48

## Natalie

I was feeling unbearably tense by the time the afternoon meal finally rolled around. Everyone was already at the end of their tether, and with Jesse announcing the cut to rations at breakfast, people were even angrier. Iris was unusually quiet, and it was only once Declan and Brendan came back that her sullenness began to ebb. Despite vague reassurances that Brendan was still working on the cords, there was a light in Declan's eyes that couldn't be mistaken for anything other than hope. If he thought we had a chance of booting up the computer, then not all was lost.

Most people were already seated at the table, waiting for their turn to go up. It'd been months since we had served anything family style, since some people always took more than their share, and everyone watched Iris with unblinking intensity as she carefully divided whatever was on offer, ready to hurl an accusation at her if she misjudged someone's portion and gave less than she'd given someone else. Today's meal consisted of three spinach leaves per person, since that was all we had been able to find, a quarter ear of corn, and a thin slice of venison. Iris was just about to serve Glen when Ed stumbled through the gates. He looked dirty and disheveled, his face barely recognizable.

I left the table and hurried to meet Ed. "What happened?" I cried. "Were you attacked by an animal?"

"You could say that," Ed muttered. His lip was split, his eyes bloodshot and swollen, and there was dried blood on his nose, chin, and shirt.

Having overheard the conversation between Iris and Jesse that morning, I wasn't feeling well disposed toward Ed, but I was a nurse, and I couldn't ignore Ed's need for medical attention. The least I could do was clean his wounds. I reached out to take Ed by the arm, but he shoved me away so roughly, I nearly lost my balance.

"Hey," Declan cried, springing to his feet and coming toward me, but Ed ignored him. He fixed his angry gaze on Glen and Sam, lifting a shaking finger to point in their direction.

"They attacked me. Said I stole food," Ed said hoarsely. "They beat me up and left me in the woods."

Everyone turned to look at the two men, probably expecting them to deny the accusation, but they didn't. Sam looked at his hands, which were folded on the table, while Glen glared at Ed, his nostrils flaring, his breath coming in short gasps.

"You deserve everything you got and more, old man," Glen bellowed. "You not only stole food, but you hardly contribute anything other than endless prayer. No one gives a damn about your sermons. I don't even know why we still make a pretense of keeping up with the Sunday services. Not like anyone is watching." Glen was so angry, spittle was flying from his mouth as he spoke. "You don't work, you don't eat. Got that?"

"I do work," Ed replied, though a few heads had nodded in agreement with Glen.

Ed was a dead weight as far as they were concerned. It wasn't that he was too old to be helpful, but he always found ways to avoid doing his chores, and his main contribution was the occasional fish that he delivered to Iris after nearly a full day of fishing. Iris had said that he probably napped for hours and missed half the fish that nibbled at his bait.

"Listen up," Jesse said as he stood and held up a conciliatory hand. "We are not going to resort to violence. If Ed stole the food, then we will work out a punishment. You have no right to gang up on him and beat him to a pulp."

"Oh, really?" Sam demanded, his head snapping up at Jesse's words. "What are you going to do about it, *Governor*? If I were you, I'd be careful. Look what happened to the first two pompous morons to hold the position."

This was so unlike Sam that a hush fell over the table, but I supposed now that food rations were involved, the gloves were off, and even Sam, who was happy to let Glen take the lead when it came to bullying the others, was ready to come into his own.

Declan, who had been standing next to me, hovering like an avenging angel, strode toward the table and glared at the assembled group, his eyes blazing with anger. "We are *not* going to descend into anarchy and violence," he said. "The only way forward is together."

"Stay out of it, Supercop," Glen hissed.

"I will not. None of us can survive on our own, so you'd better get on board real quick, or you two will find that you're the ones bleeding in the woods."

Glen balked, and Sam looked away, clearly not man enough to stand up to Declan when he knew he was outnumbered and could only lose the argument.

"Fine," Glen conceded, "but there have to be some rules. Stealing food results in loss of rations. Same goes for lack of contribution. I propose that Ed be denied rations until this time tomorrow."

"I second that," Sam said.

Declan turned to Ed, who stood rooted to the spot, his eyes glowing with resentment. Between the blood covering his face and his swollen lips turned down at the corners, he looked like a character in a horror movie instead of a mild-mannered minister.

"Ed, you are a man of God, and I ask for the truth in His presence. Did you help yourself to food from the shed?" Declan asked.

Ed's face fell and he looked like he was about to cry. "I have low blood sugar," he said. "I feel weak and dizzy if I don't eat. The sugar in the corn helps to keep me going."

"You took more than corn," Iris said.

"I know, and I'm truly sorry. I didn't take much, just enough to stave off the hunger."

"We're all hungry, Ed," Declan said. "A half packet of oatmeal doesn't cut it for me either, but you don't have the right to steal from the collective. We have a pregnant woman, and she's not stealing food, even though she probably needs it more than you."

Shelby sat with her head bowed, clearly unhappy to be singled out.

"I'm sorry," Ed said again. "I never meant to hurt anyone."

Everyone was looking to Declan, who glanced at Tim. Tim gave a small nod, and Declan turned back to Ed.

"Ed, you are to go without rations until dinner tomorrow. You're free to eat whatever you find in the woods, or any fish you catch, but the communal rations are off the table."

"Fuck you," Ed said. It was clear he meant all of us. He turned on his heel and strode toward the gates, heading to the beach.

"Well, that went well," Iris said sarcastically, her gaze fixed on Jesse. "You could have been more discreet."

"I didn't tell them," Jesse said defensively. "But I did have a word with Ed."

"He didn't say anything," Sam said. It was clear he was avoiding Iris's gaze. "Glen overheard Jesse speaking to Ed."

I was angry with Ed for putting everyone in this awful position, but what Sam and Glen had done signaled a new low in group relations. This was the first time anyone had taken the law into their own hands and resorted to violence, and the fact that Ed would be denied rations but the two people who'd worked him over would suffer no consequences was disturbing. Jesse looked like he wanted to say something but seemingly changed his mind and turned his attention to the venison and his three leaves of spinach. Declan resumed his seat after I sat down, but I could see the worried looks that passed between him and Tim. They were all too aware that things had changed, and we could never go back. Martial law would prevail if anyone else joined Glen and Sam.

# Chapter 49

In the women's house that night, I thought there might be some discussion of what had happened, but no one said a word. Everyone got ready for bed in silence and pretended to go to sleep. I lay in the dark, sweaty and angry, and feeling more than a little sorry for myself. I would have given anything to be in my cozy little condo with the air conditioner on and my cool, comfortable sheets against my skin. I desperately missed my parents and Dee and wished I had never clapped eyes on that awful ad. What had I thought was going to happen? Even if everything had gone according to plan, people would still turn on each other sooner or later. People always did when they became frustrated and angry, and twenty-first century people were simply not equipped to deal with constant hunger and a total lack of options.

I must have fallen asleep because I woke with a start, the reek of billowing smoke permeating the still air inside the house. It was surprisingly light outside, and for a moment I thought that what I was seeing was a particularly vivid sunrise—but the sun did not smoke as it came up, nor did it roar like a rapacious beast. I exploded out of bed and ran toward the door, yanking it open in my desperation to get outside.

I wasn't the first one in the square. Declan stood in the center, wearing nothing but his breeches. His sweat-dampened skin reflected the glow of the flames as he stared at the inferno that engulfed the church and painted the sky an apocalyptic red, as if the ground beneath were exhaling the vapors of hell. Declan turned, and when I saw the alarm in his gaze, I knew what he was thinking without exchanging a word. This was no accident. Someone had torched Ed's church, and if we didn't put the fire out, sparks could land on the thatch of the other roofs and burn our houses to the ground. If things were bad, they'd be considerably worse if we had no shelter.

Declan sprang into action and raised the alarm. We had to put the fire out before it had a chance to spread. As the rest of the group spilled from the houses in various stages of undress, there were grumblings of discontent, and a few people expressed the opinion that we should just let the church burn, but once they realized the danger, everyone got to work without further comment. Every bucket and pitcher was utilized, our chain stretching to the well.

I think we were all on autopilot, filling buckets and pitchers and passing them along the line in the crimson-tinged darkness. People's stares were blank, their movements mechanical. Declan and Tim were at the front, dousing the beams with water since the plaster walls had already melted away from their supports and the roof had gone up like a torch, the leaping flames curling and incinerating the thatch, the heat searing.

A familiar smell overlaid the acrid breath expelled by the glowing ruin, but my mind was too tired to place it. My arms and back ached, and my legs felt like rubber after what seemed like hours of battling the flames. Shelby came around with a pitcher of water and a cup and gave each of us a drink. Her face was covered with soot, and her hair and clothes smelled like smoke. I grabbed the cup and gulped down the cool water, but my throat still felt parched, and the water tasted like ash. Shelby moved down the line, giving each person a cupful before coming back around. She looked up and down the line, her brow creasing with confusion.

"Where's Ed?" she asked no one in particular.

A murmur traveled down the line, and everyone turned to look at the people on either side of them. We had all been so focused on putting out the flames that no one had taken a roll call.

"Ed?" Jesse called out as he looked around the square. "Ed?"

I half expected Ed to materialize out of the darkness, but he never appeared.

"Did he go to bed?" Iris asked. "Has anyone seen him since this afternoon?"

"I saw him," Jesse replied without breaking his stride. "He went to bed as usual, but he didn't speak to anyone."

"He was there," Brendan confirmed. "I tried to talk to him, but he was still upset."

I glanced at the gates. They were locked from the inside, so Ed couldn't have left during the night. That was a relief. I didn't want to imagine him out there on his own, while his church burned to the ground.

"We have to put out the fire before we can spare the manpower to search for Ed," Jesse said as he hauled out yet another bucket of water.

The bucket made its way to the front of the line, along with Shelby, who drifted toward the church.

"Shelby, stay back," I called out. "Smoke inhalation can be dangerous."

Both Declan and Tim had covered their mouths and noses with wet kerchiefs as they battled the flames, but Shelby wasn't protected from the acrid smoke, and she was standing way too close, her eyes reflecting the flames.

She didn't appear to have heard me. She was staring at the charred remains of the building, and then she began to scream.

"What is it?" Iris cried, running to place her arms around the terrified girl and trying in vain to draw her away. "Shelby, what is it?"

The whites of Shelby's eyes looked unusually bright in her soot-covered face, and tears left streaks of cleaner skin as they slid down her cheeks. She couldn't seem to find the strength to speak, but she pointed toward the church, her finger trembling with the effort.

"Shelby, what are you saying?" Iris asked gently as she took Shelby by the shoulders.

"Ed," Shelby whispered.

"You think Ed was inside the church?"

Shelby nodded, then seemed to find her voice. "I saw him going into the church when I got up to pee. I thought he was going to pray," she wailed.

Everyone stared at the church, unable to believe that Ed might have been inside. Had he started the fire, or had someone else set the building alight? Either possibility was so horrific that I simply couldn't bear to entertain it and actually felt grateful for the numbing fatigue that had settled over my mind like a heavy blanket.

I looked up and realized that the sky had begun to lighten. We'd been at it nearly all night, but the fire was finally out. The church was nothing but smoldering beams and smoking thatch. Clouds of ash swirled in the predawn breeze and settled on our hair and skin like snowflakes falling from a winter sky, except that it was already hot and humid, and we were all drenched in sweat and smelled like burned kebob. The stench was overpowering, but at least the rest of the houses were intact. The group began to disperse, everyone ambling toward their respective houses to collapse on their cots and grab a few hours of sleep. If Ed had been inside the church, there was nothing anyone could do for him. No one could have survived that inferno. And if he wasn't, he'd hopefully turn up. At any rate, the ruins couldn't be searched until the ash had cooled.

Craving solitude, I set down my bucket and stumbled toward the gates, my feet carrying me toward the cleansing peace of the ocean. Nothing made sense, and I was honestly too traumatized and exhausted to try to understand what had happened or attempt to assign blame. I was pulling off my reeking clothes before I even reached the water and dove naked into the waves, closing my eyes as the silky coolness embraced me and soothed my overheated body.

It was only when I came up for air that I realized Declan had followed me. He was in the water beside me, his hair dripping seawater into his smoke-reddened eyes. His lips were chapped from the heat, and his skin was flushed from the fire's searing proximity, but it was no longer covered in soot, and his shoulders looked like marble in the bluish light of the coming dawn. I hadn't realized Declan had a tattoo, the ink encircling his bicep reminiscent of the crown of thorns worn by Christ.

Declan reached out, and I came into his arms, wrapping myself around his body as if he could save me from drowning. He was naked as well, and I felt his arousal pressing against my inner thigh. Without thinking, I disentangled one arm and brought it down, guiding Declan inside me and wrapping my legs tighter around his waist as I gloried in every hard inch as he slid deeper inside. When I kissed him, I tasted the salt of the ocean, a hint of smoke, and the wetness of his tongue. I allowed myself to get lost in this moment of exquisite pleasure, desperate to erect a barrier between reality and my fragile psyche. I needed to be shored up, recharged, and Declan was the only person I trusted enough to surrender to both physically and emotionally at a time when I felt completely undone.

I had made love before, but this was the most intense and emotionally raw sexual experience of my life. Every cell in my being seemed to be on heightened alert, my nerve endings electrified after months of unrelenting fear and self-denial. To finally let go of my self-control and unravel in Declan's arms left me feeling emotionally bare but thrumming with ripples of pleasure in the aftermath of our joining.

I slumped against Declan, utterly depleted, but continued to hold on for fear that he'd let me go. I couldn't bring myself to speak or even open my eyes, but I didn't need to. Declan held me tight as he walked out of the water and bent down slightly to pick up the blanket he'd brought. He threw it over me and laid me carefully on the sand, wrapping me in the scratchy wool. Declan pulled on his breeches and lay down beside me, holding me close and kissing the top of my head.

"Go to sleep," he said hoarsely. "I'll watch over you."

There was so much I wanted to say, but my tongue was as thick as wet wool, and my muscles ached with the effort of lifting buckets of water all night. I drifted on a cloud of drowsy contentment, feeling safe in Declan's arms as I finally fell asleep.

# Chapter 50

## Declan

My muscles ached with fatigue, my throat felt raw, and my eyes were gritty and dry. All I craved was a few hours of oblivion, and normally, after such prolonged exertion, I'd be out like a light, but I couldn't manage to quiet my mind. Putting out the fire had been the easy part; dealing with the aftermath would be a lot more difficult. At the time, it hadn't registered that what I was smelling was burning flesh until I heard Shelby's agonized scream, and then the truth of what we were dealing with hit me like a runaway train. Whether Ed had committed suicide or been murdered, his death would have been horrific, and the realization of what he must have endured if he was aware of what was happening left me feeling as if I had reached the end of my emotional endurance.

Will and Mark would have died relatively quickly. Ed's death would have taken time. Victims of fire usually die of smoke inhalation before the fire reaches them, and I hoped that Ed had been unconscious when his heart gave out. The thought of him struggling to breathe as the fire raged all around him was enough to bring tears to my eyes.

Once the embers cooled, I'd be able to examine the scene and retrieve Ed's remains for burial. I was no arson expert, but it would mean a great deal to me if I could determine whether foul play was involved. I had to admit that some part of me was ready to accuse Sam and Glen, but I didn't think they had it in them to leave a man to burn to death—but maybe Ed had already been dead, and they had set the fire to cover their tracks. Would they have murdered him in cold blood over a small amount of missing food? And why would they jump him twice in one day?

I could understand their anger. I was angry too, mostly because I was hungry all the time and felt my body turning on itself as it searched for nourishment, but I didn't think they had done it. A cop has to trust his instincts, and my instinct told me there was something else at play here, something I didn't yet understand. What I did understand was that I loved Natalie and needed to protect her. She had felt so fragile in my arms, so vulnerable. What had happened between us hadn't just been about sex. It had been about intimacy, and it had been urgent and raw and life changing. I wanted Natalie more than I had ever wanted any woman before, but would she still want me once she had recovered from the shock, or was this a one-off, a desperate act after a harrowing night?

I wanted nothing more than to proclaim to the rest of the group that Natalie was now my Jamestown wife, and we would cohabitate until this was all over, but I had no right to pressure her. She was terrified and absolutely devastated by what had happened last night. Much as I wanted to, I wouldn't have made my move had Natalie not taken matters into her own hands. Having sex with an emotionally vulnerable woman wasn't the way to start a relationship. Natalie needed to figure out what she wanted and might decide that she couldn't handle any more complications. But that didn't mean I wouldn't lay down my life to protect her. We had already lost four people. As tiredness overtook me and I finally began to drift, I couldn't help but wonder who might be next.

# Chapter 51

## Natalie

When I woke, the sun was fully up, and I was too warm in my blanket cocoon, but I could hardly throw it off since I was completely naked, and someone might come along at any moment. I was terribly thirsty, and my body ached, my every muscle sore after hours of trying to put out the fire. My prevailing emotion was shattering grief for Ed, but beneath that was a twinge of embarrassment and tender affection for Declan.

Declan was asleep next to me, his skin still flushed from the heat of the flames, his hair falling into his face. I had thrown myself at him and had no idea how he would feel about me in the cold light of day. I'd given him little choice, and although Declan had never made a secret of his feelings for me, some would call my actions sexual assault. I didn't think Declan had been a reluctant participant, but he had been in no emotional state to make rational decisions. Neither of us had been.

I couldn't help noticing how sharp his cheekbones appeared when he was lying down or how hollow his cheeks had become. His stomach dipped below his ribs, and his hip bones jutted through the worn fabric of his breeches. While I spent my time on domestic chores, Declan walked miles every day in search of food and carried back his kill, hauling a dead weight over uneven ground in clothes that were inappropriate for the weather. And last night, he had battled the flames for hours, never stopping to take a break until the settlement was safe.

I'd dated my share of guys back home, but I'm not really sure how many of them I would describe as honorable, trustworthy, or even caring. Declan was all those things and more, and suddenly, I wanted nothing more than to call him my own, even if the circumstances of our meeting and the current situation were weird enough to make for a Stephen King novel.

I looked up when I felt Declan's gaze on me. He pushed a lock of hair behind my ear and smiled lazily, his eyes warm with tenderness.

"Good morning," he said. Despite everything that had happened last night, he seemed calm and totally in the moment.

"Morning," I whispered. My throat was still dry from last night, and I would have given up my three spinach leaves for a cup of cold water. "Declan, I—"

"It's whatever you want it to be, Natalie," Declan cut across me. "If you tell me what happened was just an emotional response to shock, then I will accept that and leave you alone."

"And if it wasn't?" I asked shyly.

Declan grinned at me. "Then I will be very happy. You know how I feel about you."

I didn't ask exactly how he felt. Back home, things would have been simpler, but here, whatever attraction we felt toward each other was tainted by fear, anxiety, mistrust, and violence. And also acute embarrassment. The men had fared considerably better than the women in the personal grooming department. They had learned to shave using their hunting knives, and none of them looked any less attractive with slightly longer hair. The women, on the other hand, looked considerably the worse for wear. After months of washing with lye soap, my hair was faded and brittle. My face was sunburned, my skin parched without the benefit of moisturizer. And I didn't want to think of all the areas below the neck that had not received any attention since I had arrived at the homestead in Virginia. Au naturel didn't begin to describe it, and I suddenly felt so self-conscious, I averted my face and buried it in Declan's shoulder.

"Natalie, I want to be with you," Declan said softly. "Here, and at home. My every thought on this island is for you, and I will do whatever it takes to keep you safe."

"Do you think I'm in danger?" I asked, his words chilling me despite the heat.

"I think we all are."

"Do you think Ed was murdered?"

"I don't know yet. But I do need to get back," he said apologetically.

I looked around. There was no one on the beach, and I couldn't see anyone through the gates. The smell of smoke still hung in the air, and I wished I could take another dip before putting on my stinking clothes, but now wasn't the time to cavort in the water. I threw off the blanket, ignored the spark of desire in Declan's eyes as he took in my naked body, and pulled the chemise over my head. I decided to forgo the wool skirt and bodice. They were covered with soot and smelled so acrid, they made my eyes water. I'd wash them as soon as I got the chance.

Declan picked up the blanket and threw it over his arm, and then we walked back to the settlement in silence, each of us bracing for what awaited us this day. My stomach felt hollow, not only with hunger but with trepidation, and I felt a wave of nausea as Tim came forward to meet us.

"Did you check the site?" Declan asked.

Tim nodded. His gaze slid toward me, but he seemed to conclude that whatever he had to say didn't need to be in private. "I have removed Ed's remains from the church. I have no reason to believe that he had suffered an injury before the fire started or had been restrained in any way, but I would appreciate it if you would take a look at the body."

"I intend to," Declan said. "Did you question everyone?"

Tim nodded tiredly. "They're all understandably tired and upset, but Theresa remembered seeing Ed inside the church. She said she went to the well because she was thirsty and wanted cold water and saw him clearly through the doorway. Ed had set a candle on the altar. She assumed he wanted to pray or maybe just needed a moment of private contemplation after the day's events."

"This would be after Shelby had seen him," Declan said.

"We have no way of knowing what time it was, but Ed was alive, and he was alone both times."

"Might someone have joined him afterward?"

Tim sighed. "I was dead to the world. I have no idea. Did you see anyone around before you raised the alarm?"

"I smelled smoke and came outside to see what was happening. I didn't see anyone until Natalie came outside."

"Natalie, did you see anyone?" Tim asked.

"I was asleep. I didn't hear either Shelby or Theresa leaving the house."

"So, once again we have no witnesses and no idea what happened," Tim said angrily.

"I'd like to see the body now," Declan said.

"I'll come with you," I offered.

"No," Declan said firmly. "I won't let you. It's too horrible."

I was about to protest and assert my independence when Tim smiled wearily at me and said softly, "Listen to him, Natalie. It's not something you can ever unsee. He's only trying to spare you something awful."

"All right," I said, and realized I was deeply grateful to them both for caring enough to spare my feelings. In truth, I was afraid to see Ed's remains and knew there was little I could do to help.

The two men walked off toward the shed, and I headed for my house, my clothes under my arm. Not for the first time, I reflected on how much modern-day society relied on technology to safeguard their sanity. TV, books, social media sites, and even mindless games all served as a buffer between the individual and their reality. They helped keep the monsters at bay when the mind was desperate for a distraction. I would have given anything to focus on something else, but all I could think of was Ed's death and what awaited Declan in that shed.

# Chapter 52

## Declan

My breath caught in my throat and my stomach dropped as Tim and I approached the shed, my mind unhelpfully going back to the time my dad had left the ribs on the grill too long and burned them to a crisp. The odor emanating from the shed wasn't much different, and the thought made me feel even sicker. We thought we were so superior to the animal world, but we were nothing but meat, our only advantage being that we were at the top of the food chain.

I shouldn't have spoken to Natalie so rudely, but I was relieved she had returned to her house. Seeing Ed's remains would have stayed with her for the rest of her days, as it would stay with me. I steeled myself for the horror and entered the shed, determined to examine the body as dispassionately as I could for any signs of foul play.

When I emerged about ten minutes later, I barely made it around the side of the shed before my stomach emptied itself out, not that there was much there to vomit. I hadn't eaten since early afternoon yesterday. My insides twisted with dry heaves, and I broke into a cold sweat as my body and mind rebelled against what I had seen. I was shaking with both shock and fatigue and would have given anything to erase the past few minutes from my mind.

"Here," Tim said. He handed me a cup of water, and I gulped it down, desperate to wash away the sour taste of bile in my mouth.

"Thank you."

"No problem. Let's take a walk. You look like death warmed over." I glared at him, and he smiled ruefully. "Sorry. Just slipped out."

"I need to eat something," I said. I felt like I was going to pass out.

"Breakfast sandwich and a large latte?" Tim asked sarcastically.

"You're on a roll, aren't you?"

"It's just my way of dealing with shock," Tim said. "This is the most disturbing thing I've ever seen."

"Me too."

"You think he was murdered?"

"How should I know?" I exclaimed, my anger and frustration mounting. "There's nothing to go on. I don't see any injuries. His skull is intact. There are no knife wounds or evidence of garroting. But that doesn't mean he wasn't poisoned like Mark or strangled with bare hands. It's impossible to make out any bruising when he's…he's…" I couldn't even utter the words. It was too horrible.

"I know," Tim said soothingly. "Come. I want to show you something."

We walked across the square toward the burned-out church, and Tim pointed to something near what had been the front bench. "You see that? That's a puddle of wax on the floor."

"So?"

"There's no accelerant to be found in the settlement. The only thing that could work is animal fat. I checked the stores, and nothing was taken. It takes a long time to start a fire with a single candle. Ed would have had plenty of time to call for help or even crawl toward the door if he was conscious. His body was at the front, near the altar."

"So either he was already dead, or he started the fire himself," I concluded.

"Exactly."

"Would he really kill himself?"

"We've all been operating under great emotional stress," Tim replied. "Perhaps he simply snapped. People do all the time."

"And if he didn't commit suicide?"

Tim shrugged. "All we can do is speculate. Honestly, I see no reason anyone would want to murder Ed, but if they did, why do it smack in the middle of the settlement, where they might have been seen, when they could have just as easily ambushed him in the woods?"

"You mean the way Glen and Sam had?" I asked.

"I questioned them both," Tim replied wearily. "I don't think they are responsible. They were angry and wanted to teach Ed a lesson, but murdering someone and setting their body on fire in full view of the rest of the settlement is a crime of an entirely different caliber. Besides, both Sam and Glen are in my house. I didn't hear either of them leave."

"You just said you were dead to the world," I pointed out.

"I was, but Sam is not exactly known for stealth. He crashes around like a bear woken from hibernation. I would have heard something."

I sighed, simply too exhausted and heartsick to continue to speculate on what had happened, but I could see there was something Tim wanted to say.

"If Ed was already dead when the fire was set, my money would be on Theresa. She admitted to being awake and seeing Ed, and she knows about poisons."

"Which is exactly why she is not the one," I replied. "If Theresa wanted to kill Ed, why would she admit to being outside just before he died? She could have said she'd slept soundly until she was woken by my shout of alarm."

"If someone had seen her leave the house, this would be the perfect explanation. Maybe she simply preempted someone recalling seeing her outside."

"But why would Theresa kill Ed?" I asked. "I have never noticed any friction between them, and she's the most serene person here."

"She's not serene; she's detached. There's a difference," Tim replied. "Besides, it could be an act."

"Could be, but I just don't see it, Tim."

"Me neither, if I'm honest," Tim replied. "Look, I'm just grasping at straws, like you. I can't imagine anyone murdering Ed over some stolen food. People were angry, but this?" He made a sweeping gesture to encompass the still-smoking church.

"Let's talk later," I said. I still felt sick and needed to get away from the stench of death and the reminder that Ed's charred body rested just on the other side of the wall.

"All right. Let's catch up after the funeral."

"Are we burying Ed today?" I asked. Brendan would need time to cut down some wood and make a coffin. That took days.

"I think it's best for everyone if we just use his blanket as a shroud and get him in the ground as soon as possible. It's too upsetting, and Brendan is needed in the bunker."

"Agreed," I said.

Tim walked away toward the beach, and I headed to the trestle table, where Iris was dishing out a breakfast of a piece of cheese and a corn fritter. She gave me a pitying look and served me a double portion of cheese.

# Chapter 53

## Natalie

The rest of the day passed in near silence. No one was in the mood to talk or speculate about what had happened to Ed. We washed our clothes and bedding and hung them to dry in the hot sun, then turned to our usual chores. Theresa, who still preferred to go out alone despite repeated warnings, headed into the woods to look for berries and edible plants, and Iris and Nicky remained at the settlement to grind more corn. Shelby sat in the shade of a nearby tree, her legs sticking out before her, her eyes closed, and her mouth slack. She didn't look well, but other than letting her rest and encouraging her to stay hydrated, there wasn't much we could do for her.

The men had dispersed as well. Declan and Brendan headed back to the bunker. Sam and Glen went fishing, and Tim and Jesse had started digging the grave. We'd bury Ed at sunset, since it had been his favorite time of day.

I watered the garden and headed back to the beach in my chemise, a basket slung over my arm. I told everyone I'd collect some seaweed, but in truth, I just wanted to be by myself. I should have been scared to be on my own, but at this point I was just as afraid to be around the others, so I took my chances. At least I didn't have to look at the burned-out church or choke on the horrible smell that emanated from the overheated shed where Ed's body awaited burial.

It was hot and humid but peaceful on the beach, and I rucked up my chemise and rolled up the sleeves, making something that resembled a summer dress. I walked along the shore, allowing the water to cool me as each wave submerged my feet and swirled around my ankles. As a child, I had dealt with anxiety by quietly humming to myself. At this stage, I was probably suffering from PTSD, but the only coping mechanism available was to either talk things out with the other members of the group or hum to myself. I opted for the latter.

I simply couldn't bring myself to talk to the others, both because it was all too raw and because I no longer trusted anyone except Declan. What did I really know of these people or what had brought them to the island? Sure, they had shared their stories, but there was no way to verify anything, and just because they looked harmless didn't mean they weren't capable of committing an atrocity. The people who committed the most heinous crimes rarely looked the part and knew how to meet societal expectations in their daily lives.

It was hot as hell by the time I returned to the settlement with my basket of seaweed. I hung it up to dry in the storage shed and went to check on my clothes. Everything was dry, so I dressed, made up my bed, and came out to join Iris and Nicky, who were preparing corncakes and roasting a piece of venison. My stomach growled, and I wished I could pilfer a cake, but there was only one per person. If I ate mine now, I'd have nothing to eat with my venison later.

It had to be around two by the time everyone returned. Sam and Glen silently handed over the fish they'd caught. It was obvious from their demeanor that they felt remorse about what they'd done to Ed and were probably terrified that they would be blamed for his death. No one said anything, and the two seemed to relax after exchanging conspiratorial glances. I didn't think they worried too much about the right and wrong but were afraid to be cast out of the settlement. Life was hard enough within. To survive without tools and shelter and with no support from the others could prove fatal, and the two men were nothing if not practical.

Tim and Jesse looked dusty and exhausted, their faces grim. They left the shovels propped against the wall of their house and washed their hands and faces before joining the others at the table. Theresa proudly handed over a few handfuls of raspberries, and Shelby ambled over and silently took her seat. She looked a little better, but not by much, and her movements were slow and uncoordinated.

Declan and Brendan were the last to arrive, and we all held our breath, desperate to hear if Brendan had been able to mend the cord. The two men looked angry and hot, and we crowded around them, searching their faces for clues to what had happened.

"Someone's been in the bunker," Declan said, his voice dangerously low. "They smashed the hard drive and shredded the cord Brendan fixed yesterday."

Our faces mirrored each other's shock.

"Who would do such a thing?" Shelby cried desperately, her chest heaving as she began to sob. Of all of us, Shelby had the most reason to be afraid if we remained on the island for much longer, and I felt her despair as if the cry had come from my own breast.

"We don't know, but it could have been anyone. Brendan and I searched the area but found no clues." Declan looked around the group, his lip curling with derision. "Is there someone here who's so afraid to return to the mainland that they would endanger the rest of us intentionally?"

No one said a word.

"Come on," Declan exclaimed. "There's no one else on the island. So it must be one of us."

"You said you heard a motor a few nights after Gael left," Sam said softly. "Maybe someone is watching us and wanted to make sure we didn't get off this island. There was such chaos last night, we wouldn't have noticed a helicopter landing on the beach. Besides, we were all here, fighting the flames."

"The hard drive could have been destroyed before or after the fire," Declan said. "It wouldn't have taken long."

"Why would you leave our only chance of escape unprotected?" Shelby screeched.

Declan looked haunted, Shelby's words clearly having hit home. "You are right, Shelby. I should have remained at the bunker, but I honestly didn't think anyone would go that far to destroy our hopes. It was my mistake."

He looked at the angry faces, all turned toward him. "The bunker had been there from the start," Declan said. "And no one had bothered to smash the hard drive. It was only once Brendan managed to fix the fridge that someone felt the need to destroy it. Sure, there might be someone watching us, but the logical explanation is most often the right one. It was someone here, a member of this group." He glared at each of us in turn. I was surprised that no one looked away or showed any signs of a guilty conscience.

"So, who do you think it is, Declan?" Glen demanded. "Come on, say it. You must suspect someone."

"I don't know, Glen. Did you do it?" Declan said, getting up in Glen's face. "Who do you suspect?"

Glen instantly backed down. "I was only saying…"

"Saying what?" Declan looked too tired to argue.

"There's something here," Shelby said quietly, her clouded gaze sweeping around the settlement.

"Have you seen something?" Iris asked.

"No, but I felt it. There's a presence here, and it's evil. It won't let us leave."

"Oh, come on, Shelby," Nicky interjected. "There's no such thing as an evil presence. People make a place evil, not earth and trees. The island didn't claim four people."

Shelby looked like she was about to cry. "You might not feel it, Nicky, but I do. I feel it all the time."

"Shelby, honey," Iris said in her most soothing voice. "It's normal to feel emotional when you're pregnant, especially when you find yourself in a situation you can't control. We will do everything we can to make sure you and your baby are safe."

"You can't protect us, Iris," Shelby cried. "No one can."

Nicky put an arm around Shelby. "I'm sorry, Shelby. I didn't mean to doubt you. Of course you're scared. I would be too. What you're feeling is perfectly normal."

"I want to go home," Shelby wailed louder. "I want my mom."

I felt Shelby's plea down to my bones. I wanted my mom too, and my sister. I wanted to curl up on Dee's couch, wrap myself in one of her colorful chenille throws, and watch some silly comedy on Netflix. I wanted to hug Maddy and debate politics with my dad. And I wanted to feel Declan's warm gaze on me as he came into the room—my other half, now a part of my family. But none of those things were going to happen now that our last chance of getting off the island had been destroyed.

"How about a dugout canoe?" Tim suddenly said. Everyone turned to look at him. "The computer wasn't our last chance. We're surrounded by trees." He gestured toward the tall pines beyond the palisade.

When no one replied, he continued. "There's no way to navigate a raft, so it can get swept out to sea, but a canoe can get us to the mainland. My grandfather told me how our ancestors used to make canoes out of tree trunks."

"Tree trunks?" Nicky echoed.

"They used to cut down a pine tree with a thick trunk, then carefully burn out the middle by keeping a low fire going and covering certain areas with chunks of bark to make the fire burn downward. The workers would shift the burning embers from one side to the other and scrape out the section that was already burned. It took time and skill, but the canoes were unsinkable."

"What made them so special?" Glen asked. It was hard to tell if he was genuinely interested or just being sarcastic.

Tim decided to take his question at face value. "The idea behind it was that the canoe was made from one solid piece of wood, so there could be no leaks."

"How long would it take to make such a canoe?" Theresa asked.

Tim turned to Brendan. "What do you think?"

Brendan lifted his shoulders in the universal gesture of ignorance. "I don't know. I'm sure there's a science to it, and if I had access to YouTube I'd find a tutorial, but this would have to be trial and error."

"I'd be happy to help," Declan said. "I've heard about those canoes, although I've never seen one up close."

"The more people helping, the faster we can make one that's seaworthy," Tim said.

"Well, we need to do something," Declan agreed. "No one is coming for us, and if we're still here come winter, we'll starve."

"I think you had better put a watch on your canoe," Iris said. "If someone felt the need to destroy the computer, they can just as easily destroy the canoe."

Jesse nodded. "I think Iris is right. We can't take any more chances with our survival. But we must also focus our energies on finding food. This might take weeks. In the meantime, we still need to eat."

"There are fewer mouths to feed," Sam said gleefully. "So that's something, I guess."

"You're such an asshole, Sam," Nicky snapped.

"I just have the balls to say what all of you are thinking," Sam retorted. "For a skinny guy, Ed could sure put it away."

"Shut up, Sam," Jesse said angrily. "Ed's death was a tragedy that could probably have been prevented if you two didn't decide to take justice into your own hands."

"Or if you knew how to keep your mouth shut," Glen snapped. "Ed's death is on you." He pointed a finger at Jesse. "You were the one to paint a bullseye on his back when you decided to discuss his food stealing within earshot of houses that have no windows. You might be a nice guy in the real world, but here, you're nothing more than a thoughtless meathead."

"And you're a dickhead, Glen, both here and in the real world," Jesse replied, and stalked off.

"Good to know that some things never change," Iris said with obvious disgust. "Men resorting to calling each other by various body parts always solves the problem."

"You should be grateful no one called you a body part," Sam replied. "I can think of a few that fit."

Iris looked shocked, but Nicky stepped forward and pointed a finger at Sam's chest. "If you can't be civil, then get the fuck out, Sam. Go live in the wilderness. Let's see how long you can survive on the occasional fish you catch." She sneered at Sam's shocked expression. "What? A hard no? Then shut up and stop biting the hand that feeds you."

Sam looked like he was about to reply but wisely shut his mouth. "I'm sorry, Iris," he muttered instead.

"Look, everyone is on edge. Let's take this down a notch, shall we?" Tim said. "Fighting amongst ourselves is not going to solve our problems."

Everyone ate in silence, then dispersed, retreating to their respective corners to sulk until it was time for the burial.

Declan waited until we were alone, then turned to me. "Natalie, I want you to move into my house. We can take the double bed." Seeing my appalled expression, he hurried to reassure me. "It's not about sex. I just want to know you're safe. I don't trust anyone."

"Not even Tim?"

"I would like to say that I'm a good judge of character, but I'm in no position to be arrogant. Three people are dead. Gael's whereabouts are unknown. I never saw any of it coming, and I don't have any idea who is responsible."

"You don't think Gael killed Will and Mark and then got off the island?" I asked.

Declan shook his head. "Given what happened to the hard drive, I think there's something else at play here." He reached out and took both my hands in his. "Please, Natalie."

"I wouldn't feel right to leave the other women unprotected."

"They won't be. I'm going to speak to Tim. I think he should move into the women's house, to keep an eye on things."

I wanted to point out that two murders and a possible suicide had taken place right under Tim's nose but decided that would be unfair. It might actually be a good idea for Tim to move in. At least Shelby would feel safer.

"If Tim agrees, then okay," I said.

Declan smiled down at me. "Thank you. I'll speak to him after the funeral. In the meantime, I think you should go lie down for a bit. You look near collapse."

"So do you," I pointed out. Declan's eyes were still red from the smoke, and his skin had a grayish pallor beneath the unnatural flush.

"I am," Declan confessed. "Why don't we go lie down together?"

I would have declined his offer, given that there wasn't an ounce of privacy in the settlement, but I was so tired and so unnerved by what had happened in the bunker that I agreed. Declan and I went to the men's house, climbed into the double bed, drew the curtains against the sun blazing through the window, and fell asleep in each other's arms as soon as our heads hit the pillows.

# Chapter 54

## Declan

Ed's funeral was a depressing affair, mostly because there was no one to eulogize him. We all stood in silence, heads bowed, unsure what to say about this man we'd barely known. Without a minister to take the service, there was nothing to do but fill in the grave and leave. We didn't even have any ale left to raise a glass to his memory, and no one really wanted to remain in each other's company any longer than was absolutely necessary. The group pulsated with anger and fear, and nothing anyone could say would make any difference at this point. Either someone among us was a remorseless killer or we were being picked off one by one by some outsider we had yet to identify.

I pulled Tim aside after the funeral. As if by mutual agreement, we didn't talk about anything that had happened within the past twenty-four hours. There was nothing new to add, and we were both cut up by our helplessness in the face of such relentless adversity. Tim had no objections to moving into the women's house, and I think the ladies, when we informed them, were relieved to have a night watchman, even if he planned to sleep on the job. Shelby, especially, seemed to feel comforted by Tim's presence and kept thanking him for agreeing to take Natalie's cot. No one suggested that Tim and Nicky shack up in the double bed, and I think they were both relieved not to have to make that decision or inch any closer toward a public commitment.

Once everyone went to bed, I would have liked nothing more than to make love to Natalie, but I could hardly expect her to feel comfortable when there were other people in the house. Even with the curtains drawn, they could still hear us, and she wouldn't be able to relax or enjoy herself. We would have to make use of the woods if we wanted privacy. I thought it'd be best to allow her to take the lead, since I didn't want to pressure her or make her feel objectified by my desire for her. I was pleasantly surprised when Natalie snuggled up to me and pressed her lips against my neck, her hand moving downward with obvious intent. I looked down at her in the darkness and could see her seductive smile.

"We'll be very quiet," she whispered.

I responded by kissing her and setting off on an exploration of my own. I had yet to get to know Natalie's body and what she liked in bed, and although we'd have to keep it down, knowing that we weren't alone added to our mutual excitement.

By the time Natalie fell asleep in my arms, I felt, if not completely happy, at least as content as I could hope to be under the circumstances. I hadn't realized how desperate I had been for emotional intimacy with another human being, something I had denied myself since the day Noah died. I felt like a hermit who'd done his penance and was ready to return to the world, even if that world currently resembled *The Twilight Zone* or a really twisty psychological thriller. At this point, I think I would have preferred a slasher because then I'd at least know who was behind the murders.

I hadn't prayed in a long time, but I closed my eyes and begged God to let us off the island and allow Natalie and me a chance at a normal life, a gift I had taken for granted before but never would again. I fitted my body to Natalie's back and closed my eyes, hoping sleep would come. I couldn't take another sleepless night. I was simply too worn out.

Morning seemed to come too quickly, and life in the settlement went on. After a breakfast of cornmeal, Jesse went hunting, Sam and Glen slunk off to fish, Brendan went to check the lobster traps, and Tim and I set off in search of that perfect tree trunk that would make for a wide enough canoe. The ladies remained at the settlement and locked the gates behind us per our instructions. Tim and I needed to know they were safe, in case someone was on the island with us, but I didn't believe anyone was there. And I didn't think Tim did either. Except for the severed cords, we hadn't seen or heard any evidence of an outside presence, and we had walked the length and breadth of the island many times. All signs pointed to the fact that the saboteur was among us, and if we hoped to avoid another death, we had to flush them out.

Tim and I walked in silence for a while, each lost in our own thoughts. What was there to say, anyway? It seemed silly to make small talk while we were literally fighting for our lives, and we were tired of talking in circles when it came to our theories. Without evidence, we had nothing, and without supplies, we wouldn't last the winter. Our outlook was bleak.

The idea of the canoe was a good one, but what were the chances it would be seaworthy when none of us had ever done anything like that before? Or that someone wouldn't try to destroy it before it ever got wet? After what had happened in the bunker, we all felt even more vulnerable and scared. To finish us all off would be as easy as shooting fish in a barrel. There was nowhere left to hide.

"Once we find the right trunk, we should bring it to the settlement and then lock the gates at night once we start working on it," Tim said. Clearly, his thoughts were running along a similar path.

"We should probably take turns guarding it at night as well. If someone fans the flames, it'll burn like a Yuletide log."

Tim nodded. "I'll take the first shift. You can play house with Natalie," he said with a suggestive smile.

"Not like you've been denying yourself," I said.

"It's different with Nicky."

"How?"

"I don't love her," Tim said. "Nicky and I will go our separate ways if we ever get out of here."

"Will you go back to your wife?" I asked carefully.

Tim sighed. "My wife shacked up with someone else before I left. She said I was a crap husband and an absentee father.

She was right," he confessed. "If I get the chance, I will try to win her back and work at becoming the giving partner she deserves. And if I can't, I will still spend the rest of my life being the best dad to my daughter."

"I guess a stint on this island has helped people get their priorities straight," I said.

"I don't know about that. I think Sam and Glen will be the same assholes they were before coming here."

"What about the rest?"

"Hard to say. I'll be the first to admit that I'm not a very outgoing guy, but it seems that everyone here is a closed book. We've been here for months but know almost nothing about each other." Tim gave me a sidelong glance. "How well do you know Natalie?"

"Not as well as I'd like, but like everyone else here, she's scared and guarded. Can't say that I blame her."

"Neither do I. I'd sleep with one eye open if I wasn't so damn tired by the end of the day." Tim was quiet for a long moment, then spoke again. "Do you think Gael found a way off the island?"

"He must have, since we've found no trace of him these past few weeks."

"And the only reason he'd need to do that is if he is guilty of murder."

"If he is, then he was also prepared to sacrifice a dozen people to save himself," I replied.

"Some people are truly evil," Tim said with disgust. "There's a darkness in them that no light can reach. In Christianity, you call it the work of the devil. Many Native American tribes believe in the Trickster or the Wendigo, but I don't buy that. I think we all make conscious choices, and we can't blame them on some mythical demon."

"I saw evil every day back in Chicago," I said. "Some people were truly without conscience, while others were trapped by their circumstances. It's much easier and more profitable to sell drugs to kids than to work at some burger joint for minimum wage and know this will be your life unless you find a way out. Some do. Most don't."

"We're very philosophical this morning," Tim said, a half-smile tugging at his lips.

"I'm not sure what else to be. I've never felt so helpless in my life."

"Me neither."

"Do you really think we can make a seaworthy canoe?" I asked.

"You have a better idea?"

"No."

"Then we might as well try. Let's head for the old cabin. There is a nice, thick pine just behind it."

"I know the one you mean," I said. "There's something about that place…" I let the sentence trail off since I could hardly admit to Tim that it creeped me out.

"Yeah, I know. Something terrible happened there. I can feel it every time I get near. Even the animals seem to avoid it."

Tim was right. We'd never seen a deer or even a rabbit near the old cabin, which was why we hardly ever went that way. I didn't believe in restless ghosts or vengeful spirits, but I did think that places sometimes absorbed echoes of tragedy into their very walls. And those echoes reverberated through the centuries unless the place was torn down and reinvented, like the many locations where blood had once run in the streets but now tourists strolled

along happily, pausing to take countless selfies. The Burnett cabin
had not been reinvented, and although we had no proof that
anything tragic had happened there, a shiver of apprehension ran
down my spine, and I wished we could find another tree.

# Chapter 55

The cabin was lost in shadow despite the brightness of the morning. The crows perched in the nearby trees cawed madly as we approached, and then exploded into the cloudless sky in obvious panic. Once again, I wondered why someone would build a cabin so deep in the woods, with no ready access to the ocean or arable land. There wasn't even a well or a creek nearby to serve as a source of clean water. Had these people died of hunger? And if someone had buried them when they died, who'd done the same for the last person left alive, or had they left the island, never to return? We'd never explored the remains of the cabin, partly because no one really wanted to set foot inside and partly because, incongruously, the door was padlocked even though the structure was a strong gust of wind away from tumbling.

The tiny cemetery was just as forlorn as before, the three stones at the edge of the clearing leaning sideways as if they were tired of standing after all this time and wanted to lie down. My gaze went to the weathered inscriptions, but Tim was off, already measuring the tree he'd had in mind with his arms. I was just about to join him when something caught my eye, and I felt a wave of nausea as the understanding of what I was looking at sank in.

"Tim," I called softly, as if the dead could hear me and would object to the disturbance.

"This one is perfect," Tim called over his shoulder. "It'll take us all day to chop it down, but it'll be worth it."

"Tim, look at this," I called louder.

Tim must have heard something in my voice and turned around, walking toward me when I beckoned him to come over. "Jesus," he cried when he finally saw what I was staring at. "What the hell?"

We stood side by side, staring at the grave that hadn't been there before. It was perfectly aligned with the other three, the soil of the mound still dark and moist. We hadn't brought shovels with us, only axes, but it was imperative that we find out who had been buried at the ancient cemetery.

"There might be a shovel inside," Tim said, tipping his head toward the cabin.

Tim strode purposefully toward the cabin, and I followed. He used his axe to strike off the rusted padlock, shoved it aside with his foot, and pushed the door open. It complied with a whiny creak and opened onto a dark, musty-smelling space. The single window was partially covered with a leather shade, but enough light came in through the door to see inside. The cabin consisted of one rectangular room that contained a curtained bed, a scarred wooden table and four chairs, a small dresser with several shelves of mismatched cups, plates, and cast-iron pans, and rusted tools that hung on nails along one side of the stone hearth. A pile of mangy skins were stacked in one corner, the leather so dry it was cracked, and an antique rifle hung above the mantel.

"Think that still works?" Tim asked as he approached the bedstead and pulled aside the moth-eaten curtain. A cloud of dust filled the air, and he coughed before peering into the dim confines.

"Jesus," he said again, this time with disgust rather than surprise.

The remains of a man rested on what had once been a mattress but was now a stained sack filled with moldy straw. He must have been tall and powerfully built once, but now he was nothing more than bones held together by what was left of his leather buckskins, vest, and boots. The fabric of the shirt had rotted away ages ago, as had most of his skin, but the gleam of a wedding ring was still visible on the skeletal finger, and he had a fine set of teeth that although tobacco-stained were all present and intact.

I joined Tim by the bed and studied the remains. What was left of the pillow and bedding were rust brown beneath the head, and there was a wicked-looking blood-stained knife on the floor by the right side of the bed.

"What do you think?" Tim asked.

"I'm no pathologist, but I'd say the guy was fairly young, based on the condition of his teeth, and that he died by suicide."

Tim nodded. "Maybe he couldn't bear the loss of his family."

"Or maybe he knew he was dying from whatever illness had carried off the rest of them and decided to put himself out of his misery."

"Could be," Tim agreed. "Well, rest in peace, buddy," he said, and pulled the curtain closed once again. "No wonder someone padlocked the cabin. Didn't want the contestants seeing this."

"They could have buried him," I said.

"Clearly, they didn't think it was worth the bother." Tim grabbed a shovel that stood propped up against the wall and jutted his chin in the direction of the cemetery. "Let's get this over with."

I helped myself to a garden trowel and followed Tim out the door. We had our answer quicker than we had anticipated since the body was buried less than two feet down. I stared at the hand that had emerged from the ground first and stopped digging. Tim looked at me, then back at the protruding hand. When he saw what I had seen, the Aztec sun tattoo on the inside of the wrist, he sucked in his breath.

"Guess now we know what happened to Gael," Tim said.

"We don't, though, do we?" I retorted. "Someone murdered Gael and buried him in a shallow grave. But we still don't know who did it or why."

"I think we should leave him, Declan," Tim said. "The body has been decomposing for several weeks, and we don't have any protective equipment. We both have open blisters on our hands from fighting the fire. We're vulnerable to bacteria, and we don't have any antibiotics."

"I need to know how he died," I said stubbornly. "I'll wear gloves."

I had brought leather gloves to protect my hands while chopping down the tree, so I pulled them on and used my hands to clear the dirt away from Gael's face, revealing what was left of his features. Decomposition was well under way, but he was still recognizable, and the deep cut to his throat was unmistakable.

"His throat was slashed. Probably from behind."

"The poor guy never stood a chance once the carotid artery was severed," Tim said.

"It's small comfort to know he didn't abandon us," I said as I gently covered Gael's face with the dirt I had removed. "We should put a marker on his grave."

Tim nodded. "Much good it will do him."

"It's the least we can do."

"Okay. We'll make him a cross. He was probably Catholic. But let's chop down the tree first. We have to focus on the living before we deal with the dead. Unless you want to say a few words."

I hadn't felt the need to speak at Ed's funeral, but finding Gael out here, dumped in a shallow hole without even a marker to identify his final resting place, I felt moved to say something. I had done a reading at my grandfather's funeral a few years back, and the words were etched into my memory.

I bowed my head and intoned, "Jesus, my Rock and my Redeemer, I am a sinner and unworthy of Your love. I have gone my own way and walked my own path away from You. And yet You loved me still. You paid the debt of my sin, and You bore it all for me on the cross. You took away the sins of the entire world.

You rose again giving me a new life and the promise of rising again in heaven. Have mercy on me, precious Jesus. Help me leave my old ways behind. Help me surrender completely to You. I trust in You, Jesus, for all that I am and all that I will ever be. Thank You, that no power on earth can now separate me from Your love. Amen."

"Gael would have liked that," Tim said, probably more to comfort me than because he had any clue what Gael would have preferred when his time came. "Shall we cut down the tree now?" he asked, and I turned away from the grave and followed Tim across the clearing, wishing all the while that I could return to Natalie and expunge the look of horror frozen on what was left of Gael's face from my memory.

It took several hours to chop down the tree, decide on the approximate length of our canoe, and cut away the remainder of the trunk. We were left with a six-foot log. The only way we could get it back to the settlement would be to come back with Wilbur and have him drag it over the uneven ground since we had nothing with wheels that would make transport easier.

"I hope no one decides to torch it," Tim said as he patted the log affectionately.

No answer seemed to be expected, so I didn't give one. I wouldn't be at all surprised if we returned tomorrow to find the log reduced to kindling.

"What do we tell the others about Gael?" Tim asked as we followed the narrow woodland path back to the settlement.

We hadn't spoken about Gael all afternoon, but it was impossible not to address what we had discovered now that we'd had some time to absorb the shock.

"Nothing," I replied.

"Are you serious?"

"There's no doubt that Gael was murdered. I think he was probably lured to the cabin and then ambushed by his assailant from behind. Whereas the other killings appeared opportunistic, this one seems premeditated. Will and Mark were left for us to find, while this time, the killer buried the body in a spot they thought it wouldn't be found. Everyone thinks Gael got off the island. Perhaps it's kinder to allow them to believe it."

"Is that the only reason?" Tim asked.

"I want to avoid causing a panic," I said. "We don't know who did it, or why, and we have absolutely no evidence to go on."

"Are you thinking that if we tell the others, one of us might be next?"

"There is that," I replied, not bothering to hide my sarcasm. There was no rhyme or reason to the killings as far as I could see. In truth, I was surprised that whoever had taken out Gael hadn't gone for me or Tim first.

"The killer doesn't see us as a threat," Tim said, and I wondered if I had spoken out loud without realizing.

"Why do you think that is?" I asked.

"Probably thinks we're a joke."

"And not a very good one," I said morosely. "A TV cop would have solved this in an hour, even with commercials."

"Don't be so hard on yourself, Declan. Even the greatest detectives have help. No one solves a case using nothing but their ability to speculate. That only works in dated fiction. In real life, detectives follow the science and factual evidence, of which we have none." Tim chuckled mirthlessly. "And speaking of science, do you know anything about profiling?"

I turned to look at him, taken aback by the question. "The only thing I know is that profiling is rarely as effective as it is on TV, and neither one of us is a qualified psychologist."

"Hey, don't get your panties in a twist. I was only asking."

"Sorry. I didn't mean to jump down your throat. I'm just on edge."

Tim chuckled. "You know, when I signed up for the series, the worst I thought might happen would be a game of musical beds. *Survivor* meets *Love Island*. But four people are dead, we have no way to call for help or get back to the mainland, and we're facing a very real threat of starvation. Not exactly how I thought my little sabbatical would play out."

"Are you going to tell the others about Gael?" I asked.

"I think they deserve to know the truth. Either way, the killer will know we found the grave as soon as he or she visits the cabin."

Tim was right, so I simply nodded. In truth, it didn't really matter. If the killer wanted to claim another victim, there was nothing to stop them.

"Okay," I said under my breath as the palisades of the settlement came into view.

# Chapter 56

"What the fuck?" Glen yelled. "If Gael didn't murder Will and Mark but was also a victim, then who the fuck is doing this?"

"I don't know," I said, cringing inwardly at my own powerlessness.

"What *do* you know? You and Tim are cops, but you're worse than useless. You know nothing."

"Simmer down, Glen," Jesse said, a warning in his tone.

"No, I don't think I will, *Governor*. We're being picked off one by one, and there's not a damn thing we can do about it. We're sitting ducks."

I couldn't argue with that. Any one of us could be next.

Glen looked around the group and pointed a finger at each person in turn. "Is it you? Or you? We know it's one of us. There's no one else on this island."

"How do we know it's not you?" Iris demanded, rounding on him.

"Why would I kill Gael?" Glen snapped.

"Why would I, or anyone else?" she countered.

"I don't know, but someone has killed three times that we know of. Maybe four. And all the victims were men, *Iris*," Glen said.

"Are you suggesting the killer is a woman?" Nicky asked.

"There's no evidence it isn't," Glen replied. He was breathing heavily but appeared to be calming down.

"Declan, Tim, could the killer be a woman?"

Tim and I exchanged glances, but there was no point in keeping anything back at this stage.

"Yes, the killer could be a woman," Tim said.

"You said Gael was attacked from behind," Brendan said. "Surely not every woman here is tall enough." His gaze slid toward Theresa, who was hovering at the edge of the group, as usual.

"No, not every woman here is tall enough to slash Gael's throat from behind, but if he was down on his knees, then she'd have no problem," Tim said.

"Was he down on his knees?" Brendan asked.

"Impossible to tell. There was dirt ingrained in the wool of Gael's breeches at the knees, but he might have fallen to his knees afterward, as he was dying," I said.

"So there's really no way to tell who might have had the ability to kill him?" Iris asked.

"No," Tim replied.

The conversation was brought to an end by Shelby, who covered her ears and began to wail, rocking back and forth as if the motion could somehow soothe her terror. Iris immediately went to her, and Shelby buried her face in Iris's shoulder and began to weep.

"Come on, honey. Let's get you back inside," Iris said soothingly. "I'll sit with you for a while."

Shelby shook her head without lifting her face. "I'm scared," she moaned.

"We're all scared," Sam said, sounding sympathetic for once. "No one has any reason to hurt you, Shelby."

Shelby raised her tear-stained face. "What reason did anyone have to hurt the others?"

"There must have been one," Jesse said. "I can't imagine that someone would randomly kill an innocent person."

"Why not?" Theresa exclaimed. This was the first time she'd appeared truly angry. "This is not a cozy mystery, Jesse. There isn't a quaint cast of characters in a picturesque setting, with each one nursing a secret grudge against the victim. This is real life, and in real life people do inexplicable, horrible things."

Theresa's eyes swam with tears, and we all stared at her, wondering if she was frightened by what had happened or if this had something to do with her own past.

Theresa looked around the group, tears sliding down her lean cheeks. "My daughter hanged herself," she said hoarsely. "One moment she was there, alive and with her whole life ahead of her, and then she wasn't. She had been attacked on her way home from school," she panted. "A random victim of a man who saw an opportunity and took it. He dragged her into a dark alley and raped her. She didn't want to report it. She was so ashamed," Theresa cried, shaking her head as if she still couldn't understand what had happened. "We didn't press her. We thought that with time, she would begin to heal, but she didn't. She couldn't live with what happened." She was trembling now, her voice quavering as she spoke. "If she hadn't gone to the college library that day, she would still be here, in this world, with me." Theresa raised her eyes to meet Jesse's horrified gaze. "So, yes, Jesse. People do inexplicable things, and they don't care who they hurt. They don't care that they break someone into a million pieces."

Natalie went over to Theresa, but Theresa waved her off, then simply walked away, heading toward the gates. We all watched her go, a small, solitary figure striding down to the beach. Something about the set of Theresa's shoulders and her bowed head said that she didn't really care if she became the next victim. She was half dead already.

# Chapter 57

"Come, let's take a walk," Natalie said once she'd checked on Shelby. I nodded, eager to get away from the palpable tension that permeated the settlement. The sun hovered just above the horizon, the ocean shimmering beneath the golden rays. Seagulls circled overhead, and the surf frothed as the waves gently rolled onto the sand. It was an idyllic scene, and if I were on vacation with the woman I loved, I would have felt happy and relaxed, but instead, I was tight as a bowstring, and Natalie could probably feel the frustration bubbling away inside me.

"How's Shelby?" I asked as Natalie fell into step beside me.

"Emotional. Terrified. Desperate," she said on a sigh.

"I feel horrible," I said.

"It's not your fault, Declan."

"Then why do I feel like it is?"

"Because you're a good man, and you want to save the world."

"Am I a good man?" I asked, needing reassurance.

"You are. Look, Glen is lashing out because he's scared. We all are. And what happened to Theresa's daughter has nothing to do with Gael's death."

"Doesn't make it any less tragic," I muttered.

"No, it doesn't," Natalie agreed.

"Natalie, what if Theresa is right and the killer is choosing the victims randomly, based on location rather than motive? Will was alone on the beach. Mark was alone in the woods. Ed was alone inside the church. Gael was probably also alone. They had no reason to suspect the person."

"Do you now believe Ed was murdered?"

"My gut feeling says no, but given that we've had three murders, I can't discount the possibility that Ed was the fourth victim. I can't know anything for certain without a postmortem."

"But you think someone in the group killed the others?" she asked.

"I don't believe for a moment that someone's coming on the island and murdering the contestants. There's absolutely no evidence of that. The murderer is among us, but for the life of me, I can't figure out who it is."

"Let's go through the suspects one by one," Natalie suggested.

"I've already done that with Tim."

"I might be able to offer a fresh perspective."

"All right," I agreed. "Let's start with Glen and Sam. They are a classic example of a bully and his sidekick. They jumped Ed. But they were both accounted for at the time of Will's death, and neither one of them seemed to have an issue with either Mark or Gael. Plus, they didn't kill Ed, just worked him over. There's a giant leap between kicking the shit out of someone and murdering them in cold blood."

"I agree with you," Natalie said. "Being a bully or an idiot doesn't necessarily make you a murderer. And whoever killed Will, Mark, and Gael was clever enough not to leave any clues or evidence behind. Jesse?"

"Jesse is an upstanding guy, or at least he comes off as one. I didn't see him leave the house the night Will was murdered, and he never left the settlement the day Mark was killed, at least not for any prolonged period of time. We don't know exactly when Gael died, so it's difficult to determine who has an alibi for his murder. And I don't think Tim is our man."

"Are you saying that because of professional courtesy or because Tim has a solid alibi for at least two murders?" Natalie asked.

Now that she had asked that, I suddenly wasn't sure where Tim had been the day Mark was murdered. He knew about the properties of jimsonweed and understood enough about forensics and police procedure to avoid making a rookie mistake. But Tim had absolutely no reason to kill anyone, as far as I knew.

"You're not sure," Natalie said.

"Factually, no, but as a cop, I have to trust my instincts, and my instincts tell me that Tim is not our man."

"All right. What about the others? Theresa knows about poisons."

I considered that. "Theresa is not tall enough to have hit Will over the head. She does know about poisons, and she did leave the settlement the day Mark was murdered. But what would be her motive? Likewise, she's not tall enough to have attacked Gael from behind, and what would be her reason for killing him?"

Natalie sighed. "She might have done something to get Gael on his knees, but I agree, I can't think of a motive, unless Gael was the one who had assaulted her daughter."

"And she would have waited all this time to murder him? I never saw a spark of recognition in either of them, and they're from opposite ends of the country. Theresa as our mastermind just doesn't add up."

"We know so little about everyone," Natalie said.

"And they're not talking," I agreed. "What about Iris?"

"Iris is a sweetheart. And she spends most of her day bent over that bubbling cauldron. She hardly leaves the settlement, so when could she have murdered three men? It would have taken time to bury Gael, even if she killed him there in the clearing. I think we would have noticed if Iris disappeared for several hours, especially if she just happened to grab the shovel." Natalie shook her head. "No, not Iris. What about Shelby?"

"I really can't see it," I said.

"Why? Because she's a beautiful woman who likes to play at being helpless?" Natalie challenged me.

"Shelby is impulsive and emotional. I can see her wanting to get back at Mark for humiliating her, and perhaps she was attracted to Will, if she has a thing for controlling older men. But I don't think Gael was a serious contender for any sort of relationship, not unless she needed someone to mow her lawn or clean her pool."

"You think that Shelby couldn't have been attracted to Gael because he was Hispanic?" Natalie asked. She didn't seem overly surprised by this observation, and I wondered if she knew something of Shelby's romantic history.

"She always spoke to him like he was her cabana boy. Besides, Shelby was accounted for the night Will was killed and the day Mark died."

"Okay. Nicky?"

"Nicky has the intelligence, the height, and the physical strength to take on a grown man, but I can think of absolutely no motive aside from the fact that both Mark and Will were pompous white men given to occasional bouts of casual racism. If Nicky were to kill every person who ever said something offensive, she'd have left a trail of dead bodies a mile long. And she seemed to genuinely like Gael. Besides, as far as we know, Nicky was at the settlement both the night Will was murdered and the day Mark was poisoned."

"I agree. And I genuinely like Nicky. I don't believe she's capable of murder. What about Brendan?" Natalie asked.

I exhaled deeply. "Brendan is a carpenter from New York. Will was from Texas, Mark from Massachusetts, and Gael from California. I can't imagine that there was a previous connection there, and I witnessed no tension between any of them. In fact, Brendan and Gael were friendly. I saw them chatting together several times. Laughing," I added.

Natalie nodded. "I think that maybe Brendan felt drawn to Gael because they were both artistic. Gael had his music, and Brendan told us he made carvings and wood sculptures besides furniture. Gael actually joked that Brendan could make a surfboard and Gael would teach him how to ride the waves," she said sadly. "I bet he was a great surfer. He was so graceful."

We both looked out to sea, as if we could imagine Gael on his surfboard, wet hair falling into his face and his dark eyes sparkling with triumph as he effortlessly rode a massive wave.

"Brendan was on good terms with Will and Mark," Natalie continued, "but I did notice that he tended to avoid Ed."

"Why do you think that was?" I asked. I had noticed that Brendan didn't seem to like Ed, but I had never witnessed an altercation between them.

Natalie sighed. "Ed once mentioned in Brendan's hearing that he didn't welcome homosexuals into his church."

"Did he? Why did you never tell me before?"

"Ed didn't die until we found out he was stealing food, and he'd made that comment months ago. I didn't think his death had anything to do with his views on the LGBT community." Natalie stopped and looked up at me. "You know, there could be another possibility that we never considered. What if Ed killed Will, Mark, and Gael, then couldn't live with the guilt and committed suicide?"

"What reason would Ed have to kill three men?" I asked. Natalie was right, I had not considered that possibility, and was now turning it over in my mind.

"I have no idea, but just because he was a minister doesn't mean he should automatically be ruled out as a suspect."

"Being a minister doesn't make him a saint, but I just can't see a possible motive," I mused. "Why would Ed want to murder those three?"

"Why would anyone?" Natalie countered.

"So, that's it, then," I said, now even more at sea than I had been before.

Natalie inhaled deeply and fixed me with her shrewd gaze. "There's me."

"What about you?"

"I want you to be certain I'm not the killer."

I shook my head. "You were never a suspect."

"Why not?"

I was embarrassed to tell her the truth, but I had to reassure her that I didn't suspect her. "I've kept an eye on you ever since we landed on the island."

"Because you thought I was a psychopath?" Natalie asked, her mouth quirking at the corners.

"No, because I was attracted to you. I knew where you were most times, and as far as I can tell, you haven't had an opportunity to kill three men. Or a motive," I added hastily.

"That leaves you," Natalie said, and grinned up at me.

"All I can do is give you my word of honor that I didn't do it."

"Is that how it works at Chicago PD? Suspects offer their word of honor and get to go home?"

I knew she was teasing me, but I still felt a bit riled. I'd never actually met a guilty person who had admitted to committing a crime. Everyone always did the "I'm innocent, Officer" song and dance because they knew that a good or even halfway decent lawyer could find a way to invalidate the evidence or cast doubt on the methods that were used to obtain the result, even if their client was as guilty as sin. The evidence had to be strong enough to bring a case to court, and all too many cases ended in either a dismissal of charges or a plea deal. In this day and age, a word of honor meant nothing, even coming from a law enforcement officer, but I could offer Natalie no proof that I hadn't been involved in any of the deaths.

Theoretically, I could have killed all of them because not only had I had the opportunity, I could very easily have found the means. It didn't take too much strategic thinking to pick up a rock and bash someone over the head, or to use a hunting knife to slit someone's throat. I had the height, strength, and training to get away with murder. And so did Tim. But a human being longs for an emotional connection and someone to trust, and we have all put our faith in people we believe to be innocent. I'd opened myself up to Tim and Natalie, and Natalie had put her trust in me and the women of our settlement. And we could only pray that our trust wasn't misplaced.

Natalie's face grew serious as she watched the emotions play out on my face. "I was joking, Declan. I didn't mean to suggest that you might be guilty."

I reached for Natalie's hands and held them in my own. "Natalie, promise me you'll look after yourself."

"What does that mean?" she asked carefully.

"It means that you shouldn't trust anyone on this island."

"Not even you?" she asked, her eyes large with confusion.

"Not even me if you have reason to doubt me," I said.

Natalie looked at me for a long moment, her gaze intent as she studied my face. "I have no reason to doubt you. Do you trust me, Declan?"

"I do," I replied, and felt like I was making a vow.

She lifted her face, and I leaned in to kiss her. That was when we heard the screams, the sound of Natalie's name carried on the wind. Natalie hitched up her skirts and took off at a run, with me sprinting behind her, my heart hammering in my chest.

# Chapter 58

## Natalie

The screams came from the women's house, and before we got to the door, Nicky came running toward us.

"What happened?" I cried.

"It's Shelby. Her water broke, and she's in a lot of pain."

Declan and I exchanged looks of alarm. That could mean only one thing. Shelby was having the baby. I hadn't examined Shelby since that day by the creek, but despite the weight loss and fatigue, she seemed to be doing as well as could be expected under the circumstances. But she still had about two months to go.

Declan must have read the panic in my eyes because he took hold of my wrist before I could disappear into the women's house. "Natalie, is it possible that Shelby is further along than she thinks?" he asked quietly.

"Anything is possible," I panted as I tried to catch my breath, "but it's not probable. Based on when Shelby first felt the baby move and her own account of the timeline, I think she's around seven months."

Declan nodded his understanding. "Call me if you need me."

"I will."

I left Declan on the doorstep and stepped inside the dim confines of the house. Shelby lay on the double bed wearing nothing but her linen shift. Her face was flushed, her skin glistening with sweat. Her eyes rolled in her head like those of a spooked horse, and there was blood on the towel between her legs. There was such naked pleading in her gaze when she looked at me, I would have given anything to promise her that everything would be well and know it to be true, but I couldn't do that. I had no idea what the next few hours would bring.

"Shelby, tell me what happened," I said with as much authority as I could muster.

"I started getting cramps, like period cramps. And then there was some blood, and my water broke."

"The blood was probably just the mucus plug."

Shelby looked at me in horror, and I realized she didn't know much about what was about to happen. She hadn't had the benefit of the books other expectant mothers had access to or the internet so she could Google anything she wanted to know. The only two women among us who'd had children were Iris and Theresa, but Theresa had mentioned that both her girls had been born via scheduled Cesarean, so she'd never gone through labor and delivery. Shelby turned to Iris, who was sitting on the edge of the bed, her fingers intertwined with Shelby's. Iris nodded and smiled encouragingly.

"All perfectly normal," she said in a soothing tone.

"May I examine you?" I asked. Shelby nodded.

I placed my hands on her belly and moved them around, trying to feel the child within. I thought I could feel the hips and the elbows pressing against Shelby's taut skin. I had performed a pelvic exam once, when I was still training, and tried to remember every detail as I slid my hand between Shelby's legs. It was mortifyingly intimate, and when I failed to pull my hand out in time, it was trapped by a contraction that was as long as it was powerful. I gritted my teeth as I wondered if I would be able to feel my fingers after the vicelike grip of the contracting muscles. As soon as it was over, I slid my fingers into Shelby's cervix, then yanked out my hand before another wave could trap me inside the birth canal.

"What's going on?" Shelby moaned. She looked worried, probably because I had failed to reassure her immediately, and her hold on Iris's hand tightened visibly. Iris and I exchanged glances, since we both knew what was happening and neither of us relished the prospect of sharing it with Shelby.

290

"Shelby, the child is in position for delivery, and your cervix is slightly dilated," I said. I thought it was about two centimeters but didn't know for sure and didn't want to spout anything that wasn't completely factual.

"No!" Shelby screamed. "It's too soon."

"Is there any way you might have become pregnant earlier than you thought?" I asked.

Shelby stared at me, obviously confused by the question.

"Look, some women carry very small, especially when they're not getting proper nutrition. Is it possible that you became pregnant in October or November?" I asked, praying that Shelby was at least thirty-six weeks and the baby's lungs were fully developed.

"Matt and I always used protection, except that one time in December. I'm seven months along," she wailed. "It's too soon."

"Shelby, plenty of babies came early long before we had hospitals and neonatal units," Iris said. I thought she was striving for an authoritative tone, but her voice quavered. "Many of them survived."

"And many of them didn't. I want to go home," Shelby cried desperately. "I need my mom."

If I were honest, I needed my mom too, desperately, but I was in no position to give in to the fear that was gnawing at my insides. My one job was to help Shelby through this, and any assistance I was able to offer was better than nothing. This baby was coming whether we were ready or not, so all I could do was mobilize my foot soldiers and prepare for this inevitable battle.

"Theresa, may I speak to you?" I asked. I hadn't realized she was back until I saw her hovering by the door, her wraithlike silhouette part of the shadows.

Theresa followed me outside. On closer inspection, I noticed that her shoulders were squared with tension, she was pale, and her breathing was shallow. I led her further away from the open window.

"Are you all right?" I asked.

Theresa nodded. "I'm just worried for Shelby and the baby. She's so scared."

"I am too," I admitted. "I know very little about obstetrics."

"You're Shelby's best chance," Theresa replied quietly. "You are a trained nurse."

*A trained nurse with no access to anything, not even frigging YouTube*, I thought savagely.

"Theresa, what can we do to help Shelby?" I asked. "I know that delivery is certain once the water breaks, but it can take up to a week. If we can manage to delay the birth, we can increase the baby's odds of survival. Every day counts. Every hour even."

Theresa resembled a cornered rabbit, and I felt a wave of panic when her gaze slid away from my face and seemed to focus on the tips of her shoes. I had hoped she might be able to offer some advice. As a practicing homeopath, surely she knew of natural remedies that might slow down labor. We might not have access to them on the island, but her practical knowledge had to be worth something in this situation. I needed to know that I wasn't alone and could consult with another medical professional.

"Theresa," I tried again.

Theresa's head snapped up, and I saw that her eyes were filled with utter desolation. "I don't know. I don't know anything, Natalie," she exclaimed in a stage whisper.

"What do you mean?" I whispered back.

"I was a schoolteacher before I became a naturopath. Seventh grade social studies. I hated teaching. I couldn't deal with the endless bureaucracy and unreasonable parents, who thought their children could do no wrong and everything was always the teacher's fault. And the kids were just awful. Loud and rude and so defiant," Theresa said. "They would talk right over me and call me names behind my back. Hurtful names."

"What does this have to do—?"

Theresa didn't let me finish. "I don't know anything about homeopathy," she cried desperately, then immediately lowered her voice. "I bought the business from a friend's auntie. She was ready to retire, and no one in her family wanted to take it on. They already had two restaurants, and everyone was working six days a week."

"So how…?" I allowed my voice to trail off as the reality of what Theresa was saying began to sink in.

"Auntie May had a notebook that detailed which supplement was used for what complaint and where to order more once I ran out. She bought them wholesale from a vitamin distributor and glued on her own labels."

I stared at Theresa, horrified by what she was admitting to. "So you knowingly defrauded people?" I hissed.

"I didn't defraud them," Theresa said defiantly. "I sold them the same supplements people bought at a higher price at legitimate retailers. If they were often sick, I gave them vitamin C. If they were anemic, I prescribed iron. If they suffered from constipation, I sold them a natural laxative, like senna, and advised them to eat more fiber. And if they complained of something that sounded really serious, I referred them to a medical doctor."

"And this was a cash business, I presume?" I asked. Theresa shrugged.

"So you misled people, took their money, and didn't even pay taxes?"

Theresa's gaze flared with resentment. "Let him that is without sin cast the first stone," she quoted. "Are you so innocent, Natalie? Do you have no secrets?"

I didn't bother to respond since Shelby let out a low, rumbling growl inside the house, and I turned to go back inside. I didn't have a watch to time the contractions, but they had to be about five to seven minutes apart. I prayed that this was a false alarm, and the labor would stop on its own, but deep down I knew that wasn't going to happen. This baby was coming, and I was completely unprepared. If I had hoped that Theresa might offer a suggestion, no matter how unorthodox, and help me through this, I now knew that Shelby and I had to tackle this on our own.

"Is there anything I can do, Natalie?" Iris asked as soon as we came back inside.

"Let's keep Shelby hydrated and comfortable," I said, trying to sound like I knew what I was talking about.

"Should I boil some water? They always do that in old movies."

"To be honest, I have no idea what they used the boiled water for," I replied. "But sure. Let's have some sterilized water on hand should we need it. We'll need towels and something to wrap the baby in when it comes."

"On it," Iris said, and hurried from the room.

I turned to see if Theresa was there, but she had not returned to the house with me. Only Nicky remained, standing quietly by the window. It was the first time I had seen her look really frightened.

"What can I do?" she asked.

"Just keep us company," I said. "It's going to be a long night."

# Chapter 59

## Declan

Since the women were focused on Shelby and no one had eaten, I thought the men should make dinner. Sam and Glen brought back four good-sized fish, and there was some cornmeal. Tim and I cleaned and gutted the fish and set it to fry in lard and then made cornmeal with butter. The food smelled amazing, and my stomach growled with hunger, but once we divided everything among the eleven plates, everyone got about two ounces of fish and less than half a cup of cornmeal. I ate my portion in about three bites and felt even hungrier once I had finished. It simply wasn't enough, especially when I hadn't had anything since breakfast that morning, and that had been half a cup of cornmeal and a clump of dried seaweed. I was so hungry most of the time, my stomach felt like it was sticking to my backbone. Regardless of what happened tonight, Tim and I would go hunting tomorrow. We needed meat, and we needed enough of it to fill our bellies.

Once everyone had eaten, Tim and I collected the dirty dishes and set off for the stream. Tim took the pans, and I went to work on the plates and cups. We worked in silence for a while, focused on washing away the grease.

"What's on your mind?" Tim asked once the silence became uncomfortable.

"I'm worried about Natalie."

"Why? She's not the one in labor."

"Because if anything happens to Shelby or the baby, Natalie will feel responsible."

"Women have been having babies since way before modern medicine. She'll figure out what to do."

"Shelby isn't due for two months."

"Or so she said."

I lowered the plate I was washing and looked at Tim. "You think she lied?"

Tim shrugged. "Who knows? Maybe she knew she was pregnant when she came on the show and thought she'd get a sympathy vote and a hefty prize. She couldn't have known we'd be abandoned here, and she'd have no access to medical support."

"Still, Natalie has nothing to work with, not even alcohol."

Tim nodded, but he seemed to have lost interest in the topic. He set the pans aside and sat down on the bank, and I suddenly noticed how tired and gaunt he looked. His hair hung around his face in black sheets, his eyes were glazed with fatigue, and his shirt hung from his shoulders like a sack, the material bunching around his concave stomach.

I sat down next to him. "There's something I want to run by you," I said.

"Sure. Go on."

"Remember when you asked me about profiling?"

"And you nearly bit my head off," Tim replied with a tired smile.

"Well, I think you may have been right."

"What about?" Tim asked, turning to face me. He appeared a little more animated, and I was glad to have jolted him out of his melancholy.

"You don't have to be a trained profiler to realize that the MO was completely different in each case."

"What are you suggesting?"

"I think we're dealing with multiple killers."

"Go on." Tim didn't appear surprised, even though the odds of having several individuals capable of murder in a group of fifteen were infinitesimally low.

"Let's leave Ed out of the equation for now and focus on the murders we are sure of. The first murder seemed entirely opportunistic. Killer follows Will to the beach, grabs a rock, and bashes him over the head. Could have been a crime of passion. The second murder required more forethought. The killer had to have the poison ready and was waiting for an opportunity to administer it. Also, in both cases, the victims might have lived long enough to name their killers unless the person hung around to ensure they were well and truly gone."

"I'm with you so far," Tim said.

"The third murder was the height of sophistication compared to the first two. We never would have found Gael had we not gone to the cabin and passed close enough to the cemetery to notice the new grave. Whoever killed Gael left nothing to chance. He had brought a weapon and a shovel, knowing he'd need both. That's as premeditated as it gets."

"And Ed?"

"With Ed's remains so badly charred and the church burned to the ground, it's impossible to tell whether this was a murder or a suicide, but the more I think about it, the more I'm leaning toward murder. There are easier ways to kill yourself, and Ed never struck me as a masochist. If anything, he was all about self-preservation."

"So, you think someone incapacitated or killed him, then burned the church down around him?"

"I think it's a definite possibility."

Tim was quiet for a long moment, then turned back to face me, a speculative look in his dark eyes. "There are two possible scenarios here. First, we have one killer who grew more confident and creative once he or she realized they were safe from persecution. Or we have multiple killers who used different methods to dispose of their victims. Given our unique situation, it makes more sense that it's one individual who's grown bolder with each kill. To entertain the idea that there are several people in such a small group who are capable of murder is truly terrifying, Declan."

"It is, but we can't rule it out."

"Did the victims have anything in common?" Tim asked.

I took a moment to consider the question. "Will and Mark were both white, well-educated, middle-aged men, who held positions of respect and came from well-to-do families. Gael was young, Hispanic, and came from a working-class background. Ed was a black, middle-aged, middle-class man. We don't know anything about his upbringing, but we do know that he was a minister of his own church, a family man, and a pillar of the community."

Tim sighed. "I can see how Will and Mark could get under someone's skin, but Gael was personable and unobtrusive." Tim let out a tired chuckle. "In all fairness, Ed's sermons could easily drive someone to murder. I had considered it myself once or twice." We both smiled at the memory of those never-ending diatribes.

"It all comes down to motive," I said. "I seriously doubt that someone killed them for fun. Whether it was one killer or several, they had to have had a reason to kill these particular men."

"If someone had a reason to kill them, why wait until we were on the island and the pool of suspects was tiny?" Tim asked.

"Simple. With the cameras disabled, no one could prove a thing. By the time someone comes out here, if they ever do, the majority of the physical evidence will have been destroyed. We have no scenes of the crime, no murder weapons, and the bodies would have decomposed considerably. A forensic team might be able to collect samples from Gael's grave, and a postmortem and a tox screen might establish the cause of death for Mark and Ed, but any other evidence will be long gone. Even the shovel that was used to dig the grave won't tell them anything since we've all held it at some point, so they won't be able to isolate the fingerprints of the killer."

Tim fixed his dark gaze on my face, his brows knitting together as he studied me. "You must suspect someone," he said.

"I don't have anything concrete to go on except a gut feeling."

"And what is your gut feeling?"

"Poison is traditionally a woman's weapon of choice," I said.

"So you suspect Theresa," Tim concluded.

"Theresa knows about plants, and she was on her own for hours the day Mark was murdered. But why would Theresa suddenly decide to kill Mark after several weeks on the island?"

"Theresa is from New Hampshire, and Mark lived in Boston. Their paths might have easily crossed."

"They might have, but my path has crossed with many people, and you don't see me poisoning them. And Mark displayed no signs of recognition when he met her."

Tim scoffed. "To Mark, all Chinese people probably looked the same."

"I don't believe Theresa had anything to do with Will's or Gael's death."

"Neither do I," Tim said.

"I feel like we're going in circles," I said. "And we're no closer to figuring out who's responsible. And whoever it is knows that and feels safe around us, which is probably why we're still alive. But what if they have no intention of stopping and will keep going until there's no one left?" I asked, finally voicing my biggest fear.

"If they have a motive, then they must stop because they can't possibly bear a grudge against all of us. If they don't, and this is just a fun way to pass the time, then we're screwed," Tim said darkly.

"Thanks, Tim. That's very encouraging."

"Hey, what do you want me to tell you? We're hardly Holmes and Watson, bro. I can't look at Theresa and say, 'Oh, her thumb and forefinger have some discoloration so she must have used a pincer grip to pick up a poisonous plant that she then pulverized to a pulp using a seashell. She secreted away an inch of intestine to make a casing and then administered it to Mark by giving him the kiss of death,'" Tim intoned, using what he probably thought was a British accent.

I couldn't help but laugh. "Would be nice, though, if we could use our powers of deduction."

"To use your powers of deduction, you have to have facts you can work with. We have none," Tim pointed out unhelpfully.

"So, what do we do?"

"Finish washing the dishes and try to keep from becoming the next victim," Tim said, and pushed to his feet. "And protect our women."

"We'd best get back, then," I said, bending down to pick up the plates. "Natalie might need our help."

# Chapter 60

## Natalie

The hours passed slowly, the humid, heavy darkness of the July night enveloping us in its sticky embrace. A lone candle burned next to the bed, and Iris and I kept our vigil over Shelby, whose contractions were still coming about five minutes apart. Theresa and Nicky had gone to sleep in the other room, their presence not needed for the moment. Declan had offered to take a shift, but I'd told him to go to bed. There was nothing he could do.

Shelby moaned miserably and threw her head back, her pale throat gleaming with sweat in the candlelight. She was tired and weak and drifted off between the contractions, her body desperate for rest. Iris and I exchanged worried looks as I pulled a linen towel from beneath Shelby's hips. She had already soaked several towels with blood, and we were running out of clean linen. I had no idea what to do to stem the bleeding, or why Shelby was bleeding to begin with. Was this normal in some women? Once in a while, I laid my hands on Shelby's stomach in the hope that I could feel the baby's legs moving within, but the last two times, the child had been ominously still.

"Here, have a drink," Iris said, and held a cup of cold water to Shelby's lips.

Shelby took a few sips and lay back, the room once again silent except for the screeching of the cicadas outside and Theresa's rumbling snores coming from the other room. I inwardly cursed her for being a fraud. There had to be some natural remedies that might aid Shelby in her delivery or slow down the bleeding, but now that I knew the truth, I wouldn't trust Theresa even if she suggested something. Her concoction might do more harm than good. Not for the first time, I reflected on how little we knew of the natural world. We relied on doctors and pharmaceutical companies, taking drugs that contained ingredients we couldn't even pronounce. It wasn't that I wasn't grateful for modern medicine. If not for big pharma, my dad, who'd had high blood pressure since his twenties, might not be here, and my grandmother, who'd had diabetes, might have died long before I was born. Modern medicine was saving lives and helping people not only to live longer but to enjoy a quality of life they might not have had if they had to deal with the full extent of their illnesses, but just now, I would have killed for some ancient wisdom.

"I'll go wash out the towels," Iris said softly as she picked up the pile of bloodied linen. "They won't dry quickly; it's too humid, but at least they'll be clean."

"Thank you, Iris," I said, and meant it. I appreciated her stalwart presence and her calm, no-nonsense attitude. She didn't cluck like a nervous hen but picked tasks that needed doing and focused on them. There was real comfort in that, and in her unwavering support. Just having her there, in the darkness of that stifling room, gave me strength.

Shelby opened her eyes when the door closed behind Iris. Her pupils looked very black in the candlelight, and her face was so drawn, I could almost see the skull beneath. She had about four inches of dark roots now, and it looked as if she were wearing a brown skullcap over her blond hair. Shelby bared her teeth as another contraction rolled over her, then exhaled deeply once the pain receded. I held out the cup of water to her, and she took a small sip, then pushed my hand away.

"I don't want it," Shelby said suddenly. "I don't want this baby."

"You don't mean that," I said in my best soothing tone. "You are just scared and in pain. Once it's born, you'll feel differently."

Shelby shook her head stubbornly. "I do mean it. I've cheated and lied and hurt people. I'm not fit to be a mother, and all I will ever do is warp this kid."

"No one knows how to be a mother, Shelby," I said. "People learn as they go along. And the children guide them. They show their parents what they need."

Shelby shot me a dubious look. "You don't even have children."

"No, but my sister does. We talked about this often when my niece, Maddy, was still a baby. Dee had her doubts. She still does."

"There are so many unwanted, abused children in the world," Shelby said, her voice quavering. "I don't want my baby to be just another kid that falls through the cracks."

"Your baby will never fall through the cracks as long as you love it," I said gently.

"But that's the thing, Natalie. I don't love it," Shelby said quietly. "If I thought it would get Matt back, then maybe I'd feel more interested in it, but Matt made his feelings very clear. He didn't want me, not in any kind of real way, and he won't want his baby. Even if this baby survives, it'll be nothing but a burden, a constant reminder of my humiliation."

"Why don't you try to rest, Shelby? Things will look better in the morning," I said.

I didn't believe that for a minute, but there was nothing I could say that would make Shelby feel better. She was exhausted, terrified, and in pain. Nothing I said would make a difference. Many women said things they didn't mean while in labor, but once they saw their beautiful baby, they forgot the pain, the doubt, and the rage they felt against their partners for subjecting them to such suffering. All they felt was love, and I hoped Shelby would be the same.

"Will they look better in the morning?" she asked.

"They always do."

"You sound just like my mother, spewing platitudes instead of confronting the truth," Shelby said bitterly.

"What would you like me to say?" I demanded.

"I'd like you to tell me the truth, Natalie," Shelby spat. "Tell me that I'm a worthless whore who went after another woman's husband and got pregnant with a kid she didn't want in an effort to guilt him into leaving his wife."

"It's not for me to judge you, Shelby, but I think you're being too hard on yourself."

"What about you, Iris? Do you think I'm being too hard on myself too?" Shelby was panting now, her teeth bared in a grimace of pain as she stared down Iris, who'd just come back into the room.

"None of us are blameless, Shelby," Iris said. "You can atone for the wrongs you've done by loving this baby."

"If it lives," Shelby cried, tears sliding down her face. "What chance does it even stand?"

Shelby turned her face away from us, staring into the darkness. As much as I wished I could say something encouraging, there was nothing I could promise that wouldn't be a blatant lie. I was powerless. I couldn't absolve her of her sins, nor could I offer her any real help. I had nothing but a bucket of water and a few linen towels at my disposal. I had no experience as a midwife, and the last serious injury I had treated before coming on the show was a scraped knee, the result of a fall from the swings in the school playground.

"Natalie is right, sweetheart. You should try to rest," Iris said.

"Is that the best you can do? Tell me to rest?" Shelby hissed.

"I'm sorry, Shelby. I wish I could do more," I said.

"Yeah, me too."

Shelby went quiet after that, and Iris and I sat in silence.

"You should get some sleep," I told Iris. "No sense both of us staying up."

Iris looked nearly as worn out as Shelby, her jowls sagging and her eyelids drooping over reddened eyes. She'd aged noticeably since arriving on the island and was much thinner now, but not in a flattering way. She looked like those heart-wrenching images of women during the Irish Potato Famine or the gray-faced mothers during the Great Depression, who stood in line for hours just to get a small loaf of bread for their hungry children. God, what I wouldn't have given for a piece of bread. My mouth watered at the thought of a bagel with cream cheese or a piece of greasy garlic bread dripping with melted cheese. I'd thought I had understood hunger, but no one truly understands hunger until they've experienced it on a daily basis for months on end. My stomach was so empty, it hurt.

Iris smoothed back Shelby's damp hair and smiled down at her. "I'm just going to rest for a little while, and then I will come right back. You hang in there, Shelby. You're stronger than you know."

Shelby gave her a watery smile, and Iris retired to the other room. I heard the groaning of wood as she lay down on one of the empty cots.

The hours passed. My eyes burned with fatigue, and I was sweating profusely even though I'd taken off my wool bodice and skirt hours ago. I felt as if I'd just come out of a sauna. But Shelby no longer seemed hot. She shivered and wrapped her arms around herself, her eyelids fluttering as if she were just waking, or falling asleep.

"Shelby," I said softly. "Shelby, can you hear me?"

"I'm tired," she whispered. "So tired."

She didn't make a sound when the next contraction gripped her and barely stirred after that. She was so exhausted that she had managed to sleep through the pain. The minutes ticked by, or would have if we had a clock. I thought it was probably around three in the morning. A fresh breeze blew through the window as the wind outside picked up, the air fragrant with the scent of the ocean and heat-dried grass. Shelby groaned, her eyes opening wide and her hand going to her belly.

"What is it?" I asked.

Shelby didn't reply but let out a low, agonized moan. Something had changed, and the contractions began to come closer together. It was as if Shelby's body had received some coded message that it was time to deliver the baby. I was glad Shelby had gotten some rest since she'd need all her strength in the coming hours. She panted like an oncoming locomotive and arched her back every time a contraction rolled over her.

"It hurts, Natalie," she cried.

"I know it does, but it won't be much longer now."

Shelby looked terrified at the prospect of actually delivering the baby, but there was no turning back now. This kid was coming out whether she liked it or not. Shelby's cry had woken Iris, and she exploded into the room, looking bleary-eyed and disheveled, her frizzy hair like a halo around her head.

"Is it time?" she exclaimed, her gaze fixing on Shelby.

"Not yet, but soon, I think," I said, keeping my voice calm. My heart was pounding against my ribs, all my attention focused on Shelby. In my mind, a prayer was going on a loop like a meditation mantra. *Dear God, please let them live*, I begged. *Please let there be no complications.*

Shelby was panting hard now, her forehead glistening with perspiration. Her hair hung limply around her face, and her shift was damp and bloodied.

"I have to push," she cried, and grabbed Iris's hand.

Iris winced but didn't try to pull back her hand. "You just hold on, baby girl," she said.

I placed the two pillows behind Shelby's back and came around the other side, taking hold of her other hand. "Come on, Shelby. You're nearly there."

Shelby squeezed hard and bore down, and I repeated my mantra again and again as Shelby strained and pushed. Angry spots appeared in her cheeks, and I was momentarily taken aback when the white of her left eye turned crimson red.

"Oh my God," Iris exclaimed.

"It's all right," I said with as much authority as I could muster. "It's just a broken capillary. It's normal."

Theresa and Nicky appeared in the doorway, both looking ghostly in their white shifts. Nicky looked scared, while Theresa seemed to be annoyed. I thought she was angry with me for forcing her to reveal her secret, but her gaze was fixed on Shelby, who was fading fast.

"I can't anymore," Shelby wailed. "I just can't."

"You can, and you will," Iris assured her.

"Take a deep breath, hold it, and bear down as hard as you can," Theresa said.

I stared at her. She'd said she had no experience with labor and had delivered her own children via Cesarean.

"I saw it on the Learning Channel," Theresa muttered.

Shelby took a deep breath and bore down with all her might.

"Again," Theresa ordered. She sounded like a prison guard ordering someone to do push-ups. "Again," she commanded.

The scream that tore from Shelby as she pushed was almost inhuman, but a tiny head finally slithered out between her thighs, and I breathed a sigh of immense relief. The tiny neck was not wrapped in the umbilical cord, and the baby's face wasn't blue.

Shelby was roaring like a lioness now, but the end was near, and she knew it. She pushed two more times, and the shoulders came into view. A few more seconds and the baby slid out of the birth canal and into my waiting hands.

Iris cut the cord, and Shelby fell back with an exhalation that sounded like air escaping a balloon. She didn't ask about the baby, and I was grateful for that small mercy because the child in my arms wasn't breathing. I quickly cleaned the mouth and nose and slapped him on the behind, but no angry yowl followed. I laid the baby on the bed and began to very gently palpate the narrow chest, hoping to stimulate the heart.

"Please, baby," I begged. "Please, wake up."

But there was no response. The baby was silent and still, the little body growing cooler beneath my fingers. Iris handed me her shawl, and I wrapped the baby in it and held it close, hoping my body heat might warm it. I recalled holding Maddy the day she was born. There had been so much joy, so much hope. And the baby had been cute and pink and surprisingly heavy, not like this little scrap of a boy that felt almost weightless in my arms. Was he going to be the next victim of this failed experiment, a tiny grave in a cemetery that should never have existed?

Shelby lay back on the pillows, her face waxy, her eyes closed, her hands limp. I stared in horror as blood gushed from between her legs, soaking into the linen sheets and the straw mattress. It quickly saturated the thin mattress and began to drip onto the floor, the puddle spreading beneath the bedstead. The blood was almost black, and I blinked back tears as grief overwhelmed me. This sort of hemorrhaging wasn't normal, and even if the bleeding miraculously stopped on its own, which wasn't likely, the damage was already done.

"Shelby, honey," Iris called to her, but there was no response. "Shelby."

Nicky grabbed Shelby's hand and squeezed her fingers, but Shelby didn't stir. Her chest had been gently rising and falling but it had stilled, and her hand slid out of Nicky's fingers.

"Oh, God!" Nicky cried. "Shelby, please."

Iris grabbed Shelby's wrist, her eyes growing wide with horror.

"Natalie, do something," Nicky screamed.

I shook my head. "I don't know what to do, Nicky," I muttered as I stared at the pool of blood beneath Shelby's hips. "I don't know what to do."

Theresa turned on her heel and fled, unable to watch. Perhaps seeing Shelby like this had reminded her of her daughter when they'd cut her down from where she'd hung herself. My legs trembled, and I plopped into a chair and closed my eyes, needing a moment's respite from the horror. I was so startled, I nearly dropped the baby when it mewled miserably in my arms, its tiny chest expanding beneath my fingers.

"He's alive," I whispered gratefully. "He's alive."

"But for how long?" Iris asked as tears streamed down her pale cheeks. "Shelby is gone. He has no source of food, and there are no other nursing mothers on the island."

I looked down at the tiny boy in my arms. I didn't realize I was weeping until tears fell on his fuzzy dark head. He stared at me, his gaze still clouded, then he began to root for a nipple.

"We must find a way to feed him," I said. "We'll give him cow's milk."

"How?" Nicky asked quietly. "We don't have a bottle."

"We'll spoon it into his mouth," I replied. "It's our only option."

"Babies are not supposed to drink cow's milk," Iris said. "And he'll choke if you use a spoon."

"All right. Let's soak a corner of a clean towel in milk and let him suck on it."

"I washed that towel using lye soap," Iris protested. "We'll poison him."

"Well, unless one of us starts lactating, it's either that or the spoon," I snapped. I had failed Shelby. I wasn't going to fail this helpless little boy.

"He needs a name," Nicky said. "It's important that he has a name."

"We should name him after his mother," Iris said softly.

"I doubt he'll thank us for naming him Sheldon," Nicky said. "What about Hunter? It's a strong name that's synonymous with survival."

"Yes," I said. "I like that. Hunter."

Iris nodded and pushed wearily to her feet. "I'm going to milk the cow, then we're going to try to feed Hunter."

"What about Shelby?" Nicky asked, her voice small with shock and grief.

"There's no longer anything we can do for Shelby," Iris said. "I'll ask the men to dig a grave. It's too hot to delay a funeral."

Nicky nodded. "I will prepare her for the burial," she offered. "Shelby wouldn't want to be buried looking like that."

Iris patted Nicky on the shoulder. "We'll wash her, dress her in a clean chemise, and brush her hair. She'd like that."

"What she'd like is to be alive and at home, with people who love her," Theresa said softly from the door. "Death is so final."

We all took a moment to acknowledge this, then Iris went out to milk the cow, Nicky went to fetch a bucket of water, and Theresa brought Shelby's spare chemise and her comb. Life didn't stop for death, not in our settlement.

# Chapter 61

## Declan

I was glad I wasn't asked to dig another grave. The physical work would have been a release, but I just couldn't find the strength to hold the shovel. My first sighting of Hunter just broke something in me. He was so tiny and helpless, all I wanted to do was to hold him and keep him safe. But he didn't need me. He needed his mother. The rest of the women looked like ghosts, their gazes haunted by the tragedy they'd just witnessed. We hadn't seen the others die, but they had stood by helplessly as Shelby tried in vain to cling to life. Theresa and Nicky were still inside with Shelby, and Iris, who looked like she'd aged ten years since last night, was making breakfast. Natalie was walking, the baby in a makeshift sling on her chest. I couldn't hear what she was saying to him, but I could see her lips moving. Her eyes were red and puffy from crying, and she looked diminished somehow. Unable to stop myself, I followed her down to the beach.

"Is there anything I can do?" I pleaded.

Natalie shook her head. She looked like she was about to drop. She'd spent about an hour trying to dribble milk into Hunter's mouth with a spoon. We weren't sure how much he'd actually swallowed, but he'd seemed content for the time being and had fallen asleep.

"Why don't you let me hold him and you lie down for a little while?" I suggested.

"That's okay. I don't think I can sleep anyway. Not yet."

"Natalie, it's not your fault," I said.

"I know, but I wish I could have done something to help Shelby. I have never felt so helpless in my life."

"We all feel helpless," I said.

Natalie looked down at the sleeping baby. "I don't know what to do, Declan. I have nothing: no formula, no diapers, no medicines of any kind should he get sick. I don't even know if he can survive outside the womb."

"What about Theresa? Can't she help?"

Natalie shook her head. "Theresa admitted to me last night that she knows nothing about homeopathy. She was buying over-the-counter supplements and slapping her own labels on them in order to sell them to gullible clients who believed they were getting homeopathic cures," Natalie said bitterly.

"Why am I not surprised?"

"You suspected?" She looked up at me questioningly.

"I haven't seen her come up with anything useful, and she tried to avoid answering even the most basic questions. She didn't seem to be familiar with jimsonweed or any other poisonous plants that grow on this island. Anyone can tell you not to eat mushrooms you find in the woods and not to chew on holly berries. The most Theresa did to help us was find some spinach and advise us to eat seaweed. Again, common knowledge."

"No one seems to be who they said they were," Natalie said miserably. "I've never had reason to mistrust people before, not on this scale, but everyone seems to be harboring secrets."

"Are you?" The question escaped before I had a chance to stop it.

"No one is an open book, Declan," she said sadly, and walked away from me, her head bowed, her arms around the baby.

I wanted to follow her, to apologize, but I wasn't sorry I had asked. No one is an open book, that's true, but some books are a lot more disturbing than others, and not every book has a happy ending.

Letting Natalie walk away, I turned back toward the settlement. The canoe was our only hope, and now we had Hunter to think of. I couldn't bear to think of putting him in the ground next to his mother. So I hitched up the horse, and Brendan and I set off for the cabin to retrieve the tree trunk Tim and I had felled yesterday. We'd get it back to the settlement and get started. I didn't know how long it might take, but failure was not an option.

# Chapter 62

## Natalie

It's an awful thing to say, but Shelby's death has given me purpose. Even though everyone offered to help, I have taken over the care of Hunter. I must keep him alive. If he can get through the first month, I think his chances of survival will increase considerably. I feed him approximately every two hours, carefully dribbling milk into his mouth so he doesn't choke. He swallows dutifully but cries between feedings. I think his belly hurts from the cow's milk, and the acrid smell emanating from his cloth diapers is worrying. We don't have any spare fabric, so we had to utilize anything that belonged to the four murder victims to make diapers and little gowns for Hunter. He looks like a Victorian child, wearing nothing but white smocks. It's too hot to wrap him in a blanket, but I must protect him from sunburn and bug bites.

Tim, Declan, and Brendan have been working on the canoe for two weeks, and it's really coming along. It's a slow, painstaking process, but they don't want to rush it in order to prevent a mistake that would force them to have to start over. The log smolders all day long, with the men taking turns shifting the glowing embers and scraping out the burned wood. The cavity grows a little bit wider and deeper with every passing day, but it's nowhere near what it should be to allow two men to sit comfortably. Declan hopes to have the canoe ready by mid-August.

There have been several debates about who will go once it's finished. Brendan and Declan are the strongest swimmers, so it will probably be the two of them. I'm terrified to be left behind, but I can't ask Declan not to go. He's the one everyone is pinning their hopes on, but with Hunter to take care of, I hardly sleep, and the fatigue is making me paranoid. Perhaps lying with Declan in the double bed, Hunter between us, is the closest I will ever get to having a family of my own.

Declan tries to speak to me and draw me out, but something has broken inside me since Shelby's death, and I'm not the only one. Everyone has been subdued. They just don't seem to have any will left to fight. No one talks about what they'll do once they get back to civilization or reminisces about the past. They just go about their tasks like zombies, coming together at mealtimes to eat the few bites we're allocated in silence. Will we die on this island like those forgotten people buried by the cabin? Will anyone ever find our graves?

I know this kind of thinking will only push me deeper down the rabbit hole, but I just can't seem to find a foothold that will help me to raise myself out of this trap. I'm suffering from depression and using Hunter as a crutch to keep me from sinking deeper into the darkness. I don't even feel a spark of desire when Declan touches me. I'm just too tired, and too hungry. All I want is for him to hold me. That's the only time I feel safe.

As I walk around with Hunter, I inwardly chant, *Dear God, please help us!*

# Chapter 63

## Declan

Brendan watched the canoe smolder from a shady spot beneath a leafy tree, his gaze glazed with fatigue. Except for meals and brief trips to the beach to take a dip to cool off, Brendan had not left it unsupervised in days, taking turns with Tim to stand guard. He even slept outside, fearful that someone would try to sabotage our efforts. Thankfully, everything had been quiet and peaceful the past few weeks, and no one had so much as approached the canoe without express permission from either of the two men. After the first few days, it was decided that I should still go out hunting nearly every day. If I didn't kill something, or if Sam and Glen failed to catch a few fish, we didn't eat.

"I think we're getting there," Brendan said when I stopped by to check on the canoe's progress. "About five more inches and we'll be able to sit low enough not to tip the canoe over once it's in the water. I'll start to work on the paddles tomorrow."

"Need my help?" I asked.

Brendan shook his head. "Thanks, I got it. The best you can do is make sure the rest of them have enough to eat until we send help."

"You seem confident," I said.

"I am. This was easier than I had imagined. As long as the bottom is not too thin, we should be okay."

"Let me know if there's anything I can do to help," I said before walking way. For the first time in weeks, I allowed myself to feel a glimmer of hope.

I want to be the one to go with Brendan, but I can't leave Natalie behind. Shelby's death devastated her, and Natalie seems even more fragile and fearful. She has good reason to be scared, but Shelby's death, awful as it was, was the result of natural causes. Women died in childbirth all the time before the advances in modern medicine, and without emergency surgery, there was nothing Natalie could have done to save Shelby's life. She's obsessed with Hunter, though. On the one hand, taking care of that little boy gives her renewed purpose. On the other hand, she will lose it if he doesn't survive. I think we all will.

We've gone several weeks without losing anyone. The thought is comforting, but my cop's instinct will not permit me to grow too complacent. I can feel it in the pit of my stomach and the marrow of my bones. We're in danger, and whoever is responsible has not been satiated. They're waiting, biding their time, choosing their next victim. I pray that victim is not Natalie. I know everyone on this island has their secrets, but there's a purity to Natalie you don't often find in people these days. She has a sense of honor, and duty, values that have been instilled in me as well, first by my parents and then by the tenets of the police academy. Natalie is the first woman with whom I could envision a future.

I couldn't help but search for Natalie among the knot of contestants as they made their way over to the table for our afternoon meal. She was there, standing next to Iris, gently rocking Hunter as she listened intently to something Iris was saying. Natalie instinctively turned sideways when Theresa approached, protecting the baby from anyone who got too close.

Will she be able to part with him if we are rescued? And will we ever get the chance to build a future together, or will I forever remind her of the tragedies that have occurred on this bloodthirsty strip of land?

# Chapter 64

## Declan

## August

We were halfway through August by the time Brendan was finally satisfied with the canoe. Brendan and I tested it by paddling around the island to make certain it didn't leak and didn't sit too low in the water and start taking on water. Once we were certain the vessel was seaworthy, a meeting was held by the group. Everyone sat around the table, their empty plates before them, since it didn't take too long to eat a few ounces of venison and a handful of beans from our garden. Despite the unsatisfied hunger, the mood around the table was jovial, people smiling openly for the first time since Shelby's death. Hunter slept in Natalie's sling, just his little fist visible over the edge of the fabric.

Jesse stood and looked around the table. "First and foremost, I'd like to thank Brendan for his ingenuity and craftsmanship. We'd never have done it without you, Brendan."

I thought that was a little unfair since Tim had guided Brendan those first few days and had helped Brendan daily, along with some of the others, but it didn't really matter. Brendan had devoted the most time to the making of the canoe and had made the paddles that would help us navigate the canoe to the mainland.

Everyone clapped. Brendan blushed and smiled shyly. "Thank you. I'm only doing what anyone would do in my position and with my skillset."

"Brendan will be ready to leave tomorrow morning, so we must choose one person to go with him. Declan is a strong swimmer, but he's also our best hunter, and the gunpowder and shot are almost gone. We can't afford to waste even the tiniest bit," Jesse reminded us. "Do we have any volunteers?"

Glen's hand instantly went up. Tim also raised his hand.

"I would prefer to go with Declan," Brendan said. "I trust him to have my back should anything go wrong. Besides, Tim is a skilled hunter, and Glen is the best fisherman. They're needed here to feed everyone until we can send help."

"And with Declan being a cop, he'll be taken more seriously than a civilian," Iris said.

I stole a look at Natalie, who looked terrified, but she gave me a small smile. "It must be you, Declan," she said. "We all trust you to save us. And Brendan," she hastily added, realizing how she must have sounded.

"I will prepare some food for the journey," Iris said. "You must keep your strength up if you're going to paddle for hours. And you must have a hearty breakfast tomorrow."

"I won't say no to a hearty breakfast," Brendan said. "I'm sick of seaweed. I would love me some bacon and eggs with toast smothered in butter. And hash browns," he added.

"You could be having that as soon as tomorrow," Jesse said.

"I can't think that far ahead. I'm a carpenter, not a sailor," Brendan replied. "I'm a little nervous, to tell you the truth."

"You have nothing to worry about," Tim said. "That canoe is solid. As long as you don't decide to lean too far to either side, you should be fine."

Once the meeting was over and everyone dispersed, Natalie and I walked down to the beach. Since she took care of Hunter, she didn't have to wash the dishes or launder piles of soiled diapers. That duty fell to Nicky, who swore she didn't mind.

"Can you ask one of the others to take Hunter tonight?" I asked. "I need to be with you."

Natalie nodded. "I've already asked Iris and Nicky. They'll take turns feeding him during the night." Natalie gave me a searching look. "Are you worried?"

"I'm worried about leaving you."

"Don't be. It's going to be okay. As long as you reach the mainland, we'll all be saved."

I nodded. I had memorized Natalie's mom's cell number and promised I would call her as soon as I was able.

"I bet the next time I see you will be back at home." Natalie laughed softly.

"No way," I said, shaking my head. "I'm coming back here for you myself. I'm not going to leave the rescue mission to some hot guy in a uniform. You might never want to look at me again."

"You are the only hot guy in a uniform I'll have eyes for," Natalie replied with a flirtatious smile. "I can't wait to see you in full police regalia."

"Will you really be there?" I asked, my voice catching. "Will you still want to be with me once this is all over?"

Natalie looked up at me, her eyes luminous. "Yes. I will be with you for as long as you want me."

"What if I want you forever?"

"You might feel differently once we get home."

"I won't. I want it to be me and you against the world, Natalie. I've never been more sure of anything in my life."

Natalie nodded. I could see that she had her doubts. People make promises when they're afraid and they need to hold on to something good, but once the situation changes, they often go back on the promises they'd made. I didn't press her. There'd be time enough for that once we were talking about an actual future, not just a beautiful dream shared by two people who were still stranded on a deserted island.

"I think you need an early night," Natalie said. "Let me feed Hunter, and then we can go to bed."

I wasn't about to argue, even though I wished someone else would feed Hunter for a change. Each feeding took a minimum of an hour, and I was eager to have Natalie all to myself. But I would wait.

"Come get me when you're ready," I said.

I sat down on the sand and looked out to sea. I had never mastered the art of meditation, but I did my best to quiet my mind and not let my fears take over. Tomorrow would change everything, one way or another. Brendan and I would make it back and get help, or we would either die trying or find ourselves back on the island with no hope of rescue. I sat there for what felt like hours, but eventually Natalie came back and held out her hand to me.

That night, Natalie didn't care that we weren't alone. We pulled the curtains closed and made love as if it were just us in a luxurious bed with clean sheets and soft pillows. After months of hunger and hard physical work, she felt insubstantial in my arms, and I knew that she wouldn't last much longer without proper nutrition. None of them would once the powder and shot ran out.

Dawn came all too soon, and I chose to say goodbye to Natalie within the confines of the bed. I couldn't bear to put my feelings on display in front of the others, and I think she was grateful not to have to watch me leave. Natalie hurried to the women's house to take charge of Hunter, and I dressed and joined Brendan for our farewell breakfast. Iris gave us plates filled with leftover slices of venison, squares of cheese, dried seaweed, and buttered beans. This was the most I'd had for breakfast since the chickens had been savaged and there were no more eggs.

Everyone inhaled their own breakfast and then followed us to the beach, the entire group eager to watch our departure. Glen was talking loudly. Jesse was offering last-minute advice, and Tim was utterly silent, his gaze burning with intensity. He clapped me on the shoulder and nodded but didn't say anything.

What was there to say? We're counting on you? Don't let us down? What will happen to us if you don't make it?

The responsibility weighed heavily on me, but I dutifully hugged the women and shook hands with the men before getting into the canoe and getting a good grip on the paddle. Brendan beamed as we cast off amid the cheers and well wishes of everyone left on shore.

"Here we go," Brendan said as we rounded the island and turned the canoe westward. We quickly fell into a rhythm, and I put everything from my mind but the goal. If nothing went wrong, we could reach the mainland within a few hours.

# Chapter 65

It was a calm, peaceful day. The best we could hope for when canoeing in an ocean rather than a lake or a river, but it was also very warm and bright. We should have waited for an overcast day. The light was blinding as it reflected off the water, and the sun beat down on my head and shoulders, the heat searing my skin through the grubby linen of my shirt. Without sunglasses, an appropriate hat, or sunscreen, we were half-blind and roasting alive. Brendan sat in front of me, his shoulders tense, the muscles in his arms bunching as he paddled steadily. I wasn't really in the mood for conversation, but after a while, the silence became oppressive, and I needed something to distract me from my thoughts.

"Brendan, you all right?" I asked.

Brendan turned back to look at me. His expression was tight, his jaw clenched with tension.

"Yeah. I don't like being out on the open water. Hated the ocean since I was a kid. Every summer, my mom used to drag us to the beach at Coney Island. It took ages, with several train changes, and then we spent hours baking in the hot sun. There were no umbrellas or even a clean bathroom. And I was too afraid to swim in the ocean. I was convinced I'd drown, so I'd run in, cool off, and return to our blanket. By midafternoon, I was begging to go home." He turned back so that he could continue to paddle.

"Sorry. That sounds awful," I said. I had much more pleasant memories of family outings on hot summer days.

"That's when I realized I was gay," Brendan said without turning to face me. He never spoke about his personal life, and I was surprised that he suddenly felt like sharing.

"On the beach?" I asked.

"My brother used to ogle all the women and point out anyone who had a nice rack or a fine ass. I looked and tried to appreciate their assets, but it was the men my gaze kept straying to. Most of them were hairy and fat, and some wore Speedos that were truly cringeworthy, but there were always a few who were just right. Young and fit and beautiful," Brendan said dreamily. "I'd close my eyes and try to imagine them without their bathing suits. I guess I was testing myself to see if I would be embarrassed or turned on. And that's when I knew."

"Have you ever been with a woman?" I asked for lack of anything better to say.

"A few times. I just wanted to be sure I wasn't missing out and assuming that a childish fantasy defined who I was, but it never felt as good, or as right. I'm not ashamed of who I am," Brendan said, defensiveness creeping into his voice.

"Nor should you be."

"Are you in love with Natalie?" he asked.

"Yes," I said simply. "If anything good came out of this experience, it was finding a woman I want to spend my life with."

"Does she feel the same?"

I couldn't help but smile. "Yes, I think she does. But getting back to real life will be the true test of her feelings."

"And yours," Brendan said. "You might feel differently once you're back home."

"I don't want to go home." That was the first time I had verbalized my feelings on the subject. "Too many bad memories. If Natalie will have me, I'll move to her town and apply to the local PD."

"Sounds like you have it all figured out."

"I don't, but it's a start. Will you change anything when you get home?" I asked.

"I think I'd like to move away from New York. I want to go somewhere rural, with woods and lakes and scenic hiking trails. I would have really enjoyed the island had it not been for the hunger and the uncertainty. I'd have liked to stay."

That came as a surprise, but I could see how someone like Brendan might not feel at home in a city heaving with people. As a carpenter, he could probably find a demand for his talents anywhere he went.

"Can I have some water?" he asked.

I laid down my paddle across my lap and reached for the bag Iris had given us. I could use a drink myself. I was sweating profusely and probably a little dehydrated.

"Look, land," Brendan said as I handed him the leather bottle.

I peered into the distance, and sure enough, there it was, the shoreline, and not just some puny island but miles of commercially developed real estate. We had to be about a mile offshore, but we'd be on solid ground in about a half hour.

Brendan passed the bottle to me, and I took a swig. The water tasted warm and leathery, but it was better than nothing. Just as I was about to stopper the bottle, Brendan turned toward me and raised his paddle. I barely had time to duck as he used both hands to ram the paddle toward my head. He missed my face, but he got me in the neck, and I felt the breath still in my throat as stars began to dance before my eyes and I choked. I couldn't manage to draw breath or see what was happening, since my eyes were stinging with tears of pain, but I knew Brendan wouldn't stop. He wasted no time and used the paddle to hit me hard on the side of the head. Everything went hazy, my stunned brain unable to formulate thoughts or utter words. I grabbed onto the sides of the canoe, desperate to regain my equilibrium, but Brendan hit me again, and I felt thick, warm blood sluice down the side of my face.

The world tilted but I held on tighter, knowing it was my only chance to come out of this alive. I opened my eyes a crack and the sunlight momentarily blinded me, but I refused to squint. I needed to look at Brendan, to understand what was happening. Brendan's face was contorted with rage, his normally warm brown eyes blazing with the sort of hatred I could never unsee. The guy everyone thought of as a cuddly teddy was more like an enraged bear whose only instinct was to protect itself.

"Brendan," I choked out. "What—?"

I never got to finish the question. Setting aside the paddle, Brendan grabbed me by the ankles and forced me over the side of the canoe, then used a paddle to shove me roughly beneath the water. The salt water stung my eyes and burned the cut on my temple, but I tried to come back up before I ran out of air. I had hoped I was far enough away from the canoe that the paddle wouldn't be able to reach, but I was groggy and disoriented. I had miscalculated. As soon as my head broke the surface, Brendan brought the edge of the paddle down, striking me on the side of the head. He then drove the paddle between my neck and shoulder, and my right arm went numb, my vision going in and out from the agony. My ears were ringing, and as I opened my mouth in a gasp of pain, water poured inside, choking me and burning my throat.

I couldn't see anything beyond the blood-tinged seawater that swirled around my head. My lungs were bursting with the need for oxygen, but I found the strength to move away from the canoe. Brendan put the paddle in the water, and the canoe was instantly upon me, Brendan stabbing me with the paddle every time I tried to draw breath. I tried to dodge the blows, but my vision was blurred with the blood that was pouring out of my head, and my arm was still as numb and heavy as a wooden log. I was dizzy and disoriented, and growing weaker by the moment. The paddle came down once more and struck me hard on the temple. There was an explosion of excruciating pain, and then everything went dark.

# Chapter 66

## Natalie

That day, there was little pretense of going about our chores. We kept looking out at the ocean, waiting for something to happen, but the hottest part of the day soon passed, and twilight settled over the island, the purpling sky twinkling with stars and the ocean turning a deep blue as night approached. Too afraid to go to the beach on my own, I stood by the gates, Hunter in my arms, and looked out to sea. There was nothing. No approaching boat or the sound of helicopter rotors. All was quiet and still.

"They had to have made it by now," Iris said as she came to stand next to me. I nodded, unable to speak.

"Maybe rescue will come in the morning," Iris reasoned. "It'd be too late for them to set off now."

I knew Iris had a point, but something inside me had come loose, and my heart slammed against my ribs as I felt an overwhelming desire to scream and scream until I was hoarse. Something wasn't right; I just knew it. I tried to tell myself that it was just fear talking and that Declan would never give up and leave us here, but gut instinct is a powerful tool if you listen to it, and my gut instinct was shrieking, begging to be heard.

"What is it, Natalie?" Iris asked. "What's wrong?"

"I don't know," I whispered. I was so breathless, I could hardly speak.

"Come. You're exhausted and need a cool drink. Let me take Hunter."

"No," I cried, unwilling to part with the baby. His solid presence kept me tethered to reality. If Hunter were gone, I'd snap.

"All right," Iris cooed soothingly. "I know you're worried about Declan, but he's tough, and resourceful. He'll be all right. I'm sure of it."

She wrapped an arm around my shoulders and maneuvered me back inside the settlement and toward the square. Iris pushed me onto a bench and poured me a cup of water.

"Drink," she said.

I gulped down the water and sputtered as it went down the wrong way. Hunter, whose face got wet, began to cry, his outrage bringing me back to my senses.

"Something is wrong," I croaked. "Iris, something is wrong."

"You can't think like that. That canoe was sound, and if they paddled long enough, they'd encounter someone. You must have faith."

"Faith?" I cried. "Five people who had faith will never leave this island. Hunter will never know his mother. How can you remain so calm?"

"Because I don't have much choice," Iris said reasonably. "If I start to panic, I'll never stop, so I focus on the things I can control, like what I'm going to make us for breakfast tomorrow."

"You know what you'll make us for breakfast tomorrow. Corn mush and seaweed," I cried.

"That's right. But at least we still have cornmeal, which is something."

"If Declan and Brendan don't bring help, we'll starve."

Iris nodded. "I know that, Natalie, which is why I can't bear to think about it. Now, have some more water and give me the baby. I'll feed him and get him ready for bed."

I reluctantly surrendered Hunter, who smiled groggily at Iris. "Hello, you," Iris said sweetly. "Let's get you a fresh diaper and some milk, and then we'll tuck you in for the night. I think Natalie needs a rest, don't you?" She kept up the one-sided small talk as she took Hunter into the women's house.

I remained where I was, staring through the open gates until my eyes began to water. Iris was right; I was exhausted, both emotionally and physically. I wished more than anything that I could climb into bed and press my back to Declan's chest as his arm came around me and his hand settled on my breast. I wanted to feel his breath against my neck and hear his heartbeat. I didn't think I would ever feel safe on the island again unless he was there, holding me.

Nicky came out of the house and held out her hand to me. "Let's get you to bed."

She was talking to me as if I were a small child, but for some reason, I responded to that. "All right," I muttered.

"Sleep in your old bed tonight, where we can keep an eye on you. He'll be back, Natalie," she said softly. "He'll be back for you."

I simply couldn't find the strength to verbalize what was in my heart and allowed Nicky to lead me into the house. She untied my laces, and I stepped out of my skirt and removed my bodice before lying down in my shift. Tim would have to take Shelby's cot.

It was too hot to cover myself, so I just lay there, staring up at the star-strewn sky through the open window until, hours later, I finally fell asleep.

# Chapter 67

The day started like any other, except that there were two fewer people than yesterday. We were down to eight adults, and we congregated around the table as Iris served us the cornmeal. Each person got half a cup, and we savored it, reluctant to get up from the table and begin our day. Everyone kept peering at the gates, hoping that they'd see a boat on the horizon, but there was nothing but empty water and clear sky.

Even Sam and Glen, who usually had something to say, were silent. Hunter snuffled at my breast, his blue gaze studying me intently, almost as if he could sense my distress.

"Right," Jesse said at last. "Keeping busy will make the time go by faster, so let's get to it, people. Tim and I will go hunting. Sam and Glen are on fishing duties. And the ladies will do what they do best."

"I think one of the men should stay behind," Iris said. "We're not safe here alone."

Tim and Jesse exchanged eloquent stares. "You stay," Tim said to Jesse. "I'll go alone. I'll just check the traps today. Conserve powder and shot just in case."

"All right," Jesse agreed. "Ladies, I'm at your disposal. I can chop wood, weed the garden, fix anything that needs fixing, and even take Hunter for a walk if you need a break."

"Patronizing much?" Nicky grumbled under her breath.

Jesse ignored her comment and smiled reassuringly. "Use me," he said.

"You can start by chopping wood," Iris said reproachfully. "And then you can weed the garden. I think we should do the laundry today, girls. Wouldn't do to be all smelly when rescue comes."

No one commented on that as they left the table and set off in different directions. Since I wasn't needed in the garden, I settled in a shady spot and sang to Hunter until he fell asleep. I couldn't help but smile at the serene expression on his face. At least someone was happy this morning. Hunter was still scrawny and looked like the preemie he was, but he did feel a little more solid in my arms. His belly seemed to have accepted the cow's milk, so he was thriving. His color was good, and there was a new awareness in him that hadn't been there before. He really had a chance now, and that made me feel marginally calmer. As long as I concentrated on Hunter's needs, I would get through the next few days without coming undone.

Still, the hours dragged by with excruciating slowness. The laundry was done and dry. The rabbits Tim brought back were cleaned, and the fish gutted. Even though we got more food for our evening meal because there were fewer men, I could barely swallow my portion of the rabbit. Where was Declan? The men had been gone for nearly two days now, but still no one had come. What was happening?

Theresa sat down next to me and laid her hand over mine. She didn't say anything, since there really was nothing she could have said to make a difference. We just sat together for a while, each one thinking her own thoughts. Once the sun set, everyone silently walked off to find their beds, their shoulders stooped with crushing disappointment.

# Chapter 68

I wasn't sure what time it was when I woke. It could have been before midnight, or it could just as easily have been close to dawn. I had no way of knowing. All I knew was that I was desperate to get some air. The house was stifling despite the open windows, and my neck and face were damp with perspiration. It probably wasn't even that hot, but the humidity made it feel like we were sleeping in a rainforest. I stole a peek at Hunter, who was sleeping peacefully in the little box Brendan had made for him, and crept toward the door.

It was a little cooler outside, but not by much. Still, it was more pleasant to be outside, and I sank onto a bench and turned my face up to the sky. There were times when I found solace in looking at the heavens, but what I felt this night was hopelessness. Compared to the vastness of the universe, I was a speck of dust whose fate didn't really matter to anyone except my immediate family. And they'd have no reason to suspect that anything was wrong for a while yet. Intuitive as my mother and sister were, I didn't think they'd give in to panic, since they didn't expect to hear from me until the middle of September. A whole month.

I glanced toward the gates. We'd left them open in case rescue came, but all I could see now was the black water of the Atlantic, the ocean as vast as the sky above me. Not a single light floating in the darkness to identify a boat or even a plane. I hadn't meant to give in to my despair, but tears began to flow, and I didn't think I could keep my weeping to myself, so I hurried toward the gates and away from the sleeping people within. I just needed a few minutes to vent my grief, and then I would go back inside and pretend that I was all right and that now it was just a matter of waiting patiently for our rescue.

I hadn't heard the footsteps behind me, nor was I able to fight against the strong arm that came around my chest and pushed me first to my knees and then face down on the ground. My assailant had one hand over my mouth to keep me from crying out and slid the other arm from beneath me to hurriedly yank up my shift. He didn't say a word, but when he forced his knee between my legs, I knew what was about to happen. The body atop me was hard and lean, the firm shaft pushing against my buttocks hot and throbbing with lust. I struggled harder and tried to scream, but the hand moved up to cover my nose, and I had to stop because I couldn't breathe.

My thoughts started to fragment, as the lack of oxygen made me lightheaded and confused. Colorful bursts of light exploded before my closed eyes, and I thought I might die here, on the ground, beneath this man who was willing to let me suffocate just so that he could get his rocks off. I felt his hand between my legs as he tried to guide himself inside me. I tried to rock my hips from side to side to keep him from accomplishing his goal, but he ground my pelvis into the dirt to prevent me from moving.

Thankfully, he loosened his hold on my nose and mouth, and I was able to suck in some air. One breath, then two. My mind began to clear somewhat, but there was little I could do. He attempted to push into my unwilling body, and I could feel his hot breath on my cheek and smell the reek of his sweat as he grunted with effort. All I could do was remain as tense as possible, making his efforts at penetration more difficult. I knew he'd get there eventually, but I hoped that he'd grow frustrated enough for his lust to cool.

My assailant withdrew his hand, spit on his fingers, then tried again, using his saliva to ease his passage. By this point, I knew exactly who he was but refused to allow his name into my thoughts. That would make it personal, and I needed to think of him as someone faceless, otherwise I'd lose whatever tenuous hold I had on reality since I would have to face him once the sun came up, and we'd both know what had happened. I didn't think he planned to kill me. He was simply taking advantage of Declan's absence to take something he must have craved for some time. Or maybe he would have gone for any of the women if they happened to be outside alone in the middle of the night. In the darkness, any hole will do the job.

My face was pressed into the pebbled dirt of the path that led to the beach, and I could feel the sharp edge of every little stone as it dug into my cheek and temple. I could breathe, but just barely, and it was that pain that kept me tethered to the moment. I couldn't afford to pass out. I needed to know exactly what was happening and wait for my chance to fight back. My attacker had placed himself at a disadvantage by trying to take me from behind. It would have been much easier for him had I been on my back, and he could force my legs wider apart and ram himself inside me. To his detriment and my good fortune, he wasn't well-endowed enough to gain entrance without raising my hips, so I tried to press myself into the ground, making it more difficult for him. He swore under his breath and tried a different tack. I let out a muffled cry as he shoved his stiff prick between my buttocks in an attempt to sodomize me. He succeeded, and I felt searing pain as he pushed into my unwilling body. He moaned with satisfaction, but his pleasure was short-lived.

I barely registered the thud, but the hand that was pressed over my mouth and nose suddenly fell away and the weight rolled off me, the sweet release followed by a number of grunts and dull thuds. I couldn't bear to look but remained prone, my eyes shut tight, my face pressed to the ground, unable to find the strength to move. Hot tears ran into the dirt, and I shuddered, my body so tense I thought my bones would snap. A gentle hand lowered my shift and wiped the tears away.

"I got you," Jesse said. "I got you, sweetheart."

I didn't think I had the strength to stand, but Jesse lifted me into his arms and held me close. The warmth of his body felt reassuring, and I rested my head on his shoulder. I didn't want to look. All I wanted was to bury my face in Jesse's chest and hide, but I needed to know what had been done in my name. As Jesse turned toward the settlement, I forced myself to take a backward glance. Glen lay on his back, his eyes open to the starlit sky. I averted my gaze from his unlaced breeches, looking away from the pale skin of his hips and the dark thatch of hair that resembled a nest filled with a fat slug.

Instead, I focused on his face, and the dark stain that spread from the back of the skull that rested at an odd angle against a sharp rock. I knew Glen was dead, and I also knew that Jesse had killed him, and that knowledge brought me a measure of peace. I couldn't bear to be responsible for the loss of yet another life on this island. By morning, everyone would know what had happened, and once again we would have to adjust to an altered reality.

# Chapter 69

The morning dawned stormy and gray, the waves slamming against the shore with violent frequency. I clutched Hunter to me as I stared out to sea, and if it wasn't for the tiny boy whose hand lay like a starfish on my breast, I might have just walked in and kept on going. But I would never succeed. Jesse and Tim would try to save me. They hadn't left my side since Jesse brought me back to the men's house and laid me on the double bed, where only two nights ago I had lain in Declan's arms. Jesse had gently cleaned my face and wiped the dirt from my mouth, then brought me a drink, covered me with a sheet, and pulled the curtains around the bed before going to wake Tim.

They must have talked outside because by the time they returned to the house, neither one mentioned Glen. Instead, they kept vigil over me while I lay there, trapped in a state of delirium that kept me from falling asleep. Horrible images raced around and around in my mind until I thought I would go mad with the horror of it. But eventually, I must have fallen asleep, because when I woke, I found Iris sitting on the side of the bed, her round face creased with concern.

She didn't ask me any questions or spew any platitudes. She simply handed me the baby, who snuggled against me as if he'd missed me. I held on to him while the men disposed of Glen's body. They didn't offer him the sacrament of burial but tossed him out to sea, happy for his body to get smashed on the rocks, his flesh eaten by fish until there was nothing left where once a human being had existed. They thought it would make me feel better to know that his body had been desecrated, but I didn't care. It made no difference to me what happened to Glen's remains. The only person I worried about was Declan.

A wave crashed onto the shore, the foaming water swirling around my bare ankles. I drew a shuddering breath but didn't move back, bracing myself for the next wave. In my peripheral vision, Tim moved a little closer. He had stood silently behind me the whole time, far enough back to give me space but close enough to reach me in three strides if I attempted something stupid. I was neither angry nor grateful. For the first time in my life, I wasn't sure I wanted to live. My limbs were sore, my head ached as if someone had split it with an axe, and my lips and cheek were swollen and caked with dried blood where the scratches from the pebbles had scabbed over, but it wasn't my physical state that bothered me. My body would heal. I would even recover from what Glen had done to me, but I couldn't seem to find any reason to go on. Without Declan, not even Hunter was enough to give me hope. The other women would look after him and love him. He didn't need me.

I didn't resist when Tim wrapped an arm around me and bodily turned me away from the roiling sea. We walked back to the settlement in silence, only Hunter making smacking noises with his lips to let me know he was ready to eat. I handed the baby over to Nicky and went inside the men's house, where I lay down on the double bed. It still smelled of Declan, and I buried my face in his pillow and shut my eyes, trying desperately to summon his spirit. I was sure I'd know if he was dead, but I felt nothing, no connection, just a gaping void.

Eventually, Iris brought me a cup of milk and some corn mush. After I had eaten, Nicky came in with the baby. She placed Hunter next to me, and then the two of them walked away, leaving us alone. Rain lashed outside the window, and the house was blessedly quiet and dark, so I curled around the baby and eventually fell asleep, too emotionally and physically drained to remain conscious. I don't know how long we slept, but when I woke, it was no longer dark. The rain had stopped, the wind had stilled, and a watery sunshine was trying to break through the stormy clouds.

I heard a shout from outside but couldn't tell who it was or what they were yelling about, so I just ignored them. The men often shouted to each other. It was their preferred mode of communication. Then I heard a feminine shriek of terror and pushed myself up on my elbow, peering through the window and into the square. What I saw left me breathless. A group of men—at least I thought they were men—streamed into the settlement, their faces covered with plastic face shields worn over surgical masks. They were dressed in what looked like paper suits and wore black holsters over the disposable fabric, their weapons clearly visible. Only the first two had their guns drawn, the black metal stark against the bright blue of their latex gloves. The rest followed cautiously, as if expecting the contestants to mount an attack.

Everyone stood still, staring at the white-clad figures, unsure what to do. The scene was surreal, like something out of a sci-fi movie, or one of those disaster films where a deadly virus kills indiscriminately until some action hero aided by a nerdy scientist and a gorgeous female doctor save the world.

"Identify yourself, please," Jesse called out as he stepped forward. I was impressed with his composure given that a gun was pointing at his chest.

The man in the white coveralls lowered the gun and said something. It sounded muffled but not unfriendly.

"Sorry, can you repeat that?" Jesse asked. "Preferably without the mask."

The man didn't come any closer, nor did he lower his mask. Instead, he spoke louder across a distance of at least six feet, which made his reply clearly audible.

"I'm Captain Blake Donaldson of the U.S. Coast Guard," he said. "We have been dispatched to pick you up from this island."

"Why are you dressed like that?" Iris demanded, clearly outraged by the antics of the men. "And why are you waving your guns around, Captain Donaldson?"

Captain Donaldson sighed heavily. "Please don't come any closer," he said as he returned the gun to its holster. "We are in the midst of a worldwide pandemic. More than a million people have died, and hundreds of thousands are currently under quarantine."

"Is this a joke?" Iris scoffed. "Is someone filming this?" She looked around as if expecting a camera crew to materialize.

"Unfortunately, this is no joke, ma'am," the captain said. "The United States, as well as most of the world, was under lockdown for several months, which was lifted only recently. We're mandated to wear face masks and shields to prevent the spread of infection and to maintain social distancing."

"Fuck me," Sam muttered under his breath.

"A worldwide lockdown?" Nicky asked, the journalist in her unable to resist the need to learn more.

"Yes, ma'am. Everything but essential businesses were mandated to close."

"What constituted an essential business?" Nicky asked.

"Just what you would imagine. Food stores, pharmacies, medical offices and hospitals, funeral homes, and the like," Captain Donaldson replied.

"The restaurants were closed?" Iris asked, her eyes wide with amazement.

"Only drive-through or curbside pickup was permitted."

"Curbside pickup?" Iris echoed.

"What about travel?" Jesse asked. "We haven't seen any planes or boats since we've been here."

"That's because most commercial travel was suspended," Captain Donaldson replied. "Everyone was instructed to shelter-in-place in order to slow down the spread."

"But surely some people still went out on their boats," Sam said.

"I'm sure they did, but you're miles from the mainland here. No reason for anyone to come this far."

It was obvious that Captain Donaldson was becoming exasperated with all the questions, but he continued to reply politely as he scanned the group. "There are only seven people here," he said. "I was led to believe I was picking up eight."

"Eight," I said as I emerged from the house, Hunter snuggled in my arms. "What happened to Declan Carey?"

Everyone turned to stare at me, Captain Donaldson's eyes widening when he realized I was holding a newborn. "He's in the hospital in Norfolk, ma'am."

"Why?" I exclaimed, tears blurring my vision. "Was he exposed to the virus?"

"No, ma'am. He was badly injured and nearly drowned. He was spotted by a passing boat. The captain got him aboard and notified the Coast Guard."

"And Brendan Taft?" Jesse asked.

Captain Donaldson shook his head. "Still at large."

"What do you mean, at large?" Jesse demanded.

"I'm sorry, but that's all the information I have at present," Captain Donaldson said. "Now, we will take you off the island and bring you to a secure medical facility, where you will be treated."

"Treated for what?" Iris cried. "We weren't exposed to this virus. Are you going to put us in isolation?"

"No one is going to put you in isolation, ma'am," Captain Donaldson said. "But you are clearly malnourished and need to be seen by a doctor. And that baby needs to be examined by a pediatrician."

"And then what?" Jesse asked.

"What happens after is not my jurisdiction, sir, but I'm sure some form of transportation will be provided to take you home.

Now, please pack whatever you wish to take back to the mainland and meet us on the beach."

Captain Donaldson motioned to the man standing behind him, and the man produced a handful of surgical masks.

"Please put these on before approaching my men," Captain Donaldson said. "There's no proven treatment against the virus."

"What is this virus, and how does it manifest itself?" Iris asked.

"The virus is called Covid-19. Some people are asymptomatic, some experience flu-like symptoms, while others need to be put on a ventilator. Once that happens, they're not likely to recover."

Iris and I exchanged an incredulous look. We had heard about the virus on the news and had even discussed it briefly when we first met, but when we had left for our training in February there were only a few isolated cases in the United States and no government measures were being implemented to prevent the spread. We had no reason to suspect that this virus would be any different from the other outbreaks we'd been warned about over time and wouldn't burn itself out after a few weeks. To discover that it had turned into a worldwide pandemic was truly shocking.

"What percentage of people die?" Sam asked.

"I don't have access to that data, sir."

"But most recover," Sam said, watching the captain with narrowed eyes.

"The majority of those affected recover after a few weeks. Some experience lingering symptoms."

"So not everyone dies?"

"No, not everyone dies," Captain Donaldson replied.

"I won't be muzzled," Sam growled. "I'm strong. I'll take my chances."

"It's for your own protection, sir," Captain Donaldson said.

"And if I refuse?" Sam asked belligerently.

"Then we will leave you here," the captain said, his tone brooking no argument.

Sam looked dubious but accepted the mask and put it on, his movements jerky with irritation.

Captain Donaldson peered at the now-empty houses. "Where's the eighth adult?" he asked.

"He drowned," Tim said. "Slipped on the rocks while fishing and hit his head. We were unable to retrieve his body for burial."

Everyone nodded in unison, and I thought with an inward hysterical giggle that they resembled a bunch of bobbleheads.

"Were you informed of the murders, Captain?" Jesse asked. "The island is a crime scene."

Captain Donaldson looked exasperated. "Our orders are to get you back to civilization. The rest will be handled through the appropriate channels. Now, if you would get your things."

"There's nothing to get," Iris said. She put on her mask and marched toward the beach, followed by Nicky and Theresa.

I put on my own mask, then tried to fit a mask over Hunter's face. It was too large, but I was able to cover his nose and mouth and tie the mask behind his head. He'd stand no chance if he became infected.

"Can I see Declan? Which hospital is he at?" I asked once I joined everyone on the beach.

"He's at Sentara Norfolk General Hospital, but no visitors are allowed in just now."

"What, no one?" Tim asked. "Declan would want to see Natalie."

"No one besides the patients and medical staff are allowed on the premises. The hospitals were overrun with Covid cases the past few months, so all precautions are being taken to prevent contagion within the wards. Even funerals are being conducted over Zoom."

"Over what now?" Jesse asked confusedly.

"Zoom," Captain Donaldson repeated. "It's a meeting site where anyone can join if they've been invited electronically."

"How does that work?" Theresa asked. "Is it like Skype?"

"Not exactly. Remember the game *Hollywood Squares*?" the man behind Captain Donaldson asked. "Where every person was in their own square?"

"Yes," Theresa replied dubiously.

"That's how it works. You can see everyone in their own box on the screen and speak with them directly."

"Fuck me," Sam said again under his breath. "What next?"

"Have our families been notified?" Theresa asked.

"I'm sorry, I don't know. We really must get going."

We were herded aboard the boat that was moored at the jetty and asked to go down below, while the crew remained on deck. I experienced a wave of panic as I made my way down the narrow stairs. This was just like before, on our way out to the island, only now the crew was armed, and some part of me couldn't believe the story they had told us. The whole thing sounded too fantastical, too unreal. A worldwide pandemic? What were the chances of that? There had been deadly viruses before, but they had always been dealt with in a timely manner. A months-long lockdown? I couldn't even begin to imagine how that looked, but it was too out-there to make up. And the boat looked legit, although at this point, I wouldn't put anything past Varlet.

What if we were being taken elsewhere? And what if the men were Varlet employees tasked with disposing of the rest of the group before criminal charges could be filed? With all of us gone, no one would be able to prove a thing. We'd become known as the Lost Colony. Just another unsolved mystery that people would speculate about for a while, then forget, our memory kept alive only by those few who had cared about us in life.

Tired of fruitless speculation, I handed Hunter to Iris and headed to the bathroom. It was small and utilitarian, but the electric light and running water nearly brought tears to my eyes. I washed my face and hands after availing myself of the flushing toilet, then sanitized as I had been instructed to do. Despite my unease, I wished the crew had offered us something to eat, but it was clear they hadn't thought that far ahead, or maybe they had intended for us to remain masked the entire time we were on board.

Shortly after I returned to the group, one of the men came down to ask us to come up on deck since we were about to dock. Thankfully, the trip back wasn't nearly as long as the trip out since the vessel was powered by an engine. When I saw the port of Norfolk, I did cry. It was quieter and emptier than one would expect, but still blessedly there, as were the houses and shops we saw in the distance. Everyone we saw wore a mask, and several people also sported plastic shields and rubber gloves despite the August heat and even when alone in a car. In fact, most people were on their own. There were no crowds or even small groups of pedestrians. People went about their business with a furtive purposefulness and barely looked at anyone they encountered, as if they could get infected just by meeting someone's gaze. Many stores were closed, and there was a pervasive air of desolation, the kind I had never experienced before leaving for the island.

We were loaded into a small bus and sent to some out-of-the-way Urgent Care clinic, where several masked and robed doctors were waiting to receive us. Hunter was instantly taken from me by a motherly nurse, but I was assured that he would be returned to me shortly. It was a relief to get out of my tatty woolens, take a hot shower using fragrant soap and real shampoo and conditioner, then change into the cool, breathable coveralls we had been issued with. Once we were ready, we were led away to various rooms, where we were examined, asked endless questions about our experience, and had blood drawn to determine just how much damage we had all suffered over the past few months. It felt odd to be treated like a curiosity, but at this stage, I really didn't care. All my thoughts were for Declan and Hunter.

Once the doctors finished with us, we were given prepackaged lunches and juice boxes and brought back to a waiting area. Half the chairs were turned toward the wall to prevent people from getting too close, and we were instructed not to sit together and put our masks back on right after we had eaten. A ham and cheese sandwich, apple juice, and a banana had never tasted so good, but I was only able to eat a few bites and saved the rest for later, hoping all the while I wouldn't become sick and vomit this desperately needed nutritional bounty.

Most of our questions were met with blank stares, since no one seemed to know anything about our families, Varlet Entertainment, or Declan and Brendan. The only thing we were told was that the police were coming to speak to us. It took several hours for the officers to show up, by which time Hunter and I had taken a short nap after I had given him a bottle of formula. He was now wearing a cotton onesie and a blue hat and was wrapped in a thin blanket against the chill of the air conditioning. He seemed content.

The police officers, who were also clad in head-to-toe PPE, spoke to us one by one. The officer who interviewed me was Officer Jeffries. He was in his thirties, his deep brown skin and warm eyes at odds with the fluorescent lights and the white coveralls he wore over his uniform. He smiled at me sympathetically, and the only reason I knew that was because I saw his eyes crinkle above the mask.

"I know you've been through a lot, Ms. Osborne, and I wish I could tell you more, but I honestly don't know anything about what happened. An investigation has been launched into Varlet Entertainment, and a forensic team has been dispatched to the island."

"What about my family?" I pleaded. "Do they know where I am?"

"I'm sorry. I don't know if your family has been notified."

"And Officer Carey?" I asked.

"Officer Carey is still in the hospital. He sustained severe head wounds and initially wasn't able to speak since his voice box was badly bruised. He was also suffering from malnutrition and exhaustion since he'd had to swim for over a mile in his condition. He just barely made it. Had he not been so determined to get help, I think he might have given up."

"Declan is strong."

"That he is," Officer Jeffries said, and I could see the admiration in his dark eyes. "He was desperate to get back to you."

Tears stung my eyes, but I wouldn't cry. Declan was alive and improving, and we were saved. At least for now. I had no idea what to expect once we were released from the Urgent Care facility, but for now, my concerns were more immediate.

"What will happen to Hunter?" I asked.

"Hunter will need to be immunized and monitored for a few days, but he's in fairly good physical condition, all things considered, and he has you to thank for that."

I waited, my heart pounding against my ribcage, and Officer Jeffries's gaze became sympathetic as he noticed my distress. "Hunter's grandparents have been contacted," he said, leaving me to infer the rest.

"I will never see him again," I whispered.

"Perhaps the grandparents will allow you to visit once the pandemic is over."

"I doubt that," I said, and wiped away the tear that threatened to roll beneath my mask.

Officer Jeffries nodded in what I assumed was agreement.

"Please, can I call my parents?" I pleaded. "I need to hear their voices."

Officer Jeffries looked conflicted, then took out his own cellphone and asked me to put on a pair of surgical gloves. "Keep your mask on while you speak. I hope you remember the number by heart."

"Thank you," I cried. "I do."

I dialed my mom's number and waited. She answered on the third ring, her voice quivering with anxiety. "Hello? Who is this?"

I wondered what her call screen showed and if she thought she was being contacted by the police.

"Mom?" I cried. "It's me."

"Oh, Natalie, thank God," my mother exclaimed. She sounded like she was crying. "We couldn't get any information. No one was picking up the phone or replying to our emails."

"Mom, I'm okay. I'm in Virginia. How are you all? Has anyone been sick?"

"Your father was in the hospital, but he's all right now. He's at home."

"And Dee? And Maddy?"

"They all had the virus, but thankfully, they recovered quickly. Maddy was completely asymptomatic."

"And Dee?"

"She lost her sense of smell and taste for about two weeks and had flu-like symptoms, but she's fine now. And Craig had the equivalent of a bad cold."

I breathed a sigh of relief. "Mom, I'm going to be coming home soon. I can't wait to see you."

"I love you so much, Natalie. I can't wait to see you in person," my mom exclaimed.

"I love you too, Mom. I really missed you."

"Natalie—"

"I have to go. I'm using someone's phone. I'll call you as soon as I can."

"All right. I can't wait to tell everyone I spoke to you. Bye, darling."

"Bye."

I ended the call and handed the phone back to Officer Jeffries, relieved that my mom hadn't asked about what had happened on the island. There'd be plenty of time to tell my family, but right now, my concerns were more immediate.

"When will Declan be released?" I asked as I watched the policeman carefully sanitize his phone. It was surreal to see people taking such precautions, but then the last five months of my life had been surreal. I really shouldn't have been surprised by anything at this point.

"I really don't know, but I will find out for you," he said as he stood to leave. "We'll speak again soon."

"Can I say goodbye to Hunter?" I called after Officer Jeffries as he headed for the door.

He turned and nodded, his gaze sympathetic above the mask. "You'd better do it now since he's going to be moved to another facility today."

"Thank you," I muttered as my chest tightened with grief at the thought of the separation.

I found Hunter in one of the examining rooms with a nurse called Terri. She was a kind, motherly woman who'd taken charge of Hunter as soon as we arrived and had been the one to look after him while I was examined and questioned by Officer Jeffries. Hunter, who looked unbearably cute in a light blue onesie patterned with fluffy sheep and a matching hat, was asleep in a plastic bassinet, while Terri made notes in his chart. She closed the chart and turned to me.

"Doesn't he look precious?" she asked. "I popped out to Target and bought a few things. We could hardly leave him in that soiled gown and cloth nappy."

I tried to reply, but the huge lump in my throat prevented me from saying anything, so I just nodded, grateful to Terri for taking care of the practicalities and wondering if she'd paid for everything with her own money. There was a fluffy yellow blanket, several bottles and pacifiers, a pack of Pampers, two more outfits, and a diaper bag to hold it all.

Terri followed my gaze and smiled. "We all chipped in," she said. "Everyone wanted to help. It's heartbreaking about his mother. He was lucky to have you."

The past tense wasn't lost on me, but there was nothing I could say. I had known Hunter would be taken from me as soon as we boarded the boat.

"I was about to make him a bottle. Did you want to feed him?" Terri asked. I nodded again, and she gave me a sympathetic look. "I can only imagine how hard it must be," she said. "You get attached, even when they're not your flesh and blood."

"When are his grandparents coming?" I asked, having finally swallowed the lump.

"They'll be here tomorrow. They're driving up and will take him home once he's released."

"Do they sound nice?" I knew it was a silly question, and Terri probably hadn't been the one to speak to them anyway, but I needed to know that Hunter was wanted and would be loved, not merely tolerated.

"They're devastated to have lost their daughter, but they're excited to meet their grandson. I think Hunter will be happy, Natalie," Terri said. "You have to trust in that, or you'll never let him go."

When I didn't reply, Terri turned toward the door. "I'll be right back."

She left the room and returned with a bottle of formula, which she handed to me once I had settled in a chair with Hunter. Awake now, he looked up at me, and I was sure he recognized me and would have smiled had he known how.

"I'll be just down the hall if you need me," Terri said, and left us alone.

I was grateful to her for her sensitivity and held Hunter close. Hunter held my gaze as I gave him the bottle, and I wondered if he was able to sense that things were about to change. There were so many things I wanted to say to him, but my throat seemed to close up the moment I tried to speak, so I just hummed a song he liked as I clung to his tiny body and inhaled the baby smell that brought tears to my eyes. Sitting there, I tried to recall the things Shelby had said about her family. I couldn't remember the details, but I could see Shelby's nostalgic smile as she talked about her parents and the fond memories she had of her childhood, and I knew that Hunter would be all right. He'd have a happy, safe childhood, and perhaps form a bond with his dad. With her competition out of the way, I couldn't imagine that Matt's wife would keep her husband from seeing his son.

Eventually, Terri returned, and I could tell from her apologetic smile that it was time for Hunter to go.

"They'll take good care of him at the pediatric unit," Terri promised.

I kissed Hunter's soft cheek, then raised one of his hands and brushed my lips against the tiny fingers. "I know you won't remember me, but I hope you'll know that you were loved," I whispered, then resolutely got up and handed Hunter over to Terri.

I could hear her cooing to him as I left the room. Tears blinded me as I stumbled down the hallway in search of Iris. I walked straight into her outstretched arms and buried my face in her shoulder, and she held me as I cried.

# Chapter 70

Not everyone was in a fit state to be released, but the clinic couldn't keep us any longer than necessary since this was an outpatient facility. We were given supplements to boost our weakened immune systems, instructions on how to eat over the coming days, and sent packing. I wasn't sure who was responsible for us at that point, but we could hardly be left on our own, since we didn't have so much as a dollar or a phone between us. The police must have involved some branch of social services and dispensed with the barely creaking wheels of bureaucracy because we were given previously worn but clean modern-day clothes, driven to an out-of-the-way motel, and provided with enough credit at the motel eatery to last us a few days.

No one was sure what would happen once the credit ran out or who was footing the bill, but we had been assured by the police that the bags with wallets, phones, and clothes that we had surrendered upon arriving at the homestead for our training would be returned to us so we could begin to make our way home. But for the time being, we were as good as migrants since everyone seemed to be short-staffed and a bunch of reality show castaways were at the bottom of the totem pole when it came to the priorities of the police department. I did hope that a team had been dispatched to the island as Officer Jeffries had promised, but no one had bothered to update us, and I didn't expect to hear anything in the next few days. Given the current situation, the only thing we could do was enjoy a few days of rest and plentiful food.

The motel's greasy spoon restaurant didn't allow anyone inside, but there were several tables set up facing the parking lot, and we were able to eat our fill since we were the only guests. Everyone got sick that first day, since we couldn't resist the desperate need to order nearly everything on the menu and eat way more than our emaciated bodies could tolerate. I didn't care, though. That first taste of burger and fries was heaven, and I would do it again despite the vomiting and excruciating stomach pains that dogged me the rest of the evening as I lay in a fetal position on the double bed in my room.

It was strange to be alone after months of sharing a house with multiple people, but I was grateful for the privacy. I hoped that those of us who had survived would remain friends for life, but realistically, I knew that wouldn't happen. As soon as we parted ways, we'd reassimilate into our very altered lives and try to forget what had happened on the island. The doctors at the Urgent Care had advised us to seek therapy but had also mentioned that mental healthcare professionals were stretched to the breaking point after the months-long lockdown. A good portion of the population was having difficulty adjusting to the new reality they'd woken to once they realized the virus was sweeping through the country like wildfire and would affect every single person and household in one way or another.

We all hear of terrible things that happen to other people and know that life can turn on a dime, but deep down, most people don't believe it can happen to them. There's that cockiness, that certainty that they can weather any storm and come out on the other side unscathed, but some things remain with you forever, even if you survive. What happened on that island and the reality we had come back to would take me and the rest of the group some time to process. I couldn't honestly say that I grieved for Will, Mark, Gael, or Ed. And certainly not for Glen. I had barely known them and would probably not have missed them had the show progressed as planned and we had eventually been taken back to the mainland and recompensed, but since their deaths had been unexpected and violent, and any of us could have been next, I was reminded just how little control I had over my life.

Acceptance and healing would take time, and I didn't expect to walk away profoundly unchanged. The aftershocks would reverberate for months, if not years, but now that I was alone in this utilitarian room, a sense of unreality had settled over me, and I decided that the best thing to do would be to allow myself a short period of emotional detachment. I turned on the TV, found reruns of *Grey's Anatomy*, and settled in to watch until I was ready to go to sleep, grateful to have someone else's problems to focus on instead of my own.

# Chapter 71

I had been at the motel for two days, and although I had promised myself that I wouldn't obsess and would wait to be contacted by the police, I couldn't help it and watched the news obsessively in the hope that there would be some mention of our ordeal and an explanation, no matter how inadequate, as to why we had been abandoned on the island. I almost expected to see Justin Rogue led away in handcuffs or at least hear a snippet of a statement issued by Varlet Entertainment, but there was nothing.

With no chores to occupy me and nowhere to go, time passed slowly. I watched a few more reruns as I lounged on the bed with the air conditioning blasting, partook of running water liberally, ate a little something every two hours until my brain caught up to the current situation and realized that I wasn't starving and didn't need to gobble food around the clock, and went for walks at a nearby park with Iris or Nicky.

I called my parents and sister every day from the room phone but kept the conversations brief, unable to dive into all the things I really needed to say. I didn't want to relive my time on the island, and there was no sense in subjecting them to the horror and fear I had lived through. I never mentioned Hunter's name, unable to talk about the baby without crying. Instead, I wanted to hear about their days and revel in the normalcy of hearing news of people I knew, speculating about when the pandemic would finally be over, and hearing Dee's accounts of hunting for toilet paper and sanitizer during the lockdown.

Those conversations kept me grounded at a time when I ceaselessly worried about Declan and wished I could speak to him, but although I had called the hospital, I had been told that since I wasn't a family member, they couldn't give me any information on his condition. The nurses were too busy to waste time on calls, and I couldn't blame them.

On the evening of the second day there was a knock on the door. I yanked open the door without bothering to put on my mask.

A police cruiser was parked in front, Officer Jeffries behind the wheel. He gave me a friendly wave and drove off, job done. I let out a shriek of joy and threw myself into Declan's arms, holding him so tight, he actually yelped at one point. He looked like absolute hell with his bandages and livid bruises, but he was alive, and he was there.

I pulled Declan inside and shut the door just as he tore off his mask. Our kiss was urgent and hot, and neither of us gave a second thought to the virus as we stumbled onto the bed, tearing each other's clothes off with single-minded determination. The conversation would come later, but just then, we needed to be close to each other and to celebrate the miracle of being alive and together.

Declan smelled different than he had on the island, the musky smell of sweat and wool that I was so accustomed to replaced by the scent of bodywash and shampoo and that smell particular to hospitals that lingered on his clothes. I was glad to see that his injuries did not affect either his libido or his desire for me. Our lovemaking was frenzied, our need for each other life-affirming after nearly a week of constant worry. I wasn't sure how much Declan had been told of our rescue or who was back on the mainland but hoped that no one had told him about Glen.

I knew Declan well enough to realize that he'd feel responsible for what had happened to me and blame himself for leaving me and not allowing someone else to take his place in the canoe, which was why I had begged the group to stick to the story that Glen had drowned accidentally. It hadn't been difficult to get them to agree, since full disclosure would put Jesse in the frame for Glen's death, and the rest of us for disposing of the body and denying Glen a proper burial.

Afterward, we lay intertwined, our bodies cooling in the frigid blast from the AC. I wished we could remain that way for a while, but the need to catch up quickly dispelled the joy of our reunion. We started with the basics, with Declan asking about the rescue and our arrival on the mainland. He knew of Glen's death but thankfully didn't ask for the details, and I didn't volunteer any information. Instead, I asked about what had happened once he and Brendan had left the island. I needed to know, to understand what had transpired. Declan's voice was a bit hoarse, both from the injuries to his throat and the effort it took to recount those awful moments when he'd thought he was going to die.

"I never suspected him," I said. "Brendan was always so kind and eager to help."

"He was biding his time," Declan said. "Waiting for his opportunity. And he got it once we were within sight of land."

"Did he not realize you hadn't drowned?" I asked, my voice quavering with emotion.

"Thankfully, I was only out for a few seconds, but once I came to, I remained below the surface for a while, only raising my face above water to breathe. Once I was sure Brendan had gone, I began to swim toward the shore. To be honest, I don't know if I would have made it had a passing boat not spotted me and fished me out. The captain alerted the Coast Guard, and there was an ambulance waiting to take me to the hospital as soon as the boat docked. I tried to explain what had happened, but I couldn't speak, and at the hospital, they gave me something to knock me out. It took a while to make them understand," Declan said apologetically. "And by that time, Brendan was long gone."

"He was going to leave us to die," I said quietly, still unable to believe that sweet, cuddly Brendan had managed to hide his dark side for so long. "Did he murder Will, Mark, Gael, and Ed?" I asked shakily.

A part of me hoped that Brendan was responsible for all the crimes because then at least everything that had happened would make some sort of sense, but I still couldn't see why he would want to kill any of those men. I couldn't identify a motive.

"I don't know, Natalie, but I don't believe he did," Declan replied hoarsely. "I thought of little else as I lay in that hospital bed, but I couldn't connect the dots. And I still can't. Unless

Brendan is a serial killer who targets random men, I see no reason he'd want to kill four people."

"Might the connection be homophobia?" I asked. "The victims all treated Brendan with civility and respect, but perhaps he sensed their underlying disapproval."

"If that were the case, Brendan would have left a string of bodies as long as the Oregon Trail before he'd even arrived on the island."

"So what's your explanation for what happened?" I pressed. "You must have settled on a plausible theory."

"I still think we're dealing with multiple killers, but we won't know anything until a Crime Scene Unit takes that island apart."

"Have the police told you anything?" I asked. Since he was a cop, I thought Declan might get preferential treatment, but he shook his head.

"I told them everything I knew, but given the current situation, I think it will take time for us to get any answers."

"Declan, I want to go home," I said. "Please, take me home."

"We can leave tomorrow," Declan said. "Officer Jeffries said our personal items will be returned to us in the morning. And I have reserved a rental car since using public transportation is not advisable right now."

I raised myself on my elbow and looked down at Declan. "How did you manage that?"

"I was able to call my parents from the hospital. My dad reserved the car in his name, since I didn't have a credit card, insurance paperwork, or my driver's license. Once I get my wallet back, I'll be able to pick up the car."

I breathed a sigh of relief since I'd had no idea how we would go about getting home or if Declan would be coming with me.

"What happens after?" I asked carefully. "Will you continue on to Chicago?"

"That depends on you."

"Well, if it's up to me, then I would like you to stay," I said. "Forever."

"I thought you'd never ask," Declan said, and pulled me close. "I accept."

"Can we leave as soon as we get our stuff?"

"If it's not too late. To be honest, I don't really want to drive at night. I don't have my glasses."

"I didn't know you wear glasses," I said.

"I need them when driving, especially at night."

"What else have you never told me?"

"Oh, loads of things," Declan said as he rolled on top of me and pinned my arms, smiling devilishly. "I never told you about all my sexual fetishes."

"Do tell," I replied coyly.

Declan kissed me soundly and proceeded to show me just how imaginative he could be when not performing before an audience.

# Chapter 72

The next day was one of the hardest but also the happiest of my life. I was thrilled to have my things returned to me and couldn't wait to put on my own clothes. My jeans nearly slid off my hips and my top hung as if on a hanger, but I wasn't worried about it. I'd never had trouble putting on weight. I'd be back to my normal size in weeks. And so would Declan, who simply belted his jeans tighter and didn't pay any attention to his too-large T-shirt.

We gathered in the parking lot to say goodbye before Officer Jeffries gave us a ride to the rental car office. Our parting was bittersweet. Declan and I were the first to leave, since we had already made plans, and we both felt a little guilty about leaving the rest of the group behind to figure out their own travel arrangements. We kept our masks on, just in case, but no one objected when I went in for hugs. Iris and Nicky were last, and I clung to them and made them promise to stay in touch. I had never grown close with Theresa, but the older woman teared up as we wished each other well. I couldn't help but wonder if she would return to her homeopathy business as if nothing had happened.

Declan and Jesse shook hands, but when it came to Tim, there was sincere emotion and promises to get together. Declan and Sam barely looked at each other, and Sam avoided my gaze when I said goodbye. I think he felt genuinely disturbed by what Glen had done and wished he had kept his distance from the other man.

All in all, I felt a sense of relief when we finally left the motel and the diminished group in the parking lot. We had a lot of miles to cover, and I looked forward to our first car trip together, even if it was under the weirdest of circumstances. I also couldn't wait to get home, sleep in my own bed, and order everything on the menu from my favorite Italian restaurant. I had checked, and they were still in business, open for delivery and curbside pickup.

As we got onto I-95, Declan held out his hand to me, and I placed mine in his, sealing our commitment to each other. We were finally on our way home.

# Chapter 73

# September

It took a few weeks to adjust to the new normal Covid had wrought. I had to learn how to use Zoom so I could participate in the many meetings the Board of Education conducted before the start of the new school year and had only seen my family once—outside, wearing masks, and appropriately distanced. My dad looked frail and tired, and my mom had noticeably aged since I had last seen her. Dee and Maddy seemed okay, but Craig moved slower, his breathing labored. Dee said he was a long-hauler and had yet to fully recover his pre-Covid health. He'd also lost his senses of taste and smell due to the virus and said he was just now starting to get them back.

Declan had applied to the township's police department, and they were eager to have him, given that they had lost two officers to the virus. We had no difficulty finding our rhythm as a couple and both felt as if we'd been living together for much longer, which I supposed we had been, if what had transpired on the island counted as cohabitation. I met Declan's family over Zoom, and we made promises to get together once some of the travel restrictions eased and we didn't have to take a Covid test before getting on a plane. Given what we'd been through, we were happy to wait and nest in my cozy condo, content to enjoy the little things like takeout, movies and books, and my lovely mattress.

I didn't really talk to Declan about it after the first few days, but I pined for Hunter. He wasn't biologically mine, but the month I had spent as his mom had left me irrevocably changed. I longed for a baby of my own, and whenever I fantasized about becoming a mom, the face that looked back at me was Hunter's. The only thing that made the separation bearable was that I knew Hunter was with Shelby's parents, and he was loved and cared for. I had spoken with Shelby's mom and told her everything I could about Shelby's time on the island and her untimely death and listened to the other woman weep at the loss of her beautiful daughter. Mrs. Bryant had thanked me, though, and had sent me adorable pictures of Hunter, which I would treasure forever.

Our one source of frustration was that we had yet to find out anything about Varlet Entertainment and the investigation into the deaths on the island. I Googled the murders obsessively but wasn't able to find any concrete information. Even with his contacts in the police, Declan couldn't get any information either. We were told we would be briefed once the investigation was complete, and that could take months, so we had no choice but to accept the lack of progress and focus on living our lives while navigating the guidelines mandated by the authorities. I had introduced Declan to my friends when we got together for socially distanced drinks, and we had even driven out to Connecticut to visit Tim, who had resumed his position with the tribal police and was working to mend fences with his wife. He didn't know anything either but had reached out to Gael's wife to make certain she was coping with the loss of her husband.

None of our group had contacted the families of the other victims, and as the weeks went by, we spoke less and less to other surviving members. Everyone was busy. Nicky was recording a series of podcasts about her experience on the island. Iris was working as a part-time chef at a local restaurant and casually seeing her ex-husband, and Theresa had not replied to anyone's emails. We found no trace of her business online, so perhaps she had decided to close up shop now that she had revealed the truth of her fraud. She was probably afraid that one of us would report her to the Better Business Bureau and she might be prosecuted.

The men were even less communicative. We never heard from Sam, and Jesse had replied to Declan's email but made it clear that it was time to move forward and put what had happened on the island behind us. I'm sure he also worried about the consequences of his actions, even though Glen's death had been an accident. But Jesse would have to live with the repercussions of that night for the rest of his life, as would I. I hadn't told Declan the truth of what Glen had done, and didn't plan to, but I had spoken to our school therapist, who was a friend of mine and was happy to help.

I still had nightmares about Glen and woke up drenched in sweat, a scream on my lips because I had dreamed that his hand was over my nose and mouth, and I was choking and felt him pushing into me as if it was actually happening. I wasn't sure what I feared more, dreams about the rape or the sight of his dead face, his staring eyes bathed by the moonlight, his mouth slack, and a pool of blood spreading behind his smashed head. But I was talking about my experience and knew that in time, the memories would recede, and I would be able to put everything that had happened firmly behind me. Life went on.

# Chapter 74

## Natalie

## October

It was toward the end of October that we finally got some answers. Agent Anthony DeVaney of the FBI made an appointment to speak to us. When he came, we settled in the living room, our masks on and our seats socially distanced at six feet apart. The agent removed his mask, giving us permission to do the same. This was a conversation that needed to happen face to face, and since I had left the windows open, I didn't believe we were at risk. I offered to make some coffee, but the agent shook his head, and I got the impression he wanted to get this over with.

"After taking your statements, examining the evidence, and following up on the leads you and Timothy Branham provided, Officer Carey, Norfolk PD had no choice but to bring in the FBI," he said. "What we were dealing with was much bigger than anyone had originally thought. This wasn't just a murder investigation, but also a case of massive fraud and several related offenses."

Agent DeVaney took a deep breath. "First and foremost, I would like to inform you that Brendan Taft was apprehended several weeks ago and was denied bail. He is being held at a maximum-security facility in Upstate New York, where he will remain until his trial."

"Is this for the attempted murder of Declan?" I asked.

"That and more. We were able to find traces of his DNA on Gael Ramos's neck and hands. And there was also evidence of sexual intercourse."

"They were lovers?" I asked, shocked.

"We believe Brendan Taft had intercourse with Mr. Ramos shortly before his death. Mr. Taft confessed to us that Mr. Ramos had rejected his advances, so he lured him into the woods under

366

the pretense of needing his help. Brendan Taft knocked him out, tied him up, then raped him and slit his throat."

"Oh my God!" I exclaimed, but Declan remained silent, only the muscle jumping in his jaw letting me know how deeply upset he was.

"Will the evidence stand up in court?" Declan finally asked.

"It will, unless he tries to plead insanity," Agent DeVaney said. "But a good legal team will tear that defense to shreds since there's nothing factual to back up the claim. You see, we have also found the remains of Mr. Taft's lover, Jon DeLuca, hidden in a metal chest in Mr. Taft's storage unit in Flatbush. He murdered him after Mr. DeLuca ended the relationship."

I felt sick, but Agent DeVaney wasn't finished. "That's not all, I'm afraid. Once we looked into Gael Ramos, we discovered that he was living under a stolen identity. The real Gael Ramos died at the age of five from leukemia."

"So, who was he, then?" I asked.

"His real name was Raúl Aguilar, and he was in this country illegally. Mr. Aguilar's father, José Aguilar, was a captain in the Policía Federal Ministerial in Mexico. He was working to curtail the activities of the drug lords and was tortured and executed after he was kidnapped by the cartel. His wife and two young sons, Raúl and Mateo, were smuggled into Texas before the cartel could come after them as well."

"Texas?" Declan asked. "Did Raúl have dealings with Will Abbott?"

Agent DeVaney nodded. "Not directly. Mateo was arrested for trying to sell a nickel bag to a fellow student. He came up before Judge Abbott, who ordered him to be deported back to Mexico, despite being made aware of the family's history and the very real danger Mateo would face. The boy, who was seventeen at the time, didn't last a week. The cartel has a long memory," Agent

DeVaney said with a shuddering sigh. "Mateo was executed, his body dumped in the desert. After that, Raúl took on the identity of Gael Ramos and moved what was left of his family to California. We believe he killed Judge Abbott, who would not have remembered him since they had probably never met in person, to avenge his brother's death."

"But what were the chances of the two of them winding up on the same show?" I asked, but I saw in the set of Declan's jaw and his narrowed gaze that he'd already figured out the answer to that question.

"Gloria Lawson and Justin Rogue made a killing in cyber espionage, but they started out as private investigators, so they had the skillset needed to dig up dirt on potential targets. They also had a contact at the police department who was able to feed them information they wouldn't have been able to find online, such as any arrests or links to cases where the police were called in. They did careful research and vetted every applicant thoroughly, working to find people who had a previous connection to each other and who could be counted on to react if that association became obvious to them. Because of this, they had several shady investors lined up for their reality show, people who hoped to capitalize on the carnage that would ensue once the situation got out of hand, and it would eventually. The sponsors even funded the construction of the replica colony, certain that their investment would pay off as soon as the show aired."

"Why did they take back some of the supplies?" I asked.

Agent DeVaney was painting an ugly picture of Justin and Gloria, but I still needed to fully understand why they had done what they did, even if their objective had always been to make millions off their investment, and it was obvious they didn't much care who got hurt in the process.

"When questioned, Gloria Lawson said that the reason they removed some of the supplies was because they had found evidence of mold and Varlet had always meant to replace them, but as no one ever returned to the island, the contestants were left with a fraction of what they would need to survive for six months."

"What about the island?" I asked. "Does it have a name? And what of the people who are buried there?"

"The island is one of many small, nameless islands found in the Atlantic, but in the documents we recovered, Justin Rogue refers to it as Barnett Island. We believe that the land originally belonged to Gloria Lawson's ancestors, who came to America sometime in the eighteenth century. No one knows why they chose to settle on a tiny piece of land so far removed from civilization, but it's possible that they used the island several months out of the year, or perhaps they had tried to escape an epidemic or attacks by the Natives." Agent DeVaney sighed. "At this stage, we can only speculate, but it seems that at least part of the family died on the island, probably because someone was already infected by the time they arrived at their cabin. At least one member of the family survived and went on to continue the branch that spawned Gloria."

"But what happened to Varlet?" Declan asked. "Surely they never planned to abandon their investment and leave us to die."

Agent DeVaney shook his head. "Justin and Gloria had anticipated every eventuality and couldn't wait for the fireworks to begin, but what they didn't figure in was a worldwide pandemic. Justin, who thought the whole thing was a government conspiracy, became ill early on and died after a week on a ventilator. He had diabetes, which put him at higher risk," Agent DeVaney explained. "Gloria also got sick and spent several weeks in the hospital. All the employees you met were freelancers that Varlet had hired just for those few weeks. No one had been contracted to remain on the island for the duration of the shoot. We believe they always meant to leave you on your own and watch what happened from afar."

"Did no one think to ask what happened to us?" I demanded, anger welling up inside me at the callousness with which we had been treated.

"The temps had no reason to think you were in danger," Agent DeVaney explained. "They were told it was all part of the plan and once their stint finished, they were always going to move on. But once the pandemic escalated on the mainland, they had other things to worry about."

"So, Justin always meant to leave us alone on the island?" Declan asked.

"The insufficient supplies and sense of being abandoned would have fed right into his agenda," Agent DeVaney replied. "Besides, he didn't want to get caught in the crossfire once hostilities broke out."

"Did he not realize the cameras had been disabled?"

"I'm sure he did, but by that time we were already in lockdown, and he wouldn't be able to get anyone out to the island to repair the damage. And then he got ill," Agent DeVaney said.

"And the cameras and severed cords? I presume that was Raúl's handiwork," Declan said. He looked worn out, and I thought that some part of him didn't want to hear any more, but being a cop, Declan needed closure before he could close the case in his mind and get on with his life.

Agent DeVaney nodded. "We found plans for the island on Raúl's laptop. According to his wife, they were having financial difficulties and Raúl applied to the show in the hope of winning the grand prize. He planned to hack into Varlet's systems and learn all he could in order to get a leg up on the other contestants. When he realized that one of the men in the group was the judge who'd sentenced his brother to certain death, he used his insider knowledge to disable the cameras and wipe all footage from the backup computer inside the bunker. He also cut the cords on the computer and the fridge to make it look like an act of vandalism should someone come looking, but it's more likely that he had hoped the computer would be useless should someone try to extract the data stored on the hard drive, in case it should implicate him in the murder of William Abbott. He probably assumed that someone would come out to fix the cameras and replace the computer and the show would continue sans William Abbott."

"But who cut the cord the second time, after Brendan had fixed it?" I asked.

"Brendan," Declan announced with the air of a man who'd pieced together all the evidence and was angry with himself for not seeing how the clues fit together sooner. "He couldn't risk a police presence on the island. Raúl's body would be found, and he'd be implicated based on the forensic evidence."

"He wanted off the island, but he wasn't about to allow the rest of you to be rescued. He attacked Declan once they were within sight of land, since he wanted to be sure he wouldn't find himself stranded at sea," Agent DeVaney clarified.

"Too bad for him he didn't finish the job," Declan said grimly.

"For what it's worth, most people would not have survived what Brendan did to you."

Declan smiled wryly. "I couldn't afford to die. Everyone on that island would have died with me."

"So, Gael—I mean, Raúl—murdered Will Abbott, and Brendan killed and buried Raúl, but what about Mark?" I asked. "And Ed?"

"We found a link between Mark Beasley and Iris Maddox in Varlet's files. Mark Beasley seduced Iris's daughter and got her pregnant. She was seventeen at the time and in her first semester at the school where he taught. He had a history of sleeping with his students, several of whom were still minors. Iris urged her daughter to report Mr. Beasley for statutory rape, but her daughter refused, even though he denied any responsibility and tried to blame her for coming after him.

"Miss Maddox terminated the pregnancy, dropped out of college, and applied to a school in Cardiff. She hasn't seen her parents since. We believe that Mark Beasley's assault on Shelby Bryant brought it all back, causing Ms. Maddox to poison Mark with jimsonweed, which she added to the ale that Theresa Zhang unwittingly brought Mark while he was sulking in the woods."

"How did Iris know about the jimsonweed?" I asked. "We thought it'd be Theresa who'd know about poisonous plants."

"Iris was interested in botany before she decided to apply to culinary school. When questioned, Iris admitted that she was the one who added the poison to the ale but claims that she only wanted to make Mr. Beasley sick, not kill him."

"What will happen to her?"

"She's been charged and is currently awaiting a bail hearing."

"And Edward Barnes?" Declan asked.

"Edward Barnes was a fraud. He was not an ordained minister, and he had used his phony credentials to embezzle thousands of dollars from families who could ill afford to spare the money. Nicky Jackson's mother was scammed by Edward Barnes five years ago when he charged her a thousand dollars for a drug rehabilitation program that never existed and failed to return the money when Ms. Jackson asked for it back. He threatened to inform the police that she sold sex in order to buy drugs."

"Did Nicky know about this?" I asked, my stomach twisting with anxiety. I wasn't sure how much more I could stand.

"She claims not to have known anything about it since she hasn't resided at the same address as her mother in over a decade, but I'm sure Nicky is well aware of her mother's lifestyle."

"And the autopsy?" Declan interjected.

"The autopsy showed no evidence of foul play. We believe Edward Barnes committed suicide once he realized he'd be getting no money from the producers. When his family had become aware of the fraud, they gave him an ultimatum. He could either repay the money he stole or face a public accusation, which would almost certainly lead to jail time. Without the money, Ed Barnes was going down. Hard."

"What about the rest of them?" Declan asked.

"Every contestant on that island had a past. Glen Grisham routinely helped himself to stock from his company's warehouse and sold it online, and several accusations of sexual assault had been logged against him with Human Resources. The complaints were never followed up since the HR manager was one of Glen's drinking buddies," Agent DeVaney said.

"Theresa Zhang is not licensed to practice homeopathy and has been charged with medical fraud. Samuel Murphy failed to report a Native American burial ground on his land and destroyed the evidence in the hope that no one would call for the site to be preserved. It seems his neighbor saw him excavating the grave and ratted him out. Charges are pending."

Agent DeVaney sighed heavily and continued. "Jesse Milford faces charges of tax evasion, and Timothy Branham was implicated in the disappearance of a man whose remains were recently discovered on tribal land. Shelby Bryant was guilty of blackmail and extortion against the town sheriff, with whom she'd had an affair, and Nicky Jackson has a history of plagiarism and copyright infringement. Iris Maddox's restaurant was closed due to ongoing Department of Health violations, and William Abbott accepted a bribe to expunge a friend's son's criminal record."

I was surprised Agent DeVaney stopped there, tactfully leaving me and Declan off the list. I could feel Declan's gaze on me as he absorbed this information. It wasn't until Agent DeVaney finally left that Declan faced me across the silent room.

"I told you about my gravest mistake, Natalie," Declan said, his gaze radiating pain and betrayal. "Surely you weren't the only person on that island who didn't harbor a secret."

"No, I wasn't," I choked out. "When I was in high school, I became involved with my math teacher. He was an attractive, fun-loving man. A real favorite with the students. Guy Nixon seemed much older to me then, but he was only twenty-six at the time."

"Did you sleep with him?" Declan asked.

"Yes, but it wasn't just that. He was very persuasive and talked me into posing for some intimate photographs and videos, even though I told him repeatedly that I didn't feel comfortable. He told me they were just for us, and no one would ever see them."

I angrily wiped away a tear that slid down my cheek. I'd thought I was over it, but the pain of Guy's betrayal was as much a part of me as what had happened afterward, and I knew it would always live in some remote part of my brain, the emotions dormant until some unexpected trigger brought them to the forefront, and then it was all as raw and fresh as if it had happened last week.

"Guy posted them on a website where he charged a membership fee that allowed the members to view pornographic images and videos of minors. I had a breakdown when he was taken into custody and the names of the girls he'd exploited were leaked online. It took two years of therapy and heavy-duty antidepressants to finally find the strength to take the first step toward reclaiming my life."

"What happened to the teacher?" Declan asked. He looked outwardly calm, but I could feel the rage building inside him.

"He was never charged, since the police couldn't conclusively prove the site was set up by him or that he had been the one to upload the videos. The payments and subscriptions went through so many encryptions and anonymous VPNs that they couldn't prove ownership or even participation. Guy Nixon was released, but he lost his job, and his reputation suffered because even though he never served any time, there were girls who later came forward and said he had been grooming them. He was blackballed and had to leave town."

"Let me guess, he's still teaching and has access to young children," Declan said, his lip curling with disgust.

I shook my head. "He committed suicide five years ago. Jumped off the roof of his building."

"Did he really jump?" Declan asked quietly.

I'm not sure what Declan saw in my eyes, but he'd asked the one question I had been dreading, and I knew that if we were to have any future together, I'd have to tell him the truth. Still, I stalled, unable to speak the words out loud.

"They were never able to prove otherwise."

"Did he jump, Natalie?" Declan's voice was still quiet, but there was a steely edge to it, and I knew I couldn't afford to avoid the truth any longer.

"No. I went to see him after my last serious relationship broke up. If I was to ever truly move on, I needed to say my piece and tell him how I felt, even if he didn't care. He asked me to come up to the roof for a drink. It was a beautiful night, and he had always been keenly aware of esthetics. I didn't want a drink. I just wanted to get it over with, but he had a glass of wine, and it wasn't his first of the evening. He was unsteady on his feet."

"What happened between you?" Declan asked.

"I accused him of ruining my life and demolishing my self-esteem, and he laughed at me. He said I was stupid and gullible, and I had no one to blame but myself. And then he went for me. He grabbed me and kissed me hard and slid his hand between my legs. I think he wanted to prove that even after everything, I wasn't immune to his charms and would respond to his drunken advances. I tried to push him away, but he wouldn't let go, so I stepped on his foot, and when his hold on me slackened, I shoved him away. He stumbled backward and fell off the roof. I never meant to kill him. It was an accident."

"Were you ever questioned in connection to his death?" Declan's tone was softer now, and his eyes filled with sympathy.

"No. No one knew I had gone to see him, and we hadn't been in touch for years, so there was no reason for the police to suspect that I was anywhere near him that night. Guy didn't have a door camera, and there were no security cameras on his block. His roof wasn't overlooked by any windows." I took a deep breath. "The police found no evidence of foul play, since there were no scuff marks or any indication that he had resisted. He must have turned as he fell, because when they found him, he was facedown, as if he'd jumped. The verdict was suicide."

"Would you have admitted that you'd been there had you been questioned?" Declan pressed.

"No. It really was an accident, but the police would not have seen it that way. I had a strong motive and an opportunity, and there was no way to prove that it wasn't premeditated. They would have locked me up."

"Do you regret it?" Declan asked. He sounded strangled, his face tight with tension.

"I regret my part in it, but I'm not sorry he's dead," I replied truthfully, pinning Declan with an unblinking gaze. "Guy was a predator who preyed on trusting young girls. I wasn't the only one he'd filmed. There were girls as young as twelve on that website. Seems Guy taught middle school before getting the position at my school."

I faced Declan, my chest heaving with the injustice of it all. "Will you report me, Declan?"

He shook his head. "No."

"Will you leave me?" I choked out.

Declan stood completely still, his gaze sliding to the window because clearly, he couldn't bear to look at me. I could only imagine the arguments playing out in his mind. If I

376

understood Declan at all, I knew that he was a cop to the core of his being and couldn't simply overlook a suspicious death. He was dutybound to report me, but he also loved me, and I prayed that his love was stronger than his sense of right and wrong. After all, he'd taken a life, but the difference was he deeply regretted it. I didn't.

Neither of us moved, and with every second that passed, I thought Declan was closer to walking out on me, but he didn't. He turned to face me, his gaze now clear and focused. And full of love.

"I will never leave you, Natalie," he said softly. "I believe in the rule of law. Without law, there's only chaos. But I also know from experience that the law sometimes fails the victims, and the guilty often get off on a technicality. Guy Nixon should not have gotten away with what he did. I wish you didn't have to carry the weight of taking his life, but I'm pretty sure the world is a better place without him in it."

Declan crossed the room, took me into his arms, and held me tight. "We are both damaged. Let's be damaged together and hope to be better in the future."

I nodded into his shoulder. "I'd like that."

# Epilogue

I'm not sure what prompted me to suggest it. Maybe it was a need for closure since I still dreamed about the island frequently and my thoughts often strayed to that damaged group of people that had changed my life forever, but I decided that I wanted to make a pilgrimage to the island on the anniversary of our rescue.

Declan was reluctant at first. His memories of those days were traumatic to say the least, but he eventually agreed, probably because he realized this would help us both to finally move on. We invited the contestants still at liberty to join us, and surprisingly, nearly everyone agreed.

We were a diminished group, and the island seemed even more hostile than when we had last been there, probably because strips of yellow police tape flapped in the wind, holes excavated by the forensic team had turned into deep tidal pools, and the colonial dwellings situated behind the tumbledown palisade looked even smaller and creepier than when they had been occupied by the contestants. But there was also a strange sense of peace to finally being there in person.

Much had happened in a year, and although the pandemic was still with us, we had learned to adjust and appreciate the things we had previously taken for granted, like spending time with family and friends, and going out to those public places that had been adjusted or converted to fall within CDC guidelines and allow us that small bit of normalcy. Many a relationship had imploded due to the pandemic, but Declan and I were going strong, our bond only strengthened by the hardship we had endured. Perhaps that was why I needed to see the island. I was ready to close the chapter on that period in our lives and begin a new one that included a family of my own and a future in which Declan and I were ready to forgive ourselves for past mistakes.

The rest of the survivors had adjusted as well, and those not behind bars were thriving. Jesse had settled his debt with the IRS and was in the process of expanding his ranch. Tim had been cleared of all suspicion in the death of the man found buried on tribal land, since there was no physical evidence to link the victim to any of the Branhams. It was assumed that the man had been killed elsewhere, his body buried on the reservation by someone who had hoped to implicate members of the tribe.

The sheriff was still recovering from the aftereffects of Covid, so Tim was now the acting sheriff of the tribal police. He and his wife were still separated, but they were on good terms, and Tim thought there was a chance of them working things out eventually since she had ended the relationship with her boyfriend and was once again single.

Nicky had published a series of podcasts detailing our experiences on the island and our subsequent rescue and was writing a book. She also had a new man in her life. They were taking things slowly, but Nicky was happy, and I detected no awkwardness between her and Tim. They were simply glad to see each other and reminisce about their island romance.

Sam had paid a hefty fine for destroying a historic burial and was now hosting an archeological team who were excavating on his property. He wasn't happy about it but was glad things hadn't gone worse for him. We didn't talk much, but he seemed gentler somehow, and I hoped he'd find whatever it was he needed to make him happy.

I never heard back from Theresa, but I had communicated with Iris, who was serving her sentence at a facility in Upstate New York. Her lawyer had been able to get the charge down to manslaughter, and Iris had agreed to a plea deal, so she would be out in about five years. Coincidentally, Brendan was incarcerated at a maximum-security prison just down the road, where he would probably spend a good portion of what was left of his life. He had been found guilty of the murders of Jon DeLuca, Raúl Aguilar, and Rich Tanner, his previous partner who had been thought to have left the country to take up a position at a mission in Africa. His badly decomposed remains had been found in Brendan's storage unit, and the police had been able to identify him through dental records.

I also updated the group on little Hunter, who was now known as Shiloh Bryant. I was still in touch with Mrs. Bryant, and she periodically sent me pictures of Shiloh, now thirteen months. He was absolutely adorable and surprisingly looked nothing like Shelby. Mrs. Bryant had confided in me that Shelby's ex, Matt, had demanded a paternity test, and it turned out Shiloh wasn't his. Shelby's parents had no idea who the father might be, so they'd applied for and been granted legal guardianship and would raise Shiloh in a way that would have made his mother proud. Everyone oohed and aahed over the pictures, but I could see that they had moved on and Shiloh was no longer of any real interest to them.

We brought a picnic and spread out on the beach after a brief but poignant tour of the island. It was obvious that once we'd caught up with each other's news, there really wasn't anything more to talk about. We had been thrown together by providence and we had survived, but I was relieved to realize that both Declan and I had moved on long before this impromptu reunion. We were getting married next month, and although I didn't tell any of our fellow contestants, I was expecting our first baby.

"I don't know if you guys already heard, but we're to receive compensation," Jesse suddenly said. "My lawyer told me last week."

"Really?" Nicky asked, lowering her bottle of beer in obvious surprise.

"Yeah. Justin's estate has finally gone through probate, and since we signed a contract in which we were promised fifty thousand dollars for our participation, each contestant, living or deceased, including Shiloh, will receive a sum of fifty thousand dollars."

"God, he must have been loaded," Nicky said.

"Yes, but clearly the money wasn't enough. Justin wanted to play God with people's lives."

"And look where that got him," Sam said.

"I'm glad the families of the deceased will get their share," Declan said. "Especially Raúl's wife and Ed's family. I think both Will and Mark were pretty well off."

"Shiloh will have a nice little college fund set up for him," I said, wishing I could see the baby in person just once.

"Any word on Gloria?" Nicky asked.

"According to my lawyer, Gloria moved to North Carolina," Jesse said. "That's where she's originally from, and her parents still live there. She works in their laundromat. Gloria and Justin weren't married, so she has no claim on his estate."

"Oddly, I don't feel bad for her," Nicky said. "At least she survived."

"As did we," Tim said, and raised his bottle of beer. "To us, the survivors of the Lost Colony." We all solemnly raised our bottles.

"I think it's time we went home," I said, and everyone jumped to their feet.

No one glanced back as we motored away from the island. And I knew that I'd never look back again.

**The End**

# Notes

I hope you have enjoyed The Lost Colony. This story is a bit of a departure for me since the historical overtones are purely superficial. The original idea was inspired by And Then There Were None, my all-time favorite Agatha Christie mystery. It had left quite an impression on me when I read it as a teenager and again when I watched the TV adaptation a few years ago.

I love the idea of a group of flawed individuals coming together in a setting from which there's no escape and being forced to face their deepest fears and long-buried secrets. However, unlike Agatha Christie, I had allowed a few of them to live. In real life, not everyone gets the punishment they deserve and not everyone's true nature is exposed.

I would like to thank Linda Robertson for allowing me to use her real-life ancestor, Captain Thomas Osborne and his ship, the Bona Nova, as part of Natalie's family history. I'm always a little envious of people who can trace their ancestry that far back and have amazing stories to tell. If any of my ancestors were swashbuckling heroes, their exploits are lost to history.

I love to hear your thoughts, so feel free to reach out to me. I can be found at

irina.shapiro@yahoo.com, www.irinashapiroauthor.com,

or https://www.facebook.com/IrinaShapiro2/.

Made in the USA
Monee, IL
08 May 2025

17116738R00225